# DEAD WORLDS

# A ZOMBIE ANTHOLOGY

## VOLUME 3

### EDITED BY
### ANTHONY GIANGREGORIO

**OTHER LIVING DEAD PRESS BOOKS**
BOOK OF THE DEAD
FAMILY OF THE DEAD
DEAD WORLDS: UNDEAD STORIES VOLUME 1 & 2
REVOLUTION OF THE DEAD
DEAD RECKONING: DAWNING OF THE DEAD
THE MONSTER UNDER THE BED
DEAD TALES: SHORT STORIES TO DIE FOR
ROAD KILL: A ZOMBIE TALE
DEADFREEZE
DEADFALL
SOUL-EATER
THE DARK
RISE OF THE DEAD
DARK PLACES
VISIONS OF THE DEAD
END OF DAYS: AN APOCALYPTIC ANTHOLOGY
**THE DEADWATER SERIES**
DEADWATER
DEADWATER: Expanded Edition
DEADRAIN
DEADCITY
DEADWAVE
DEAD HARVEST
DEAD UNION
DEAD VALLEY
DEAD TOWN
DEAD ARMY
**COMING SOON**
BLOOD RAGE by Anthony Giangregorio
DEAD WORLDS: UNDEAD STORIES 4 and 5
DEAD CHRISTMAS: A Zombie Anthology
BOOK OF THE DEAD VOLUME 2

# DEAD WORLDS: A ZOMBIE ANTHOLOGY VOLUME 3

Copyright © 2009 by Living Dead Press
All stories contained in this book have been published with permission from the authors.
ISBN    Softcover    ISBN 13: 978-1-935458-26-5
            ISBN 10: 1-935458-26-4

This book was printed in the United States of America.
For more info on obtaining additional copies of this book, contact:
www.livingdeadpress.com

# Table of Contents

# FOREWORD

Welcome to the third installment of the Dead Worlds series.

The stories in this volume are filled with what you have come to expect from Living Dead Press and myself.

I have personally chosen each undead story and I know you're going to enjoy them. We have a bunch of return writers who have been with me since the beginning and also there are many new ones to add to the undead fold.

Each story has that little something that makes a zombie story great, whether it's a story filled with lots of blood, action and guts (my personal favorite) or a clever twist at the end, they all have a spark that makes them good enough to be in this anthology.

So sit back, get comfortable, and get readin', because the zombie apocalypse could come at any time, and when it does, I doubt any of us are gonna have time to read.

Anthony Giangregorio
August 2009

# THE LIVING END

## KELLY M HUDSON

The *biter* slipped up behind Joe and nearly got the drop on him before he heard it at the last second, spun, pipe wrench in hand, and bashed it upside its head. The biter staggered to the left, its expensive Italian suit exploding thick dust into the air.

Joe took a step back and gathered himself as the biter moaned in front of him. The zombie was shorter than he was, but not by much. Joe stood just under six feet tall and was pudgy, with a balding head and a long, scraggly beard that he didn't see the point in shaving. He wore a baggy pair of ragged jeans and a tan t-shirt, just like he had in the past, before the apocalypse happened.

The biter, in stark contrast, had probably been a businessman back before the dead owned the Earth, and had been tanned and in good shape. Now the zombie had brown, shriveled skin, like a mummy, and was wizened and dry, like a raisin, making his expensive suit look ridiculous on him.

Joe hit him again, this time sending the biter stumbling off to his right. Joe had to readjust his swing. He heaved the wrench over his head and crashed it down on the top of the biter's head, crunching the skull and smashing it flat. The biter's brains burst out of its ears, dark and thick, and they reminded Joe of the blackberry jam his grandmother used to serve him with his toast when he was a kid. The brains dribbled out and puddled on the zombie's shoulders as the biter hissed a last breath, dropped to his knees, and then pitched forward; dead forever.

Joe took a step back and let the biter hit the floor. He called them *biters* because they were aggressive zombies, and you didn't see them much anymore, not like when the dead first rose and the entire world ignited in a fury of gunfire, blood, and carnage.

Now most of the zombies were sort of docile, tranquilly walking around as if the world belonged to them. And Joe guessed it probably did. There weren't many humans left—none that Joe knew of or had seen in months—and the zombies roamed the streets free and unhindered. It was funny to think back on those days, when there was more of him than there was of them. It was like some vague dream of sunshine and cookies that got slapped away every morning when he woke up to gray skies and long days spent foraging for food and working in the garden out back of the farm he'd taken over two years ago.

Had it really been two years? Time was a strange concept anymore. It felt like the days dragged on forever, and yet they added up rapidly. Two years he'd been out on that farm and it was like yesterday to Joe.

He'd gone in, swept it clean of the living dead, and taken over. He took stock of the supplies there, figured he had a good couple of months before he'd need food, and then journeyed into the nearby town. He didn't know its name and didn't care because, honestly, it didn't matter anymore.

The old world was quickly slipping away.

Joe snuck in during the day, when he could see best and when the biters moved slower, got a bunch of books on farming, some seeds and essential items, and set up shop. His first crop had been crap, but that had been expected. What he hadn't counted on were the animals, or critters, as his daddy used to call them.

They were everywhere. Without humans to hold them back and keep them in check, they were plentiful and it was all Joe could do to keep them out of his garden.

He set up traps and poisons and salvaged what he could. The next summer he did better. This year was going to be the best. He'd expanded from tomatoes, carrots and lettuce to add potatoes and green beans. Joe found out he had quite a green thumb and was pleased with his meager existence.

He still needed to go into town sometimes, though, for supplies. The people had long since been killed and raised as dead folk, or fled, so he didn't have much trouble. The biters, over time, had lost some of their edge and hunger. Joe wasn't sure whether it was the rot that was eating them or if they were just satisfied with owning everything.

Over time, he could come into town and walk right through them without drawing much interest. There were a few new ones in town that had drifted in and got the idea to eat him, like the one today, but Joe took care of them as needed. Mostly, though, the dead left him alone.

It was disturbing at first. After all the days and nights on the run and fighting for his life to one day reach this point where the living dead barely got a rise out of seeing him. Sure, they'd follow him sometimes, but they'd lose interest and go back to what they were doing. And what they did fascinated Joe to no end. Because, if the truth be told in its entirety, Joe didn't really go into town anymore for canned goods or whatever supplies he needed to scrounge up. He came to town to watch the dead.

He'd sit on a fire escape on the third floor of the abandoned Savings and Loans building and spy on them. Joe would sit on the edge of the fire escape, looking directly over the middle of the town, and observe the zombies as they went about their days, acting for all the world like they were living, breathing people and not what they really were, the walking dead.

Eventually, this was all Joe cared to do, to sit and watch, and except for the farming to keep him in food, this was how Joe spent his days.

He developed names for them and imagined where they'd come from and what they were up to every day. There was Mr. Postal Man, the zombie dressed in a postman's uniform. He was old, with wispy gray hair dotting the sides of his rotting skull and the remnants of a white mustache, torn in half for some reason, sitting under the hole where his nose used to be.

Mr. Postal Man carried his mail bag up and down Main Street all day long, stopping at each building and reaching into his bag like he really had letters in there to deliver. Joe watched as Mr. Postal Man nodded his head and then moved on to the next building, carrying on silent conversations with ghosts. It was this way every day. Come sunset, Mr. Postal Man would shuffle off into the Post Office and didn't come out until morning. Then he went about his routine again.

Every day, rain or shine.

There was Elaine Cromwell, the wealthy town benefactress. Well, Joe didn't really know her name, but that was the story he'd created for her. She was older, too, and was dressed in what must have been a stunning outfit back before the world changed: pleated pants, a smart dress shirt, a short tie designed for women, and red high heels.

All in tatters now.

Elaine still wore her pearls; seven strands that wound round her neck and weaved in and out of the rotting flesh of her chest cavity. Her face was gone, long ago ripped off and eaten, probably, leaving her teeth exposed and gleaming in the sunlight. And her eyes, never blinking, looking back and forth like she was watching a tennis match. Elaine went in and out of buildings, doing her duty as caretaker of the town.

And then there was Tommy Edwards, named after Joe's old, almost certainly dead, best friend. Tommy was the high school football team quarterback. He walked around, every day, up and down the middle of the street like he was in a homecoming parade. Tommy wore his old ball uniform, a dingy blue shirt with a faded number 23 over pads and pants that used to be bright white but was now stained with age, blood and God only knew what else.

Tommy's cleats would echo between the buildings as he scraped along, always searching for his homecoming queen.

It was a surreal scene in a world that had lost all meaning of the word.

On and on it went. He had a name for everyone, and there was upwards of a hundred of the living dead wandering about town on any given day. Sometimes new ones would come into town, like the ones that tried to eat him, but they usually drifted through and on, searching the highways for whatever it was they were looking for.

And then there were the biters, of course, the ones that were still aggressive. But they were thinning out by the day.

Joe walked amongst the dead Townies—that's how Joe liked to think of the zombies—several times a week, until they got used to him. The first time he'd done it in a fit of despair. He was lonely and lost and longing to end his life. The desire overcame him and he crept out of the shadows and walked right up to Mr. Postal Man and stood next to him, daring him to bite him.

Mr. Postal Man looked at Joe, hissed, and walked away. He went back to doing his rounds like Joe wasn't even there. Joe couldn't believe it, of course, so he went up to the next zombie and then the next, and all of them practically ignored him. One or two snapped their teeth together like dogs do when they're warning someone away, but none of them attacked him. Joe left the town that day, shaken and confused.

He came back nearly every day since then. Sometimes he walked with the zombies like he was one of them. He strolled alongside Tommy one day and tried to take away the flat football that Tommy always carried in his arms. Tommy hissed at him so Joe let go and never tried that again.

"I was only going to play catch with you," Joe had told Tommy.

He learned their patterns and their behaviors and did their tasks with them and the zombies never once tried to eat him. Far from it, they almost seemed to welcome him after a time. Most days, though, he sat up on that fire escape and watched. Just like he had come to do that day, when the biter attacked him, and the scavengers rode into town.

They rode bicycles with carts attached to the backs of them and these scavengers were armed to the teeth. They came that morning, just after Joe killed the biter, when the sun was peeking over the horizon.

Joe had just killed the biter, found his seat on the fire escape and opened his thermos of coffee, when they appeared. He heard them before he saw them, the squeaking of their wheels riding the air, giving fanfare for their entry into town.

Joe didn't move. He sat there, stunned, and watched as they rode in full of whoops and hollers. He hadn't seen a living human in over a year now and they were a strange sight to see.

There were thirty of them; twenty-two men, six women, and two children, both boys. They gesticulated wildly, their arms and legs doing crazy somersaults in the air, a manic opposite of the living dead who just sort of shambled along, oblivious to their arrival.

They came in and rode right down the middle of Main Street, carrying machetes and axes and baseball bats. They parked their bikes and stormed into the stores, rooting through them as Joe sat on the fire escape and watched, his coffee growing cold next to him. He wasn't sure what to do. There'd been scavengers before, of course, but they were usually very few and they moved on quickly.

This group, however, was much more organized. They took their time, going through every building and coming out mostly empty handed.

This must have sparked a rage within them, because by the time they reached the end of Main Street, they came out of the last buildings full of anger. They cursed and spit and waved to each other, their verbal language skills almost non-existent. One man, their leader, called the scavengers over with a whistle and spoke to them in guttural grunts and gestures. He stood over six feet tall, and was skinny, like a walking skeleton. He wore a thick black leather jacket, torn blue jeans, and a pair of motorcycles boots with the heels worn off. The Leader was missing his two front teeth and had scrawny patches of hair that grew along his jaw line like rolling tumbleweeds blowing across a ghost town. His eyes were pale and milky and clearly insane. This was what these people had been driven to, in their long months of survival and terror-filled nights; they were completely mad.

The entire time the scavengers were busy searching and getting angry, the Townies carried on with their normal activities, moving around as if nothing was different about that day.

Joe could sense some irritation in them, however. He watched as Mr. Postal Man hesitated at the entrance to a building some of the scavengers had gone into. He seemed almost put out by the new arrivals, because he bunched his shoulders and hissed more than Joe could ever remember seeing him doing before. But Mr. Postal Man moved on. As did Elaine and Tommy and the others. They minded their own business and kept to their tasks.

The scavengers, though, weren't satisfied. They'd obviously ridden into town with high hopes and were furious at getting stumped. They broke from their meeting with the Leader, each of them brandishing some type of weapon, and looked around, their eyes glinting with malice, eager to get some satisfaction. The scavengers spread out, shattering glass store fronts and smashing doors down. They broke into the few cars that were parked along Main Street, the tanks long-since drained of gas, and tore out the seats and dashboards. They even set a series of small fires.

None of this riled Joe to the point of doing something until he saw one of them, a female with wild, frizzy hair, punch Elaine in the face with the business end of a toy bat, the kind they used to give away free at baseball games. This woman, who wore a catcher's mask over her face and an umpire's black, scarred pad across her chest, shrieked wildly and swung the toy bat around again, knocking out Elaine's remaining teeth. They clattered on the ground as Elaine stumbled back and raised her hands and moaned.

Joe had heard this kind of moan before and it chilled him to hear it again. The moan brought back echoes of the apocalypse, of when the dead were first birthed, and he shivered at the reminiscence. This groan was a very specific cry to others of her kind, to bring them to her, telling them that there was food in the offing. Joe knew that call, and although in the past he'd dreaded it, and despite the chill he'd just gotten, he felt Elaine's moan enter his chest and rally him.

Joe scampered from the fire escape and into the building, running past the destroyed body of the biter and down the steps, dashing through the empty entrance to the Savings and Loans and bursting onto Main Street, right into the middle of the chaos.

He didn't know what came over him or why. He just knew that he was suddenly consumed by an irrational rage, a driving need to kill every one of those bastard scavengers. This was his town, where he lived with his friends, and even as he thought this, Joe realized how insane it sounded.

The walking dead; his friends?

Choosing them over living, breathing humans? How could he side with the zombies over his own kind? Joe didn't know the answer and didn't care.

He charged down the street, brushing past Tommy and rushing past Mr. Postal Man. Joe aimed straight for the bitch who'd hurt Elaine, honing in on her like she had a target drawn on the pad across her chest. He leapt at her, a growl erupting from between his clenched teeth, and slammed his lowered shoulder into the woman, surprised both at how strong he was and how weak she seemed. Her ribs snapped on impact and she flew up into the air and then back down, landing on her rear. When she hit the pavement, Joe heard one of her legs crack underneath her and realized that the woman had no more substance than the zombies roaming the streets.

Elaine turned and looked at Joe. She stopped moaning. The woman on the ground screamed, and as she did, help from the scavengers came.

They ran to her, weapons raised and ready as Joe stood next to Elaine, his fists clinched and his jaws grinding his teeth together in rage.

The scavengers formed a line in front of Joe and the Leader stepped forward. He bent down to look at his woman and then looked up and glared at Joe.

He grunted something and waved his baseball bat around.

"You go to hell!" Joe yelled. "Get out of this town, it's mine!"

Joe took a step back and bumped into Mr. Postal Man. Joe spun, shocked to see that Tommy was standing next to Mr. Postal Man as were most of the Townies, gathered behind Joe like supporting neighbors. It was the damndest thing Joe had ever seen. There they stood, two rival gangs, ready to go to war over the small town.

The Leader shrieked and waved his bat over his head. He charged Joe and swung the bat, smacking Joe on his left arm and smashing him to the ground. The Leader jumped on Joe, kicking and swinging the bat, slamming it into his legs and back as Joe rolled on the ground, screaming and trying to get away.

The scavengers roared and attacked, following the Leader. They crushed forward, using their knives, sickles, pipes and bats as they attacked the living dead.

They trampled many of the Townies into the ground, beating them mercilessly. It was a slaughter, as the living overtook the dead by sheer speed and ferocity. But more and more dead were arriving, heeding Elaine's call. They came in from the side streets and the outlying suburbs, all rotted, shambling, and moaning. They numbered in the hundreds, these zombies, and they steadily moved forward, slowly but surely creeping up on the marauding scavengers.

The ranks of the dead swelled with soccer moms, community leaders, children, teachers, firemen, and police; all living dead, all peaceably minding their own business, until the call of one of their own, until the scavengers arrived.

Soon, the tide began to turn.

In the midst of the initial melee, Mr. Postal Man grabbed the Leader by his neck as he was attacking Joe and dug his fingers in, ripping out a chunk of the Leader's flesh.

The Leader screamed and dropped his bat, his hand flying up to his wound as his warm, wet blood sprayed across Mr. Postal Man's chest.

Joe scooped the bat from the ground and cracked it across the Leader's knees, shattering them. The Leader shrieked and crumpled and Tommy and two other Townies, Meter Maid and Businessman, descended on the fallen Leader. They drove their hands into his soft parts, tearing open his stomach and ripping out bunches of his intestines. Tommy bit off the Leader's right nipple and slurped it into his mouth like a piece of candy.

Joe lurched to his feet and stared down at the Leader lying helplessly at his feet, being torn apart by the Townies. He raised the bat over his head, screamed with triumph, and sliced it down, crunching the Leader's screaming face. Nose, eyes, bits of teeth and bone exploded, the Leader's head splattering like a popped water balloon.

Joe stumbled back as Tommy and the Meter Maid and the Businessman feasted on the Leader's still twitching body. They pulled pieces of his liver and kidneys out as other Townies joined them, their hard, shriveled, gnarled fingers and rotting teeth stripping the Leader of his flesh and vital organs.

The dead surrounded the scavengers now as the zombies from the suburbs and outlying areas arrived. The scavengers, however, fought on with savage brutality.

One of the scavengers, a man with long hair that wore stained white leather pants and a pair of pink sneakers, used a pipe to batter a resident of the town, a Stay At Home Mom. She was on her back, wearing a torn and blood-stained apron over a checkered blouse and short skirt as Long Hair whacked her chest with the pipe, her oven-mitt covered hands clawing at his arms.

Elaine slipped up behind Long Hair and dug her fingers into his mane, tangling her fingers into his locks. Long Hair jerked his head to try and pull free of Elaine's grip, forgetting about Stay At Home Mom. She sat up, face-level with his crotch, and buried her teeth into his inner right thigh. Stay At Home Mom wrenched her

9

head back and tore free a chunk of white, leather-covered flesh and gobbled it down. Long Hair screamed, his hair still intertwined in Elaine's fingers, and smashed the top of Stay At Home Mom's head with the pipe. Elaine yanked backwards, exposing Long Hair's throat as another zombie, a Plumber, dove in and chomped on Long Hair's Adam's apple. Blood foamed from the burbling wound as Elaine hauled Long Hair down to the ground to be feasted upon by the Plumber and the other Townies.

Another group of scavengers, just off to the left of Long Hair, all male and shirtless with tribal markings painted on their torsos, formed a circle to combat the pressing dead on their every side. They killed a dozen zombies only to have dozens more replace them, fodders for the bats and sickles the Painted Scavengers wielded.

The Painted Scavengers fought ferociously, slicing skin and splintering bone, but the dead were unaffected by these attacks and pushed forward until the Painted Scavengers were all squashed up against each other, their arms and legs pinned and their weapons useless. The dead kept pressing against the Painted Scavengers on all sides until their spines snapped and their chests caved in as they were compacted together.

Ribs cracked and interlocked with the ribs of others, cheeks mashed together until teeth met and then broke, noses snapped and then skulls and flesh tore. The dead pushed them together until the Painted Scavengers became one huge lump of flesh, pulped together like a mass of sculptor's clay. And then the dead dug in, greedy fingers and teeth rending flesh and bone.

In the meantime, over to the left of the pulverizing, Joe joined his dead comrades, swinging the bat amongst the scavengers that were grouped around him, cracking arms and legs and fracturing bones. He danced among them, as much an enemy of the living as the dead were. For each scavenger he took down, three of the dead fell on the crippled humans, chomping and tearing at their delivered feast.

Joe was beside himself with manic fury, fully caught up in the moment, at one with his neighbors and friends.

Until he spun one time too many and impaled himself on a drawn knife. At the other end of the knife was a Boy, his face grubby and his blue eyes wide with primitive anger. The Boy laughed and spat in Joe's face and jerked the knife out and stabbed him repeatedly with relentless rage.

Joe doubled over, blood pouring from his stomach and pattering the ground like rain drops. He fell to his knees as Mr. Postal Man shambled up behind the Boy and jammed his fingers into the Boy's eye sockets, grinding his fingers in until the eyes popped out. They slid down the Boy's screaming cheeks and hit the ground with a wet slap. Mr. Postal Man dug his fingers in deeper, got a good grip with his hands, and then yanked. The Boy's grubby face split in half and his brains spilled out, slithering down his chest like a lumpy, bloody snake, followed by a deluge of blood and viscera.

Joe fell on his rear, in shock, as some of the Townies slid in on their bellies and slobbered up the eyeballs and the brains of the Boy. Mr. Postal Man jammed his fist down the open head and kept shoving until his hand passed through the Boy's throat and into his chest. Mr. Postal Man went as deep as his elbow before he clenched his fist and heaved, tearing the Boy's heart out of the top of his head. The Boy's body fell to the side, into the waiting fingers and teeth of hungry Townies, as Mr. Postal Man looked down at Joe. He raised the Boy's heart to his lips and bit into the still-pulsing muscle.

Joe looked down and watched as his own blood poured from his wounds and he felt weaker by the second. He held his hands over where the Boy had stabbed him but he knew it was useless; the kid had gotten him good and there was no recovering from this wound. Joe felt the warm wetness of his life spill out and run through his fingers, staining Main Street.

The entire time, as Joe bled out, not one zombie turned his way to attempt to feast on him.

The scavengers fought their losing fight, and as Joe watched, the dead thundered over them, stampeding the humans under the sheer weight of their numbers. Within minutes, it was all over.

Joe fell to his side and gazed as his neighbors feasted, their lips smacking together over wet and warm flesh, their teeth grinding on bones. The sounds of the banquet filled the Town Square, echoing between the empty buildings.

Joe smiled and thought of the barbecues his dad used to throw when he was a kid, when the entire neighborhood would come over and dig in and enjoy the party. This was much like that and Joe was happy that in his dying moments, he could have such a joyful sight to see.

Mr. Postal Man shuffled over and sat down next to Joe and looked at him. Joe met his eyes and they stared at each other. Mr. Postal Man, his fingers thick with gore, reached over and took Joe's right hand into his. He held Joe's hand as Joe's breathing slowed and eventually stopped.

Half an hour later, Joe rose. He sat up and looked at his neighbors and their feast and at Mr. Postal Man, still sitting next to him. Joe moaned and crawled over and tore a strip of stringy flesh from one of the corpses and stuck it in his mouth, chewing vigorously.

When the eating was done, Joe got to his feet and walked into the Savings and Loan building and went up the steps and out the window of the third floor and sat down on the fire escape.

From there, he watched his neighbors go about their daily tasks, as he would every day until he rotted away and was no more.

# THE HIGHWAY MAN

## ERIC S BROWN AND MARK M JOHNSON

Lucas stood in the middle of the road blocking the coach's path. He'd already said all he had to say. What happened now was up to them. His eyes drifted from the driver of the coach to the man who sat beside him holding a shotgun. A third man stepped out of the coach itself. He wore the long coat of a professional killer, which was pulled back to show the revolvers resting in holsters on his hips. Lucas hadn't planned on there being three men to deal with but facing the unexpected was just another part of the job when you made your living stealing. Either you were good enough to handle it or you were dead. The look on their faces told him there was going to be blood in the dirt today.

The third man moved first. His hand twitched, telling Lucas he was going for his gun, but Lucas' hands moved with the speed and grace born of countless gunfights and encounters like this one. His revolvers cleared their matching holsters before the other man's even got close to his own. He put a bullet into the gunfighter's throat and sent him sprawling onto the road, spraying blood. His second shot struck the man with the shotgun dead-on in his forehead, blowing a gaping hole in the backside of his skull where the bullet exited. By this time, the driver had leapt sideways to the left off the coach as the bullet Lucas had intended for him smacked the spot where he'd sat as wooden splinters flew into the air. Lucas cursed. Age was catching up with him.

Inside the coach, a woman was screaming as he sprinted around to get another shot at the driver. The man had lost all his nerve and was fleeing up the hill by the side of the road. Lucas hated shooting him in the back but the man's cowardice left him with little choice. His pistols boomed three more times as the driver cried out and toppled down the hill, a trio of wet, red patches growing on the back of his shirt. The man's corpse rolled to within a few feet of Lucas and lay still. Lucas scowled and spat

# DEAD WORLDS

into the dirt, holstering one of his guns as he moved to the coach's door.

A woman dressed in the fine clothes of a 'lady' sat inside. She was in her early forties but attractive for her age. Not attractive enough for Lucas to spare her life however. She didn't appear to be worth the time and struggle of having his way with her. Ignoring her pleas, he calmly shoved the barrel of his pistol into her stomach and pulled the trigger. Gut wounds were the worst and she was really annoying him with her crying and carrying on so she deserved this. She was still conscious but dying as he tossed her from the coach and pulled out the heavy, locked box from beneath her seat. He hoped it was worth the effort.

Evans had told him the lady was the wife of Bob Pilkington, the fat little pig who now ran the boom town of Gold Flats, and she was supposed to be bringing a large amount of their savings with her, thus the guards he'd squared off with.

The box was small enough to be carried. He would break the lock and go through it later. Right now, he wanted to put as much distance between him and this place of gun smoke and death as possible before some idiot rode up the road and he had to kill them, too.

Tucking the box under his arm, Lucas started back for where he'd left his horse on the other side of the hill. As he turned from the coach, he saw the driver getting to his feet.

*What in tarnation?* he thought.

Talk about a stubborn S.O.B. He jerked his other revolver which still had three rounds left in its chamber and shot the man a fourth time. The bullet impacted with the driver's sternum and put him down in the dirt once more. For good measure, Lucas walked over and added another round straight to the man's skull. There was no point in taking chances. He smiled with the satisfaction of a job well done but the smile quickly fell from his lips when a low, hollow moan coming from behind him.

He turned to see the other two men he'd killed on their feet and shambling towards him, the fronts now covered in mud and blood. The coach's horses were amazingly well trained but the men's unnatural odor of offal and death must have spooked them.

14

They took off, taking the coach with them, filling the air with dust that clogged the nasal passages and caused a man to gag. The sudden movement of the two men made Lucas jump out of instinct. Combined with the utter shock of seeing dead men walk, even his experience failed him. The weight of the box under his arm threw him off balance, beyond the point where he could right himself, and he spun where he stood, dropping to the ground like a falling tree. The box bruised his side where he landed on it and he grunted with pain. He looked up to see the men drawing closer.

Lucas had heard the stories about dead men returning to life as ghouls that ate the flesh of the living but hadn't believed them. Who would believe such drunken nonsense? The stories were everywhere though. In the last three towns he'd passed through there was always at least one drunken fool in the bars he visited babbling on about the End Times and God's judgment upon the Earth. He'd laughed off as foolishness.

Lucas didn't believe in God. There was nothing after death but darkness and the void. But these men were certainly dead. To claim less would be to insult his to skill as a killer.

He raised his guns towards them. "Back off, fellas," he warned, "I'd hate to have to put you down twice in one day."

If they heard his words or had any fear of the weapons he held, they didn't show it. They kept shambling towards him, their cold voices crying out with moans of longing and hunger.

Lucas scrambled to his feet, taking in the situation with practiced ease.

"They're so slow," he muttered, backing away from them. "Damn slow."

His confidence began to return and he aimed and blew out the closest one's kneecaps. The walking corpse collapsed into the dirt, still moaning. Lucas laughed. "You're even slower now, aren't you, fellow?"

Lucas did the same to the second man with his last round, now both sprawled in the dirt.

He watched them crawl towards him for a second with morbid fascination before he snapped out of it. Picking up a large, heavy rock from the road side, not wanting to waste any more ammo on the bastards, he moved towards them. Lucas carefully moved up to the first one, grabbed one of its arms as it reached for him, and wrestled it to its back. He sat down on top of it, striking its head over and over with the rock until its skull was completely smashed in. The men didn't seem to have much strength so it was easier than he'd expected.

Lucas did in the second man the same way. He stood up, tossing the rock aside, and wiped at the blood which was now smeared over his clothes. Sweat ran from his head in rivulets that cut through the dust coating his face. He pulled a handkerchief from his pocket, cleaning up his hands from the ghoul's blood.

Finally, Lucas walked back towards his prize and bent to pick up the box from where he'd dropped it.

No sooner was his hand on the box, then something heavy threw itself onto his back and his face struck the box as he was forced to the ground. He spat teeth and blood as dirty fingernails tore at his flesh through his shirt.

Crying out in pain, he rolled over to find the woman he'd gut shot on top of him. He stared up into her cold, soulless eyes as she buried her teeth into his throat. White hot pain filled his mind and he howled like a dying animal as she tore into him like a rabid dog, slinging his blood and her saliva everywhere around them as they struggled. His vision became filled with the redness of his own life as the world faded away and the darkness descended.

Once before upon his birth, his eyes had opened to life, and they now opened into a new life in death. Lucas groaned as he sat up from the bloody, dust-covered road and turned to gaze at the woman who he had now joined.

She had lost interest in him as soon as he had revived and moved off into the brush.

As Lucas looked around him, a new and strange second life filled his body. He heard an animal whiney in the distance and then it screamed as the woman tore into his horse which had somehow gotten free and wandered into the road. He watched with dull eyes as she gnashed at the animal's hide with her teeth, tearing away large chunks of flesh from its side with each bite, her hands holding tightly to its reigns so it couldn't escape.

*That's my horse*, he thought. He remembered! His thoughts were foggy and his motions slow, but he remembered. That 'lady' done tore my throat out and killed me as sure as the sun rises, but for somehow I ain't stupid like those other fools were. I can still think.

Lucas struggled to his feet and stood swaying as his undead mind slowly remembered how to walk. The lockbox he had coveted so much lay broken open at his feet. It wasn't the sparkle of gold that glistened from within but an ancient stone tablet that glowed with an ethereal green luminescence. It was eerie, magical, and utterly useless to him. He had no interest in the box or its tablet any longer; something else ruled his desires now.

A hunger filled him unlike anything he'd ever felt. It burned at his entire body, demanding to be fed.

The old familiar aches, pains, itches, and needs that once defined his existence were newly absent. Lucas's undead body felt numb, light as air and completely lacking its old limitations. He did feel something though, an emptiness that bordered on shear agony burned within his stomach.

The sound of the distant yet approaching hoof-beats reached his dead ears and new memories surfaced as his natural instincts took over.

*My shooters are darn near empty as my aching stomach*, he thought.

He stumbled towards the dusty road, while his dead fingers fumbled and dropped several fresh rounds as they attempted to do what they had done thousands of times before. It took terrible effort to load the rounds into the tiny holes of the weapon's chamber but he finally managed it. With his loaded pistols back in their holsters, Lucas stood in the center of the road and waited.

He didn't have to wait long.

Two riders came around the bend in the road at a break neck gallop, leaving a cloud of dust behind them. When they spotted Lucas standing in their path they both reined in their steeds and stopped.

"Well, well, well," said the larger of the two men as the sun glinted off the tin star on his chest. "What do we have here?"

Lucas stared at the sheriff coldly, drool and blood running down his chin.

"As I live and breathe, if it ain't Lucas Maynard."

Lucas remembered his name as the man spoke it and his mouth twitched in a smirk.

"Looks like you got what was coming to you already, boy. I won't have to take you in after all."

Lucas's hands dropped down over his pistols, hovering.

"Whoa there, son," the sheriff shouted as he and his deputy reached for their guns. "You draw down on me, and you're gonna come up short and dead all over again, you rotting piece of horse dung."

But Lucas did draw, but his dead hands lacked the unnatural speed he possessed in life. His guns had barely cleared their matching holsters when two bullets slammed into his chest and he staggered backwards but failed to fall.

"Gosh darn, Sheriff," the deputy said as he looked over his smoking barrel. "Why ain't he dead?"

The sheriff lowered his gun and glared at the outlaw highway man, the turned to his deputy and said, "Hey, boy, I ain't never seen no dead man who could shoot back. Something ain't right about this one, even as messed up as he is. Put a dang bullet in his head and let's get this over with before he starts up with them six shooters again."

"You got it, Sheriff," the deputy replied as he drew his revolver and lined up a shot with Lucas' head.

"No," Lucas gurgled out of his torn throat. His voice was full of pain and rage as he raised his guns and aimed his shots to maim. He managed to put a few rounds into each them, ignoring the bullets which tore into his flesh once more.

Lucas didn't feel any pain from their shots but they sure as hell did from his.

Both lawmen lay on the ground, bleeding and whimpering from the gut shots Lucas gave them.

He dropped his guns to the road and staggered towards the two wounded men, wondering if the bullet holes in their bodies would make it easer to tear their stomachs open with his fingers.

It had been a long day and now, it was time for lunch.

# HEAD ON

## FRANCESCO COLLIA

Connor Mason knew he was going to crash. He didn't believe in much, let alone that he was psychic, but it had become a bore to argue with the precog déjà vu that had intermittently freaked his game over the years.

It wasn't a vision so much as a feeling, a split-second flash of his immediate future. But just because he sensed things didn't mean he sixth sensed them. Other people got them, he knew. It was just another quirk of our frustratingly uncharted brains. Either way...

The truck broke hard in front of him then cut left into the on-coming lane. It was a dated pickup modded for handyman side-gigging, the kind with motley tools skidding about the bed and, always, a six-foot ladder looming over the back gate. It was the latter that raised Connor's dread and it was little consolation that he had been correct when it came untethered and airborne. Even with this foresight he couldn't do more than slide down just low enough in his seat a blink before the ladder speared through his windshield.

Connor burrowed into the leg well as far as his seat belt would allow, all his weight resting on the accelerator. His car raced forward. And he remembered. There was something in the road. In the snapshot between when the truck swerved and when he lost his head with the panic of decapitation, he had seen something, some-one, in the road. There had been another accident. That's what the truck was attempting to avoid. That's what, who, he now clipped with his front tire at such a speed that it lifted the left side of his car off the pavement, depositing it 180 degrees later with a sicken-ing metallic crackle.

His first thought upon regaining consciousness was that the world was different. He knew being upside down had something to do with it, but there was an ominous tapping at his memory. Not as if trying to get in, but to warn him to wake up, to remember. His vision centered on the two cars across from him, one humped up on the other's trunk. Twisted steel and sex appeal. That classic pro wrestling interview braggadocio, a random connection by a brain clawing its way back.

Then he saw it. Him. It.

"...the hell?" he said, quickly swallowing the thought of making another sound. The self-preservation of silence kicked in. Or was it nausea clamping his mouth shut. A woman was hanging backward out of the passenger window of the bottom of the two cars, the hem of her dress flipped over covering her upper body, and the thing that was camped out over her head. The thing, a person, it had to be. A person, a bystander, a rescue worker, someone coming to the aid of an accident victim. This was a crash site, and an awful one from the little he could see. Of course, it was that. Yet it wasn't. The tapping got louder. The thought that such assumptions were no longer an option seeped in. That such assumptions would get him killed. And then the thing lifted its head out from beneath the dress. "...the fuck?"

Human. Past tense. A man, dressed casually, khakis and a polo, the former ripped at the knees. He got to his feet, slowly, his movement more rote than willful. Then he turned and the tapping stopped. This was Connor's reminder. This was what he needed to understand. The world was not just different, but very likely, over.

The top half of the man's face was ashen, empty, his eyes tiny black pits. The bottom half was crimson, mottled with blood and skin, bone and hair. His chin dripped gore, dripped the remnants of that woman's head. He shuffled toward the second car and Connor knew if he didn't start acting instead of reacting he was the next station in this cannibalistic buffet.

The first step was to assess his health. He had been so distracted by the visual stimuli upon waking that he hadn't bothered to figure out if he was injured. His head pounded, throbbing with rushing blood. He felt his legs, arms and chest and allowed himself a relieved sigh for being intact. But he needed to free himself from his seat, to get upright, or he risked passing out again. And next time, he was sure, he'd end up with a bit more wrong than a headache.

He stuck one hand through the rungs to use as a brace on the ceiling and unbuckled his seat belt with the other, sliding onto the metal ladder. His head rest was gone, lopped off, but the seat still reclined and he maxed it out for as much squirm room as possible, ducking under the steering column and bringing himself up onto his knees. He was jammed in tight, the car's cabin essentially cut in two. But he was thankful for being able to extricate himself, for his generic size at last being useful for something other than just buying clothes off the rack.

The man, the ghoul, was rummaging through the broken window of the second car. Connor closed his eyes, dizziness overcoming him. Deep breaths. Focus. It was survival hour. He needed to run, to escape, and when he started he couldn't stop. Or allow anything to get in his way. If he had to fight, he would. But what would he be fighting? What else was out there?

Connor looked back to the first car, over the draped corpse of the woman, and saw her deployed airbag. He couldn't help but shake his head. He would have been pinned if his airbag had gone off, if he had one. This used car he bought on the cheap, the one he nervously joked was a deathtrap, had saved his life.

For the moment at least.

And that thought brought him back. He was alive, but was he any better off than the feasted upon woman? If he was to suffer the same fate, would delaying it just prove crueler? Then, as if to answer him, she moved.

It wasn't the wind, though that had started to pick up. And it was definitely too late for death throes. No, she moved. She dropped to the ground and began turning herself over. She moved, even with half the contents of her skull on the face of that *thing*, she moved. She rose, her dress falling back into place, exposing her face for the first time. And Connor pulled himself out of his car.

She saw him right off and stumbled forward. She was slow, he knew that from the others he'd watched, and he took a moment to survey the scene. There were the cars in front of him. The truck that had swerved off the road was crumpled around a telephone pole, its driver splayed on the hood. To Connor's right was a delivery truck on its side, now a big brown wall blocking him in. It had to be left, he thought, past the two cars. Past the gorging monster.

Connor looked back and the woman was closer. She was teetering to her right, the side with the gaping hole in her cranium. She lunged forward and fell flat on her face, inches from where he stood. And was still. He could see inside the hole, at her half-eaten brain. He tapped her with his foot, then kicked her. Hard. She was dead. *Dead* dead, he thought and somehow knew it to be true. But another thought took hold of him. He hadn't moved. She landed at his feet and he hadn't moved, hadn't made any attempt to run or defend himself. He knew that was literally the last time that could happen.

The other...*thing* pulled out of the car, its face awash in fresh carnage. Connor had stopped thinking of it as a man, or even a former man. Nor was it an animal. It was like nothing alive, nothing natural. Whatever it was, it was now aware of his presence. It was looking right at him.

Head down, Connor dashed past, avoiding the murderous outstretched arms in the narrow gap between the wreckage. As he cleared the back of the bottom car, his foot slipped off the edge of the asphalt, twisting his body and sending him to the ground. The creature continued for him at its methodically relentless pace. Connor tried to hop back onto his feet in a single motion, but failed to gain his footing and stumbled backward, smacking into the totaled pickup. The impact sent him back to the ground. He couldn't believe he was having so much trouble simply trying to run.

He dug his heels into the dirt on the shoulder of the road and slid himself up the side of the truck. The creature had stopped advancing, yet that filled him with more apprehension than relief. More fear. Why?

Something grabbed his wrist and pulled him onto the hood. Without looking, Connor knew it was the driver he had check listed as dead, knew he was paying for another assumption.

The pain was piercing as the driver's thumb pressed hard into the soft tissue beneath his palm, threatening to bore its way straight through. Connor turned and saw the driver's face, bedazzled with shards of glass. He was dead, or had been. This was something as easy to discern as whether someone was, well, alive. Life, it turns out, is quite a distinguishing feature.

The driver pulled Connor's hand closer to his mouth. Connor tried to pull free, but couldn't. He tried again. The driver responded by opening his mouth wider and, with his other hand, pulling himself forward to gain more leverage. Now no longer thinking, Connor used the vise-like grip to his advantage and hauled himself onto his stomach, bringing his free fist down onto the crown of the driver's head. This did it and he pulled loose, landed on his feet, and was off running down the road before he could even be sure what had happened.

When his mind caught up with his body, Connor pulled to a stop and looked back. He was gasping, and knew he had to control his breathing or risk hyperventilating. He was a safe distance from the pile-up, but knew everything he did from here on out, every mistake, every moment he wasn't moving, would mean they were one step closer. Who or whatever they were.

Fortunately, he knew where he was. He drove this back road every day to and from work, knew he was about a half mile away from a major thoroughfare, from the gas station on the corner. What he didn't know was what else was going to be there waiting for him. He hurried along trying hard not to dwell on the obvious whats and whys. He needed answers, but wasn't even sure he could wrap his head around the questions.

He stopped again, his temples pulsing, eyes tearing. His adrenaline was waning and he began to worry. He couldn't relax, not now, not here. He felt exposed, desolate. He needed to find someone to talk to. He needed some aspirin. He needed some solace and comfort and until he found all these things what he needed most of all was to stay on edge, to stay cranked.

The girl was standing there when he lifted his head.

She was off the road in a bit of clearing in front of a straggle of trees. His heart jumped. He called to her, but she didn't respond. She was facing the other way, but appeared to be ten or eleven, what marketers now called a tween. To him, she was just a kid, but he knew nothing was *just* anything anymore.

Connor narrowed the distance between them cautiously, calling to her every few steps but receiving not even a flinch. He was pretty sure what he was going to discover, but also needed to see it for himself. When he got to within a body's length of the girl, she moved for the first time, raising three arms at her sides, the odd one bigger than the other two, darker, and not attached to her body. She turned, her smeared face contorting. She let out a guttural moan and opened her mouth. There dangling between her parted lips was a finger, its skin snagged in her braces. Her tongue fruitlessly swatted at it, again and again. She didn't appear to have the motor skills or the acuity to remove it by hand and Connor thought she may very well be permanently stuck in place, locked down in eternal struggle. Sisyphus by Bosch.

Despite her evident state, despite what he had seen at the crash, Connor still felt he should help her in some way. She was a child, after all, and isn't that what he was supposed to do? He wanted to yank the finger out, but knew she would all too quickly seek to replace it with one of his own. Finally, he thought it best to just back away, and as he did, the woods came alive with the sound of death.

First, there was two, then too many to count in a quick scan. A dozen, maybe. Men, women, all ages, all sizes and races, all shambling through the brush toward him, at him. A macabre chorus groaning the same hellish dirge. Connor knew he could outrun them, but how far, how long. How would he know if he was running from or to...to what? What, what was he supposed to think?

He jogged the rest of the way to the intersection only to find he had gotten nowhere. No cars, no people, no noise. Nothing. He moved towards the gas station hoping for some sign of life, muttering the last word aloud.

"Life."

The automatic doors didn't open, so Connor tried the handles. Locked. This wasn't just your average emergency like a hurricane or even a riot, where you prep your store and hope for the best. This was of an unprecedented magnitude, a life-altering split from reality. No one would think to lock the door behind them because no one would be coming back. Unless they were still inside.

Connor banged on the glass and pleaded for help. He was fully aware that the longer he carried on the more likely he was to draw attention to his location, but whoever was inside, whoever was ignoring his pleas had to realize the same. And once they, the *things*, were here, well, that couldn't be a chance worth taking.

Yet, still no response.

"So that's how we're gonna play this?" he mumbled to himself. He picked up the metal garbage can next to the door and raised it over his head. He was getting in there one way or another, if not for shelter then at least for aspirin, water, a chance to see the prick who would leave him out here to die alone. He reared back...and saw the prick.

"What are you, retarded?" A blonde woman smacked the glass from the other side.

Connor lowered the can and placed it beside him. His eye was twitching from the pain behind it. He started to speak, to say he had no idea, but she spared him the effort by unlocking the door and sliding it open.

"Well, get in here already," she said, barely waiting for him to clear the doorway before locking them in.

"It's not like I wasn't trying," he said.

"Right. I just had to make sure."

"What, that I wasn't..."

"Gonna eat my face? Yeah," she said.

Connor walked past her knowing he wasn't coming up with a comeback to that. He headed straight for the meds aisle, having gotten to know this little quick stop quite well over the past year of commuting, and especially in the last month since they had joined the world and started brewing some decent coffee.

Not bothering to comparison shop, he grabbed the box with **EXTRA STRENGTH** in the biggest font and went to the freezer for some water.

"You gonna pay for that?"

He held the pills mid-swallow before gulping hard. He was looting. He'd just walked into a store and took what he wanted, what he needed maybe, but that's what they all say, isn't it? He was *they* now. Already. Already?

"This your place?" he asked.

"No," she said, turning her head from the window just enough to flash him a half grin.

He took another swig from the bottle before capping it and placing it on a shelf. After a full minute of silence, rather uncomfortable considering the rush he'd just been through, he finally asked, "Okay, what the hell's going on?"

"End of the world," she said, not looking at him. "What's new with you?"

"Jokes? Really?" He took a few steps toward her.

"Sorry. Nerves." She turned to fully face him for the first time since the door. She was older than him, late 30s maybe, and now, as he decelerated back to normal speed, he couldn't help but notice how nicely her tank top was clinging to her with sweat. Jesus, he thought, was he really that pathetically...male?

"So, what's your story?" she asked.

"I don't know. I was just driving home and...everything just sorta happened real fast."

"You crashed?" she asked.

He nodded. They had moved to within a standard conversational distance and Connor tried to relax, but was a fidgeting mess, hopped up on an emotional cocktail of fear, anxiety, and natural social awkwardness.

"Accidents all over," she continued. "I stopped to help someone just down the road a bit and..." She turned away again to check the window. "So much for my Good Samaritan badge..." The last word hung there, waiting. Like bait, thought Connor. Picking up on hints, *getting things*, wasn't exactly his forte, but he took a shot and offered his name.

She smiled. "I'm Andie. Are you all right? From the crash?"

"I guess," Connor said, reflecting on it for the first time since crawling out of his wreck. "I mean, yeah, all things considered."

"So, what did you hear? On the radio."

"What do you mean?" Connor asked.

"In your car. What did you hear about what's going on?"

With nothing to offer, he stammered. And shrugged. "I had my iPod on."

"Great," she sighed.

"Well, what did you hear? You were driving, too."

Andie beamed a stare at him, narrowing her eyes for effect. Then deadpanned, "Who listens to the radio anymore?"

That broke the already cracking ice and Connor steadied, gaining his bearing.

"Is there a radio in here? TV?"

"No reception," she said.

"Internet?"

"No connection. Phone's out. No cell service."

"Fuck me."

"I don't think we're in re-populating the Earth mode just yet, big guy," she joked.

"What? Oh." Connor blushed.

She was quick and funny and he knew he was in trouble, but that's not what he had meant. Cell phone? How could he not have thought to use his until now? He fished it out of his pants pocket: no bars. Fine, but still. He had to get in the game. That kind of broken link was now lethal.

"How did the whole grid get shut down so fast?"

"What's so fast? We have no idea what's happening, let alone when it started. And, really, weren't we all walking around pretty clueless to begin with?"

"So what do we do now?" he asked.

"Well, we'd talked about…"

"Wait, we?"

"Oh, crap." Andie covered her mouth. "I never told you, did I? There's somebody else in here."

"Wait, what?" It was the unexpectedness of the news, had to be. What other explanation could there be for the unease that burst in his stomach.

"God, I'm sorry," Andie continued. "It's just with all that was…anyway, we met up out there and thought it best to, you know, band together. He's in the back office. Resting."

"Resting?"

"He got hurt. One of those things bit him. I don't know; that's what he said. He was bleeding."

"He's been bit?" he asked.

"On the arm. That's probably bad, right?" She began nibbling on a fingernail.

"I don't know, maybe," he said. "I know I don't want to get bit by them or anything else for that matter."

"His name's Ted, by the way," she offered.

Connor headed for the door just off the counter, next to the coffee station. He might have to put on a fresh pot before nailing down any sort of decisive action.

"Or Jim."

"What?" asked Connor, his hand on the knob of the half-opened door.

"His name might be Jim. I don't really know," she said.

Before Connor had the chance to ignore this intelligence report, the door bashed him in the forehead. He staggered backward and, reaching for balance, came up with nothing but a coffee pot, full but luckily for him, cold, which he pulled down all over himself as he crashed to the floor. The door had bounced back, and now, standing in the opening was neither Ted nor Jim.

What was standing there had now ceased to be anyone. It was no longer human.

"Holy shit!" Andie yelled from across the store.

And that pretty much summed it up. Connor slid back and got to his feet. The thought that the door would have slammed shut if he hadn't been standing there crossed his mind, but thought it best to file that bit of irony for later.

The thing lurched out into the main room, groaning like the others had back at the pile-up. It had on a suit, nice cut, though the gnawed through sleeve killed the whole look. The man made his way past the counter and there wasn't any doubt that he knew where he was going.

Connor had made his way back to the opposite side, parallel with Andie, an aisle between them.

"A gun," he said. "There's probably a gun near the register, right?"

"Right," she said, ending the word in a long sigh.

"But...?"

"But, he has it." She pointed at old what's-his-name clumsily navigating the store's floor displays. Connor's shoulders slumped as he looked at her.

"What?" she said. "Like I saw this coming?"

"Whatever. We need to stop him."

"You think?" Her words shook as she edged her way closer to Connor.

"I think we need to go for the head," Connor said.

"How do you know that?"

He remembered the woman at the crash, how she fell dead after her skull had been hollowed out. But he also remembered something more basic. Killing 101. "It's always a headshot that will do the trick."

"Okay. With what?" she gasped.

Without thinking, he picked up a can of chili and hurled it at the man which had now cleared a pyramid of travel mugs. Direct hit. His head snapped back and he stopped.

Connor moved closer and threw again. And again. Each step he gained upped the impact. Andie joined him with an armful of cold tall boys. Together they barraged the man, knocking him to the floor. He looked dazed, out of commission. But not dead. Not for good. It would take more, it would take crossing that line. It would take finishing the job.

And Connor did.

Can after can, point blank. Pounding, caving, weakening. He wedged his heel into the crack in the skull he'd made and pressed and tore the man's head wide open.

Nothing was said for a while. Both he and Andie slowly backed away from the re-dead thing, killing the dead person once more, without being aware they were doing so. Coming together, Connor and Andie alternated cursory glances out the front window as they searched for a path past the last few minutes of carnage. They had killed. Whatever it the man was, whatever he may have done to them... It was easy. That's what was drumming in Connor's mind. So easy. And it was probably only the beginning.

Andie snapped back first with a double take. Outside, huddled between the gas pumps was a boy, seven or eight tops. He was crying and dirty. And alive. Undeniably not dead.

"That can't be good," Connor said. He hadn't even seen the boy, not yet. The sight of the two dozen or so strong horde advancing on them from the side road, from the way he'd originally fled, was an ample distraction.

"Run!" Andie screamed.

She was pale, her fingers pulling through her hair. Connor saw where she was looking, who she was screaming at. He glanced at the horde, back to the child. Back and forth, hoping a plan would somehow be jarred awake. But there was only one course of action and the more he thought he had a choice the less he had a chance. He went and opened the doors.

"What are you doing?" she asked, panic in her voice.

"What do you think I'm doing?"

Her hand was on his shoulder and the look in her eyes, the pleading, the terror, was transfusing him. He shook her off. It's not what he expected from her, but then again, he wouldn't have guessed he'd be playing the hero. It would have been a sucker's bet.

"Just make sure you let us back in." Then he turned and stepped outside and she reached for him again. But he was already out of reach.

Halfway to the pumps he remembered the gun. Too late. There was just so much to think about in so little time. Even less now that he had a better view of the property. Besides the crowd bearing down on his left, a smaller group was coming up from the direction he was running. And there were stragglers even closer. If he made it, it wasn't going to be pretty.

The boy was older, bigger than he thought, maybe a schoolmate of the finger girl from up the road. And he was in shock, wasn't moving.

*Dead weight*, Connor thought.

A groan from the other side of the pump. A hand coming into sight, clawing the air. Connor yanked the boy to the side and snatched the squeegee from the container of brown water on the side of the trash container. Holding onto the rubber wiper blade, he stepped out to face his undead predator, and then rammed the wooden handle straight into its open mouth, then out the back of its head.

The force of the blow sent them both down, him on top of the creature. Connor rolled off and went back to the boy. He was going to have to drag the kid the twenty yards back to the store. And there just wasn't time. The smaller band of things...*zombies*? (Were they fucking *zombies*?) was almost on them.

Then he had an idea. Burn their asses.

He lifted the nozzle to the pump, then let it drop back in place. He slapped his leg, reached into his pocket, pulled out his wallet, pulled out his debit card. Swiped it. No, he wasn't going to need a receipt.

Zip code. "Son of a bitch." The 3 stuck, wrong number, try again. The crowd got closer. Processing. Done. Regular, no; he decided to splurge. Premium. Then he let it rip.

He spread a long arc of gas at their feet and, as they got closer, on their legs. One-liners about seeing them in Hell jockeyed for position on his tongue.

But then he stopped cold.

His mouth hung open. There was no swear, no invective, no blasphemy ever conceived strong enough for him then.

He didn't have a lighter. Or matches. Or any goddamn way of igniting the gas, of making these things about to kill him anything more than wet.

He was out of options. He was left with desperation. The boy was lying where he had left him and Connor hooked his arms under the boy's and began to pull him away. The gas, though, had spread and he slipped, fell underneath the boy, fell and ran out of time. The first of them was only a few feet away when it jerked back and dropped away. The sound. Gunshot. Andie. Connor looked back and saw her in front of the open doors still in her firing stance. There were more coming around the building. Coming for her.

He tried again to get up, had to try. More shots rang out. Screaming. He slid his hand between his stomach and the boy's back in an attempt to turn him over, to get him off, to free himself, and he felt something wet.

He pulled his hand back. Red. Blood. And Connor knew it was over. Sensed it.

The boy's eyes flashed. He hadn't been in shock, the little bastard. He'd been in whatever transformation stage these *things* went through. He was awake now. And dead. And hungry.

# THE EXCUSE OF MADNESS

## ROB X ROMÁN

*S*PANG!

"Dude! Did you just hit my sister with a shovel?"

"It's not your sister anymore, Ben! She turned into one of those *freaky people!*" Kevin screamed as he wound up for another swing at Ben's sister's head.

Despite the blood and bone that tore through her broken scalp where Kevin had tried to bash her brains in, Jennifer still stumbled forward, baring her bloody teeth at him.

The Freese Fresh Air Mall, the premiere outdoor hangout for the small town high school crowd of Ives' Corner on Saturday afternoons, had gone from being a busy, bustling center of teen angst and hormones to a bizarre battlefield of psychopaths versus the sane.

Unlike most of their fellow classmates, Ben and Kevin didn't hang out at the mall; they worked there. The well-maintained landscaping found throughout the compound was due to their hard work. It was while he was digging a hole for the new sapling Ben was getting from inside the van that Kevin noticed something was wrong. Ben's super-hot bitch of a sister had come to visit them with her usual entourage made up of the other three hottest girls in school, commonly known to him and his friends as "The Bitch Brigade."

These girls did their level best to keep a distance of at least a hundred yards between them and the unworthy, otherwise known as Kevin, Ben and their friends. For them to be only a few feet away was bizarre. It was then that Kevin noticed the noise around him. What he had relegated to the back of his mind as the mall's usual cacophony of squeals, laughter and dueling genres of music had become the soundtrack of human carnage.

People were running and screaming while others seemed to slowly stumble about. It took Kevin another moment to realize that it was these shambling burnouts that people were running from. He saw Mrs. Harvey, his chemistry teacher, cornered by four of them. She screamed hysterically as they all seemed to just fall on top of her. Kevin thought he saw one of them bite into her arm. *What the hell*, he thought to himself when his heart skipped a beat. One of them *had* bitten into her arm ... and gnawed it off! The guy shuffled away with his prize as the others pulled and tore at the rest of her body, a lake of blood pooling beneath their handiwork. His eyes started darting about the complex only to see sights just as gruesome. Mr. Ritchie from Ritchie's Garage fought with two others as he tried desperately to pull his intestines back into his body. Ms. Corey shielded her crying baby as she was beset by more of the ravenous hordes while Barry Palmer threw his girlfriend of six months, Sheila Yost, into a phalanx of gnashing teeth and rending hands to buy himself a moment to escape. Barry was actually running toward Kevin, all the while looking back to make sure he wasn't being followed. Had he been looking to where he was going, he never would have run smack into Bridgett Hammond, long standing member of The Bitch Brigade.

Barry knocked Bridgett flat on her back, a position he had seen her in before. Kevin could have sworn he heard something break on impact. Barry tried to get up, but Stacey, Val and Kara pushed him back down, pouncing on him. He screamed as Bridgett bit off his left ear, the skin tearing through to his left eye as the supple pink flesh refused to give up its anchor to his face. Stacey's teeth clamped onto his shoulder as her head worked back and forth, slowly, methodically, but with a building amount of force as Barry's screams soared higher in pitch with each shake of her head. It was then that Kevin noticed something else.

Stacey had braced herself against Barry's back for leverage, finally tearing away the meat from his neck that she fought so long for. Her right hand was at the middle of his back while what was left of her left wrist scraped against the concrete of the mall's floor. Just as he had seen the woman's arm taken by one of the affected psychopaths, Kevin imagined the same had happened to her hand. The bone at her wrist cracked and chipped as she chewed on the meat in her mouth. No pain shown on her face, just the orgasmic expression of eating human flesh. Val had an arrow lodged in her throat making Barry's prone, but still writhing body a bit difficult to reach. Each time she aimed for his back with her mouth, the rear of the arrow would be stopped by his rib cage and her head would stop moving. She managed to push the obstruction deeper into her neck, but stopped once she decided to pull his right arm up instead and bite into it. Barry wailed again and again as Kara tugged at his freshly severed Achilles tendon. She pulled with her teeth since her left arm was useless, all the flesh and muscle having been eaten right off the bone.

Ben heard Barry's screaming and jumped from the back of the van. He saw The Bitch Brigade all over him, blood on the ground and his sister and Kevin watching.

"What the hell is wrong with you people?" screamed Kevin. Ben noticed Jennifer turn around and stumble toward Kevin. That's when he hit her with the shovel.

*SPANG!*

"Dude! Did you just hit my sister with a shovel?"

"It's not your sister anymore, Ben! She turned into one of those *freaky people!*" Kevin shouted and was ready to swing for the bleachers this time. Terror quickly overtook him when he found he couldn't move the shovel. Though a year younger than Kevin, at sixteen Ben was taller and a mass of lean, corded muscle. Kevin had called him "freakishly strong" on more than one occasion.

"How do you know she's one of them?" loomed Ben as Jennifer shuffled ever closer.

"Half her neck's chewed off. I just smacked her in the head with a friggin' shovel and she's *still* walkin' around! More than that, she ain't bitchin' about it!" Kevin kicked at Jennifer, pushing her back, but she remained on her feet. She began to close the gap again.

Kevin was pulled an inch or two into the air as Ben yanked the shovel from his hands. He closed his fists around the handle as if trying to wring the life out of it. He faced Kevin menacingly.

"I see what you mean, Kev," Ben began, "but she's *my* sister!" Ben hefted the shovel over his shoulder. In shock, Kevin could only stare at his best friend. For all Ben's complaining about her, Kevin supposed that blood was indeed thicker than water ... and much thicker than the urine that was now filling his pants. Kevin closed his eyes, hoping the blow would be quick and that no one would notice he had pissed himself. It was one thing to be dead, but another thing entirely to have people pointing and laughing at your corpse.

*SPANG*!

Kevin was amazed that his hearing was still perfect even after having his head crushed by Ben. He then heard the sound of struggling. He opened his eyes to see Ben trying to keep upright as the weight of Jennifer's body threatened to topple him over. A piece of her cracked skull had caught on the flat of the shovel. Her body, trying to fall over from the blow, was pulling him down. Kevin couldn't quite figure out what was making him more nauseous - the scraping of bone against metal as Ben tried to dislodge his cudgel or the bobbing of Jennifer's left eye as it now hung free from its socket.

"I've been...*hunh*...wanting to do this...*hernh*...for a long time, Jennifer!" exclaimed Ben as he fought to keep his balance while trying to free the shovel from her tenacious, ruined skull. "All the times you...*hernh*...told me I...*har*...I was the reason mom and dad split! All the...*hunh*...times you set me up for a...*unh*...beating from our step dad! How does it feel now?!"

With that, Ben put his back into one hefty yank of the shovel. With a crack and a pop, the annoying piece of skull fell free of the rest of Jennifer's head. Her body fell back, motionless. Not satisfied with the outcome of the morbid tug-of-war, Ben quickly stood over her body and repeatedly bashed in his sister's skull until any semblance of a human head was completely obliterated. Somehow, her left eye managed to escape the carnage only to roll over and stare directly at Kevin.

Ben didn't realize the savaging of Jennifer's head had drawn the attention of the girls feasting on Barry's torn body. They slowly began to rise from their meal. Ben was pulled out of his distraction with his sister's condition when he heard the clang and crunch of Kevin driving a post hole digger into Stacey's sternum. Ben had only a moment to notice that she didn't cry out before he was poked in the chest by Val's arrow.

She was close enough to have her hands on him, but the arrow didn't allow her gnashing teeth to reach the soft flesh of his neck. Her hands were cold, ice cold and clammy on his bare arms while her breath was hot and rank as blood and flesh slowly dribbled over her chin, continuing down her neck. Ben pushed her away with the shovel's handle and then closed the distance between them with a solid swing to her face. The arc was a little low and he ended up nailing her in the chest. The flat of the shovel caught just enough of the arrow to send it sailing through her neck and clattering harmlessly to the concrete a few feet behind her. She stopped, but she didn't fall. She raised her arms at Ben and moved toward him again. He swung a second time, landing a solid blow to her face. Her nose was crushed and most of her once beautiful teeth, work that put an addition on her orthodontist's house, were either completely missing or broken. She fell hard on the concrete, lying motionless on her back.

Ben turned to see Kevin putting all of his weight on the post hole digger, trying to bore a hole through Stacey's chest. She writhed underneath him as he strained to push the landscaping tool through to the concrete. With a strained snap and crunch of bone, Ben could tell Kevin had cut through her spine. Stacey stopped moving, but it was clear she still wasn't dead.

Kevin's eyes widened as he realized Kara was slowly pulling herself toward him. He guessed her ruined arm didn't allow her the leverage to get on her feet so she opted to crawl toward him as if she had all the time in the world. He jumped on both of Stacey's arms for leverage and, with one good jerk, pulled the tool clear of her chest cavity. He swung it over his head and slammed it into the back of Kara's skull.

Brains, blood and bone exploded everywhere under his adrenaline charged attack and she stopped moving.

Ben heard a shout and he turned around to see Val doing her best to gum old man Finney's leg to pieces. The teeth that were left in her head had a tenuous hold on her gums at best and were simply giving way to the amount of pressure she was exerting on them.

Ben kicked at Val while helping the old man to his feet. As Mr. Finney hobbled away, Ben, remembering what he just saw when Kevin caved in Kara's head, swung the shovel up and put every ounce of strength he had into a downward swing.

*SPANG!*

36

The top of Val's head completely gave way to Ben's powerful blow. Though blood spattered everywhere, the crushed shards of her skull had nowhere to go but down into her brain. She went limp.

"Aim for the head!" Ben called out.

"What?" asked Kevin, stumbling back from the gruesome scene exhausted, crashing from his adrenaline high and sitting by the hole he had dug earlier.

"Ya gotta destroy the brain. That's what stops them. See?" Ben ran over to Bridgett's writhing form. She had been helplessly pinned under Barry's dead weight, a situation she had found herself in on better occasions. Back then she just wanted to breathe. Now, she wanted to take a bite out of Kevin. Ben swung the shovel's edge hard and down into the top of Bridgett's head. The shovel half-cleaved, half-crushed her skull, but the outcome was still the same...Bridgett was now dead.

Ben worked the shovel back and forth until the top of her head was separated and her ruined brains oozed onto the concrete.

Kevin was still trying to process all that had happened, all that was still happening, and his part in it when he noticed Jennifer's disembodied eye again. The staring contest was over when a sneaker stomped on it, the eye exploding into a red and white puddle.

"Hey, guys...*whoa!*" yelled Mike as he succeeded in keeping his balance on the slick mess. "What the hell did I just step on?"

"Mike! What's going on?" Ben asked.

"Man, there's a...did you guys just off The Bitch Brigade?" Mike asked, finally noticing the mess. "Please tell me they were trying to kill you!"

"Yes, Fish!" exclaimed Ben. "Now focus!"

The boys called Mike "Fish" because he had a two second attention span. His father was convinced he had ADD and tried to get him medicated, but his mother wouldn't have it. She said Mike simply felt the need to know everything as it was happening. His mom was right.

He was still dressed in his Burger Bean uniform, an oxymoron of a place across town that sold "healthy fast food", but it was spattered with blood. Since nothing at the Burger Bean ever bled,

Kevin assumed he must have been having the same kind of day they were. To prove him right, Mike was holding an aluminum baseball bat with blood, brains and hair coating the end of it.

"Yeah, okay," started Mike, "you asked what's goin' on. Honestly, guys, I have no clue. One minute I'm taking this guy's order and the next thing I know, some dude walks up behind him and starts chewing into his neck! I mean, what the hell, man? Who does that? Then I notice there's more of this crazy cannibal shit going on out in the street, so I grabbed the bat we keep behind the counter and told Scott, the manager, to close the security gate at the front of the restaurant."

"Smart move," Ben said.

"It would have been," continued Mike, "if that asshole didn't have his stupid head shoved so far up his ass! He says, 'I'm the manager! You don't tell me what to do!' So he goes out onto the sidewalk acting all tough and demands to be told what's going on."

"And one of those crazy people got him?" asked Kevin.

"Tore his face right off!" exclaimed Mike. "Can you believe that shit?! Tore...his...face...*off*! Then more of those whack jobs started coming into the store so I started swinging for the cheap seats. My parents are off at Cabo and since you guys are the closest thing to family I got, I jumped in the car and came here."

"You mean these nuts are everywhere?" asked Kevin as he got to his feet, moving closer to his classmate.

"*Everywhere*, dude!" Mike said. "You should see the front of my car! They're all over the roads! I think my radiator's cracked from hitting so many of 'em!"

All of a sudden, shots rang out from somewhere deep in the mall.

"I never thought I'd be glad to hear the cops show up," said Kevin, an audible sigh of relief leaving his mouth.

"That might not be the cops, dude," said Mike. "I don't hear any sirens and I saw a bunch of yahoos raiding *Our Constitutional Right* up the road, trying to get their hands on as many guns as possible. That could be them trying to blow holes in anything that moves. I guess you could kill anybody here and claim they were all messed up or something."

Mike's last words struck a chord with Ben. The look on his face must have been obvious.

"What're you thinking, Ben?" Kevin asked.

"I'm thinking about what Fish just said," replied Ben, a distant stare in his eyes. "We could kill anybody."

"What?" exclaimed Kevin nervously.

"Yeah," Ben continued, "we could kill anyone whether they were one of these freaks or not. Tell me you never thought about killing my sister, Kev."

"B...b...but, Ben," Kevin stammered, "thinking it and doing it are two totally different things..."

"I'm gonna kill my stepfather," Ben announced.

The boys fell silent. All that could be heard were the screams deep in the mall and the eerie moaning of those that had gone insane.

"Well, if there were ever a son-of-a-bitch that deserved killing, it'd be him," murmured Kevin, repressing thoughts of the man they all came to hate in equal measure. "We should go see my brother about using one of his guns."

Ben looked at Mike. "Are you with us, Fish?"

Mike hefted the bat before Ben and Kevin, bringing their attention to the gore that seemed embedded at the end of it. "Ya see that? Most of that is what's left of my manager's head. That was the best and cheapest therapy money could buy. I suggest we take the van though, 'cause, like I said before, I think my radiator's had it."

Kevin pulled the keys out of his pocket, "We'll take the van."

"Shotgun!" shouted Ben.

Mike looked around, like he was searching for something.

"Why does it smell like someone pissed themselves around here?" asked Mike.

\*     \*     \*

"Johnny!" yelled Kevin standing outside of his brother's apartment. He held a shovel in his hands having decided it was the better weapon when compared to the post hole digger. Ben and Mike also stood in the hallway, weapons at the ready in case any more cannibals were roaming around.

On the ride to Johnny's place, Ben and Kevin could see the world had gone as crazy as Mike had described. Ben lost count of how many weirdies Kevin clipped with the van.

The crazies were everywhere while the sane ran as best they could. Those who were cornered used whatever was at hand as a weapon. Kevin hoped his older brother was holding his own.

"Johnny!" Kevin yelled again as he gently pushed the end of the shovel against the door. It creaked open slowly.

The boys made their way cautiously into the apartment, each of them calling out for Johnny, but getting no response.

"He must have taken off," Mike suggested.

Kevin sighed, "I wish I knew for sure, but there's no getting through on the damn cell phones. If he did take off, chances are the guns are with him."

"We've come this far," Ben said, "we might as well check. Where'd Johnny keep 'em?"

"He kept them locked up in his bedroom closet," Kevin said.

With that, the three of them walked to the bedroom. Kevin's heart sank when he saw the closet door open. Unwilling to admit defeat, Kevin headed for it and saw one of the gun cases, still locked, sitting in the middle of the large closet floor.

"All right!" exclaimed Kevin. "One of 'em is still here!" He placed his shovel against the wall, stepped into the closet and picked up the gun case.

Arms reached out for him from behind the clothes lining the back. Kevin didn't notice until they touched him, but he moved quickly enough that he avoided their grasp. Still holding the case, Kevin stumbled backwards out of the closet and fell onto the bedroom floor.

Chancing a quick glance around the room for his compatriots, Kevin only had a moment to shout something inarticulate at Mike, who somehow understood it as a warning of someone coming up behind him.

Mike turned to see three lunatics stalking after him. From their direction, he assumed they must have come out of the bathroom only about a foot away. He pushed the lead attacker away with his bat and went after him swinging.

Ben stood frozen for a moment, not sure what to do.

"Go help Fish!" Kevin yelled, still on the floor. He raised his feet and pushed at his assailant. "He's got more of 'em to deal with!"

Ben ran out of the bedroom, shovel raised. Kevin could hear it connect as metal met bone.

With the case still in hand, Kevin got to his feet, but as he reached for the shovel, the man in the closet lurched forward, cutting Kevin off from his prize. The man raised his head. As much as he'd hoped the killer before him wasn't his beloved Johnny, it was the only answer that made sense.

As Johnny loomed forward, Kevin could see the bloody wreck of his chest. It looked liked someone had sliced at it with a knife. Whether it was before or after his brother had lost his mind, Kevin couldn't say. All that mattered now was he had become one of *them* and the only thing that would stop his cannibalistic rampage was to destroy his brain.

With his path to the shovel cut off, Kevin used what was left to him...the gun case.

The flat of the case landed with a hollow thud against the side of Johnny's face, but there was no sign of the blow having fazed him. Kevin immediately corrected, turned his wrist and hit his brother again, but this time with the edge of the case. Johnny stumbled a few steps to the side as a flap of skin tore from his cheek where the case had landed. Kevin hit him again and Johnny fell, but only because he was taken off balance.

Noticing the handle of the case wouldn't survive another solid smashing, Kevin took the case in both hands, straddled his brother and started pounding. The combination of rage, adrenaline, and the unforgiving shell of the case made short work of Johnny's skull. Blood streamed everywhere as it clung to Kevin's weapon and whipped around the room with each downward strike. Bits of bone and brain were smashed together. What didn't become glued to the case's deadly edge became a permanent part of the bedroom rug.

Exhausted, Kevin stopped the onslaught on what was once his brother while whispering through a veil of tears, "I'm sorry, Johnny. I'm sorry, Johnny," over and over again.

When he opened his eyes, Kevin noticed Ben and Mike watching him from the doorway. They had all liked Johnny. He was one of the few adults that seemed to remember what it was like to be a teenager in a small town.

Kevin looked down at what was left of his brother and tore the key ring from Johnny's belt loop. He tossed them and the gun case to his friends.

"Unlock it," Kevin said. "The bullets should be in his nightstand and the other gun should still be in the closet. I'm gonna change my clothes."

\*　\*　\*

Kevin, Ben and Mike pulled up in front of Ben's house in silence. Up until this point, Ben and Mike had killed only strangers and people they hated or couldn't care less about. Kevin had killed Johnny. Johnny! He was all Kevin had left and the only adult to ever give a damn about him.

"Kevin ..." Ben began.

"No," Kevin interrupted, holding back tears. "For all we know he was already dead and didn't even know it. His chest was torn to shreds, man. How do you survive that? For all we know, whatever's affecting people around here is probably not letting their brains process the fact that they're dead already. I was only helping him along."

Kevin fell silent, dropping his head to his chest. "I was only helping him along," he whispered.

Another few moments passed. Kevin dried his tears and chambered a round into his brother's semi-automatic pistol.

"Okay, guys," Kevin said, "we came here to do a job, so let's do it."

"Yeah," said Ben, "no reason for assholes like my step-'dud' to keep on living while we're losing good folks like Johnny."

Kevin, having the most experience with firearms, took the pistol while Ben held onto his shovel and Mike, his bat. They had searched the entire apartment for Johnny's second gun, but to no avail.

"Guys, how do we know he's even home?" Mike asked.

"Where have you been, dude?" asked Ben incredulously. "That asshole hasn't worked a day in his life since my mom started sucking my dad dry with alimony. There's no way he's ever gonna leave this place until we throw his corpse out on the lawn."

They piled out of the van and slowly made their way to the front gate.

"Kevin, you go around back and see if you can get in. We'll try and keep him busy by the front door," Ben said.

"Gotcha," Kevin said, holding the gun low and in front of himself, a product of too many bad cop shows.

"And be careful!" Ben added with a whisper. "He's got a five-shot revolver in the house with him."

"Okay," said Kevin as he made his way around the side of the house.

Ben and Mike made their way onto the porch and to the front door. Ben pressed his back against the side of the house closest to the doorbell. He pushed the button.

"Ma!" he yelled. "It's me, Ben!"

"Ben?" he heard her yell from inside the house.

At that moment, Ben noticed Mike standing right in front of the door. Just as he tried to motion for him to stand against the siding, two shots rang out from inside. Both shots landed clean in Mike's face. Ben couldn't tell if Mike was still alive or had died in that instant, as he stayed on his feet, staring off into nothingness as blood began to slowly spill from his wounds.

At the same instant Mike's lifeless body fell to the ground, Ben's mother started screaming and three more shots barked from the back of the house. Ben's brute strength coupled with rage helped him bash open the front door with one solid kick. He heard more gunshots as he quickly made his way to the kitchen where the backdoor was. The action in the kitchen was over when he arrived.

Just inside the open doorway stood Kevin, holding Johnny's pistol in his right hand while tucking Ben's stepfather's revolver into his waistband. His left ear was bleeding where a bullet had nicked him. He was still pointing the pistol at Ben's stepfather who was lying on his stomach, crying in agony. It was then that Ben noticed the man's ruined knee. It was if someone has scooped it out with a trowel and smashed it to pieces with a hammer. Blood and bone was everywhere. Ben's mother sat on the floor next to him, weeping. She turned to look up at Ben, her face a muddied mess of running make-up.

"Why? *Why*?" she screamed. "Why would you do this to your father?!"

"Stop calling him that!" Ben yelled back. "He's *not* my father! I'm fine by the way or don't you care that he was trying to kill me at the door?"

"He thought you were one of those sick people!"

"I announced myself!"

"He didn't know!"

"Yeah, right, ma," Ben said. "I think he was hoping to kill me and used that as an excuse to keep out of jail."

"Dude," said Kevin. "Where's Fish?"

Still looking in disgust at the man upon the floor, Ben said, "This asshole killed him."

With tears returning to Kevin's eyes, he stomped down hard on the man's right hand, knuckles clearly crunching under the attack. The man tried to lift himself onto his elbows to cradle his hand, but the pressure it put on his nonexistent knee sent him flat to the floor again in horrific pain.

"Why?" he cried. "Why can't I just pass out? This hurts so damn much!" He sobbed into the floor. "Why are you doing this to me?"

Ben's mother rose from the floor, anger filling her face now as she wiped the tears and failed war paint from her eyes. "Yes, Ben! Why *are* you doing this? I taught you better than this!"

"Yeah, ma," Ben said sarcastically. "You taught me how to sit at home with a deadbeat and sponge off of someone who works for a living."

She slapped him but Ben didn't feel a thing. He grabbed her by the shoulder and pushed her back down to the floor.

"As for *why* I'm doing this, well, *Carl*," Ben crouched down to look into the sobbing man's face, "it's basically the same idea you had for offing me. Think of it as the bill coming due for all the shit you've put me through."

"I...I...I didn't do anything to you!" Carl screamed.

"Is that why my dad's had to pay my hospital bills, Carl? Is that why my knee still hurts when it rains, Carl? Is that why I'm missing a few molars, Carl?"

"Those were all accidents and you know it, Ben!" his mother yelled indignantly.

"Accidents?" Kevin asked. "Lady, you were *there* when we saw him knock Ben down the stairs after punching him in the face! Hell, you were there for at least a half dozen beatings!"

"They were *accidents*," she insisted.

"You keep spoutin' your bullshit, ma," Ben said, "but you don't have a jury box full of assholes who just wanna go home and a corrupt judge to believe you this time."

"So how do you wanna do this, Ben?" Kevin asked, looking back down at Carl.

"We're not," Ben stated matter-of-factly.

"We're not what?" Kevin asked.

"We're not gonna kill him. Anything we do to him is gonna be too quick. We've seen how those freaks work. They're slow and they kill slow."

Ben's mother was back on her feet, her hands clutching at Ben. "What are you going to do, Ben? What are you going to do?"

"We're going to give this bastard a fitting funeral, ma." He turned to Kevin. "Kevin, get the blanket from the couch. We're dragging him to the front lawn."

Kevin smiled as he tucked the pistol down the back of his pants and headed out to the living room.

"No!" screamed Ben's mother as she beat uselessly against his chest. "No! No! You can't do this! Stop it!"

Ben grabbed her by the arms and forcefully pushed her against the counter, where she hit with a large thud, falling to the floor while sobbing. All Carl could do was scream as Ben and Kevin rolled him onto the blanket, furious pain shooting through his leg. They slowly dragged him onto the front porch. They seemed to sober when they came upon Mike's lifeless form.

Carl's screams were starting to draw a crowd of the shambling horrors, but Ben and Kevin took a moment to place Mike's body in the back of the van so they could properly bury him later. With renewed anger and thirst for vengeance, they once again tended to their sadistic task.

As they continued to pull Carl onto the porch, the man tried desperately to grab onto anything he could, but everything that passed within close proximity was closest to his crushed right hand.

With each step the boys took, he slowly slid some more, and each inch was another nail being hammered into his nerves. He was grateful for the moment when all movement ceased. He was still in excruciating pain, but the movement aggravated it to the nth degree. He was now lying still on the front lawn looking up at the slowly darkening sky as the noon day sun began to set.

He tried to relax by concentrating on his own breathing since whatever god had decided to bless him with lucidity in the face of extreme pain was not going to let him slip into unconsciousness.

"I'm going to survive this," he whispered to himself. "I'm going to survive this, and when I'm better," Carl began to shout, "your ass is mine, you little bastard! Do you hear me, Ben? You thought it was bad before? I am going to *kill* you!"

He began to breathe easy again. He wasn't sure what he noticed first, the low murmur of moaning voices coming closer or the fetid stench of death and rot.

"Is someone there?" he called out. "Can you help me? Hello? Answer me, damn it!"

His voice became a beacon, a lighthouse in a sea of food for the damned. The more he called, the more he drew them to his location. Finally, Carl could see someone moving toward his wounded leg.

"Hello? Yes, my leg is hurt bad! Could you ..."

The man he had been talking too fell to his knees and sank his teeth into the wound. An inhuman howl of pain tore from Carl's throat. He could feel the man gnawing on his shinbone, trying to tear it from the rest of his leg. Just as the realization of that sensation registered in his mind, a new plume of pain exploded on his left forearm as he saw a child, no older than eight, tearing into it with his small teeth. Flesh and sinew were pulled away as the boy slowly raised his head. Carl's wails filled the night, a clang of the dinner bell for the world that was now insane.

He looked up to see a woman reaching for his head. Before he could shut his eyes, her forehead exploded, spattering blood into his face and clouding his vision.

"Yeah," Ben said to Kevin who had just fired the round. "Be sure no one kills him too quick. I want it to last as long as it can."

Ben and Kevin were on top of the van, out of reach and out of sight of the growing crowd, watching the whole gory show. The odd picture of Carl lying on the blanket like a picnic feast was not lost on them.

"What about your mom?" Kevin asked.

As if on cue, Ben's mother appeared at the front door, first screaming in horror over what was happening to Carl and then in anger at those who were slowly devouring him. She threw herself into the group and was immediately swallowed up by clutching and clawing hands.

"There's your answer, I guess," Ben shrugged. "She made her choice."

"So what's next after this? You know, after we bury Fish?"

"I don't know," Ben said, "who else do you think deserves to die?"

# LAX TALIONIS

## RICK MOORE

Nineteen year old Randall Fletcher ran from the abandoned apartment; rage pounding at his temples. He left the building, cut across the parking lot, and emerged onto the sidewalk. His anger hadn't abated. It consumed him. So much so he gave not the slightest thought to what started all this in the first place. An asshole's mistake if ever Randall had made one.

The man who lurched from the alley brushed Randall's forearm with his fingers; fingers so cold they were irrefutably dead. The creature, who was balding and dressed in a natty pin-striped suit, still held onto his briefcase with his other hand, oblivious that the lock had popped and the contents were gone, leaving the empty briefcase hanging open.

In spite of this, the briefcase still represented sufficient importance that he was unwilling to part with it, even now, after returning from death.

The zombie's nails raked Randall's flesh, digging in deep enough to draw blood. Running on, escaping the dead businessman, the image of the zombie's fingernails lingered inside his head. The thumbnail appeared to have been manicured as recently as a week ago, and other than the grime beneath it, had sustained no damage. The rest of the fingernails, also presumably the recipients of a recent buff and polish, had, in that time-frame, fared far less favorably. The index finger had a nail that was split down the middle, the bluish-gray flesh puffing up from underneath. The middle finger had no nail at all; some former clawing incident having ripped it clean off. The fourth nail had turned a purplish black underneath, like somebody had responded to its touch by clobbering it with a hammer. And the fifth, the nail of the businessman's baby finger, wasn't visible at all. Instead, what Randall saw at the tip was an eyeball, popped through at the front, embedded down past the tip segment to the knot of his top knuckle

(Randall had even felt it leave a cold slug-like trail across the skin on his forearm).

Moving along the sidewalk and seeing neither people nor zombies up ahead, he glanced over his shoulder. Behind him, the dead businessman had wandered in the opposite direction, either too stupid to follow his intended prey or smart enough to know he'd never catch up with it.

The zombie took a few more awkward steps, then some sound from the alley caught his attention. The businessman turned around and Randall got a front on view of him. The zombie looked at the opening to the alley, frowned, as though teased by a thought just beyond his grasp. He looked at the alley, looked at his hand, raised his hand in front of his face; becoming aware of the eyeball adorning his pinkie as if for the first time.

Randall had no sooner entertained the notion that the eyeball might be a recent acquisition, before another man came stumbling from the entrance to the alley and onto the sidewalk; one hand pressed to his head. The fingers were splayed enough for Randall to see the eye socket was empty, blood pouring through the gaps and down the back of his hand.

The zombie popped the pinkie in his mouth and bit down with teeth so perfectly aligned, they had to have cost thousands. Lately, however, it was evident oral hygiene had ceased to be high on the dead businessman's list of priorities. A grimy, red film covered the teeth and strands of flesh dangled from several of them.

*Dude*, Randall thought. *Would somebody please give that zombie a toothpick.*

Regardless of their hygienic abandonment, the businessman's choppers worked well enough for chomping; which was pretty much all that mattered these days. The eyeball withstood the pressure for a few seconds, then popped, its juices dribbling down his chin. A few lazy cow-like chews later, the zombie gulped down his snack.

The soles of the zombie's mud caked shoes scuffed against the cement of the sidewalk, taking him back toward the day's meal plan. He'd had his appetizer. Now he was ready for the main course.

Randall aimed his .44 (well, his dad's .44), and called out, "Move out of the way!"

The man turned just as the zombie businessman reached for him. Randall saw then that he'd lost more than an eye to the dead man. The t-shirt he wore was torn and wet and red where the creature had taken a bite out of his shoulder. After parting with a portion of shoulder flesh along with the muscle it clothed, the zombie in the pricey suit must have gouged out the man's eye. Randall had heard no screams, the zombie had taken him completely by surprise; so the man must have found something in the alley to climb on and had escaped additional mauling. The man must have seen the zombie exit the alley and made the mistake, no doubt in a desperate state of panic, of thinking it was safe to leave.

Randall could have killed the zombie and allowed the man to live. But he knew he could no more save the man's life than his own.

The attack that had sealed Randall's fate had been nowhere near as savage as the one on the vision impaired individual he now aimed his gun at; just the brief sinking of teeth into his ankle before he used his other foot to repeatedly stomp his attacker's head. Turned out all the zombie got was a mouthful of sock. But when he examined the ankle, he found the bastard had broken the skin; the indentation of the biter's teeth marks wet with blood that was mingled with glistening saliva.

Randall immediately cleaned the area with peroxide, but he'd seen so many die from a zombie bite that he rated his chances as slim to none.

Randall knew at the time he had three days, maybe less. Drastic actions had been called for. Were even more so now, 27 hours after being condemned to death.

Which meant Randall didn't have time to listen to the man beg for his life. He placed the bullet in the center of his forehead, destroying the brain and taking off a good sized piece of the man's cranium. The businessman zombie was close enough that his shirt and suit jacket got decorated with a spray of bone fragments, brains and blood.

The creature appraised the Pollockesque splat dribbling down his shirt, then his attention turned to the one-eyed dead man with a gaping hole in his brain pan, lying flat on his back on the sidewalk. The zombie fell clumsily to his knees, reached out and grabbed a handful of gray matter, and shoved it hungrily into his mouth.

There was no sense of disgust, watching the zombie eat. No urge to waste another precious bullet. The zombie was only doing what it needed to do to survive. And he'd already been far too generous, saving the man from that awful gnawing hunger these things evidently felt, no matter how much they gorged themselves.

Randall felt satisfied, knowing the man's death had served two purposes. Three in fact. But the only one that really mattered to him was that shooting him in the head had a nice calming effect; seriously helping to relieve some of Randall's tension.

\*　　\*　　\*

Randall arrived at his car, a butt ugly yellow piece of shit called a Yugo GV that had rolled off the assembly line around the time of his third birthday. That it was still running might have been considered a genuine miracle had its very existence not been such a genuine travesty. But for all the misery the car had inflicted, both on its owners (of which there had been many) and anyone unfortunate enough to lay eyes on it, the car was one of the few things Randall had ever owned (not counting the Goodwill bargain bin leftovers his dad dressed him in growing up) and its outcast status stirred in him an affinity that had burgeoned in the two years since he took ownership to the closest thing he'd ever experienced to love.

Angry as he was about not finding Martin Riley cowering in some corner of his parents' apartment, Randall opened the driver's side door gently and got in.

Resisting the urge to slam the door shut, he closed it with equal reverence.

"He wasn't there," Randall said to the two people sitting in the back seat. "And I really needed Martin to complete the set."

Neither of his passengers said a word. They made some sounds that might have been intended to be words, but it was hard to tell without removing the strips of tape from their mouths.

"Listen, guys," Randall said, turning in his seat to look at them. "I've already heard you beg for your lives. Remember? That's why I set you to mute."

The guy, who was the same age as Randall, fell silent, communicating the extent of his rage with his eyes.

*I'm gonna kill you motherfucker*, those eyes said (or at least so Randall thought). *Nobody does this to me and gets away with it. Nobody!*

"But I have gotten away with it, Todd," Randall said. "Just like you used to get away with sticking my head in a toilet full of diarrhea back in Fremont High. Back then, you had all the power. Hell, even until a day ago I never would've had the balls to do this. Would've gone on just keeping track of where you were at in my little black book. Stewing over how you made me suffer. Would've just gone on venting my anger on them hobos, too, picturing your face instead of theirs when I killed 'em. Well, not just yours."

Randall broke off to look over at the woman, who was bound and gagged with rope and tape the same way as her traveling companion. Unlike Todd, who'd come at Randall with a tire iron before he made him put the brakes on with a bullet to his right kneecap, Fiona had been easy to capture as a threatened insect. She'd just froze. Not what he'd expected from the bitch who used her position as his manager at Walmart to belittle him in front of his coworkers and order him around like he was the raw recruit to her domineering drill sergeant.

Maybe it was because he'd caught her off-guard, parking far enough away to maintain the element of surprise (like he'd planned with Martin), and maybe shooting her husband in the heart added to her willingness to follow his demands. Whatever the answer, she was his now. His to do with as he pleased. And Randall had plans for her. Not sex stuff. She was sort of cute for a woman as old as his mother would have been had she lived past the hour of his birth, and he'd jacked off imagining cutting Fiona's throat more times than he could count, but that was not what any of this was about.

Not now when he was going to become a zombie.

\*    \*    \*

Randall dragged Fiona across the floor of the gym and lifted her up onto the seat. Panting, he stood there looking at her, Todd, and the others. It nagged at him, seeing Martin Riley's chair sitting empty. They'd been best buds all through middle school, but in their freshman year here at Fremont High, Martin had treated Randall like he had leprosy. Two-faced motherfucker.

Still, no point dwelling on it.

"What did Meatloaf say?" Randall asked the people seated before him. "Two out of three ain't bad? I guess if you do the math and weigh the odds, seven out of eight is pretty freaking goddamn awesome."

The seven people, all gagged and bound to wooden classroom chairs, sat looking at Randall, not one of them making a sound.

"I'm not gonna waste time doing that whole previous episodes recap crap," Randall said. "Each of you did some evil shit to me. Just because you knew you could get away with it. And I can understand, I guess. I mean, in a way, just being the skinny little antisocial wimp that I am, I kind of asked for it. And I bet it felt damn good, sticking it to little loser boy Randall Fletcher. Literally for you Bobby, and you Del, and you Nick. Huh, guys?"

The question was directed at three teenagers, all of them quintessential jocks who'd opted post High School to keep partying in their own playground, what with their grades and physical prowess not quite up to snuff to get them out of it. If Randall had hoped to see regret in their eyes, he would have been disappointed.

Fortunately, he had no such expectations. The hate radiating from the eyes of Bobby, Del and Nick had the same unforgiving intensity they always directed at Randall whenever he entered their field of vision. Even now they believed they would get out of this. And when they did they would not just stomp his ass, their eyes told him, but give it another pounding, just like they had that time they caught Randall alone in the locker room.

Randall had found them holed up in Bobby's basement, along with ten other kids they regularly partied with. There was no sign of Bobby's parents, so Randall figured they must have already fled. Pot smoke hung heavy in the air and the floor was littered with empty 40oz malt liquor bottles. The whole group was so out of it that Randall corralled the trio with relative ease, ordering them out of the house and into his Yugo, his .44 keeping their retaliation minimized to the level of threats, even when he had Bobby tie up Del and Nick, and then had Bobby snap a pair of his dad's girl-friend's handcuffs around his wrists (they were the furry kind she kept for customers who liked it kinky).

His dad's girlfriend, Jane, wasn't there. No reason she should be. She'd let Randall pay her to take his virginity and the subse-quent times educated him about all the things he'd only ever experienced in magazines, on video or in his imagination.

As such Randall had a soft spot for her in his heart.

Not so for dear old dad, the low-life scumbag whose fifteen year long running gag (told to the trailer park denizens he sat around getting shit-faced with) went, "I'd like to quit whooping Randall's ass, really I would. But making that little bastard bleed, it's a major part of my workout routine. And I gotta stay in shape, so what's a guy to do?"

Right now Randall thought his old man was probably less afraid of what would happen to him than going another minute without a drink. The son-of-a-bitch was shaking and drenched in sweat, he needed it so bad.

The last in the bunch seated before him was Marcy Hillman.

Chief among her crimes was failing for eleven years to recog-nize that they existed in the same universe, a period of time during which she'd been the object of Randall's undying infatuation. Marcy perhaps wouldn't be here at all, if not for the occasion she laughed like a hyena when he finally managed to stammer enough words for her to understand he was asking her to be his prom date. And then there was when she crumpled the poem he gave her and kicked it away like it was infected with Aids.

Randall leaned in close to her face. "Who's got the last laugh now, Marcy? It's payback time, bitch. Payback to all you mother-fuckers. Lax Talionis, assholes. You hear me? Lax Talionis."

Those beautiful blue eyes looked into his glass-covered gray ones. Pleaded. Only bad feelings stirred inside him. It was funny how love could so easily turn to hate.

Randall walked slowly up and down in front of them, studying their faces, basking in his moment of triumph. Here they were, the people he loathed most in the world, all gathered together for one very special occasion. His ankle throbbed, reminding of the catalyst that had enabled him to make his darkest fantasies a reality. He took the chair intended for Martin Riley (two faced motherfucker), sat and smiled at them.

"You probably saw when I brought you here," Randall said, his voice never sounding surer, "that Fremont High has been abandoned. Nobody's going to come save your asses. The world's too preoccupied with saving its own ass these days to worry about a bunch of shitheads disappearing from the face of it."

Randall nodded to the door over his shoulder. Except for some windows fifty feet off the ground to let in light, the door was the gym's only entrance or exit. "Lucky for us," Randall said, "I found a set of keys in the custodian's office. No way I would've broke through that door otherwise. Not with how thick it is and the school installing double deadbolts after those vandals broke in here and graffiti sprayed the walls a few years back."

Hearing this, Randall's dad, Arthur, started crying and made noises into his strip of tape. Now that he had them gathered, Randall wasn't feeling quite as testy as he had while abducting them, where prying eyes could see he was up to no good. He decided to let his old man have his say; decided it might be fun to hear the old fucker beg for his life.

"Son," Arthur said, after Randall ripped the strip of tape from his mouth. "Don't you think this has gone far enough? You scared the living shit out of all of us. And maybe in some way you was even justified. But this has to end now, Randy."

Man, the old fart really knew how to lay it on thick. Knew just how to look at Randall with those big sorry eyes of his. Randall shook his head, took a roll of duct tape from his pocket, and tore off a strip. "Gone far enough? Pa, I ain't even got started."

"Then get me a drink, Randy," Arthur blurted. "Please, son, for the love of God, get me something to..."

Drurghh.

That was better. Never should've taken the tape off in the first place. Randall returned to his chair, resumed where he left off. The throbbing in his ankle had intensified, the pain worse than any Randall had known in his life (and he'd had more than his share).

"You're probably wondering what my intentions are," Randall said. "And I think you'll suffer more if you know in advance; so here it is. A little over a day ago I got bit by a zombie." Randall rolled up his pant leg, showed them the wound. His skin had turned puffy and black where he'd been bitten; his shin and calf were now an unhealthy mixture of purples and yellows.

"See, I've got this theory," Randall said, facing them. "When I return, and see every one of the people who made my life a living hell, something inside my brain is gonna spark. Maybe I'll even come back as something close to who I was. Maybe that's just wishful thinking. But one thing I have no doubt about. When I see all of you sitting here, the memory of the misery you caused will be embedded deep enough that as I eat you, I'll experience the sense of retribution I was always denied while I was alive."

Most of them had begun to sob while he'd explained his master plan, and looking at their blubbering self-pitying faces, Randall felt such happiness that he did the rarest of things.

He actually laughed.

\*　\*　\*

Around noon, the fever hit. Randall took it with a delirium chaser. At first he'd lose a few minutes with no idea where they'd gone, then he started losing whole hours. Randall came rushing up out of one such episode (a hallucination wherein he was dressed as prom queen and a bucket of pig's blood was poured on his head) and found the thunderclap that cleared the confusion of images from his mind was in fact a sound from halfway across the gymnasium.

Randall lay on the floor in the fetal position, the cool wetness his head rested in a combination of his drool and sweat. Lying there, looking across the gym, Randall found himself looking into the eyes of his unrequited love, Marcy Hillman. By trying to work herself free of the rope he'd used to tie her to the chair, Marcy had toppled over to the floor.

A jolt of panic shot through him. Marcy hadn't succeeded this time, but what if one of them did get loose while he was caught in a fever dream? They could get free and get the keys; leave him here to starve. Randall grabbed the big ring that held the labeled keys, found the one for the gym, and worked it loose. He looked at the door. There was a gap beneath it, and when his strength returned he would crawl over there and slide it under, make sure he used enough force that the key couldn't be retrieved.

But then he realized if he wasn't able to do this then the key could be found.

So he did the only thing that came to his mind.

He swallowed the key, almost choking on the coppery taste but managing to get it down without vomiting.

There, now they would never find it.

He became aware that Marcy was watching him. That all of them were.

Jesus. The looks they gave him. Even with them bound and the upper hand unquestionably his, Randall withered under the combined force of so much hatred directed at him. He felt his heart beat faster and almost yielded to the urge to get the hell away from them go find some place dark to hide.

Even with his tormentors tied up, he still feared them. But soon, all that would change.

Soon, they would be afraid of *him*.

\*　　\*　　\*

Day became night, became day, became night; became night, became night, became night.

Randall opened his eyes, saw only darkness. He was still alive. He scratched his itching chin, found it thick with hair. How many days and nights had he lain there? How could he still be alive? The fever had cooled from his skin. Could it be possible? Had he somehow survived the sickness that should have taken his life? What were the odds? One in a million? One in ten million? Was he, Randall Fletcher, king of the losers, somehow immune?

"I made it through," Randall rasped, barely able to speak. "I fucking made it."

Over by the door, there was a dull repetitive thudding sound. Someone was kicking it. Randall had no sooner wondered if someone was trying to get in, when a whisper inside the darkened gymnasium gave him his answer.

"Did you hear that?" asked the voice, so quiet it sounded like the rustle of paper.

It wasn't someone trying to get in. Someone was trying to get out. They'd escaped. Gotten free of the ropes. But how had they?

"He's alive..." the voice whispered. "He's still human..."

Randall heard them moving closer. It was not the sound of feet, but of hands and knees scurrying across the gymnasium's floor.

"Hi, Randall," said Marcy Hillman.

Bobby worked his lighter. The dancing illumination provided by the wavering flame showed seven sunken cheeked faces. They loomed over him on all fours, Todd, Fiona and his dad each brandishing splintered chair legs.

Randall went for his .44, but it was still in the car and his hands were tied together behind his back. His legs too had been bound at the knees with rope, the intention to render the zombie they'd expected (hell, he'd expected) he would come back as, a threat only to those who got too close.

Todd jabbed him in the stomach with the splintered end of the chair leg. His dad raised his own chair leg over Randall's head, sneering as he prepared to bash his son's head in.

"Wait," Marcy said. "He's alive... Don't you know what that means?"

"Means he'll know it was me who killed him."

"We're starving," Marcy said. "No telling when we'll break through that door."

"So?" Arthur asked.

"So he's not infected," Marcy said. "We don't have to perform an allotment like we discussed."

"Move back," Arthur said, adjusting his grip on the chair leg. "He's my boy. I'll do what needs to be done."

"After what he just put us through," Marcy said, "why make it easy on him?"

Arthur grasped what she was proposing, mulled it over, looked at her and nodded his approval.

Nobody else put up any objections.

Randall's intended victims appraised him in ways he'd never been looked at in his life. So this was how it felt to be wanted; needed. All seven moved in on him, saliva gathering at the corners of their mouths. Randall no longer saw hatred in their eyes. Only ravenous hunger remained.

Randall could do nothing but lie there, the seven of them keeping him pinned, his thrashing struggles useless against the rope that bound him.

"By the way, you little illiterate shit," Marcy said. "It's Lex Talionis."

"Yeah," said Todd. "Like the album by Acheron, dickwad."

"Wait, you guys," Fiona said. "You don't really mean we're...."

"Nobody's putting a gun to your head," Marcy said. "You want to go without? Go without. Me, I'm gonna do what I have to, to stay alive.""

Marcy was as good as her word. She rolled up Randall's sleeve, dipped her head and came up with a mouthful of raw flesh. Randall's first scream hadn't even begun to taper when his dad ripped off a piece of cheek with his teeth. After that, Randall's screams became one continuous loop. They each took their turn, Bobby cauterizing the flesh with his lighter when the wounds bled too freely. Only Fiona refused. Marcy returned for her third sitting and bent forward for another bite out of his bicep. Fiona beat her to it; scooting in for a tentative bite, shaking her hands while she chewed like it was some reality show survival challenge where she'd been told she had to eat bugs or be eliminated.

But Fiona didn't gag, she didn't pull away and run to the corner to puke. She kept her mouth attached to Randall's arm. Chewed into it. Now that she'd gotten started she couldn't stop.

And it was then that the eating of Randall Fletcher began in earnest.

He felt the heat of their mouths and cracked lips against his flesh. Felt their teeth sink in deep. Felt the frenzied biting and chewing and swallowing and gnawing and slurping and biting, biting, biting. They had appetites not even a horde of zombies could match.

"Oh, you taste so good, Randall," Marcy said, her mouth stuffed with a severed finger and both his ears. "So good..."

Randall's screams echoed throughout the gymnasium. If anybody gave a shit, they were elsewhere tonight. Nothing ever changed. Losers went on being losers, and those who fed on them went on feeding on them.

"Look what I found!" somebody called, and Randall, barely conscious and wishing he wasn't, raised his head and saw his dad holding the key to the door in one hand and a floppy length of his son's torn intestines in the other.

The piece of metal was coated in sticky strands of Randall's fermenting fluids, but other than that looked like it would work just fine.

Arthur wiped the key on the sleeve of his gore drenched t-shirt. Blew on it and held it aloft. "Good as new!"

All of them stopped a moment to look at the key. Then they saw Randall wasn't yet dead, and set about finishing their meal.

# PLUMBING TROUBLES

## JESSY ROBERTS

Max wiped his greasy, potato chip encrusted fingers against the rough denim of his work jeans. Despite the fame and glory the Mario Brothers brought to plumbers worldwide in 1985, plumbing was not heroic work. Instead, it was hard, filthy and thankless. There were no magical mushrooms, no pipes filled with gold coins, and certainly, there were no princesses to save.

Every once in a while, there were perks. Max always accepted the calls to the Western Nebraska State College all-female dormitory. An old building with old pipes, the plumbing was always on the fritz. The girls had to shout "flush" prior to flushing the toilet or scalding hot water doused a friend in the shower.

Max knew more about the workings of the girls' dorm than he would publicly admit. His DNA was caked all over the small hallway that housed the faulty pipes of the communal shower. He would bill the time to the boss, sometimes getting overtime pay for leaving a little of himself behind on the work site. The girls didn't know he was there, concealed within the wall, peeking at them through a small hole.

He licked salt off his lips and slowed his breathing as a blonde co-ed, wrapped in a pink beach towel, walked into the shower room. She reminded Max of the cheerleader captain that had rejected his invitation to prom. He unbuttoned his jeans and slid his hand inside, imagining the blonde's long, red-tipped fingers stroking him.

The over-sized towel fell to the floor, exposing her lush, all-natural body. Max was all for fake tits and nose jobs, but this girl didn't need any surgical enhancements.

Max closed his eyes and imagined those perfect breasts bouncing up and down as she rode astride him, screaming out his name as he pleasured her. He rubbed himself harder, faster, sweat sprouting on his brow.

"Hey, Betty. I didn't know you were still here." A curvaceous brunette walked into the shower dressed in a black push-up bra and matching lace panties. Betty walked straight for the blonde and gripped her long, wavy hair, pulling the wet bombshell against her curves.

"Betty, what're you doing? It was only a one-time thing between us."

Max smiled. It was like a scene out of an adult movie.

He closed his eyes, imagining the last time the two attractive girls were intimate.

"Betty, stop it! Get off of me!"

He heard the water splash as the girls struggled, then a loud splat as they hit the shower floor.

Max opened his eyes. The blonde was on her back, Betty slurping and groaning between her legs. This was the culmination of his peeping Tom escapades. He had always imagined how hot it would be to see two girls getting it on in the shower. He pulled himself out of his jeans, frantically stroking his erection.

The blonde started to scream, wiggling her hips.

"Ouch, Betty!" she cried, pulling at Betty's hair.

*You have to lick gently. It's very sensitive*, he silently instructed the brunette. He slowed his pace. This was not as he had imagined hot lesbian love.

Max stuffed his member back into his pants when he noticed the water swirling around the floor drain had turned red. The blonde was screaming louder now. There was no confusing the tortured shouts as cries of passion.

Max felt his heart skip a beat as fear replaced arousal. What was happening? Why was the blonde bleeding? He fought the urge to help. If anyone found out about his secret spot or self-indulging activities, he would lose his job. His wife would leave him again. She was pregnant with their first child.

"Help me!"

The blonde twisted her torso, clawing the tile in an effort to escape Betty's sharp teeth. He could hear it as Betty gnawed and crunched down on the blonde's most intimate area.

*Move, dammit. Do something!*

The blonde's head cracked against the floor of the shower, the sudden silence more eerie than the shouts for help. Betty lifted her head from between the blonde's still splayed legs, her face covered with blood.

He gagged when he saw a couple of curls of dark pubic hair stuck to the thick, crimson liquid.

Betty slithered up the blonde's prone body, biting a trail up to the large breasts he had admired. Max turned his head to the side and threw up his cheeseburger and fries when the brunette bit off the blonde's left, round, pink nipple, sucking at the wound.

Max leaned back against the wall, his stomach still recoiling from the cannibalistic mutilation going on in the shower.

He should just leave and notify the police, let them deal with crazy Betty. She would be easy to identify considering she was walking around with blood and pubic hair all over her face. Even Barney Fife could make an easy arrest in this case.

One, two, three, he counted. He took one final look in the shower, compelled to look at the gruesome scene despite urging himself to walk away. The blonde's hand started to twitch as Betty sucked her bottom lip in between her teeth and then tore it off with a low snarl.

"What the hell?" he whispered as the blonde's head moved back and forth.

Max screamed, slamming back against the wall when the blonde's eyes popped open. She tossed Betty aside then flipped on to her knees, her generous breasts swaying back and forth, her remaining nipple brushing against the wet tile.

She wasn't dead.

He hurried out of the hallway, then sprinted to the lobby of the dormitory. The resident advisor on duty could call the police and ambulance. He was getting out of the building and heading straight to the bar for happy hour.

The lobby was empty, like a tomb.

Max ran past a raggedy leather couch and big screen television to the front desk, picked up the phone and dialed the emergency number. A busy signal. He slammed the phone down on the cradle and then retried his call.

*Beep, beep, beep.*

How the hell could 9-1-1 be busy? He read the local newspaper. Violent crime was a rare thing in the small community. People called the police when their neighbor's teenagers played their music too loud, or a dog barked all night.

He dropped the phone onto the desk. Where were all of the students? He looked around the lobby. Complete silence.

Max had never heard a silent dormitory before.

Then a piercing scream shattered the stillness. Max hurried toward the sound, certain that someone had discovered the bloody blonde, or, worse yet, the hungry Betty. As he turned the corner, toward the communal bathroom, a slender girl with reddish-blonde hair slammed into him, knocking him to the ground.

"Run!" she yelled, leaning down to grab his arm, pulling him to his feet. "Run!"

Max jumped up and looked down the hall. A dozen college-aged girls, including the blonde and brunette from the bathroom, were staggering toward him, their flesh broken and torn. They were in various states of undress, with gaping wounds oozing blood and soft tissue. Some had sustained more severe injuries than others.

One girl's intestines were hanging out of her gaping stomach, dragging along the floor. It reminded him of his mother-in-law's spaghetti, the entrails leaving a dirty brown trail of slime and blood.

"Come on!" the girl who had knocked him over yelled. "We need to run!"

He took her hand and raced through the lobby to the front door of the dormitory where his work truck was parked in a red zone. He fished his keys out of his pocket, unlocking the door. Max shoved the girl in through the driver's side and climbed in after her.

"Hurry," she whispered. "They're coming."

Max glanced at the building, saw the dozen girls spilling onto the steps.

He jabbed the key into the ignition and pumped down on the accelerator. The engine turned over with a rumble, sputtering to life. A black puff of smoke burst out of the exhaust pipe.

"Go!" his companion yelled, buckling her seatbelt.

He thrust the shifter into drive and squealed away. His heart raced, his mind numb with fear.

"What's going on?" he asked, slowing down for a stop sign. A college professor was leaning over a student on the sidewalk. The student's throat was ripped open, blood pooling on the pavement.

"I don't know. I just got back from class and my roommate attacked me! She knocked me over and tried to bite me. I got away, ran into the hallway and found everyone was going crazy!"

"Are you hurt?" he asked, turning to look at the girl.

"No. Are you?"

"No, I'm okay. Grab my cell phone out of the glove box. Call the police."

She nodded her head, then twisted the knob on the compartment and fished out his black mobile phone. She flipped the phone shut a moment later.

"Busy," she said.

"Try again," he responded.

She dialed the number again, then shook her head and closed the phone a second time.

"Damn," he muttered. "We need to stop by my house, pick up my wife, then keep moving."

"They're everywhere," she said as they passed the elementary school. Children, blood soaking through their clothes and staining their faces and hands, were throwing each other against the hard cement of the schoolyard. One little girl, in a lacy pink dress and white tights, hunched over a little boy and snacked on his ear. Blood dripped off the ends of her flaxen pigtails.

"I think they're eating each other," she gasped.

Max nodded.

"I don't know what's going on, but people *are* eating each other!"

"Okay. Don't get bitten by anybody. Check. Anything else I should add to my *don't turn into a human-eating monster list*?"

Max barked out a small laugh. He could appreciate her sarcasm. It was better than the rancid fear burning in the back of his throat.

"I'm Max, by the way," he said, turning onto a tree-lined, one-way street. Home was a couple of blocks away.

"Kristin."

"We're almost to my house. When we get there stay in the car. Lock the doors when I go get my wife. If we're not out in ten minutes, drive away. Don't look back, don't think twice, just drive as fast as you can out of town."

"Okay," she replied, nodding her head. She looked young, more like a scared high-school kid than a college girl. She reminded him of his little sister.

He felt ashamed of his extra-curricular activities behind the shower room wall.

Max pulled his work truck up in front of his small, two-bedroom house. The yard was a mess, the lawn needing to be mowed and the shrubs trimmed. He didn't know why it mattered to him now if Kristin saw the way he actually lived, but he wished his house looked a little better. He should have done the yard work the way his wife had asked him instead of putting it off to finish a six-pack and watch football all Sunday afternoon.

He jerked the car into park and jumped out of the truck. Out of the corner of his eye, he saw Kristin scoot behind the steering wheel. Smart girl. She would drive away if she ran into trouble.

"Susie!" he shouted from the front steps. "Susie-Q, we need to get out of here!"

He slowed when he saw that the front door to his house was wide open behind the closed screen.

"Susie?" he called out as he opened the screen door. "You home, baby?"

The living room was a disaster. The oak coffee table's legs were splintered, the table cracked in half. Framed pictures were shattered on the floor. He leaned over and picked up the ultra-sound picture of his unborn daughter. He set it back on top of the fireplace mantle, then walked further into the living room, shutting off the television as he went by.

He let out a cry of loss and fear at the sight of the once white couch cushions which were now stained a deep red. He sagged to his knees in front of the wet, crimson splotches and dropped his face into his hands.

He should have been a better husband, should have protected her from everyone and everything. He wiped the wetness from his cheeks, took a deep breath, and then stood up on unsteady legs.

Max hurried to his bedroom, yanked open the closet door, and pulled out his hunting rifle, stuffing a duffle bag with boxes of ammunition. He dropped the duffle on his bed and opened up the drawer of his nightstand to grasp his handgun. It was loaded. The feel of the cool handle in his hand calmed his raging nerves.

"Max?"

He spun around, flipping the safety off the handgun. He dropped the gun to his side when he saw his wife, still in her nightgown, her right hand cradling her bulging abdomen, her left wrapped around the grip of his baseball bat.

"Susie?" he cried, running to his wife as she threw herself into his arms.

"Are you hurt?"

"No," she said, tears streaking down her flushed face. "The mailman broke into the house. He tried to kill me. I got away and locked myself in the basement."

Max stuffed his gun into the back waistband of his jeans, then flung the duffle bag over his shoulder. He grabbed his wife's right hand and pulled her out of the bedroom behind him.

"Keep that baseball bat handy, Susie-Q. Get ready to run to the truck."

Her hand tightened around his.

The truck horn sounded. Once, twice. Kristin was signaling them.

They reached the front door and stopped.

The walking dead surrounded the truck, beating their lifeless limbs against the windows, trying to get to Kristin. The horde's cacophony of moans and groans sounded like a chorus of sinners being scorched in the fiery depths of Hell. He shuddered. They were revolting, a mass of mangled flesh and missing limbs.

"Duck, Kristin," he yelled, swinging his rifle up to his shoulder, taking aim, and shooting the first assailant that came into focus through his scope.

Susie had never complained about all the hours he'd spent with his buddies at the shooting range, or the weekends he spent out in a tent hunting during deer season again. He was the protector, the provider.

The bullet collided with the back of one attacker's head, flesh and blood spurting all over the truck. He aimed at a second attacker and shot again, followed by a third and fourth. If he shot them through the head, they stayed in a dead heap on the ground.

He found out quickly that bullets to the rest of the bodies didn't seem to affect the mindless things. They continued their slow, steady onslaught against his work truck. He looked down both directions of the street. Dozens of the hungry undead headed straight for them.

"Follow me," he hollered to his wife, drawing the handgun again. The Winchester was out of bullets.

He emptied his clip into the heads of the zombies, gobs of flesh and brain matter splattering all over him. Kristin leaned over and unlocked the passenger side door, allowing them access to the interior of the vehicle.

He slammed the door shut behind him, slicing off the fingers of one of the zombies as it tried to grab him. The fingers fell to the floor of the truck, landing in an empty fast food French fry container.

Kristin revved the engine, then peeled away from the curb, the front end of the truck smashing into the hordes of undead approaching them.

Max pulled the duffle onto his lap and retrieved a box of ammunition. He showed Susie how to load the rifle, then the handgun.

"Reload the guns as I shoot down these bastards!"

Aim, fire, reload. They were in a steady rhythm by the time they reached the outskirts of town, blowing the brains out of any of the zombies they came across. The side of the truck was covered with blood and brain matter.

Soon, Kristin turned down a dirt road that winded to a secluded camping spot. Large pine trees shaded their path, blocking out the glaring light of day.

"My friends and I come out here sometimes. It's really private," Kristin said. "There's a clean stream here, too. I've drank the water before and never got sick. I figure we'll head there until we figure out something better to do."

Max settled his rifle on his lap, rolled up the window of the truck, and then leaned back against the headrest. He closed his eyes, reliving his morning. He reached over and grabbed his wife's hand, grateful she was still alive.

She was ice cold.

Max jerked his hand away and twisted to look at his wife. She was picking at a small wound on the inside of her ankle.

"Where did you get that cut, Susie?" he asked in a quiet whisper.

"I'm not sure," she answered. Her fair complexion was taking on a blue pallor. "It must have happened when I fought off the mailman."

Frothy drool pooled at the corners of her mouth, dripping down over her chin and splattering on her extended belly. Kristin scooted closer to the driver's side door, trying to distance herself from Susie.

Susie's small, bloated frame started to shake and rattle, her blonde head cracking against the glass of the back window.

"She's turning, Max. We need to get rid of her!" Kristen said, keeping her eyes on the windy, rural dirt road. "She'll make us one of them if we don't."

Max buckled his seatbelt, and then maneuvered his wife onto his lap. She was shaking harder, blood trickling out of her eye sockets and ears, bubbling spittle branding his neck and cheeks.

"Hurry, Max! We don't have much time!" Kristin urged.

After a quick stroke of Susie's distended abdomen, he opened the truck door and threw his wife out onto the dirt road. In the side mirror, Max could see his wife's body tumble against the hard earth. A minute later, she rose to her knees, then her feet, her arms extended in front of her as she strutted in the stagger of the undead.

A white-tailed buck jumped in front of the truck.

"Shit!" Kristin screamed, cranking the steering wheel to avoid collision with the antlered deer. The car swerved, and then spun, the wheels losing traction with the unpaved road.

After a couple of moments, the engine stalled.

"Are you okay?" Max asked, checking himself for injury.

"Yeah," she said, brushing shards of safety glass off her lap. Kristin turned the key in the ignition, but the engine wouldn't turn over. "We're screwed, Max. Looks like we're going to have to walk."

He grabbed his bag of ammunition and guns and unlocked the passenger side door.

"Wait!" Kristen shouted, leaning over him to relock the door. Her soft, pert breasts rubbed against his face through her shirt and he instantly felt himself growing hard.

What the hell was wrong with him? He'd just thrown his undead pregnant wife out of a moving vehicle and he was already ready to bang a comely co-ed?

"Where the hell is your wife?" Kristin asked.

Mike's erection deflated. The truck had spun around, facing the direction they had just traveled. Clouds of black smoke loomed in the distance, the acrid stench of burning buildings and flesh invading his nostrils.

There would be no town to return to.

"Well, where is she?" Kristin asked again, breaking his morose thoughts.

Something hit against the side of the truck.

Bloody fingers trailed down the window of the passenger side window and then Susie smashed into the glass with clenched fists. Max could hear the bones in her wrists and hands breaking, then grinding together as she punched with increased fervor. So far the window held.

"Follow me!" Kristin cried, shoving her door open and jumping down to the road.

Max tried to follow, his movement restricted by his still buckled seatbelt.

He reached down to unfasten the safety belt, but it was stuck. He pressed the button over and over again, each time with the same futile result.

"I'm stuck!" Max cried.

Kristin hesitated for a brief moment and then jumped back into the truck.

"Help me!" he whimpered as his wife's broken, mangled fists destroyed the window. The glass was splintering, cracks webbing

70

out across the surface, bits of flesh sliding down to collect on the rubber weather stripping.

"Sorry, Max," Kristin whispered while grabbing the ammo and the guns. "You're on your own."

Max grabbed her arm as she backed away from him.

"Why? I saved you!"

The window gave way to Susie's violent demands. She grasped his arm, pulling it out of the opening and into her mouth. He cried in agony as her teeth ripped through the soft flesh of his forearm.

"I'm not going to risk my life for the Peeping Plumber. Did you think we didn't know what you were doing while we showered?"

Kristin picked up the handgun and centered it between his eyes. Visions of her naked, scrubbing her nubile flesh with a pink loofah sponge, floated through his mind.

She squeezed the trigger.

# DEFILEMENT

## MICHAEL SIMON

"Damn, John, we can't go back. It's a fucking nightmare!"

I crept up beside Brian, glanced into hell and shuddered. My business partner was right; the 501 leading into the city looked like something out of the movies. Smashed cars, downed telephone poles and broken glass covered the road. Across the city, sirens wailed and a plume of black, tarry smoke was coalescing into a single immense cloud above the hotels. But the worst was the bodies, the ones torn apart on the pavement, the ones that should have been dead but still twitched and spasmed unnaturally and the ones that were dead and yet staggered between vehicles in a mindless hunt for living flesh.

As we watched, a camper side-swiped a stalled Lincoln and fish-tailed into the ditch. The dead converged on it before the parents, or the kids, had a hope of getting away.

Brian turned his head and vomited. It was all I could do to keep the bile down as I put a hand on his shoulder.

"Let's get out of here."

He managed a nod and we both crawled back until we reached the small clearing where Theodore waited. Our client was rubbing his fat hands together anxiously.

"What did you see?"

"More of the same," I said disgustedly.

"It's worse," Brian said, slumping to the ground. "What we saw on the golf course doesn't compare. Myrtle Beach is full of them."

"Any sign of Ray?" I asked. Our second client, the owner of a major Midwestern manufacturing plant, had been obsessed with retrieving his cell phone from his car after we ran into the woods. We hadn't seen him since.

Theodore shook his head. "Nothing. I thought I heard some noises earlier but...." He shrugged. "They're gone now."

"What the hell are those things?" Brian asked. He found a thick trunk to lean his six-six frame against. "They're just like the ones on the fairway."

Our overweight client resumed rubbing his hands together as he paced between us. "They're flesh eaters," he said nervously. "The way they tore into the foursome ahead of us... my God, they're zombies!"

The name seemed obscenely funny and I giggled nervously. "Just like in the movies, eh? Zombies."

Brian stared at me. "What do we do, John? If we can't get into the city...."

I took a deep breath. We had created our company in the back of his garage fifteen years ago, with a small bank loan and big idea. Now we serviced a dozen states and major customers like Theodore and Ray. Since the beginning, we complimented each other. I was the idea man, the brains behind the operation while he was my counterpart, the front man with the bright smile and firm handshake.

"We'll stick to the woods but parallel the road until we can steal a car," I decided. "Since they can't go into the ocean, those things will start moving out of the city...."

Theodore's eyes widened. "My God! They'll head in this direction. We have to escape! Now!"

Brian stood up and nodded at me. "Sounds like a plan." He showered our customer with a look of disdain. "Sorry about your golfing expedition but it's officially over. You can come with us if you like but you'd better be quiet."

Theodore licked his lips nervously and his double chin quivered like a turkey neck.

"I'm coming," he whispered.

I glanced back at the sky before following them into the woods. The smoke cloud over the city looked as big as the Rockies back home.

*   *   *

I grimaced. "Couldn't you have found something a little larger?"

My buddy just shook his head tiredly. We had walked for three hours and the thick scrub brush and low-lying branches had exacted a toll.

"Every vehicle we saw was either smashed or in a ditch, or crawling with those damned zombies," he said wearily, wiping his brow. "Either we try for that Mustang or we move on."

I glanced up and down the road. Ten miles out, the 501 was still a disaster, with multiple smash-ups and the undead thicker than flies on shit. Corpses and parts thereof littered the road and even the dead things seemed to quiver and tremble like a child's play toy with dying batteries.

Theodore elbowed his way between us and peered through the grass reeds.

"It's getting dark," he said. "Did you find something?"

I sighed and glanced at Brian. "It might be a standard. You're going to have to drive."

He raised his eyebrows. "You sure?"

I wasn't sure at all. He was the ex-football player...the man of action. I was the brainy nerd behind the desk.

"Just be quick," I said.

He nodded. "I'll be there."

I took a big breath and did the stupidest thing in my life. I ran towards the road, towards the mass of zombies who were in the midst of ripping bodies into mouth-sized morsels and scooping up mounds of bleeding flesh. In the blink of an eye, I felt dozens of black rimmed eyes swivel to track me and every undead within sight started lumbering in my direction. And there were a lot of them.

I reached the pavement and shifted east, away from the car. I ran past bodies mutilated beyond description. The first few zombies I encountered were clumsy and easy to avoid but then they began to converge and my ability to dodge and weave was put to the test. I was not the athlete my partner was.

Ducking under the outstretched arms of a hobbling, blood stained teenager, I nearly ran into a businessman in a ripped, pin-stripped suit.

"Brian!" I yelled.

I sensed the mob closing in. A black woman in a red dress lunged at my face, her fetid breath making me gag as I backed away. A kid missing half his neck, with his head tilted precariously to one side, grabbed hold of my leg. I kicked him off but tripped over a corpse and landed heavily on my side.

"Ugh!" The impact left me momentarily stunned and I felt hands and teeth tearing at my clothes.

"Brian, now!" I screamed.

I punched and kicked like a madman. I had a brief image of a man in military fatigues; lips sliced away revealing shards of broken teeth, straining for my neck. I elbowed him in the face and felt bones snap. Another zombie fell across my chest and I punched him in the head, my fist pushing into tissue that was unnaturally soft and mushy.

"Dear God!" I breathed.

I sensed the approach of death when the zombies abruptly hesitated. Like a jet plane coming in for a landing, a huge roar washed across the road, just as the Mustang surged into the mass of zombies, smashing bone into pulp and catapulting bodies skyward.

The car screeched to a stop inches away from my head.

"Get in!" Brian hollered through the open window.

My head still reeled as I found my feet and dived into the open window. Hands that more resembled claws ripped through my pants, searching for my flesh. Stumbling corpses fell against the car even as Brian shoved the gas pedal to the floor and seventeen-inch tires painted black stripes across the pavement.

Brian didn't take his eyes off the road. "You okay?" he asked, weaving between undead.

He shifted twice in the span of several heartbeats.

My clothes were torn but I felt fine. "What took you so long?" I asked, breathing heavy.

"There was a kid in the front seat of the car," Brian replied. "He was feeding on the remains of the driver. He almost bit Theodore's fingers off."

I glanced into the back seat to where the fat man was trembling like a virgin on her wedding night.

"Christ," I muttered. "This is a fucking nightmare."

DEAD WORLDS

\* \* \*

We slept in the car that night, parked halfway up a logging road that branched off the highway. Or at least we tried to. Sports cars aren't campers and Theodore's constant whimpering didn't help. Not to mention the low grade headache I had inherited since grabbing the Mustang.

By dawn I had enough. I opened the door.

"I gotta take a leak."

The other two were already awake and followed me out.

"How's the gas?" I asked as we relieved ourselves against a tree.

"About half a tank," Brian replied, his voice still thick with fatigue. "What's our next step?"

I finished and zipped up. "We have to get away from the coast. Best bet is to take the interstate inland."

Theodore took another minute to do up his fly. How he found it below that sagging gut was beyond me. "How come we haven't seen any police?" he asked.

I shrugged. "Maybe this thing is more widespread than we thought."

He looked around nervously for a moment, biting his nails. "Do you think we can find something to eat?" he asked suddenly. "I'm starving."

\* \* \*

We couldn't get within a mile of the onramps. The entire road was clogged with dead vehicles and roaming zombies. In desperation Brian took us up a side road where we managed to find an abandoned farmhouse just before the gas ran out.

"There's plenty of supplies," Theodore announced from the storeroom in the back. "We can survive for weeks."

Brian checked the barns in the backyard and returned with some hammers and a box of nails. "I found a woodpile next to the shed," he explained. "Should be enough to turn this place into a fort."

"We can't stay here forever," I pointed out. "We may be off the main route but they're still bound to get here."

He gave me a cracked smile. "Well, until you come up with the next part of the plan then?"

I shrugged and grabbed one of the hammers. "I'll start with the doors."

By the time we finished, boards covered every square inch of the windows and doors and even Theodore managed to put in a few nails, when he wasn't fretting like an old women and pacing back and forth. After supper we each commandeered a bedroom on the second floor. That night, as I was getting undressed, I first noticed the rash, a fine, irregular redness that had spread up the back of my left calf. And at its source, a tiny scratch.

"Bastards," I murmured. One of them must have got their fingernails on me as I jumped into the car.

I had seen things like this on TV, a small, innocent looking cut that had the potential to spread into a severe skin infection or even the dreaded flesh-eating disease. I abruptly went to the bathroom and, using the soap and a tub of hot water, proceeded to scrub the hell out of it.

After thirty minutes there was a bang on the door. "Hey, John, are you going to stay in there forever?"

"Relax Theodore," I said. "I'll be out in a minute."

That night I still didn't sleep well. In addition to the headache I was plagued by nightmarish dreams, visions of Debbie, her wedding dress covered in blood, her flesh being devoured by mindless zombies. I awoke repeatedly to the sounds of her screams. By the morning, however, the leg was looking better, less red and the cut itself had scabbed over.

Theodore served up some eggs and toast and I ate a little of both.

"Well, I finally had a decent sleep," Brian said.

Theodore nodded with a mouthful of food. "Me, too."

I didn't comment.

\*     \*     \*

Brian and I resumed working on the windows while our client wandered off after fiddling with a few pieces of wood. After a couple of hours, he returned looking as proud as a peacock.

"I found a short-wave radio in the attic," he announced. "Son of a bitch works, too. I just spent the morning talking to people across the state."

"What did you find out?" I asked.

"This infection, disease, whatever... is everywhere." He spread his hands wide. "It's gone global. This country is supposedly under marshal law but there's been no word from the President."

Brian glanced at me expectantly.

I shrugged. "That settles it. We're staying put, at least until we run out of supplies or the zombies find us."

That night I scrubbed the leg again. This time the scab tore open and a torrent of yellow pus poured out. It smelled horrible and I opened the bathroom window so the guys wouldn't notice.

\* \* \*

My headache was still firmly intact when I found Theodore alone at breakfast. He was trying to sneak a second helping and turned red when I called him on it.

"Brian went out to scout the area," he said, trying to change topics.

My partner came back an hour later. "I found a cop car about a mile down the road. What's left of the trooper still has a gun on its hip. What do you think?"

With my head pounding like a pneumatic drill it took a few seconds for his words to register. "Uh, I think we need that gun," I said.

"Good," He looked relieved. "That's what I thought. Theodore, mind the fort. We should be back in a couple of hours."

\* \* \*

The trek to the patrol car was mostly across level ground and yet I had trouble keeping up with my partner. My left leg seemed heavy and slow, twisting outwards unexpectedly and threatening to give out.

"You're kind of quiet," Brian remarked at one point.

I forced a laugh. "I'm not quite as sure footed as you, Mr. Ex-quarterback."

He snorted but said nothing more.

There were two zombies stumbling around the cruiser and the piece of road kill that used to be a human being.

Brian leaned close. "My turn to distract them," he whispered. "You grab the gun."

"Okay." I really didn't want to repeat yesterday's debacle.

He took off at a sprint, waving his arms and shouting as he hit the road. The pair of undead, a woman in a stained, blue jogging suit and a male teenager with only half a face, immediately turned and lurched towards Brian. I waited a few seconds before starting for the gun... and quickly stumbled into the ditch.

"Damn leg!" I cursed. What was wrong with it?

I hobbled over to the side of the car. The cop was missing a head and it looked like someone had taken a huge ice cream scoop to his insides. But the gun was in the holster so I undid the belt and took everything.

"John!"

I glanced over at the sudden cry. Brian was almost surrounded by zombies and more were coming out of the woods.

"Help!" he shouted.

I automatically raised the pistol and tried to aim at the nearest zombie. But for some reason my eyes refused to focus. Everything was fuzzy and indistinct. I squeezed my eyes shut, took a deep breath and tried again. But all I saw was a gray blur.

"John, for God's sake, shoot!" Brian screamed.

I pulled the trigger and prayed.

A moment later the gun was ripped from my hand. I blinked and stared into the angry face of my friend.

"What the hell were you thinking?" he demanded. "You almost hit me!"

My vision seemed to settle back to normal and I recognized the mass of zombies staggering towards us.

"At least you got their attention," he continued still, fuming. "It gave me a way out."

I finally found my voice. "Hey, you're the hunter. I barely know how to hold the thing."

He gave me a dubious look. "Let's get out of here."

My leg seemed to work better as we headed back towards the farmhouse but I was still left with a host of unanswered questions.

Before bed I was shocked to see the red rash now stretched up to my thigh. My ankle was swollen and mottled in places like a three-day old bruise. It wasn't painful but, rather, incredibly itchy.

I scrubbed it again in the tub and even found a bottle of penicillin in the medicine cabinet. I took a handful of the pills.

A fever started about midnight and kept me up all night with alternating bouts of chills and hot sweats. In the morning I felt a little better but the thermometer I found in the bathroom still read one-hundred degrees.

\* \* \*

"You don't look so well," Theodore said as I forced downed some pieces of toast.

"I think I'm coming down with something," I replied, shivering as the fever spiked again.

"I might go back to bed for a few hours."

Brian came in through the back door. "I moved the tractor to the side of the house. If we lug those pieces of old fence around we can block off the entire backyard." He looked at me. "What do you think?"

I saw his mouth moving and yet I had to really concentrate to understand the words. "Sure," I said finally. "Let's start this afternoon."

I retreated to the bedroom but couldn't sleep. The thermometer read one-hundred-and-four and the rigors and muscle pains left me feeling exhausted. After an hour of trying I gave up and forced myself to help Brian and Theodore with the pieces of fence. If they noticed anything unusual they didn't comment. I begged off early and went back to bed, skipping supper as my stomach felt like it was on fire. I tossed and turned as the sweat poured off me in waves. In the wee hours I stuck my mouth under the bathroom tap and sucked up a gallon and then promptly threw it all up in the toilet.

"Damn," I muttered, sliding back against the tiled wall. I took another handful of penicillin and managed to keep that down though I wasn't sure it was doing any good. My entire leg looked like a beach ball wrapped in elastics, the skin so stretched in places it had actually split, exposing clear, fatty tissue beneath. The splotches of color had coalesced into black, tarry skin, like gangrene and yet there still was no pain and even the itch had faded.

My stomach looked bloated like I was four months pregnant and that damn rash was creeping up my chest.

I stood naked in the bathroom for twenty minutes until I remembered it was a bath that I had originally come in here for.

*   *   *

Brian slid into an empty chair at the table.

"How you feeling, buddy," he asked. "You haven't been looking the best these past couple of days. Theodore is a little...concerned."

I shook my head ruefully and forced a laugh, "Isn't he always fretting about something? No, I'm fighting off a flu bug or something. Plus I... haven't been sleeping all that well."

He looked surprised. "I thought getting back into a real bed would help. I know that night in the car was tough..."

"No, the bed's fine," I said, forcing my thoughts through the ever present headache. "I'm having bad dreams, nightmares about Debbie and the wedding." I shrugged. "I guess I'm really worried about her."

"Hey man," Brian leaned forward and flashed me a reassuring smile. "If there's one broad who can take care of herself it's Debbie. She'll be fine until this thing blows over and we can get back. Don't forget, we got a bachelor's party to attend."

"And you're still going to stand up with me?"

"Wouldn't miss it for the world." He slapped me playfully on the shoulder and stood up. "Now go grab a few hours sleep and get better. I have to finish up the barricade in the back yard."

I watched him go, acutely aware of the sudden itch spreading across my back.

\* \* \*

I paced the floor in my bedroom all night, exhausted and yet unable to sleep. I tried to put together coherent thoughts but my mind kept coming back to the picture of the mutilated cop. For some reason it didn't seem as awful as before.

At some point I took my temperature but the mercury went right to the top. Annoyed, I crushed the thermometer under my left palm. It was only in the morning that I noticed the pieces of glass still wedged in the skin.

\* \* \*

Brian left the table the moment I came down for breakfast.

"Where's he going?" I asked.

Theodore waved a dismissive hand. "He wants to finish the work in the backyard." He put down a plate of pancakes in front of me and waited.

I looked at them and felt my stomach recoil. "Ug, you can have them. I'm not hungry this morning."

He flashed me a disarming smile and took them away. "No problem, John."

I walked to the front of the house, unsure why I wanted to go there. I didn't feel right. Every time I moved I felt my vision shift. One minute I was seeing double, the next the room was spinning unmercifully and I had to hang on to the nearest wall.

The windows in the front rooms were heavily boarded but I could still peer through a thin crack at the driveway that snaked towards the road. I spied it immediately, a zombie crawling towards the house.

Partially shielded by the long grass, the undead dragged itself forward, hand over hand, two protruding bones all that was left of its lower legs. Tendrils of dirt-covered flesh dragged behind in a parody of a tail. Its face was bloated and burnt like someone had held a blowtorch to it.

So mesmerized was I by its approach that I nearly forgot there was something I was supposed to do. The thought lingered on the fringes of my consciousness for several minutes before I finally remembered.

"Brian!" I shouted. "There's one out front."

Both he and Theodore ran into the room. Brian peered through the crack. "I'll get the gun."

I straightened. "I'll come, too. We'll have to dispose of the body in case it attracts others."

The other two seemed to consider this for a moment. They exchanged a look before Brian nodded. "Good idea. Let's go."

We went out the back door and through the sleek little opening Brian had made in the barricade beside the tractor. The zombie saw us the moment we stepped around the corner and immediately angled towards us. Brian cocked the gun and walked behind it.

"You ever use one of those things before?" I asked. My vision kept fading in and out and it took a supreme effort to get the words out.

"Only rifles. My dad never let me touch a handgun," he said. "But how hard can it be?"

He pointed the gun at the zombie's head and pulled the trigger.

Nothing happened.

"What's wrong?"

He stepped back as the undead reached for him. "I don't know." He examined the weapon and tried again. I heard the faint click of metal on metal.

"I think the bullets are bad," he said. "Wait here." He jogged back around the house.

The zombie immediately turned to me, raising its blood encrusted arm like a student asking to be let out of class. It pawed at the earth before hesitating, the eyes, burned and red-rimmed, focused for the briefest of seconds. Then it turned back towards the house.

Just then Brian returned with a long spade. He stepped up and jammed the tip into the back of its neck. A low moan escaped the burned lips. Brian applied more weight and then stepped on the shovel, driving it deep. The spade cut through skin and muscle before severing the spine. The zombie's body twitched in one massive spasm before the spade completely severed the head.

The body flopped over, limp.

"Son of a bitch!" Brian exclaimed. "It's still alive!"

I looked down. The damn thing's mouth was still working, the eyes focused on Brian. No sound emerged from the crushed larynx but the malevolent intent remained.

"It's the b...brain," I said. "That's where it s...starts."

He stared incredulous at me for a second and then raised the shovel high. He brought it down hard on the zombie's forehead with a sickening thump. The skull sunk in an inch but the mouth kept moving.

"Die...you...piece...of...shit!" Brian brought the shovel down again and again, beating the head into a congealed mass of gray matter and bone. Bits of flesh and clotted blood sprayed outwards with each swing, covering my shirt and face. I should have turned away or stepped back but I was mesmerized by the violence. The adrenaline surged in my veins, my vision cleared and my senses actually tingled. I felt hungry for the first time in days and I swear I could actually taste food. I smelled the decay of the zombie's flesh, the sweat on Brian's brow as he beat the skull into blood-stained jello, and even the fear in Theodore's mind as he stared out the front window of the farmhouse.

It took me several seconds to realize I was chewing on something that had landed on my lip and I had to spit out the chunk of dead flesh.

Brian finally stopped and wiped the sweat off his forehead. "It's dead now," he said, more to the unrecognizable lump at his feet than to me.

My mind was crystal clear, my senses razor sharp. I could even sense more of the undead out there in the woods, stumbling around, searching for food.

"Let's g...get it off the lawn," I said.

He nodded tiredly before grabbing the shoulders as I took hold of the protruding leg bones. The white husks felt cool in my hands and I was acutely aware of the succulent marrow beneath my skin. My fingers moved as though they had a mind of their own, scraping inside the open end...until I saw the rash extending over my wrist and I hastily pulled the hands back and under the cover of my sleeves.

I helped Brian bury it in a shallow grave behind the barn. By the time we finished the adrenaline rush had faded and I was having problems thinking clearly.

It took me a moment to realize Brian was talking.

"S...Sorry, what was that?"

"I said, I'm going to take a closer look at the gun. Can you close the barricade?"

"Uh, sure."

He went into the house and I stood there immobile for several seconds as I tried to recall his instructions.

What's wrong with me? I was the brains behind a national company, making million dollar decisions daily, and now I could barely put together a cohesive thought.

I felt the headache return and with it the fever. I forced myself to complete the barricade. But instead of returning to the house, I caught myself walking towards the freshly dug grave.

What am I doing? My left leg almost gave out as I spun around angrily and limped upstairs before the other two saw me.

In the bathroom, I ran a bath and stripped off my clothes, but what I saw in the mirror shocked me. The rash had spread across both arms and up into my neck. The black skin on my legs had faded to a deathly gray but the swelling had moved up with the redness, splitting skin and exposing muscle and tendon across my chest. I probed several openings, feeling not pain but rather simple curiosity.

Blood leaked out of several holes, brackish blood that clotted the second I touched it.

What kind of infection is this? I wondered.

A knock on the door interrupted me.

"John, are you okay?" I recognized Brian's voice.

"Y...yes...." I stammered. I was having a hard time enunciating. "Need to wash...off...blood."

He paused. "All right." His footsteps disappeared down the stairs.

But I didn't get into the bath. Rather I stood there for a long time, staring at my diseased body. Around midnight I gathered my clothes and snuck back into my bedroom, locking the door behind me.

I didn't have any dreams that night, and my headache settled into a dull throb that stole away any coherent thoughts. It didn't bother me as much as before...and I was beginning to feel an incredible hunger.

I could hear Theodore and Brian whispering softly in the kitchen.

My lips were dry and cracked and I futilely tried to lick them with a tongue composed of sandpaper.

What was happening?

Something tasty was on my shirt. I shoved it into my mouth and consumed it with reckless abandon. I searched for other tasty morsels and hurriedly swallowed them.

There was a soft creak on the stairs. Someone was coming up. I felt fear and hid in the corner of the room, listening as the footsteps went past. A second body followed and paused outside the room. Something tested the doorknob but stopped when the lock resisted. It walked away.

Who was it? I scurried from one side of the room to the other. I was ravenous. I tried to open the door myself but it wouldn't budge. Then I remembered it was locked.

How to open?

I pulled again but it didn't move. I smelled food and fear and wanted to get out. I needed to get out.

No! I can't do that. What's wrong?

My thoughts became lost in a rush of primitive emotion as I tried and failed to control my mind. I sat down on the bed and attempted to put my shoes on but I forgot how to tie the laces. After a few minutes of frustration I whipped them across the room.

I grabbed the doorknob again and somehow got it open. I lurched towards the bathroom.

In the mirror I barely recognized the figure staring back. Its entire skin was chalky and pale, edematous with numerous ulcers that drained yellow, purulent globs. The eyes were milky white and black rimmed, the face haggard with stained teeth. A huge abscess perched like an egg on one shoulder. Without conscious thought I grabbed and squeezed it, releasing brown ichor that oozed between fingers that now resembled claws. I scooped it up with my free hand, marveling at the texture.

I turned at a sudden sound and recognized Brian standing in the doorway. Another figure, it took me a moment to remember Theodore, stood behind him.

"John, say something," he said quietly.

"Ah..." My mouth refused to form words. "J...Jooww..." It came out as a moan.

I looked at the thing in his hand. What was that thing?

I felt so hungry.

"He's gone, Brian," Theodore whispered. "We can't wait any longer."

I reached towards them, my claw-like hands imploring... I needed them... needed food...

"John, please...." Brian whispered.

I smelled their fear, smelled the warm blood coursing through their veins... I was so hungry.

My fingernails brushed his skin just before the weapon roared and spat flame. I had a brief view of the ceiling before my vision narrowed and faded utterly.

\*　\*　\*

"I told you I could fix the gun, Ted," Brian said quietly.

"I never doubted you," Ted replied. "It was the matter of pulling the trigger."

Brian just stared at the lifeless corpse on the bathroom floor. Blood dribbled from the neat little hole in its forehead. "He was my friend," he whispered.

Ted put a hand on his arm. "Hey, it happened just the way the guys on the short-wave said it would. You had no choice."

Brian glanced up at his former client. "But what are we going to do now?"

Ted just smiled. "Don't worry about that. I'm pretty good at making plans, too."

# EATERS

## KEITH ADAM LUETHKE

David Stowe was running out of food and hope. He'd taken residence in a townhouse near a working gas station. The idea was that if he needed gas for the car, he could fill up the tank and high-tail it out of the infected zone. But the television had gone out a few months ago; its last broadcast was of a bunch of policemen shooting at...well, he still had a hard time believing in the zombies.

When the undead hordes reached his suburban home, he waited outside for them with a roaring chainsaw belching smoke. He thought they wouldn't dare approach him, but the rotters just kept coming. The first one to feel the spinning blades was Debra Houston. She was a young bank teller who he'd chatted with about the weather every Friday when he cashed his check to buy a meager supply of groceries, and as the chainsaw dug through her vacant expression, he screamed.

The others that came for him were easier to dispatch. The chainsaw cut through them like a knife through melted butter, separating flesh, bone, and stringy muscle with an uncanny ease. When a pile of dismembered corpses littered his lawn and no more zombies were in sight, Stowe packed his chainsaw, water, and a few slabs of dried beef into his van and drove for hours, figuring he'd eventually find a place the zombies hadn't soiled yet. He settled for the townhouse and hadn't moved since. He hadn't seen a soul, living or dead, in a week, until today, the day that changed his life forever.

He started everyday with a slice of beef. But this morning, the slabs he'd munched on for the duration of his exile were all gone, only a sliver remained, and he swallowed it without even chewing. His stomach growled. There was only one thing left to do: raid the gas station and hope they had something besides candy bars left to eat.

Stowe peered through the blinds in the window and noticed four rotters milling around outside. Three of them were male and shuffled from side to side searching for fresh meat; the other was an old woman with a fork sticking out of her forehead. Apparently, the fork hadn't gone far enough or she would've been dead for real instead of roaming around with the other rotters. Stowe would fix that problem for her, and deal with the others as well. He found his chainsaw right where he left it on the kitchen table, the gas tank was full and he'd oiled the blades late last night.

Before the world went completely to shit, some behavioral scientist warned not to dispatch the undead with a noisy weapon because it would only attract more and more zombies. He knew the guy was right, but didn't heed his words. The chainsaw was the only power he had left, and it was the only thing he was good at. He'd worked at a lumber yard six days a week for the past ten years. In those long years he'd come to respect and rely on the chainsaw for everything. He marveled at the way it kicked up sawdust as the blades worked through ancient trees; he relished the way the machine made his hands shake when he held it, as though it were a living/breathing entity. He would never give up on the chainsaw, never. If it drew more zombies to him then that was fine, he'd just have more easy flesh to rend and rip.

Stowe grabbed his sunglasses and headed outside. He flung the door open with carefree ease and looked toward his prey.

"Hello, meat," he chuckled.

The zombies moaned and raised their withered hands toward him. They dragged their feet, but would be upon him in less than a minute.

Stowe curled his fingers around the chainsaw's choke cord and yanked. The engine growled and churned to life. He squeezed the trigger, making the blades whine and beg for something to bore into.

The woman with a fork in her head was the first to reach him.

He pressed the chainsaw's blade to her chest and pulled upward, sending bone chips and decayed flesh into the air. The sharp metal blades ripped through her chest and upward through her head, sending the fork clattering to the pavement. Content, he moved in on the rest of them. There was no challenge for him, it was slaughter. The zombies tried to rake their skeletal hands along his skin, but he sawed away their hands before they reached him. He quartered them, taking the arms, then the legs, and finally their ragged heads. Stowe grinned at the mess he'd made and continued to the gas station.

He saw two abandoned cars beside the pumps and revered his chainsaw. If the dead were here, they'd hear him and come out. He wasn't one for surprises, unless it was on his terms, and he was positive he could handle a zombie horde easily. The first car was a Volvo, beaten to hell. Inside the vehicle were stacks of plastic storage boxes housing clothing and food. He would come back for it later. As he approached the second car, a black Firebird, he saw something stir within. Stowe inched forward, raised the whining metal blades, and waited. But nothing came out to greet him. Curious, he peered through the windows and what he saw in the passenger's seat would haunt his dreams for many nights to come.

A bloated girl, with corn silk hair, stared at him with hollowed-out eyes while fat rats gnawed away at a gaping hole in her stomach.

He had seen just about everything, but this appalled him to no end. The blond girl twitched as the rats stripped her flesh; it was like watching the rotters' feast, only worse, because they'd stop eating after the corpse had animated. His cheeks started burning as he pried the door open, thankful it was unlocked. It was worse up close, there were at least twenty rats crawling in and out of her body. Stowe resisted the warm urge brewing in his throat to puke. He squeezed the chainsaw's trigger, giving it more gas, and sliced into the rats. Their fat bodies jerked as he severed them and the fresh blood splattered on the dashboard and blinded his sunglasses. It only took a few minutes to deal with the pests but it felt like hours. He tried to avoid desecrating the female's body, but sometimes the rats would sneak into her rib cage, and one even slinked from her gaping mouth. He ripped and tore, rending animal and human flesh alike. When he was finished, he killed the chainsaw and leaned against the hood; the coppery taste of victory hung in the air.

"Oh, God..." Stowe gasped, and took off his sunglasses. He wiped the blood off them with his shirt sleeve and closed his eyes. "When will all of this end?"

From behind, a thick southern voice answered him.

"That's hard to say, partner. Some folks say it already has."

Stowe slowly opened his eyes. A tall man in a cowboy hat stood no more than five feet away. Stowe went for the cord to start the chainsaw, positive he was hallucinating and a zombie was coming for him.

"Whoa, hold up, slim," said the cowboy, and raised his hands to show he meant no harm. "I'm not one of them, you can relax."

Stowe gave him another look. The man wore clean jeans, shirt, shoes, and looked...healthy.

"Who are you?"

"The name is Shane, but folks around here call me Bowie on account of the knife I carry around with me."

Stowe's grip slackened on his chainsaw.

"What folks?"

Bowie chuckled. "Well, shit the bed Ethel, how long have you been hiding?"

Stowe thought back to the endless sleepless nights he'd spent in the townhouse oiling the chainsaw and stuffing pieces of leftover meat into his mouth.

"I don't know," he answered, honestly.

"That's fine. Why don't you follow me? We've got a place set up not far from here. I'm sure the others will shit a brick when they see you coming."

Stowe nodded, at a loss for words. His stomach grumbled and the thirst in his mouth was unbearable.

"Do you have anything to eat or drink?" he asked.

Bowie patted him on his back, and quickly withdrew his hand because it came away bloody. He took out a blue handkerchief from his back pocket and cleaned up.

"Well, yeah, we've got all kinds of things to drink, and plenty to eat. You'll be stuffed and happy tonight, friend. What's your name, cuz?"

"You can call me Stowe," he answered. "Do you mind if I get some gas before we go?"

Bowie gave the chainsaw an uneasy glare.

"Sure thing, but don't take too long. I don't want to be late for supper."

\*  \*  \*

Stowe was brought to a three-story house a mile down the road. Bowie sang a tune he'd never heard before on the way there and they never saw a single zombie. The house was constructed of red brick and white siding, comfortable and modest.

"Here we are," said Bowie. He rapped the front door with his knuckles.

A woman, no more than twenty, answered.

"Well if it isn't Bowie. I thought you might be running late on a count of the time."

Bowie smiled at her.

"I ran into a survivor. His name is Stowe. Would you like to meet him, Mary?"

On cue, Stowe strolled up to the door.

The woman recoiled at the sight of him.

"My word..."

"Hello," Stowe greeted, and shuffled his feet in an attempt to look less menacing.

"You weren't joking now were you," said Mary. "You look...famished."

Stowe cracked a smile, "I could use a good meal or two."

Mary seemed to snap out of her stupor at the sound of his voice.

"Yes, yes, come in, come in. Do take off your shoes first though." She parted for him and gave Bowie a wide grin.

Stowe entered and slid his shoes off. The house was bigger on the inside than it looked outside. Book shelves adorned every nook, a plush red couch sat in the living room, and he spotted a kitchen table long enough to sit ten people.

Bowie locked the door behind him.

"Well, don't just stand there. Come on in, I'll get you a drink."

"Thank you," Stowe replied.

Bowie vanished around the corner, whistling happily.

"Well, where were you hiding? I thought we found just about everyone in this town," giggled Mary.

"I was in a townhouse east of here. I never really went outside unless I had to."

"Oh, well," she sighed. "Here, let me take that thing off you," Mary replied and reached for the chainsaw.

Stowe jerked back.

"Don't touch me!"

Mary gulped.

Bowie rushed back, a Coke bottle in hand.

"What's going on here?"

"I...nothing," Mary said.

"I'm sorry," Stowe muttered. "It's been a long time since I've been around people."

An awkward silence hung in the air.

"No trouble, hoss," said Bowie, and handed him the Coke.

Stowe broke the cap off and drank down the soda in one gulp. He sighed, relishing the taste.

"Do you have another?" he asked.

"Well sure, fella," Bowie replied, and went back to the kitchen.

Mary backed away.

"Would you like to take a shower? We have running water here?"

"You do?"

"Yeah," she grinned, and licked her lips. "Why don't you clean up before dinner?"

"Okay."

Bowie returned with another drink and Stowe finished it quickly.

"Where's your bathroom?"

"It's around the corner," answered Bowie. "Take your time. The water's hot."

"I will, and thank you again."

As Stowe walked down a narrow hallway, he heard other voices coming from various rooms in the house.

*How many people live in here?*

Bowie clamped his hand down on his shoulder.

"Why don't I take that thing off your hands for now?" he insisted. "We don't want to dirty up the bathroom."

Stowe felt his grip lessen on the chainsaw.

"Can you put it somewhere safe?"

"Sure can, slim. She'll be safe with me."

Stowe nodded and relinquished the chainsaw.

Bowie heaved the machine in two arms.

"Hot damn, this thing is heavy. How'd you haul it around everywhere?"

"You get used to it," he replied, and went into the bathroom, shutting the door behind him.

\* \* \*

After a hot shower, Stowe dried off and stared into the mirror. His collar bones were poking out of his shoulders like wings and he could see almost all of his ribs.

*Bowie had it right to call me slim*, he thought.

Stowe discovered a number of fresh clothes in a closet beside the shower and he found a descent pair of pants and a white, button down dress shirt to wear. He couldn't help but smile as he dressed; things were finally starting to look up. When he exited the bathroom, Bowie was waiting to greet him.

"Well, just look at you."

"That shower felt great. I haven't had one since this mess started."

Bowie nodded. "Welcome to paradise, buddy. Now let's get some grub."

He led Stowe to the kitchen where a number of people sat around a long table. Where every stranger sat was a plate with a cooked human arm or leg bone. In the center of the table were two blackened corpses cut up like a turkey on Thanksgiving Day.

"Dinner time," Bowie said, and patted Stowe on the back.

Stowe's hands suddenly ached for the roaring chainsaw. He took a few steps back.

"What's the matter, slim?" Bowie grinned. "You shy?"

The people at the table smiled. Most of them were twenty or a little older. He focused on two young girls and an older gentleman

94

with a baby on his lap. The girls waved at him. All of the people at the table were healthy and in great shape; it was as though the outside world hadn't touched them.

"Where's my dinner?" asked one of the little brunette girls.

"In a minute dear," answered a slender woman to her right.

Stowe took a few more steps backwards.

*What's going on here?* he thought.

Bowie took a seat and gestured for Stowe to come sit down beside him.

"We won't bite, promise," he smirked.

"Cannibals..." Stowe groaned, barely audible.

"Hey, I resent that," scolded the man with the baby on his lap. "We're opportunistic." To Stowe's horror, the baby was eagerly reaching toward the dismembered limb on the man's plate.

Stowe's stomach churned.

"Please sit down for the mealtime prayer," instructed Bowie. "We can't start dinner without you, it just wouldn't be polite."

"Fuck this," Stowe said, and bolted for the door. He expected the thunder of Bowie's feet to chase after him, or for an uproar from the people at the table. But to his astonishment, nobody gave chase. He reached the door and tried the knob; it wouldn't turn. He kicked and screamed, banging on the painted wood.

"Quit while you're ahead, cuz," chuckled Bowie from across the room. "Why don't you just come and sit down and we'll explain everything."

Stowe broke away from the door and headed down the hallway. He had to find his chainsaw and rip through that door and anyone else standing in his way. Behind him, he heard somebody curse.

"Why do they always run away?"

"I'm on it," sighed Bowie.

As Stowe ran, he attempted to open every door along the hall, but all of them were locked. He came to the end of the hall and the last door.

*Come on, open up dammit...*

Like the others, the door was locked.

Bowie strolled up to him casually, his hand resting on the knife his name derived from.

Stowe bashed the door with his shoulder.

"I wouldn't do that, friend. You might not like what you find in there."

"Get the hell away from me, you sick bastard!"

Bowie withdrew his knife and slowly approached.

"Come back to the table, please."

Stowe bunched his fists and pounded on the door. The frame splintered under his relentless blows.

"I won't tell you again," Bowie warned.

Stowe gave one last shove and the door slammed open. He leaped inside and regretted it at once. The square room was crowded with zombies. Dozens of hungry eyes found him and shambled closer, raising decayed fingers and snapping their blackened teeth.

"Dammit, Stowe, now you've gone and done it."

Bowie heaved himself past Stowe and dug his long knife into the vacant eye socket of an approaching zombie. The blade slipped through the orb and into the brain.

Stowe made for the hallway.

Three rotters reached for Bowie and he batted them away, slicing fingers and pushing them back with his free hand as he fled.

Once Bowie was in the hallway, Stowe slammed the door shut.

Mary was waiting for them with a hammer and nails. She drove nail after nail into the door, sealing it against the frame.

Stowe exhaled.

"What's going on here?"

"What's going on here?" mimicked Bowie. "You almost got me killed in there, that's what's going on, slim. I told you to stay out of there. Do you want all of our food supply to get away?"

Stowe gagged. "You...eat them?"

Mary finished securing the door and wiped a few beads of sweat from her forehead.

"What do you expect, huh? We certainly don't want to eat you, sir," she giggled.

"What about disease? What if you become one of them?" Stowe questioned, disgusted.

"We ran out of food months ago. Instead of starving we decided to roast a few of the zombies and eat them. It's kind of funny if you think about it, seeing how they always want to eat us. So we turned the tables on their asses. And none of us got sick. We grill 'em, mostly. Mary adds seasoning, and then it's mealtime," Bowie explained. "Now, if you'll excuse me, I'd like to sit down and eat."

Stowe froze. He couldn't move, couldn't breathed.

"Come on," Mary urged. "You can sit next to me if you want."

Stowe was led back to the table with the others. Bowie traded seats with one of the girls and Stowe sat beside Mary.

"Finally," said the man with the baby. "Everyone bow your head, please." The group complied and stared at the table for the prayer. "Bless this meal, O Lord and the arrival of the newcomer. In your name we pray, Amen."

"Amen," everyone but Stowe said in unison.

At once, Bowie grabbed a chunk of blackened arm and pulled the skin off, stuffing the flesh into his mouth. The others did likewise, munching and slurping on the corpse before them. Only Mary resisted. She looked toward Stowe, and took his hand.

"It's not so bad really. You get used to it. You can get used to anything, but I'm sure you've already discovered that." She smiled and took a thigh bone, sunk her small teeth into the meat, chewed, then offered some of the meat to Stowe.

Stowe took the thigh bone in one hand and examined the grilled flesh; it had a vague scent of basil mixed with burnt poultry.

"Go on, give it a try. You'll never go hungry here."

Stowe closed his eyes and bit into the flesh. The taste filled his mouth, rich and delicious, like the seasoned chicken he got at the deli. He continued to eat, and smiled at Mary. He was one of them now and could never go back. He was an eater of zombie flesh and relished the sudden idea of the thousands of shambling undead stalking the streets, ripe for the picking.

"Mmmm, not bad," Stowed said. "Tastes like chicken."

# THE BRIDGE

## MICHAEL PRESUTTI

The two men watched from afar as the massive group of zombies moved through the small town. They seemed to come in waves now, one minute the streets would be empty, the next, filled with freshly raised corpses.

To Manny this scene played out daily, a routine that made him want to puke just watching them. His partner Jake looked at it like a sporting event, never hesitating to make it a game as to which zombie he could shoot a certain way. To Jake the whole world had gone straight to Hell and it was his job to clean it up, one corpse at a time. Manny had warned him that one day his foolish behavior would come back and bite him in the ass, but Jake would only laugh and shrug off the rebuke.

Today was their food run for the group. Each day two were chosen from the group and sent out on a scavenger hunt to find food and water. In the beginning, it wasn't difficult. But as the days went by after the virus hit, it became more and more difficult, forcing the scavengers to go further out to find what they needed. The town of Farmingham was small, with a population that once went as high as eight thousand. After the virus hit, the death rate skyrocketed to the point where the dead outnumbered the living by two to one. As the months went by the percentages changed. Only small pockets of people existed in the town, with hordes of zombies as their neighbors. For Manny and Jake the town still held memories of homes with mothers, fathers, brothers and sisters, all dead but not gone.

It all seemed as if it were only yesterday.

Manny remembered going down these familiar streets every day from work. It would be easy to stop into a Starbucks or McDonalds and grab a bite to eat. Now those places were empty establishments and the population in the town was the walking dead. They had no need for such places. The rest, if there were any others living, were MIA, missing in action.

The leader of their group, a man named Riker, called it 'The plague from God' to teach mankind that they had gone too far, messing up the Earth and the people in it. But Manny knew otherwise. He remembered the day when the news came out that the dead were rising. That some chemical spill caused by the military somewhere in California had created the virus, plague, disease or whatever you wanted to call it. It all seemed like some ridiculous Hollywood prank.

But the news reports began to come in making it quite real and the scenes of the dead feeding off the living were very real and horrifying. All he knew was that it took only one month for the world to go to Hell with Jake, himself, and a few lucky survivors that now had to live in it.

So now here he was, scavenging with the irresponsible psycho Jake, the one person he hated scavenging with above all others.

Jake watched the zombies through binoculars, scanning the group, looking for what he called 'prime targets'. He was told by the leader of their group to conserve ammo, but Jake never listened. He stood on an abandoned car while chewing on a candy bar he'd found, looking down on his personal hunting retreat.

Manny dragged the large duffel bag filled with canned goods behind him and stopped by the car to look up at Jake. The man was making himself a prime target also. It was his turn to hall the sixty or more pounds of goods while Jake made shooting noises with his mouth as he aimed his rifle at potential targets.

"Too damn easy, you know that, Manny? Man, they are slower than molasses in winter. Tell me, Manny, how it is that those dead puke bags can kill so many of us when they can barely function? I mean, look at them!" yelled Jake as he pointed to a batch of them milling about an old store in the center of town. Manny looked and saw what Jake was talking about. The small gathering of the dead looked lost as they stumbled about. Every once and a while one would pound on a window or door, trying to get inside but most of the time they walked around moaning or growling their inhuman speech. They were nothing more than shell's, empty disgusting shells, bumping into this and that. That is until they saw you.

Then, like some radar-seeking vampire, they ascended on you in force. It was the reason you followed the three laws of Riker. If you followed those you lived.

"Remember the three things Riker told us Jake. The three things that get you killed?"

Jake gave Manny a tired, bored look and rolled his eyes.

"Do I remember? Hell yeah, he drills it into our heads every damn morning. Riker will stand there like God almighty and spout out enough warnings to scare the crap outta anyone that even thinks about goin' out here. It's amazing that anyone still volunteers to do the scavenger hunts at all."

Jake jumped down off the car while Manny dragged the bag behind him, making scraping noises that any zombie within a hundred feet could hear.

"It's a warning, you idiot. You remember how many were in the group when we first found them? Thirty five. Now it's down to twenty. They didn't follow Riker's three rules. First rule, always carry a weapon. Second rule, never fall down or get close to one of 'em, and the third rule, run like hell and don't confront the enemy. You follow those rules and you'll live to see another day."

Jake snickered and shrugged his shoulders as if fluffing off his friend's advice. The sun was going down fast and if they didn't get moving they'd get caught outside. It was another of Riker's rules. If you don't come back by sunset, then you'd better find a safe place to hunker down in, because you weren't going to be let back in until morning.

"Come on, snail, we're too far out and might get stuck out here if we don't get our asses in gear," complained Jake, who held his rifle in front of him while waiting for the right opportunity.

Manny, sweating and cursing, pulled harder on the bag, leaving a dirty trail behind him. Shadows were getting longer and the air cooler. He hated being out at all and especially so with Jake. As they turned the corner, the sight of the bridge made them both stop and ponder their next decision.

The bridge was the worst part of the trip. Everyone who scavenged hated it. It was an old, covered bridge that the town restored several years back before the change and it crossed the French River that supplied the factories with water. It was an ugly bridge that made one cringe whenever one saw it. The length of it was over eighty feet and quite narrow. Traffic lights hung before and after the entrances since only one vehicle at a time could go through. Some said it was over one hundred and fifty years old and that it had always been used by the town to transport goods to and from other areas.

Now it was nothing more than a spider web of danger that stories were told about in the darkness by the fires. Many in the group had died on the bridge. Riker, their leader and advisor, warned everyone to stay away from it at dusk and at dawn, when visibility within was at its poorest. The zombies had a way of blending into the old timber inside the bridge and coming out as you entered, sometimes trapping you. Manny hated to use it even in broad daylight. He knew that his fears were mostly in his head. That nothing would happen to him if he just followed the rules. Still, they both stood there looking at it, both knowing that dusk was already upon them. The bridge was already considered a no man's land until morning.

Jake looked around, scanning the buildings and streets. They were alone and he smiled to himself, nodding as he looked at Manny.

"You ready, partner?"

Manny looked at him in utter amazement. Letting the bag drop, he moved next to Jake.

"It's too late, Jake. The sun is almost down and to chance the bridge would be plain stupid. I opt for finding shelter for the night and wait until morning."

Jake laughed and slapped the back of Manny's head with his hand, sending a shock of black hair flying upwards. Manny cursed at him and backed away.

"Such a pussy, I swear. Come on, I ain't hanging around here tonight. I'm tired and cold and really hungry. We can make it, little baby Manny."

"But Riker said..."

"Hell with what the man said," replied Jake, cutting him off angrily, his words sharp and aimed at Manny. "He sends us out here while he sits at the house eating, drinking and taking any woman he wants. We take the chances and he gets the benefits. Not gonna happen. I'm for home."

What Jake said was true and Manny knew it. But it was still a group, still a home with food, lights and comfort. So what if their leader kept most of the spoils. Manny was alive, fed and had a roof over his head and best of all the zombies couldn't get at him, at any of them.

The house's location was an abandoned police station.

"You in or are you out, baby Manny?" Jake asked, making baby sounds as he finished the sentence.

Manny grabbed the bag and hauled it hard, dragging it like an anchor tethered to him. Jake laughed and slapped his back.

"That's the spirit, Manny. Jake will watch out for you. No hungry zombies gonna take my best friend, no way."

The bridge was in deep shadow and Manny couldn't see the other end. He looked around at all the old buildings that led up to the ancient structure. Dark windows, like eyes, watched him, all of them empty. The silence in the town was eerie and chilled him more than the sight of the zombies he'd seen. The only sound was of their footsteps and the food bag as it caressed the pavement, making soft scraping noises. The sun was now hiding behind the town's taller buildings and the inside of the covered bridge was no longer discernable.

Manny had been in it before and never felt good crossing it despite the fact that sunshine blazed all about him. But this night it looked ominous, evil, like it was going to swallow them whole.

"I'm not sure this is such a great idea, Jake. We can go the long way and avoid this altogether," Manny said, his voice weak and pathetic.

Jake kept walking while shaking his head.

"No way are we going the six blocks to cross the regular bridge, too many soul eaters out that way. I know I don't have enough ammo to fight that crowd. Besides, it would take us way too long. Riker would just lock us out."

They closed in on the bridge and Manny remembered the horrifying stories told by the others about it. Riker spoke to them about the casualties brought about by those trying to cross the covered bridge at night. Yes, it was a shortcut, a direct route to the areas they found food, and yes, at times it was used by the zombies as a trap to catch them.

The dead found their way inside the enclosed spaces hidden among the many timbers that crisscrossed its ancient frame. They hid well, waiting, crawling at times along the sill and overhead beams. Riker spoke of one occasion when two in their group went out to gather water and because they didn't watch the time, they found themselves on the streets at dusk. They left the water behind, frightened. Upon seeing the bridge, they knew they had a chance to get back before the doors to their sanctuary were closed. As they entered the old structure, they had no idea that below them and above them the dead waited. They never had a chance as the dead dropped from the rafters and crawled along the bridge's wooden slats to reach them. The two people were torn to pieces in minutes.

The group searched the next day and found what was left. Riker spared no details to make his point to the group huddled about the fire that night.

Manny took it all in, fearing what he himself at the time had never done. Now he was before the 'edifice of doom' as some called it in the group and he was not at all pleased.

Darkness loomed, filling in the crevices and doorways all around them. Long shadows stretched across the streets like fingers trying to grab hold of them. As they stood before the bridge's entrance, they could hear the cries and moans from the walking dead. They were not far away and both felt the hairs on the back of their necks rise.

Manny stared at the opening filled with inky blackness and backed away. Jake saw him and quickly stepped in front of him.

"I figure we have no more than twenty minutes to make it back home. The only way to do that is to cross it. So don't go chicken on me, Manny, or I'll tell the others you're a coward. I'm not going to stay out here, no way."

In Manny's mind he saw Riker with his white beard and dark piercing eyes saying to him, "Follow the rules and live."

He saw Julie, the girl who claimed she liked him, begging him not to be late. She was so young and beautiful. He wanted so much to be with her now. He stared at the black hole before him. It beckoned him forward. Manny swore he could smell death pouring from inside the bridge. His guts were in turmoil at the thought of walking into it.

"Let's go right now, Manny," Jake commanded. He was growing tired of the little twerp.

Manny took the bag of canned goods and put them inside a doorway. He didn't want to be bogged down with the awkward weight. They could always come back and get it another time. Jake smiled and led the way. The sound of the zombies was close; no doubt they could smell Jake and himself.

Jake walked onto the old bridge and seemed to fade into the blackness. Manny hesitated, his whole being screaming from within that this was a very bad idea.

"Come on, Manny!" Jake yelled from the darkness.

Manny entered the black depths and saw Jake running ahead, leaving him behind. Incredible fear struck him, squeezing his heart like a vise. He cried out and Jake laughed as he continued to run. Manny ran, too, feeling his spindly legs moving as his feet hit the wooden slats like dead weights. It was like those dreams where you tried to run but you couldn't seem to get far. It was like that now as he tried to catch up to Jake.

Suddenly dark figures separated from the wooden structure of the bridge like wraiths appearing out of the shadows. Manny stopped to see them dangling from the ceiling and dropping to the floor of the bridge. Jake saw them too and realized that the trap was set perfectly by the zombies. He found himself surrounded by creatures that looked like someone had buzz-sawed them. Their faces were broken nightmares with bodies mutilated by endless traumas. Manny turned to see that the entrance they came in from was already blocked by a dozen dead creatures, all shuffling toward him. Some had missing limbs while others were disemboweled with their insides hanging out. Everything looked like some bizarre, surrealistic painting of the macabre come to life.

"Run, Manny, run!" screamed Jake as he fired into the first group of the dead, dropping them to the bridge's floorboards and turning them into a pile of writhing flesh. Manny pulled out his pistol and fired into the backs of some, spinning them like hellish human tops but not stopping them entirely. He realized his mistake, knowing full well what he was taught from the beginning; aim for the head. That was the only way to truly stop them.

He heard Jake scream in pain as one of the zombies crawled along the wooden roadway to attach itself to his leg by its teeth. Manny ran toward Jake, firing his pistol with each step. The creature that was ripping into Jake's leg was stopped instantly when Manny blew its head off, brains and pieces of skull flying in all directions. But Manny knew it was far too late to save Jake.

Once bitten, you turned into one of them.

Jake shot two more as they began to close in on them.

The ones behind Manny shortened the distance quickly. Above him, he heard a slithering sound and knew that there were more on the rafters. He fired his gun into anything he could see. Dark moving shadows were everywhere and he didn't have enough bullets to get them all. The exit was only five feet away and it was being blocked by dozens of the dead. They would never make it. He would never see his girl again or the rest of the group. He looked at Jake, who stared back as the creatures were reaching for him.

Jake's eyes begged him, pleaded with him. Manny would have time to perform one last act before he died on the bridge. Without hesitation, he aimed his pistol, as arms enfolded about him, as hands grabbed hold of his clothing, and shot Jake right between the eyes.

That was the last thing he saw before the creatures that dwelled inside the bridge dragged him into Hell.

\* \* \*

They found the bodies the next day hanging from the rafters of the bridge, stripped clean of their flesh. Riker stood silently while the others stared in horror at what was left of Manny and Jake. Two others with rifles found the bag of canned goods hidden in the doorway, thanks to Manny, and left to return to the house.

Riker bent to retrieve the weapons and anything else worth salvaging, handing them to another to carry back with them.

"I should burn this damn bridge to the ground," Riker said quietly. Some in the group nodded, aware of how he felt about the ancient structure.

Before he walked away from the bridge and into the sunlight, he looked back, contemplating the act of doing such a thing, but knowing it was impossible.

They needed the bridge. It was a lifeline to food and water.

Tonight, he would make a special note to talk about Manny and Jake. He would give the warnings every night to all despite their complaints.

He followed the men with a heavy heart, for now they were eighteen.

# REBIRTH

## ANTHONY GIANGREGORIO

His name was Mark Jameson...and he was dead.

Well, maybe not dead, dead, but when your heart doesn't pump, you don't need oxygen, and your hair doesn't grow; doesn't that constitute being dead?

He stared at his face in the bathroom mirror, studying the decay slowly creeping across his worn visage.

He scratched at the wound on his arm, the one he'd received when he was attacked in the subway more than three weeks ago.

Since then he'd called in sick and stayed home.

No other living souls have seen him since he'd become a hermit, but it was easy to do this as he lived on the outskirts of town, more than a half mile off the main road. No one would come to him unless they were invited.

He held a razor in his hand, wanting to shave, but as he touched the blade to his cheek, the skin sloughed off his face like wet porridge. It dripped into the sink where the red and black gore slid down the side of the basin like small snails in a race to the drain.

His eyes were not the deep blue they once were either. A haze of milky white had coated them, making him look like a geriatric with the worst case of cataracts in history. But for some reason his vision was still good; he could see.

His brow was more prominent, but some of his hair had fallen out, making him look two decades older than his thirty-odd years.

There was a new pustule on his neck and he reached up and pushed on it with the tip of his index finger. The large pimple-like globule was punctured and a yellowish, whitish ooze dripped down his neck to the middle of his chest. His eyes followed the trail of slime to study his once muscular chest; only a few black hairs between his pectorals. But now his torso was covered with oozing masses of yellow, red and black wounds. He looked like a fungal growth gone mad and it made him sick inside.

Over the past two weeks, he'd begun to detest his body odor, too. The smell of rot seeped into his sinuses, making him want to puke.

But he would lather on deodorant or splash on some after shave, anything to cover up the redolence of oppressive death.

Deciding shaving was out of the question, he picked up a towel and dabbed his face where the blade had touched flesh. After removing the towel from his face, it was now covered with gore and he tossed it into the hamper, disgusted with himself.

What had he become? How could this be happening?

After dressing, he went into the living room to watch some television. As he turned it on, he remembered the cable had been out for weeks, about when he was attacked actually.

What was odd was the radio channels were also silent and over the past few weeks he had heard an odd assortment of explosions through the day and night.

It sounded like a war was being fought in town but of course that would be ridiculous. It must be construction, road work perhaps.

As he sat down on his favorite easy chair, he sighed, finally taking the weight off of dead muscles and tendons.

He remembered the first week as the worst. This was when his body technically died and went into rigor mortis. For a full day he couldn't move, only blink as his muscles and limbs atrophied. But eventually it went away and he was able to move again, though now there was a slight discomfort whenever his muscles were flexed.

What was strange was his appetite was all but gone. At first he had eaten fine, but then when he got a look at a vegetable it made him want to vomit. After that he went through every steak and roast in his freezer until it was all gone.

He was glad his cat hadn't returned home, now missing for more than two weeks, for he truly didn't know what he might have down if it had returned.

After the fresh and frozen meat was gone, he dove into the processed meat, beef stew, and chili-with-meat a few of the choices. He found he could barely keep it down, but it did control the hunger, if barely. He didn't understand why normal food wasn't filling him, wasn't satisfying him. He had to assume it had to do with his sickness.

He wondered if he was the only one of his kind, a man who was dead and yet not dead.

Many times he had thoughts of dressing up like the Invisible man, complete with overcoat and bandages, and take a drive into town to see if he was actually the only one suffering from this ailment. He imagined visiting his doctor to see if there was anything that could be done and the doctor's mystified face as he took his dead patient's temperature, blood pressure, ect.

But in the end Mark decided it wasn't worth the risk of being discovered. He imagined what would happen if the military found out about him. Why, they would lock him up and do tests on him till the cows came home. No, he didn't want anything like that to happen to him.

So with no television or radio, he sat down and picked up a book, deciding it would pass the time nicely.


A week later found him pacing back and forth in his small home. He was restless, more so than ever before.

He was going stir crazy.

He was a social animal and being separated from the rest of humanity was driving him nuts.

His body had deteriorated more, too. Most of it was no big deal; a fingernail here, an eyebrow or eyelid there. But when he went to the bathroom a few days ago and had taken a piss, he made the mistake of shaking his penis three times instead of two.

The third wasn't the charm, however, and the member had popped off in his hand and he was so mortified that he'd dropped it into the toilet. As he'd staggered away in utter shock, his hand accidentally pressed the plunger, and before he could cry out in loss, his penis had been flushed into the sewer system, like a dead goldfish named Goldie he'd had as a kid.

The next few days after that were a blur, as any man would attest to.

So now, days later, after becoming a eunuch, he'd had enough solitude and self isolation and decided it was time to go into town and see what was going on.

After all, something was up. He hadn't received his mail in more than three weeks and the phone lines were down as well. He figured someone had had an accident and crashed into one of the telephone poles leading to his home. It had happened before. Unless he complained about it, the phone company would ignore the downed lines, not wanting to expend the man power for only his and a few other homes connected to the line.

So with this as his motivation, he got dressed. Black sunglasses, a large fedora, black gloves and a scarf made him feel like a villain in an old horror movie.

Stepping outside, he felt himself shunning the sun, but he forced his body to keep moving. His car was only a few feet away and in seconds he was inside and out of the worst of the sun's harsh rays.

It was warm out but he noticed he didn't feel the difference in temperature. Wrapped in his coat, gloves, and scarf, he should have been sweltering like a steamed clam but he felt fine.

Turning over the engine, he backed out of the driveway and made his way into town.

As he drove down the winding road, his eyes took in the telephone poles lined up like sentries, seeing they all appeared undamaged. If so, then why were the phone lines down?

He made it to the outskirts of the main road leading into town, and from then on he had to walk. The reason was the abandoned cars and two trucks that were spread across the road like discarded trash.

A few of the vehicles had what looked like blood splatter inside them and on the insides of the windows, but it was dried to a brown color and he couldn't be sure.

Taking one plodding step after another, he made his way into the town proper.

As he reached Main Street, where the most activity would normally be, he found the street was a ghost town. Some of the storefronts had broken windows and most had closed signs hanging in the doorways, that is the ones that still had doors as most were kicked in and hanging off their hinges like drunks trying to stand up.

A few placards were hanging by one hook over doorways, the wood slapping the facades of the buildings, reminding him of one single person clapping. It was all so surreal. While he'd been holed up in his house, it seems the town had gone to rubble.

Stepping over some bricks scattered across the sidewalk, thanks to a truck that had plowed into the corner deli, he side-stepped the truck, its front end half in the store, and continued onward, searching for some sign of life.

He walked for almost half an hour before hearing something other than silence. He immediately gave it his full attention.

At first it sounded like a howl, but then, as he listened with ears that were slowly sliding off his head, he heard the distinct scream of what was definitely female.

Crossing the street, he stepped over a strewn bag of groceries, the produce now a rotting mess, and moved to the next corner.

As he gazed out onto the deserted street, he spotted movement from the far left.

The woman's yelling was louder now, and as he watched, she slowly came into view, but the second he saw her he knew there was nothing *slow* about her movements.

She was hobbling, her right leg giving her trouble, and by the way she moved Mark had a feeling it might be a sprained ankle. The woman was crying out for help, for anyone who could hear her to help her, and a second later Mark saw what she was running from.

More than a score of what could only be called *zombies* were shambling down the street at about the gait of a casual jogger.

As Mark stared at the first ghouls in the line, he saw a resemblance to himself, and though he didn't want to admit it to himself, he looked just like them.

He was a zombie, too, but for some reason he was still an individual; he could think for himself.

And as the woman came closer to him, her eyes seeing him wrapped up in hat and coat, she screamed at him and began hobbling forward with outstretched arms.

Mark stared at her, saw the panic and terror in her face, and made up his mind right then and there.

He was a man, not a monster and he would do what he could to help her.

Reaching down to the sidewalk, he picked up a stray pipe, the cast iron heavy in his grip. With his gloves on he couldn't feel the metal, but with the sun shining down he believed it would have been hot to the touch. Even with the glove on he should have felt some residual heat, but his sense of touch was less heightened than before.

Still, as the woman came to him, he hefted the pipe and stepped into the street, pointing behind him to the woman.

"Get behind me! I'll see what I can do to stop them!" he growled, his voice scratchy from lack of use.

She never hesitated, desperate for any help she could find, and as she ran by him and waited near the corner of the building, Mark waded into the charging ghouls like a Viking going to war.

He swung the pipe hard to the side like a baseball bat and a ghoul's head was caved in, the blow so strong its left eyeball popped out of the socket to roll across the road like a shiny marble. The next zombie in line had been an old woman, but Mark showed her no mercy and swung the pipe overhand, bringing it down like he was chopping wood. When the pipe connected with the top of her cranium, the blow caused her dentures to pop out of her mouth. The false teeth flew threw the air to land and bounce, shattering like dice to roll across the pavement.

The next two ghouls came at Mark at the same time and he ducked low, charging into their midriffs with his shoulder. As he knocked them off their feet, he felt something pop in his shoulder but he ignored it. Where there should have been pain there was only mild discomfort.

The next zombie had been a child, no more than ten, but Mark knew the innocence of youth was now gone, as dead as the heart inside his own chest.

With a sideways swipe, he whacked the boy on the head, sending the kid across the road with a massive dent where his right ear used to be. The child flopped around on the ground, looking like a robot with its wires crossed.

Then Mark had to focus on the here and now as more ghouls came for him.

A few got past him and he heard the woman cry out in fear behind him. She backed away and when she turned to run, she tripped over some debris scattered on the sidewalk. As she went forward, her arms were at her sides and her forehead connected with the stone curb, knocking her into unconsciousness immediately.

Mark spun then, realizing there was no way he could stop them all, so he turned and dashed back to the woman.

A zombie was bending over her, looking like it was about to take a bite out of the back of her neck when Mark kicked it in the side of the head. The ghoul fell over, its face smashing onto the pavement, flattening its nose and pulverizing its facial features.

Mark reached down and scooped the woman up in his arms, feeling how light she was. It was like she hadn't eaten in a week, and as he caught a close up glimpse of her face, he saw this was so as her cheeks were drawn and her skin was pale from lack of nourishment.

Three more ghouls came at him and he swung the pipe at two of them, the tip catching a cheek and a forehead. But the minor wounds meant nothing to the attacking dead and Mark began to backpedal.

He shoved two aside and began running, his hollow breath echoing in his chest. He ran for two blocks, each corner he turned giving him more distance from his pursuers. For whatever reason, he was lighter on his feet than they were.

Across the next street was a hotel, and Mark headed for it, kicking in the large front door and slamming it closed before the first ghoul had rounded the bend in the road to see him enter.

Hunched down low, he risked a peek over the window frame of the door, and as he watched, the hordes of undead ran past the hotel. A man who looked healthy was in the street and he was caught flatfooted by the zombies. Mark watched helplessly as the crowd of undead swarmed over him, running him down like a pack of wolves. They dove in with teeth and nails, tearing the body into pieces. By the time the dead had left to continue their search for their lost prey, there was nothing left of the hapless man but a large pool of blood and a chewed up shoe.

In seconds, the last zombie shambled to the end of the street, turned the corner and was gone, leaving the street deserted once more.

Mark glanced down at the woman he placed on the floor after kicking in the door and closing it, and now he reached under her and picked her up once more. He carried her to the main desk where he picked a key for a room at random, then used the stairs to take her to the second floor.

Upon entering the room, he used his left foot to close the door and laid her gently on the bed.

As he gazed down at her, he saw she was a pretty thing. Early twenties, soft brown hair and long lashes. Her breasts were rising and falling with each breath she took and though there was an admiration in his heart for this fine looking specimen of femininity, there was no arousal.

Of course, when he remembered he had no penis, it certainly helped to douse any flames of desire that may have sparked within him.

He sat down on the bed next to her, quietly watching her sleep.

She didn't move for an hour before she finally stirred.

With a low moan she opened her eyes, and when she saw him, complete with hat, sunglasses ,and over coat, she gasped and jumped up, trying to pull away from him. She went as far the head board before there was nowhere else to go.

"Who are you?" she asked softly, her eyes wide with fear. "Are you going to hurt me?"

"I'm the guy who saved you," he replied. His voice was gravelly and he didn't recognize it as his own. He'd forgotten the last time he'd spoken aloud other than when he'd yelled at her in the street.

"Oh, I, uhm, I guess I owe you my thanks then," she said.

"Uh-huh, I guess so," Mark said.

They made small talk for a few minutes, the woman filling Mark in on what had happened and how the entire town had become zombie central. This was when he found out her name was Lisa.

Mark listened quietly, asking a few questions now and then, but for the most part just letting her talk. Finally, she pointed to his sunglasses and scarf, the latter covering the bottom portion of his face.

So why are you wearing that scarf and glasses? Is there something the matter with you?"

He shrugged, and as he did this something popped in his shoulder. He remembered his shoulder check with the zombies.

"You could say that."

"Well, I don't care how you look. You saved my life. I'm very grateful. Please, let me see your face. I want to see the face of the man who was such a hero. The way you attacked those zombies was pretty cool."

He nodded, deciding there was really no reason for more pretenses. Either he showed her what he looked like or he should just leave now.

Slowly, he raised his hands to his face, and with each hand, he grasped sunglasses and scarf at the same time.

"Okay, don't be scared now, I won't hurt you," he said softly.

"I know that," Lisa smiled. "You're my hero."

He chuckled, the sound like crackling paper. "Now that's the corniest thing I've heard in quite a while."

She shrugged herself. "Maybe so, but it's the truth."

So with one last look at her, Lisa nodding for him to do it, he took off the facial coverings.

Lisa gasped when she saw his features, the same features the walking dead wore out on the street. As she jumped off the bed, she tripped over her feet and fell heavily to the floor, whacking her head on the bedside table.

"Lisa!" he cried out and went around to her. Her left arm had fallen over her head and the other was under her body.

Carefully, like she was made of China, he lifted her up and set her down on the bed again.

After covering her up, he checked her pulse and was satisfied it was strong.

He slid off his gloves so he could feel her pulse better, and as he fixed her pillow and hair, his hand came away with blood on it. She had a small cut on her scalp thanks to the side table.

As he loomed over her, he looked at the blood on his fingers, and before he could stop himself, he touched the tips of his coated fingers to his tongue, tasting the blood like a man testing a Marinara sauce.

As the plasma slid down his throat, he felt something he couldn't explain, a tingling to his extremities.

He stared at his fingers for a moment and then tried an experiment. Reaching down, he stuck his fingers into the wound on her skull and when his hand came back coated in warm blood, he licked it off his hands like a fat man at an all-you-can-eat rib joint.

As he lapped up the blood, his body began to feel energized, more alive than ever before since he was changed.

His hearing grew better and his vision was sharper and his shoulder ceased to bother him.

As he glared down at the unconscious woman, he came to an epiphany, one that the other ghouls he'd battled in the street must have already figured out.

Human blood was life to the undead.

As he leaned over her, his mouth opening wide so he could taste her, Lisa's voice floated in his head, the words she'd said upon waking the first time coming to the forefront of his mind.

*"You're not going to hurt me are you?"*

"Oh, no, my dear, I won't hurt you," he whispered as his teeth grew closer to her throbbing jugular. "But I may eat you a little."

# Z WORD

## CATHERINE MACLEOD

She was definitely awake: dreams didn't rattle your spine and make your scalp burn. No, that was Jake, dragging her up by the hair, knee-walking her right off the bed.

She struggled to free herself and lost, stumbling after him into the hall.

"Jake, what...?"

He was supposed to be gone by now, headed for Los Angeles, or wherever the next big deal was. She didn't care as long as he left before she did; she was lousy at goodbyes.

"C'mon, Lori, we have to talk."

Talk? They never *talked*. And since when did conversation involve pulling her hair out? He'd wrapped her dark braids around his hand like a leash. When she tried to jerk free he grabbed the back of her neck and pushed hard, bending her over. Her sight was limited to his bare feet, the gold maple hardwood floor, the bottom of that ugly landscape painting he'd bought at an auction, and a corner of the big-screen TV.

"*Police are urging people to stay inside their homes,*" the newscaster said solemnly. "*The phenomena is widespread. The number of deaths...*"

Jake snatched up the remote control, changed the channel, and tossed it away in one smooth motion.

Lori squawked, "Ouch, damn it!" It bounced off her bare foot. "Watch it!"

"I've *been* watching."

"What's that supposed to mean?"

And what was all that noise outside? Sure, it was the weekend, but this wasn't the usual TGIF after-work cutting-loose. There were always sirens somewhere in the city, but not this many. And...was that gunfire?

She tried to stand as they approached the picture window. He said, "There's nothing out there you want to see," and shoved her down again, and wasn't that just like him, telling her what she wanted? She turned her head quickly, biting at his arm. Her eyes blurred as his hand circled her neck and squeezed.

"Be a good girl, Lori. Don't make this worse than it has to be."

When she could breathe again he let her look up. Eye contact was something new. So was fear.

What was *this*?

And what was *that*? She had no choice but to run around him in an awkward circle, like a kid playing crack-the-whip, as he yanked her down into the wooden chair. It was either that or fall on her face, and she had the sudden feeling that might've been all right with him, too. The chair was one of his precious antiques, wide and heavy, not meant for sitting; another of Jake's status symbols.

She drew a relieved breath when he let go of her hair.

And shrieked as he yanked her arms back, wrenching her shoulders. She pitched onto her feet, but by then her left wrist was handcuffed to the back of the chair, and he had hold of the right. Seconds later and restraint was a done deal.

There'd been a time when she could anticipate his moods perfectly. So much had depended on it. But she allowed that lately she hadn't been paying enough attention. She'd known better than to let herself be distracted, but she hadn't seen this coming.

There was no point in waiting for a better time; with him there wasn't likely to be one. "Jake," she dared, "what's going on here?'

"That's what *I'm* wondering."

She wriggled in the seat, testing for give. The chair didn't budge, didn't even quiver. She glanced around, looking for clues, possibilities, anything that would tell her what Jake wouldn't.

She thought the nail driver on the hall table spoke volumes.

He just set it there after he bolted the chair down, right? Right? He wouldn't, oh God, he *wouldn't*.

She glanced up. Eye contact.

"I'm disappointed you'd even think that," he said. "You know I'd never hurt you."

Her scalp still stung. He stepped aside.

She saw the stool, five feet in front of her, and didn't make sense of it until she looked up and saw the noose. It hung from the chandelier, that prismatic monstrosity he'd bought her for a wedding present. It was fashioned from the same cheap yellow cable her father had used to tie chicken coops on the back of his truck.

"Oh," she whispered.

Possibilities ran through her mind, none of them acceptable. She swiveled her hands, testing for give in the cuffs and finding none. "Jake, what...?"

He crouched quickly, startling her. "Sweetheart," he said, "I don't believe I'm an unreasonable man. All I've ever asked from anyone is loyalty."

Oh, God, not the loyalty speech. She'd heard it so many times at the office, usually just before someone got the axe.

"I don't think it's too much to expect in return for giving you what you want," she said.

She didn't say, "What you *thought* I should want." She knew now what this was about, and wondered what she'd done to tip him off. She closed her eyes for a moment, and opened them to find his face inches from hers.

"I expect betrayal from my competitors. That's just the way business is done. But I expected better from you. I've thought about this for a long time, and I still don't have an answer. I just don't know how I can live, knowing you've been with another man."

She also didn't say, "Bull." If he really cared about that he wouldn't have made it necessary. But she didn't answer. Carole Wisten's girl knew when to keep her mouth shut. It might've been a little late for her sense of self-preservation to kick in, but it *was* kicking. Jake waved a brown manila envelope between them, close enough to brush the tip of her nose. She jerked her head back.

"I hired a detective to follow you, and I know all about Marcus. Where he works, where he lives, how many times you went to his apartment. I have pictures, dozens of them. I know what you asked him to do, Lori."

*Talk to me? I got giddy just from the conversation, you idiot.* She hadn't cheated without reservations, and not for a very long time.

Jake held a color photo out to her. She remembered that night. She didn't know why she'd been nervous; after living with Jake she should be an old hand at control games.

*Cuff me to the chair, darling. Don't let me move.*

Marcus Crawford was obedient. She'd thought she could get to like that in a man. "These cuffs have a lot of sentimental value for me," he'd said.

"Me, too," she'd joked.

Jake snapped his fingers in front of her face. "Nothing to say?"

She actually smiled, surprising him and herself. Using handcuffs on her would be his idea of poetry. He was a great believer in motion. "What can I say that wouldn't be the wrong thing?"

He seemed to consider it, then returned her smile. "Nothing." He leaned forward and kissed her cheek, a dry, polite peck. "I guess you understand everything you need to."

"Yes, Jake." Whatever he had planned was going to happen anyway, no matter what. It always did. Maybe Marcus would get here before it got too bad. As terrifying moments went, this one was almost serene.

Until their next-door neighbor screamed.

Theresa wasn't just pounding the door, she was body-slamming it. "Lori, let me in! Let me in! Let me..."

Lori opened her mouth to yell back. Jake's hand sealed it shut.

"Don't." His tone of voice made her think of the nail driver. "Trust me, sweetheart, you don't want to do that."

The noise in the hall ceased abruptly. Jake turned away from the door as if it had never happened, and stepped onto the stool, easily finding his balance. He was a man who kept in shape.

"Jake, don't do this, please." There was no point, she knew, but she was supposed to ask.

"Oh, Lori, we all do what we have to. But you know that, don't you?"

She did. She waited to feel some kind of panic, but didn't. Same with guilt. His expression of determination as he snaked his head into the noose would be heart-breaking, if she didn't recognize it. She'd seen it in the bathroom mirror, the first time she'd cheated on him. Doing what she had to do.

Was he giving her what he thought she was supposed to want?

Lori blew out a deep breath, annoyed with herself. She should know better than to even think that. Jake knew how she feared death, and why. She'd been to one funeral in her life, and never wanted to do it again.

No, this wasn't about guilt. She'd been disloyal, and this was revenge. This was one hell of a payback.

*Done is done*, she thought.

He stepped off the stool.

*Done is done*, her father always said; Harvey Wisten's way of reminding them his word was final.

Her mother always said, *The meek shall inherit the Earth*; her way of saying, *Please don't make him mad.*

And no, Lori didn't want to make him mad. But she also didn't want to inherit the Earth. She'd shoveled enough of it for a lifetime. You didn't go hungry living on a farm, her dad said, but you damned well worked for what you got.

Lori had a motto of her own. *Say nothing*, which, of course, she'd never told anyone. It was her way of saying if they didn't know what you had planned, they couldn't stop you. She was getting out. The risks she'd taken, squirreling money away these past few years, were about to pay off. She knew it was a crapshoot; exactly how she'd manage in the city was anyone's guess. But she wouldn't be hoeing any more potatoes.

Anyone's guess wasn't even close.

She spent her eighteenth year working hard enough to keep her folks from suspecting anything. *She was a good girl*, they said. She knew her place. She'd smiled, obviously embarrassed at their praise, and made a mental list of what she could afford to leave behind, starting with them. She might miss them, but didn't kid herself; they'd keep her on the farm if they had to tie her down to do it.

The day before her nineteenth birthday, she packed. It took her fifteen minutes; she'd been planning it for a while. There were things she'd miss, but not many, and she'd had time to say goodbye to them. By suppertime she had two bags stashed in the recycling box at the end of the long driveway, a thousand dollars in her purse, and a ticket on the ten o'clock bus out of town.

At nine-thirty the sheriff found her sitting in the ditch across the road, watching as her folks' house went up in flames.

"The neighbors heard the explosion," he said.

"Yeah."

"Any idea what might've caused it?"

"Um...I heard Dad talking about getting a new furnace. Maybe...?"

"Yeah, maybe."

She had the absurd thought that dead was as meek as you could get. Her folks might not inherit the Earth, but they were about to get six feet of it.

She winced as another fire truck pulled up, siren howling. The sheriff followed suit as she muttered, "Smells like pot roast." He dropped his jacket around her shoulders, even though she wasn't cold, and took her home with him. His wife bustled her into the guestroom.

She woke during the night and remembered her suitcases hidden under the blue bags, and her purse, dropped somewhere in the ditch. The sheriff looked disgusted when she asked if he'd drive her down to get them. He couldn't blame the fire on her, but she knew he disapproved of her wanting to leave town.

She understood. The town, like her parents, lived by a certain set of rules, even if they meant she would've died in the fire, too.

A decent daughter would've kept her place.


She was definitely awake; dreams didn't kick you in the face.

She came to with cool toes bumping against her. She looked up at her husband, and yes, it was as bad as she'd thought it would be. His body was still swinging in little arcs. His face was blue.

But she wasn't screaming, for a wonder, though she guessed most of her composure came from shock. She really needed to pee, and she wouldn't be getting off the chair until Marcus arrived, but she was...sort of...okay.

Except for being confused. Jake Harrison hadn't committed suicide just because his wife was unfaithful. He was stronger than that. He was resilient. He was..

"Jake Harrison is a son of a bitch," the employment agent had told her.

"Yes, ma'am," Lori agreed.

The woman peered over her reading glasses. "You know him?"

"I've heard."

"I'm sure. Well, his secretary quit this morning. The second one this month." She flipped through Lori's file, but Lori thought it was probably just for show. The agent had that pinched look people got when their choices were running out. "It wouldn't be like temping. He's a very demanding boss. Wants everything just so." And Lori just bet his word was final, too. "Would you be willing to go?"

"Yes, ma'am."

"Your references are excellent, and you're..."

"Available?" Lori said amiably.

"Well, yes." The agent chuckled softly. "You might do all right."

She did.

She'd finally used her bus ticket. She sold the farm without regret, and after funeral expenses, and paying off her father's debts, there was just enough to rent a tiny room and pay for business college. She still worked for what she got, and, in her opinion, it was considerable.

"Good morning, Mr. Harrison, I'm Lori Wisten."

"Call me Jake."

"Yes, Jake."

His hair was graying-blonde, his eyes green like the Atlantic on a fall day. What her mother might've called a fine figure of a man, if she'd been bold enough to say such a thing.

"Do you know the secret to a successful business deal?"

"Timing?" She did know something about that.

"Very good," he said. "And?"

"Knowing when to get out?"

"Excellent. And?"

"I'm...not sure."

"Accepting your possibilities. Seeing them the way they are, not how you wish they could be."

Yes, she could appreciate that one, too.

"Yes, Jake."

Life with Harvey Wisten had been good training; she worked late, didn't mind the smell of manure, and learned to gauge his moods so she knew how far to dodge.

"Do you know what it takes to be on the winning side?" meant somebody wasn't.

"All I've ever asked from anyone is loyalty." She tried to be at least three offices away when he started that one.

"I expect betrayal from my competitors," meant she should make like Elvis and leave the building.

But when he came back from a meeting with a pleased, private smile, she stayed. Those were the days he moved real estate like a bulldozer. Jake Harrison was on the winning side and his grin said *gotcha.*

He was wearing that same smile a year later when she accepted his marriage proposal. She expected she was wearing it herself.

She wore it for a couple of years until she realized that, like so many of the things Jake loved, it was really just for show. She wasn't ungrateful; he gave her everything he thought she could want. But the cabinet full of expensive china wasn't much company, and neither was he.

She didn't blame him for being big on appearances; she'd been taken in by them herself. Small town girl swept off her feet by her handsome, powerful boss. God, she was such a cliché. She wondered when he'd started considering her possible.

She was the pretty, fresh-faced secretary who'd look up to him and make a good wife. She was, she guessed, what he thought he was supposed to want. The same way he was supposed to want antiques, and that single malt whiskey he shuddered over.

She stuck it out as long as she could. She kept her place. But living with Jake was the loneliest thing in the world.

*Money can't buy happiness, but it makes being miserable much more pleasant.*

She wondered who came up with that one. Maybe the same wit who coined the phrase, *Small town girl makes good.*

But at the moment she wasn't feeling so good, though. She ached from sitting in one position, she was thirsty, and her bladder was about to burst. How long had it been since Jake dragged her out here? Hours, but she didn't know how many. She'd dozed off once, rousing when his foot brushed against her chin. Small town girl up close and personal with the dead. Moving her head out of the way was an effort. It bumped her again.

It *tapped*.

Lori opened her eyes.

Jake opened his.

A high-pitched *something* came out of her throat. It was answered by another bout of pounding at the door.

"Marcus?" she squeaked, watching Jake. "Is that you?"

It was just some weird reflex, right? She'd heard the dead did strange things. His hands were trembling now, shaking even harder than hers. Rattling like the door.

She leaned to the side as far as she could. His gaze shifted with her. It wasn't just her imagination. He was *looking* at her.

Eye contact.

There'd been more today than in the whole ten years of their marriage, and she'd had enough of it for a lifetime. She blinked rapidly, holding back frightened tears.

Okay, fine, she wasn't getting up, he wasn't coming down. Nothing to worry about yet. Yeah, right. Here she was, avoiding his eyes and hoping he didn't say anything; just like any other evening at home.

Until the picture window exploded. Lori jumped, yelping in pain as the cuffs stopped her short. What the...? That insectile whine wasn't coming from her.

The bullet ricocheted once, and she ducked, praying for a miss. There was a shattering of glass as it took out one of the paintings. *Please let it be the landscape one.*

She drew breath to scream. And stopped, because someone outside was already doing it for her. A lot of some ones, in fact. The noise from the street was incredible. How the hell had she ever slept through that?

There were no more sirens, but the screams were unending. Someone was beating a jagged non-rhythm on a car horn, and once she heard the crash of a who-knows-how-many vehicle pileup. It sounded like New Year's in Hell. Smoke blew through the broken window, thick and eye-stinging, as if someone was having the mother of all barbecues. It smelled like pot roast.

The pounding at the door was louder now, more insistent, as if extra fists had been added to the effort. This was wrong. Everything was *wrong*. Random thoughts spun in her mind like puzzle pieces and she dreaded seeing them click together. But they would soon enough, and she had an idea what the big picture would look like. She told herself not to panic, that it wouldn't do any good. But fear was cold in her stomach, coiling like a snake, creeping determined into her throat. She swallowed hard.

She twisted in her seat again, turning as far as she could. By stretching her neck to the point of pain, she could just see the cuffs. There was no way to pick them with her hands held like this, though, even if she knew how. They looked ordinary enough, plain silver, a little scratched, pretty much indestructible.

She looked again. They weren't scratched. They were monogrammed: **MC**.

They had a lot of sentimental value.

She gazed up at her not-dead husband and watched as his swollen features arranged themselves into a familiar grimace.

*Gotcha.*


It was morning, and the constant pounding at the door was background noise. She thought she might've slept. Or passed out again after Jake started air-walking and reaching for her. He still wasn't too well coordinated, although that might come in time. Her mind was going, and she was lousy at goodbyes, but she wasn't sorry; at least part of her still knew when to get out.

She didn't need to pee anymore. The screams in the street had died. Once she heard a woman shriek, "Oh, God, no!" But it might've just been her imagination. Or it might've just been her.

She accepted the possibilities now, but still wouldn't let herself think the Z-word. She really would go crazy then, and she couldn't stand any more screeching, not even her own.

She remembered Jake telling her not to look out the window, knowing what was happening. Knowing the real estate market was bust. Knowing when to get out.

Impeccable timing, like always. Doing what it took to be on the winning side.

She yawned stiffly and let her eyes roll shut. Exhaustion grabbed her again. So did Jake.

She yanked her head back as he squeezed it between his feet. Even now he was strong and she wondered if he would pull himself down or her up.

As her eyes blurred, as the door gave and what was left of Marcus and Theresa shuffled in, she had time to think that the small town girl really had made good. Her mother would be proud.

She was about to inherit the Earth.

# THE BREACH OF SANCTUARY

## MARK M JOHNSON

Lucent dreams scrolled through President Nicholas Bedford's mind as he tossed and turned behind a thin curtain of sleep. The many troubling problems that stalked his daylight hours were haunting his dreams.

Dealing with the world's many complicated issues were a part of his everyday responsibility. In the past three years in the position he now occupied, these responsibilities had never troubled his sleep before now.

His wife of twenty-seven years, Bethany Ann, a very attractive and powerful woman in her own right, lay at his side unaware of his troubled slumber.

Isolated from the outside world by heavy drapes over sound and bulletproof windows, their room was dark and quiet. The only illumination in the room came from the clock on the bedside table that showed the time as 1:57 a.m Tuesday.

Pulled from his half sleep as if from some psychic intuition, Nicholas Benjamin Bedford, husband, father, and leader of the free world, sat upright in the bed only seconds before his bedroom door was violently opened.

For a brief moment, the man at the door was visible only as a shadow, backlit by the light from the hallway. The shadow man rushed into the room, followed close behind by several more dark figures. Nicholas reached out quickly to his nightstand as if groping for a weapon, and turned on the nightstand light.

"What the hell is going on, Steve?" the President asked, bellowing with worried outrage. Bethany sat up beside him, pulling away a blindfold to reveal shocked, sleepy eyes. "What?" she asked no one in particular as she pulled the blanket up to cover herself.

"I'm sorry, sir," Stephen said with cold urgency. "The grounds have been compromised, we have to move now!"

Nicholas and Beth were both used to this kind of drill, but still they were moving slow as they reached for slippers at either side of the bed.

"Have the riots worsened?" the President asked his protector.

"It would appear so, sir, but I don't have any confirmed Intel other than the need to move you now."

"All right, Steve, just give us a few minutes to get dressed," Nicholas said while coming to his feet. He and Beth where both dressed in full pajamas with matching slippers as the secret service men crowded around them.

"I'm sorry, sir, there's no time, the house may not be secure for much longer. We have to move now, as you are, sir." Stephen said in a firm and respectful tone. Nicholas and his wife both nodded in understanding. They put their lives into the hands of these men sworn to protect and if necessary, die for them, every day.

They were ushered out into the hallway to their waiting four-teen-year-old daughter, Angela, who looked frightened and wary amongst all the men and one woman surrounding her.

"Mommy," she said crying out tearfully as she rushed into the arms of her mother.

"It's all right, baby, Steve and the boys will protect us," Beth said, whispering into Angela's ear to calm her frayed nerves.

"We have them," Stephen said into a microphone mounted on his wrist. "We're on the move to L-Z one, E-T-A four minutes."

After moving through the house for less than two minutes, Stephen held up his hand, bringing the group to a halt; he held his hand to his ear

"Jesus," Stephen said in a whisper, listening in disbelief to the sounds coming over his earpiece. He could hear multiple machine-guns firing, and screams in the background behind the voice of the man in charge of the landing zone for the Air Force Two helicopter.

"L-Z one is compromised, I repeat, L-Z one is compromised," the man spoke loudly into his microphone with just a touch of panic in his voice. "They're coming over the fence, hundreds of them! Jesus Christ, there's too many, don't let them flank us! Fall back, fall back, goddamn it!"

Stephen could hear the pounding of the helicopter blades just under the machinegun and handgun fire. Mixed in with the gunfire and shouting voices of fighting men, he heard an almost feminine high-pitched screaming. Stephen cut off his earpiece and turned to his men.

"We have to use the alternate exit; let's move people." Everyone turned abruptly and began moving the first family back down the hall from where they'd just come from. Though it was still early morning and still dark outside, the hallway which they where running down was brightly lit. Aside from the fact they seemed to be running for their lives, the house around them was just as it always was, quiet and normal. But the situation made the normalcy surreal.

The group moved through the house with intense purpose; through a doorway into a large room. They then passed through another doorway into a large open hall, going back, retracing their earlier path. Stephen again stopped the group with a hand signal as he listened to his ear price.

"Sanctuary is breached! Sanctuary is breached!" a panicked voice told him. "We have multiple subjects, multiple points of entry! Repeat, sanctuary is breached!" Breaking glass, gunfire, high-pitched shrieking, men screaming, and more gunfire. Stephen tuned the earpiece out and turned to his group.

"Sanctuary is breached," he said to them gravely. His men were listening to the same broadcast Stephen was and they were already reacting to it. The four agents at the back of the group immediately turned to cover the rear, as two more moved to the front ahead of Stephen.

*Sanctuary is breached*; everyone in the group knew what that meant. Those three words washed over them like a slowly breaking wave of dread. Sanctuary is breached; whatever was happening outside was now in the house.

Stephen's mind worked fast. Evaluating the situation in seconds, he came to a decision, "Emergency exit!" he said loudly.

Like robots awaiting command programming, his men reacted to his order with an explosion of action. Like golden cattle, the first family was herded down the hall with haste, to the very door they had left only moments ago.

Stephen threw the door open and entered to make sure the room was still secure. "Clear," he said, as the secret service men began leading the family into the room.

Suddenly, a new sound broke through the still silence of the early morning home; it was heavy footsteps from around the corner of the hall. The two men who had moved to the front ahead of Stephen took up positions on either side of the hallway to face the possible coming threat.

Agents Michael Vicente and Anthony Edwards stood several yards ahead of the group covering the hallway. Both had their guns drawn, pointing them at the floor while standing shoulder to shoulder about five feet apart. When they heard approaching footsteps, they both brought their guns to chest height and prepared to deal with who ever was coming, be it friend or foe. However, nothing could have prepared them for what came around the corner.

A man staggered around the corner of the hallway, and after misjudging the turn, he ran into the wall at the curve. He stumbled back away from the wall, turned, and noticed the people standing at the door to the President's bedroom. His eyes were black, glistening orbs that seemed to move and shift in his head like living things. His clothes hung in bloody tatters from his body, but his face was what everyone was looking at. Most of the flesh from his left cheek and throat was torn away and missing so that the windpipe was visible and his teeth shone out from his face like a living skull. Upon seeing them, his mouth dropped open, issuing an ear-splitting shriek, and he stumbled toward the nearest man blocking his path.

"Stop right there!" Anthony hollered with authority. "Stop or we'll shoot!"

The man turned and looked directly at Michael with his glistening, black, swirling eyes. Michael looked on in disbelief at the wounds on the face and neck of the man as the man dropped his mouth open and shrieked, lurching towards Michael; reaching out with twitching claw-like hands.

Michael reacted instinctively to the trespassers aggressive approach and squeezed off four rounds into the man's chest. Every bullet hit its mark within millimeters around the man's heart. The man hardly faltered as he slammed into Michael's gun hand. The hollow point bullets had torn through the man's chest and left a bloody cavity into which Michael's gun hand sank as the man slammed into him.

Michael's mind couldn't process what was happening; the man should be lying on the floor only seconds from death with the placement of those shots. All his training told him so, and still the man continued his attack. The apparent psychopath hit him hard, slamming him into the floor and knocking his breath from him. Michael struggled to free his gun to no avail; the man stopped that insane shrieking and opened his mouth wide, baring his teeth. Michael grabbed the man by his shredded throat with his left hand, pushing snapping jaws away from his face.

The enraged lunatic snarled as he tried to bite Michael's arm, clawing at Michael's face, and his thumb sank into and popped Michael's left eye. Someone screamed incoherently as he struggled to free his gun, and in a panic he began squeezing off rounds. The bullets tore apart the man's body and Michael's gun hand burst through the man's back just to the right of the backbone. Michael realized the screaming he was hearing was his own, as the man took hold of Michael's wrist and pulled it away from his bloody and torn throat, freeing himself from Michael's hold.

Only seconds had passed since the man had appeared, six or seven at the most as Anthony watched his best friend's eye ooze around the man's thumb still pressed in Michael's eye socket. He could hear Michael screaming and wanted to help, but from this angle, he couldn't get a shot off without hitting him. The crazy man pulled away Michael's neck hold, and Anthony watched in horror as he bit into Michael's right cheek, blood spraying across the crazy man's ravaged face.

"No! You motherfucker!" Anthony screamed as he grabbed the man by his jacket and tried to pull him away from his friend's face. He heard another sound through all the screaming and looked up just in time to see a blood-splattered girl languidly approaching him. She shrieked loudly and flung her arms out, reaching for him.

The girl was young maybe sixteen or seventeen with long blonde hair around what was once a pretty face, before her nose had been bitten off. Her eyes were nothing but a cold, swirling blackness. She wore a blood-soaked hospital gown torn to shreds just below her breasts; she was naked from there down to her bare feet. It appeared that she'd been pregnant recently, but all that was left of her belly was a gore soaked hole where her organs hung out to drag behind her on the floor.

When Agent Roger Murray saw the girl come around the corner of the hallway, his mind couldn't believe what his eyes were telling him. The girl was so badly injured that she couldn't possibly still be standing, breathing, or for that matter, attacking secret service men protecting the President. However, her intentions were clear and Roger acted accordingly. Centering his aim on the target, he fired. One, two, three, shots to her heart, the blood spray from the impacts splattering the wall, floor, and ceiling. Still she kept coming. Another hit on the right side of her neck and the flesh exploded outward as if she'd swallowed a small firework and it had gone off in her throat. Still she kept coming. Another shot tore into her right shoulder, almost severing her arm. The only affect it had was that her gait shifted as she regained her balance.

**What the fuck**? he thought, open mouthed.

Anthony could hear the shots fired from behind him as the bullets hit the girl's body. Three shots hit her in the chest almost simultaneously, a fourth on the right side of her neck, vaporizing the flesh. The firing continued as a fifth found her right shoulder, destroying the joint and leaving her arm dangling uselessly from a few strands of sinew. Then she was on him. They both stumbled backwards as she grabbed hold of Anthony's left arm and tried to bite through his suit coat sleeve.

Anthony reacted in panic when he felt the girl's teeth against the cloth-covered flesh of his arm, biting, pinching, and chewing. He turned and threw his arm outwards, spinning the girl away from him and into the agent behind him whose bullets only seconds ago had almost torn the girl's arm from her body.

The girl hit Roger with her back to his front, and they both began to fall backwards. But he held his balance and stopped himself from falling. The girl turned impossibly fast and grabbed at him with her only good arm, snarling noises bubbling up from her ruined throat. She was too close and he could smell the coppery stench of freshly spilled blood coming off her body. Roger tried to push her away, but she held on tight and snapped her teeth at his face. They slowly spun as the two of them struggled in the center of the hallway like two dancers on a prom date from Hell.

Roger did the only thing he could think of to stop her; he brought his gun up under the left side of her snapping jaw and fired. Blood, brain matter, and bits of skull hit the ceiling nanoseconds after the bullet. Roger had his mouth and eyes wide open as he fired and the blood spray blinded him. He tasted the girl's putrid essence in the back of his throat. He bent over gagging, and as he tried to clear the blood from his eyes, Roger felt a hand grab him by his collar. He moved to bring his gun up and felt another hand on his wrist.

"It's okay, I got you, buddy!" Stephen's voice yelled into his ear.

Stephen gathered Roger into his arms, and turning, he thrust Roger through the door and into the waiting arms of two of his teammates already inside the room. Stephen turned and watched as the unreal scene in the hallway played itself out. He had the look on his face of a man who couldn't accept what he was seeing, yet because he was witnessing it with his own eyes, he had to believe it was real.

Anthony saw the girl's head explode from Roger's shot, and looking over Roger's shoulder, he could see more people coming from the other end of the hallway. Anthony noted at least six crazy, shrieking people coming down the hall, all staggering like drunken invading Huns. He turned back to the corner of the hallway in front of him and saw three more attackers were coming from around the bend.

Anthony, frozen in shocked disbelief for the first time in his career, heard Michael's screaming turn into a gasping gurgle. He looked down at his best friend for more than nine years as he lay under his attacker. Michael's hand still protruded from the man's back, it seemed to be growing out from it like some macabre circus freak show. He'd dropped the gun and the hand was spasming, reaching fingers gripping and opening. The man was ripping into Michael's neck like a starving man at a long awaited feast, gnawing at the flesh, growling in obvious pleasure. Michael's eyes looked into Anthony's as he gurgled out his last cry and expired.

Again, Anthony looked back over his shoulder, back to the door and into Stephen's eyes with a look of absolute horror and indecision twisting his features.

"Come on, man!" Stephen shouted to him, but the door was at least twenty yards away. Anthony knew he couldn't make it with out endangering the President. The people in front of and behind him were too close, only seconds away, and in a split second he knew what his fate would have be.

Anthony locked eyes with his commander and Stephen knew what he was about to do, and he knew Anthony had no other choice.

Stephen watched as Anthony ran forward to meet the attackers head on. He got off one shot into the face of the first, an overweight man dressed in what was once a very expensive suit. It was now covered in blood like the two behind him were; his reaching right hand had only a thumb left on it. Anthony's shot destroyed the face and most of the left side of the head, but fat man's momentum carried him into Anthony, and they both fell to the floor, trapping the Secret Service agent under the man's dead body. Strangely enough, Stephen thought he recognized the lunatic as a congressional representative, but couldn't place the name. The other two assailants fell onto them, scrambling around the body of the fat man in search of Anthony's flesh.

Stephen's eyes, tracking movement, came back to the man attacking Michael. The man appeared to have lost interest in his victim and was now looking at Stephen. As the man moved to stand, his head exploded, covering the wall behind him with what was left of his face. As Stephen lowered his gun, his mouth gaped when Michael sat up and turned to look at him with something that looked like black ink moving in and covering the whites and color of his eyes. Michael shrieked at Stephen, his cry gurgling through his ruined throat. Stephen couldn't understand what he was seeing but he knew his time was up; the last thing he saw before he slammed the door shut was Anthony bringing his weapon up and under his chin. As the multiple locking bolts clicked into place, Stephen heard the shot that killed Anthony from the other side of the door.

He backed away from the door a few steps and listened in shocked disbelief at the pounding, scratching, and screaming coming from the other side only seconds after he'd slammed it closed. The door almost seemed to be vibrating in its frame; Stephen could hear the sound of splintering wood as if a thousand rats were on the other side trying to gnaw their way through. He knew that the one-inch thick steel plate imbedded inside the door and frame and the surrounding walls made it all but impenetrable. Still, he couldn't shake the feeling that the door was going to break down at any second, allowing those *people* into the room.

"What the hell is going on out there goddamn it!"

Stephen heard the President's harsh almost panic-ridden question and knew it was addressed to him. He turned away from the door to face the rest of the people in the room though he didn't like turning his back to the door; the hairs were standing on the back of his neck.

He could hear Roger gagging and retching in the President's bathroom as he tried to wash the blood out of his eyes and mouth. Stephen had started out this accursed day with nine agents, eight men, and one woman, now only seven agents remained. The clock on the bedside table read 2:02 a.m, less than five minutes had passed since they had left this room.

"I'm sorry, sir," Stephen said, "I don't know much more than you do."

"Damn it, Stephen, I need to know what's happing out there and I need to know now!" President Bedford bellowed with frustration. He pushed past the men around him and stepped to the window.

"Sir, wait!" Stephen said as the President pulled back the drapes, revealing the world on the other side of the window.

Although no sound penetrated the room through the sound-proof window, the scene spoke volumes in itself. A large plume of black smoke rose from a massive fire only a few blocks from the Whitehouse grounds. The fire lit the early morning sky with flickering shadows and glowing ghosts of red and orange. Off in the distance, behind the black smoke obscuring the star lit morning sky, many other fiery smoke plumes reached skyward. Down on the grounds of the Whitehouse lawn, groups of rioting people numbering from three or four to as many as twenty, surged back and fourth. Their struggles were lit by the flickering light of the fires and the flashing of police lights and weapons fire. It looked as if the end of the world had begun while they'd all been sleeping.

"Mother of God!" President Bedford gasped, in open-mouthed, wide-eyed horror, at the once beautiful view from his bedroom window. "How did this get so out of control?" he said, demanding of no one in particular with the voice of a man who was used to getting what he wanted without delay. "The Guard was called in yesterday afternoon, I thought they had it all under..." he stopped in mid-sentence as the Air Force Two helicopter came into view, circling above the Whitehouse.

"Oh my God, the city's burning," Angela said. "It's all over," she sobbed heavily. Turning away from the window, she allowed herself to be held again by her mother, who looked as if, she too, were about to burst into tears. Everyone else in the room was held in rapt silence as they beheld the terrifying view.

Stephen stepped up to the window, gently pulled the curtains from the President's grasp, and let them fall, cutting off the end of the world show playing through the glass.

"I need you to step away from the window, sir, we need to get moving," Stephen said in a soft yet firm voice as he looked directly into the President's eyes.

"Where's my staff, Stephen?" The President asked unyieldingly, "I need to speak with my Chief of Staff and Defense Secretary Stratham urgently; now before we move." Stephen looked back into his commander-in-chief's eyes with deadly seriousness.

"Sir, we've been out of contact with the Sec Def and everyone else's security teams for the past half hour." Stephen paused for a moment to let this disturbing news settle into the President's mind.

"I have had no communication with the rest of the Whitehouse Secret Service team after sanctuary was breached, nothing. We have to assume at this point that they have either evacuated or were lost." He paused again, taking in a deep breath, "I just witnessed something out there in the hall that I can't explain. I just lost two good men to unarmed civilians. I don't know what the hell is happening out there, sir, but I do know that we need to get clear, as soon as possible." Stephen finished and waited for the President to reply.

The President looked down for a moment and considered his options given this upsetting news, then he looked up into the frightened eyes of his wife and quietly sobbing daughter. He turned to his protector. "Get us out of here, Stephen," he said gravely as the Secret Service man nodded.

"Yes, sir," Stephen said and turned to two of his agents. "Rodriguez, Bentler, you're on point," he ordered them. He stepped to the west wall of the room and pressed his hand against a hidden panel which fell in and slid to one side, revealing a key pad underneath. Stephen quickly began punching in the code to open the emergency exit passage. As he labored, the sound of splintering wood from the hallway side of the bedroom door changed to the soft ringing of flesh and bone on steel.

"My God, they've torn away the outer layer of wood on the door," Agent Tanner said as he backed away from the entryway with his gun pointed toward the door.

"That's one inch, thick plate-steel, man. They aren't coming through anytime soon," Agent LaSalle said, confidently. Almost as if in response, the screaming outside the door increased and the door began to vibrate within its frame.

"Oh, God," Angela said, breaking out in sobs.

"Angela, calm down, please," her mother said, trying to calm her while looking almost embarrassed at her daughter's outburst of fear. Angela's father stepped over and took his daughter's hand in an attempt to comfort her. Agent Victoria Wheeler turned and lowered herself down on one knee in front of Angela and reaching out, she took the frightened girl gently by the shoulders.

"It's going to be okay, sweetheart," Agent Wheeler said, "We'll get you out safely, right, Stephen?" she asked soft but firmly, addressing her superior. Stephen glanced over from the key pad he was working on and looked directly into Angela's eyes.

"Yes, we *will* get you clear, Angela," he said, confirming with resolute confidence, despite the anxiety in the room. Everyone's nerves seemed close to the boiling point as a five by ten foot section of the bedroom floor dropped down and slid to one side with a soft hum. It was the emergency exit. Florescent lights flickered to life, revealing a steep flight of stairs. Stephen nodded to his point men and they immediately plunged down the stairway. Seconds later they called up the all clear.

"Okay let's go," Stephen said and motioned with his hand, signaling the agents to lead the first family down the stairway. Victoria took the lead, while the three remaining agents took up positions behind the family, following them down and out of sight.

Stephen watched them disappear, and then turning his troubled gaze past the trembling door, he looked to Agent Murray.

Roger was only just now exiting the President's private bathroom after washing a dead girl's blood out of his eyes, mouth and off his face and hands. While he'd gotten most of the blood off his face, Roger's shirt, tie, and jacket still looked as if he'd just blown someone's head off at close range.

Stephen looked him up and down, mentally evaluating his condition and continuing ability to perform his duties. Roger looked shaken and just a little confused as to how this could have befallen him. Otherwise, he appeared to be clear headed and ready to rejoin the team.

"You okay, buddy?" Stephen asked his right-hand man and partner. Roger looked up from the floor and into Stephen's eyes with uncertainty.

"Steve, sir, what just happened out there? That girl, she..." Roger said, rambling as his gaze shifted uneasily to the door behind which all Hell seemed to be breaking loose.

"*Agent* Murray! I need you to focus, we have a job to do and I need you at one hundred percent," Stephen barked, interrupting Roger's nervous ramble with a forceful, authoritative and commanding voice.

"Sir, I'm sorry but we just lost two good men, two friends, to a bunch of..."

Again Agent Athens interrupted, this time stepping into Rogers's space and looking directly into his troubled eyes. "No, I don't want to hear anything else from you except, I'm ready to go; we don't have time for anything else right now."

Roger looked into Stephen's eyes. Seconds passed as Roger seemed to come to his senses and then his eyes cleared of indecision.

"Ready to go, sir, I'm good," Roger said with a slightly shaky voice.

"Okay, let's clear out," Stephen said and jerked his thumb over his shoulder to the open stairway in the floor. Roger nodded his head and hurried down the emergency exit stairs.

Roger did pause and once again gazed at the door behind which many unexplainable things continued to pound and scream, but then he moved on. With them moving again, Stephen turned and followed his people down the stairs.


Coming to the first landing in the steep spiraling stairway, Stephen pressed his hand against a large palm button on the wall, activating the closing mechanism and sealing off their escape route.

The group had already traversed the long, narrow hallway at the bottom of the first flight of stairs. The second spiral stairway was out of sight as Stephen and Roger followed. When they came to the bottom of the second stairway, the two Secret Service men found the whole group nervously waiting. They had already opened and entered the large elevator that would take them down deep into the underground world beneath Washington D.C.

Roger stepped in the elevator as Stephen paused just outside the doorway. He pulled out his communicator, switched channels, and spoke into the microphone in his jacket cuff.

"This is Good Shepherd," Stephen said urgently into the device. "I have my flock and we're heading down to the main tunnel complex, E-T-A one minute, do you read, main tunnel?" A moment of static was the only reply and then a harried voice sputtered from the speaker.

"*Negative! Negative Good Shepherd, that is a negative. We have hostiles in the main tunnel*! I repeat," there was a pause in the response as distant shrieking voices accompanied by multiple automatic weapons fire reverberated through the speaker in Stephen's ear. "*We have hostiles and we are engaging.*"

Stephen could hear John, the chief of the main tunnel station, as he held the microphone away from his mouth and called out to others, *"Fall back to the station, concentrate your fire! There's too many,"* an exasperated voice cried. The automatic fire increased in volume as the men firing them drew closer to the main tunnel station in their retreat.

*"The main tunnel isn't secure, Good Shepherd, we're closing off the elevator exit at this level; recommend you use the emergency exit level for the chariot, sir."*

"I read you, main tunnel," Steve said, almost whispering into the microphone.

*"Copy that, Good Shepherd, you get them out, and Steve, I can't explain it but, some of the hostiles in the tunnel..."* John paused as if even he could not believe what he was about to say.

"I'm listening, John," Stephen said, prompting in nervous anticipation of what he was about to here.

*"Some of the people we're fighting,"* John said, continuing his report. *"The hostiles, they're my men, Steve, it's like they've gone insane or something, I know this sounds crazy but I just don't know man, I..."* John went silent.

"John, I've seen the same thing happen and I can't explain it either," Stephen said, thinking of his fallen man in the hallway rising up with his throat torn out and screaming. Steve shook himself mentally and after taking a deep breath said goodbye to his friend

"We're heading to the emergency exit as you advised, John, good luck, main tunnel." With that said, Steve stopped transmission.

*"Copy that, Steve, we've got your back and good luck to you, main tunnel out,"* the voice of John Gerard, an old friend to Stephen and the main tunnel Secret Service commander was replaced by empty static. Stephen hastily stepped into the elevator car and the doors slid shut silently as he activated the code panel and began their descent. Switching the channel yet again, he spoke into the microphone, this time with a new and frightening urgency in his voice.

"Chariot, this is Good Shepherd, do you copy?" This time the response was instantaneous.

*"Copy, Good Shepherd, this is chariot, we've been monitoring your situation and we're holding on station for a pick up at the emergency exit L-Z what's your E-T-A?"*

"Hold your station, Chariot, I'll get back to you on that," Stephen turned to the President who was waiting anxiously behind him in the emergency exit elevator.

As Stephen conferred on his communicator, the conversation was easily overheard by everyone in the elevator. The realization that the main tunnel was overrun by rioters unsettled the President greatly and he visibly started at the information.

"How is that possible? The tunnel is one of the most secure locations in Washington," President Bedford said, asking no one in particular in an exasperated tone.

"Yes, sir, but the tunnel has many public entrances that could be taken by a determined group of people," Roger Murray answered as he turned to the President. "There're many surface and subway entrances that..." Roger stopped talking abruptly as a stabbing pain shot down his back like an electric bolt. The white hot pain then traveled back up his spine with a staggering explosion of agony behind his eyes and forehead. Roger grunted and fell back against the wall of the elevator car, grasping his head in trembling hands.

"Roger!" Agent Wheeler called out as she came to his side. "Are you okay, what's wrong?"

Roger seemed to regain his composure quickly as the unexpected pain faded as fast as it arrived. "Yeah, yeah, I'm all right, just had a little brain freeze," he said as he shook it off and stood up straight again, smiling at his fellow agent with whom he shared a secret. "I'm good, Vicky."

"Are you sure? You looked like you were going down there for a second," Vicky said, showing just a bit more concern than the situation might warrant, and earning a suspicious look from the First Lady.

"Yeah, I'm okay, thanks," Roger said as Stephen turned from his communication with the Air Force Two helicopter and stepped between the two of them so he was facing the President in the elevator car. He ended the uncomfortable exchange between the two agents with a quick look to both.

"Mr. President, sir, I need a conference with you," Stephen said matter of factly as the situation was far too urgent for normal protocol.

"Well, out with it man!" President Bedford said.

"We need to make a decision on our course of action, we have two options and ultimately the final say is yours, sir." Stephen paused for only a second to let the information settle in. "We can descend down into the main White House bunker where we'll be quite safe from any and all activity on the surface, but we may be trapped down there for quite a while as the situation gets sorted out."

"Or?" the President asked, prompting Stephen to continue.

"Or we can attempt a pickup by Air Force Two at the emergency L-Z. Which may expose us to hostiles on the surface, sir."

The President considered this information for only a few moments and made the decision with his trade mark decisive quickness. "I don't want to be trapped in the bunker, Stephen, no matter how safe it may seem. Get us to Air Force Two and get us off the ground."

"Yes, sir, Mr. President," Stephen said respectfully, "I agree." Stephen turned and again spoke into his hand communicator. "Chariot, this is the Good shepherd, we are a go for emergency pick up, E-T-A sixteen minutes."

"*Copy that, Good shepherd, be advised there are numerous hostiles on the ground. We watched them overtake the group at the main L-Z only a few minutes ago.*"

"Can you give me a number on those hostiles, Chariot?"

"*Ah, I'd say thousands, Good Shepherd,*" the air force pilot replied sounding as if even he couldn't believe what he was seeing.

"Say again, Chariot, did you say thousands?" Stephen asked in honest disbelief.

"*Roger that, Good shepherd, that's thousands, well over five thousand or more if you include the area just outside the White House grounds.*"

"Chariot, are these hostiles armed?" Stephen asked.

"*That's a negative, Good shepherd, as far as I can see they appear to be unarmed rioting civilians.*"

Stephen took a few moments to absorb this information, his brow furrowed as his mind worked out all possible strategies and scenarios.

"Copy that, Chariot, we are now fifteen minutes out," Stephen informed the pilot as the elevator slowly came to a soft stop at the selected level.

*"Be advised, Good shepherd, we're being tracked by hostiles on the ground, they appear to be following us as we circle. Possibly waiting for us to make a landing attempt, we're going to head off north to lead them away from the L-Z. When we come back in we'll be landing hot. I repeat, we will be landing hot. Good Shepherd, do you copy?"*

"I copy, Chariot, Good shepherd out." As Stephen signed off with the Air Force Two chopper, the elevator doors were opening. His two point men, Juan Rodriguez and Jerry Bentler, immediately exited the elevator car and moved away to the left and out of sight.

The narrow corridor leading away from the elevator looked old and seldom used. The concrete walls were dark and water stained and the floor was slightly damp with dark mold in the corners. Over their heads, dim flickering florescent lights only added to the shadows dancing across the walls. The air was thick with mildew laden moisture and Jerry pinched his nose harshly to stifle a sneeze. The resonance of their breathing, soft footsteps and the distant dripping of water was the only sound in the otherwise silent underworld.

Moving down the corridor like wraiths of death, they communicated with silent hand signals. Jerry took point and moved around the corner at the end of the long shadowy corridor. Jerry crouched and slid around the corner into the larger tunnel, scanning for hostiles. Juan came up right behind him, his weapon panning above Jerry's head. Together, they moved into the larger tunnel and quickly determined they were alone.

Juan keyed up his microphone, "Clear," he said into the right cuff of his suit. The tunnel that dead-ended at the opening of the elevator corridor was easily large enough to drive a small car through. The curved ceiling was twenty feet at the center; with visible I-beam supports arcing from one side to the other. Waiting for the group now exiting from the elevator corridor, Jerry and Juan stood next to three electric carts (similar to golf carts) with attached cords plugged into the wall.

Stephen and the rest of his team led the first family over and onto the middle cart.

"Rig for heavy combat," Stephen said, gesturing towards a locked weapons locker adjacent to the carts. Stephen pulled out a set of keys and tossed them to Agent Bentler, who unlocked the weapons locker and then tossed back the keys.

The team quickly passed out their Dragon Skin body armor tactical vests amongst themselves and the first family.

"Here," Vicky said to Angela, "let me help you with that." She stepped up to the first family's cart and gently helped the distraught girl get her vest on. The team around them moved with silent efficiency, the tunnel echoing with the sounds of their breathing and the dry clicks of automatic weapons being prepped and loaded.

"Get ready for some payback, you bastards," Jerry said quietly as he slapped home a fully-loaded clip. Juan nodded and smiled; his eyes hot and cold at the same time.

"It's cold down here," the First Lady said, rubbing her hands on her goose-pimpled arms. Her husband reached over and put his arms around her.

"And creepy," Angela added as all their voices echoed into the dim emptiness of the tunnel.

"Sir," Stephen said as he reached out and offered his suit jacket to the President.

"Thank you, Stephen," the President said as he took the offered jacket and draped it around his wife's shoulders. She smiled and nodded her thanks. Without asking, Agent Wheeler put her jacket around Angela's shoulders. Angela turned and smiled weakly at the Secret Service woman.

"Okay, people, let's move it out!" Stephen said. Everyone nodded and moved to their positions. Moving quickly, everyone pulled the charging cords for their carts from the wall sockets and stowed them away in their compartments on the carts. Taking the point again, Rodriguez and Bentler mounted the first cart and pulled away from the group. Stephen, Victoria, and Roger climbed onto the President's cart with Roger taking the wheel. Behind them, the two remaining agents in the Presidential detail, LaSalle and Tanner, climbed aboard the last cart and together they all pulled away into the flickering shadows of the emergency exit tunnel.


Agent Kediri LaSalle had never seen any real action in his long distinguished career and was only a few months from retirement. His wife, daughter and his three sons were waiting for him on their Montana ranch and he ached to be with them.

Agent LaSalle's partner, Ronald Tanner could see the worry on his mentor's dark-skinned, Creole face.

"They're okay, Ked," Ronald said, trying to console him. "The rioting is mostly confined to the coastal cities and the mid-east of the U.S."

Agent LaSalle looked over at his protégé, a secret service newbie from New York, and four months into his second year in the service.

"I know, Ron, but I don't *know*," LaSalle said, the slight accent in his voice giving away his Louisiana heritage. He shook his head and took a steadying breath, "I haven't spoken to them in two days."

"You have a safe room there, don't you? I remember you saying something about that," Agent Tanner said.

Agent LaSalle smiled, "We have a fallout bunker. I lived through the cold war remember."

Tanner nodded and returned the smile, "They'll be fine, man."

"Yeah," LaSalle said, "What about you, your mom and pop?"

"Talked to 'em last night, they're in Connecticut at my mom's sister's place."

"Good to hear, man," LaSalle said, casting an uncertain glance behind him into the rapidly receding shadows.

The tunnel sloped sharply down, then after a few hundred yards it leveled out to slowly begin to ark upwards again.

In less than five minutes, they reached the far end of the tunnel, where Rodriquez and Bentler awaited them in another side corridor.

"Okay, listen up," Stephen said as he climbed from the electric cart. All eyes turned to him as everyone gathered around. "I have the President with me." He turned to Roger. "And you Roger, I want you to take the First Lady." Roger nodded he understood. Stephen continued. "Victoria has Angela, and the rest of you are on point." Stephen took a deep breath and looked into the eyes of the people gathered around him.

The President's eyes were hard but uncertain, the First Lady and her daughter's eyes were terrified but trusting. As for his team, their eyes looked cool and confident, a few burning with anxious desire for payback for their fallen friends.

"When we blow the hatch," Stephen continued, "I want a defensive perimeter around the L-Z before the dust settles. Air Force Two is coming in hot so you'll have to wait until you hear them touch down before exiting the hatch. It should be only a few seconds if we time this right."

"R-O-E?" Agent Bentler asked, wanting to know the rules of engagement.

"Anyone approaching with hostile intent, obvious or otherwise," Stephen paused, considering his next words. "You put them down without hesitation. You are weapons free gentlemen, shoot to kill."

The men nodded in approval as their bodies tensed at the thought of coming action.

"One more thing," Stephen said, almost hesitantly. "If there are large groups of hostiles then go for the legs to slow them down. Small groups or individuals, use head shots." The few who hadn't clearly seen what happened in the White House hallway frowned slightly.

"No questions, okay? Just trust me on this," Stephen finished; everyone nodded again, trusting their commander without question. "All right, let's do this."

Rodriquez and Bentler took the lead into the exit corridor followed by the first family, each of them guided by their assigned agents. Tanner and Lakota covered the rear as they moved into the narrow corridor which curved slowly to the left in a spiraling ramp leading up to the surface world. Unlike the rest of the emergency exit tunnel, the surface exit corridor was dry and brightly lit.

"Has this tunnel ever been used?" The First Lady asked Agent Murray, who looked slightly troubled as he walked besides her.

Murray seemed to shake off his dilemma as he answered. "No," he said, shaking his aching head to clear his thoughts. "It was completed in the late sixties. We've never had a situation that warranted its use before now."

It only took a few minutes of hurried walking to reach the small, square room at the end. Stephen stepped past his point men and approached the code panel to the left of the pressure sealed door at the far end of the square chamber.

Stephen keyed in the proper code and with a dry click, the small box over the code panel unlocked, exposing a large green palm button with red, glowing numerals over it that read 0.60 seconds.

Stephen glanced over his shoulder. "Lock and load," he said to his team.

As his team readied their weapons, Stephen spoke into his communicator, "Chariot, this is Good Shepherd, do you copy?"

"*Copy, Good Shepherd, we're holding on station, circling just outside the L-Z,*" the pilot quickly replied. "*Surface conditions are favorable for emergency exit, but not for long. I recommend you proceed quickly.*"

"Copy, Chariot, we are ready to blow the hatch in sixty seconds on my mark." Stephen waited a few seconds for the Air Force Two pilot to get into position. "Mark!"

Stephen pressed the palm button and the readout over the button began to count down. He stepped away from the code panel and the pressure door next to it, his four point man team stepping up without hesitation to replace him.

Ten feet above their heads and six feet below, was The Ellipse, a circular grass field just south of the White House. The shaped charges over the emergency exit hatch detonated at the end of the countdown. The first family and their Secret Service detail heard a loud muted explosion as the charges detonated, instantly creating a massive fifty foot wide crater in the earth over the hatch. The detonation shook the room and sent dust and small bits of debris cascading down from the ceiling, and after a few more breathless seconds the pressure door opened with a hissing *pop*.

Agent Rodriguez threw the pressure door open and plunged through it, followed quickly by his comrades. The small chamber beyond the pressure door stank of wet earth and detonated explosives. Dirt-filtered light shone down from a round opening to the surface ten feet over their heads. Rodriguez shouldered his weapon and jumped onto the ladder beneath the opening as behind him, the rest of the point team followed. Rodriguez reached the opening and paused halfway through, waiting.

On the surface, the Air Force Two helicopter came down hard and fast, cutting through the billowing dust and debris and landing with a bone-jarring thump. The Air Force pilot set down less than twenty yards from the crater at the far end of The Ellipse from the National Christmas Tree. The hot landing strained the landing wheels and the chopper threatened to topple forward. The pilot compensated and leveled the aircraft with an expertly trained hand.

Even before the aircraft's landing gear was settled, its doors were thrown open and four marines in full battle gear leaped from the chopper and spread out around it.

Rodriguez heard the helicopter hit the earth and exploded into action. Emerging from the emergency exit hatch like angry ants, he and the point team charged up the slope of the crater. The air swam with blowing dust from the helicopter's spinning blades as they crested the edge of the crater and spread out around the chopper, joining the marines. The four Secret Service men took positions between each of the marines, filling in the gaps.

Around them, Washington burned with apocalyptic chaos and they could hear the screams of the rioting civilians coming for them.

LaSalle came up between two marines and brought his weapon up, scanning for targets. The marine to his left noticed him and nodded, LaSalle nodded back. Around them, target hostiles were advancing from every direction. The marine to his left opened fire first and by firing in short, five round bursts, he took down the two closest advancing hostiles, who immediately began to struggle to their feet!

"What the hell?" The marine said, lowering his weapon slightly and looking over the rifle's sight.

"Head shots!" Agent LaSalle shouted.

To the right of the two hostiles that were shot but not down, a larger group came lumbering onto the field. There were at least twenty or more civilians in a loose grouping and most were splattered with blood and had torn clothing; one man wore only his boxer shorts. The attackers moved towards the L-Z screaming as if they were insane and staggering as if they were all drunk or drugged.

LaSalle dropped to one knee and opened fire, stitching a line of rounds across the advancing hostiles at knee level, panning left to right and back. Shins, knees and thighs exploded in bloody sprays of flesh and bone. Robbed of their legs, the first line of attackers fell forward and the bullets tore into their shoulders and faces. Behind the first wave of hostiles, others continued forward, oblivious to the death around them, stumbling and falling over moving and unmoving bodies.

Agent LaSalle emptied a full clip and quickly popped the empty out and reloaded. Bringing his weapon back up, he began to fire in short bursts. In the massive tangle of bodies he had created, blossoms of spraying blood bloomed from almost every head that remained attached to a moving body.

The marine to LaSalle's left looked over at him and nodded, his eyes wide with respect. "Head shots," he said. The two rioters the marine had failed to stop with his first shots were still moving forward. The marine quickly dispatched them with a few well placed rounds and then panned, looking for more targets; there was no shortage.

Stephen was the first out of the hatch after the point team. Turning, he scanned for hostiles, but couldn't see the surrounding terrain over the crater's edge. The only thing he could see was the dark sky, the pointed top of the Washington Monument, a few tree tops, and the marine standing at the far edge of the crater, firing his weapon as he guarded their escape.

Stephen reached down and helped the President out of the exit hatch and holding him by the arm, he hurriedly led him up towards the waiting helicopter. Blinding wind driven soil obscured their vision as gunfire, police sirens and hundreds of screaming voices assaulted their ears.

At the lip of the crater, the President cried out as he twisted his ankle and stumbled.

"I've got you!" Stephen said, hollering above the driving windstorm of the rotor blades and chaos around them. Dropping his automatic rifle, Stephen pulled the President's arm over his shoulders and drew his sidearm.

Behind them, Agent Murray reached the lip of the crater carrying the First Lady in his arms. Setting her on her feet, he unshouldered his automatic weapon. "Run for the chopper!" he yelled.

She said something back but the churning air swallowed her voice and she turned to run after her husband and the safety of the Air Force Two helicopter.

Roger spun in a quick circle, looking for targets as he moved towards the chopper. He saw Agent Wheeler clear the lip of the crater while dragging Angela behind her, then a sudden wave of dizziness drove him to the ground.

The pain accompanying the dizzy spell was intense, a stabbing agony that shot from the back of Roger's neck to his groin and back again, settling in his forehead above his eyes. He gasped for breath and then vomited explosively onto the grass. The thick black vomit left a bitter chemical sting in his mouth and throat.

"Roger!" he heard Agent Wheeler yell and realized she had stopped beside him.

"Go, go!" he yelled, waving his hand and pointing towards the waiting chopper where the President and First Lady had already climbed aboard. He hacked and spat out the last of the lingering bile in his mouth and staggered to his feet. The pain and nausea that drove him to the ground was gone just as fast as it hit him, leaving only a dull ache in his head.

As Roger ran for the open doors of the rescue helicopter, he heard Stephen's voice in his earpiece. *"The package is aboard, fall back to the chopper!"*

When he made it to the helicopter's doors, Roger turned just in time to see the perimeter collapse under the relentless onslaught of the rioting civilians.

Agent Juan Rodriguez heard the call to fall back, but if he obeyed, it might allow the massive wave of rioting civilians to

151

reach the chopper before it could take off, and he knew he couldn't allow that. He'd already put down roughly more than five dozen assailants. Unfortunately, for every one he stopped there were two more to take their place.

*Oh God, what the fuck is happening?* he wondered, but had no time to contemplate this distracting thought so he pushed it back down. The rioters were advancing; there was no stopping their sheer numbers, the only thing he could do was slow them down.

In his peripheral vision, Agent Jerry Bentler saw the marine to his left drop his empty automatic rifle and draw his sidearm. Jerry, too, squeezed off the last rounds in his rifle and dropping it, he drew his 9 mm SIG. Somewhere in the back of his mind, he registered how many people he'd killed in the past minute but he would dwell on it later, if he survived.

So many people, so many insanely screaming and bloody faces. Men and women, young and old, rich or poor, they all fell under the hail of his bullets. He was silent, his mouth set in a determined grimace as he killed without hesitation, one after another, until a little girl's face fell under his sights.

The little girl's bloodied, thin blonde hair was matted to the left side of her head where one of her ears should have been. She lurched over several of Jerry's kills and came directly towards him. Her mouth and the front of her blue **I Love Washington** sweater glistened wet with freshly spilled blood.

It wasn't that she was a kid that gave Jerry pause, he had already killed several in the past few seconds, it was that she was so *little* and she reminded him of someone. The little screaming girl couldn't be more than five or six years old, and she looked exactly like his little sister's daughter.

"Samantha?" Jerry asked as he lowered his sidearm and looked over it. To his left, he barely registered the marine falling into the emergency exit hatch crater as he was tackled by a blood-covered attacker dressed like a mailman.

"No," Jerry whispered, "I..."

Another few seconds passed and the girl halved the distance between them. A low keening groan escaped from Jerry's lips as he raised his weapon. He could see the black of her eyes when he squeezed the trigger.

The bullet glanced off her right cheek, bone distorting her face in a crimson spray of torn flesh. Her head hardly tilted from the impact.

"Oh, God," Jerry said with a sob as he pulled the trigger again. But it clicked empty.

"Shit, shit," Jerry said and in a smooth, well practiced motion he popped the empty clip and slammed another home...and then the girl was on him.

He staggered back as the girl slammed into him and latched onto his arm. He almost lost his gun as he tried to fling her off but she held on. He screamed when she bit into his hand. He clubbed her on the top of her head and she fell away, taking away part of his gun hand in her mouth. His ravaged hand refused to cooperate and he dropped the gun. Jerry fell to his knees, scrambling to pick it up with his left hand.

The girl was coming again, but the blood on her mouth and chin was his now. The screaming in his ears was his own as he pulled the trigger and shattered the rest of the little girl's face.

Agent Ronald Tanner knew he wasn't going to make it. He saw the marine to his left turn and run when the order to retreat was given, but he couldn't follow. The fleeing marine left a gap in the line and if Ronald didn't fill it, it would be disastrous.

He wasn't going to make it. If he turned and ran, they would be on him, there were just too many. Instead of backing up, he shifted his position slightly to the left and walked forward, firing in short, sweeping controlled bursts, taking the fight to the hostiles, one head shot at a time. He was screaming now, but it wasn't a scream of fear or terror, it was a battle cry.

Agent Kediri LaSalle saw the marine to his right bug out and then he saw Ronald move to cover the retreating marine's kill zone.

Kediri was running backwards.

*I'm not going to die here, I'm not going to die here,* he chanted in his mind. Firing the last of his auto rounds, he discarded the rifle. "Ronald!" he called, shouting out to his new partner who was walking into the oncoming crazies and away from the Air Force Two helicopter.

Ronald shot a quick glance over his shoulder and then shifted his fire to cover Kediri's retreat.

"Fall back!" Kediri screamed to Ronald, but the man couldn't possibly hear him now. Kediri caught sight of close movement to his right. Upon turning, he saw a man in a torn and bloody bus driver's uniform less than twenty feet away. He tried to get his sidearm up, but the bus driver's head exploded away from him before he could react thanks to someone else's bullet.

One harried marine went past Roger and into the waiting helicopter, then another. Agent Roger Murray saw one marine falling into the exit crater, struggling with a mailman? Agent Juan Rodriguez was holding his ground but there were far too many for him to stop for long. Roger's eyes shifted and he caught sight of Agent Jerry Bentler swinging a small and bloody blonde girl on his hand like a rag doll. To his right, Roger spotted one of the marines being dragged to the ground by six or more attacking civilians. Even over the chaos around them, Roger could still hear the marine screaming. Then he saw LaSalle running backwards to the helicopter as the crazed bus driver was about to tackle him. Roger put a short burst into the side of the bus driver's skull and the man toppled over. LaSalle turned and looked at Roger incredulously.

"Come on, Kediri!" Roger screamed at him, and LaSalle ran for it.

Kediri jumped into the helicopter and Roger threw himself backwards behind him. The marine at the door slammed it shut just as one of the crazies thumped into it, splattering blood across the door window.

"Go! Go! Go!" Stephen yelled to the pilot who immediately took the advice.

The Air Force Two helicopter took to the sky with a crowd of hostile and rioting civilians gathering beneath it. Kediri pressed his face to a window and caught sight of Jerry firing the last of his ammo and dropping the handgun. He drew his backup sidearm from an ankle holster and when he glanced up at the helicopter, it seemed like he was looking directly into Kediri's eyes.

Jerry nodded, then he took flight himself, running across the tops of two parked cars and into the street.

As the chopper gained altitude, Jerry vanished from Kediri's sight and into the streets of an apocalyptic Washington D.C.

"Crazy bastard," Kediri said quietly to himself, his voice almost choking. His heart broke for the guy and his selfless act of bravery as a rare tear rolled down his dusty cheek. As the helicopter rose into the air, Washington fell away behind them.

With a helping hand from Stephen, Roger pulled himself up from the floor of the chopper and then fell forward, doubling over gasping in agony.

"Roger!" Stephen shouted as he reached out and tried to help his friend.

Roger fell onto his side and sucked in his last breath as darkness bloomed in his eyes.

# THE UNLUCKY

## GARETH WOOD

Bersi the Fair gazed out over the land from the back of his horse, and smiled. Flocks of birds rose from the shore ahead, and the forests sang with life and the promise of adventure. He inhaled deeply of the fresh clean air, and turned to his friend Valgard and laughed aloud, for Valgard wore his habitual frown.

"What's the matter with you?" Bersi asked his fellow Northman, "You look like you sucked on some fouled mead!"

Valgard's scowl only deepened, and he spit onto the ground. He looked into the forest as if he saw something there to be feared.

"Where are the skraelings, Bersi?" he asked, worry evident in his tone. "Where are the damned skraelings?"

For five days they had traveled down the coast of Vinland, searching for the skraelings. None of the natives of this vast and fruitful land had come this year to trade or fight at the small Northman settlement farther up the coast, and finally, in summer, a mission had been sent to find out why. The men rode south along the coast, and passed village after village, all of them empty.

The birds settled into the grass again after the men passed, and the sun slowly sank to the west, nearing the horizon hidden by sparse forest and low hills. Exploration had shown that this region of Vinland was the tip of a large peninsula, reaching south west into a larger landmass, possibly one far larger than Greenland.

Bersi and Valgard had come to Vinland as colonists from Greenland, part of a small but growing community. Neither was married, but Bersi had been popular with the women at home for his good looks and good humor. He turned and looked back at his companions on this adventure. There was the captain, Arinbjorn the Grim, tall and strong like any good Northman should be. He spoke seldom, but his words were worth hearing when he did. Arinbjorn rode at the left, watching the coastline pass, all the rocky fjords so like the homeland they had left behind. The young man

Runolf was at his side, pointing at something in the trees. Runolf was a cheery and energetic lad of thirteen, well liked by all the men and women of the Vinland colony. He wore a sword now, and was counted among the men rather than the children.

At the back were the last two men on the mission, Yrsa and Olvir. Olvir was the oldest man in the colony, having seen forty summers. He had few teeth, but his eyes were sharp and his mind was quick. He was dark and lean and ate as much as a man twice his size. His wife Solveig had packed him three warm shirts when he had told her that he had volunteered for the mission, and the other men teased him for it.

To his left was Yrsa the Dog, exiled from Norway three years past for murder. He had pale skin and dark eyes, and a temper that was unmatched. He was a looter and horse thief, and was not well thought of amongst the colony's women. His skill with sails and ships was the only thing that kept him in good standing.

Bersi looked to Arinbjorn again, and the captain pointed away to the south. Bersi saw that another village was in sight, this one close to the water, and there appeared to be bodies lying among the huts.

The native folk, whom the Northmen called skraelings, were a primitive people who fished and hunted and lived in small villages on the coast in summer, and then moved into the forests in winter. The skraelings painted their faces and hands red with stripes of ochre, and dyed some of their clothing with it as well. The skraelings had fought the Northmen for a year after the colony had been established, and then had started to trade food and tools for spears and knives. The skraelings had no metal, and found the iron tools invaluable.

Now a village in ruins might offer clues to why the local people had not come again. Bersi nudged his horse forward, and his nose smelled decay and blood. His horse shied from the odor, and Bersi calmed it with a firm and smooth motion, stroking its neck and whispering to it. His companions spread out beside him, as they rode slowly among the huts and corpses. This village was the first they had found with bodies in it. All the others had been empty of life, both men and livestock. The bodies lay strewn about the central clearing between the huts and the skraelings small longhouse. The huts were tall cones of branches, with laced twigs and grass woven through the tree limbs to keep wind and rain away. All the huts were round, with a single opening, except the skraeling's version of a longhouse. This structure was rectangular, and smaller than the Northmen would have built it. It was divided inside into two rooms, each with a fire pit, and had a low roof of branches and grass. In the summer heat, the walls and roof were very dry.

"By the gods," Valgard muttered, gazing about at the scattered dead. All of the corpses had been torn apart, the blood and entrails of men and animals lying on the dusty earth. Possibly twenty men and women's remains lay destroyed in the village. The Northmen had never seen such carnage, even though none were unused to the sights of war, not even young Runolf.

Yrsa climbed down off his horse and crouched by one of the bodies while Arinbjorn rode a circle around the scene, looking closely at the ground. Nothing else moved in the village except the ever present flies.

"Yrsa? What did this?" asked Bersi, staring in horror. His eyes found the bodies of two children among the dead, in such a state that he looked away.

It was Olvir who answered rather than Yrsa. He had climbed down also and stood over two of the corpses with sword in hand.

"It was men did this deed, Bersi. What manner of men, I cannot say."

"It can't be men," Yrsa the Dog growled. He was looking at a head in the dirt, a head whose skull was cracked open, and whose brains were spilled on the ground before him.

"Why do you say that? I see no animal's footprints here."

"No man can tear the flesh of another's bones like these have had done. No man would be strong enough to crack these bones open." He kicked the head and spit in the dirt.

Arinbjorn held up a hand, and the rest fell quiet. The captain looked over the shoulders of the others and into the woods. "It was men. They came on foot from this way," and he pointed into the woods. Arinbjorn was known as a good hunter and tracker. "They fell on the skraelings and then walked away on foot, that way." With this he pointed again, further to the north. Bersi looked and could see the path that a crowd of barefoot men, and some women, had left on the soft ground.

Runolf asked, "What weapons did they use? I see no spears or arrows."

Olvir shrugged. "They used none, boy. This was done with teeth and hands."

"Teeth? You are sure?"

"Yes, captain, I am sure. Look here," Olvir said, holding up an arm, most of the flesh missing from the bones. There were tooth marks on the bones, Bersi could see that clearly. He felt a chill go through him despite the warmth of the day.

"Who did that? Who could do this?" Valgard asked, looking about as if he expected to be set upon by fiends at any moment. His hands held tightly to the horse's mane.

"Maybe you could ask him," said Olvir, pointing behind Yrsa.

A skraeling had walked from the woods, and was staggering towards the Northmen. Yrsa stepped forward, and Bersi and the others could see that the man was hurt. He was near naked and unarmed, but his skin was pale and he had a bloody wound in his chest, another on his left arm. His eyes darted between the men, but once Yrsa stepped towards him, the skraeling focused only on him, and kept moving forward in a stagger, as if drunk. One arm reached for Yrsa, the other hung limp and useless.

Olvir frowned. "Careful there, Yrsa," he said, climbing back upon his horse. He looked around as the others did, to make sure there were no other skraelings waiting in ambush while this one distracted them. He saw none.

"Ho there! Skraeling! What happened here?" Yrsa called to the approaching man. The wounded man did not respond, but reached out and took hold of Yrsa's arm, and opened his mouth wide. Bloody red meat fell out from between the skraelings teeth, and the man pulled Yrsa into an embrace with his one good arm. His teeth sank into Yrsa's shoulder above where his armor ended, and the Northman shouted and pushed the skraeling away. Sword drawn, and a furious grimace upon his face, Yrsa thrust his blade into the belly of the skraeling, and was amazed when the man did not fall. He pulled the blade out and swung it solidly into the man's chest, where it crushed ribs and pulverized lung and heart. The man still stood and little blood oozed from the wounds. Yrsa swore and backed away. The skraeling advanced, arm outstretched and mouth open.

*He should be dead*, thought Bersi. He was stunned. Was the skraeling a ghost? He looked down at the man's feet, and saw dust kicked up by the moving feet.

Not a ghost then, he thought.

Yrsa recovered his wits and swung his sword again, higher this time. It struck the neck and cleaved through, and the head spun away as the body fell to the ground. It had taken only moments, once the fight began, to end it. Yrsa grimaced and clutched at his shoulder, which was bleeding freely. Arinbjorn swung down from his mount and took his pouch of tools and medicines from the bag he had stowed it in, and had Yrsa sit on a log nearby.

As the captain tended the wounded man and showed young Runolf how to clean and bandage the wound, Olvir and Valgard looked over the corpse. Bersi went to look for the head which had rolled under a bush. As he spotted it, he heard Olvir saying, "Look, the chest wound was enough to kill him, and the sword in the belly. Why didn't he fall?"

"Perhaps he was a ghost?" Valgard asked. He made a sign to ward off evil spirits.

"He looks solid to me. Look at this; his flesh is cold already and there is hardly any blood." Olvir was poking at the corpse with his finger and a knife. It was true, there was not enough blood. What there was came out slow and thick, like sap from a tree. "He stinks too, like a barrow."

"What? What do you mean?" This was Arinbjorn, listening from where he tended Yrsa.

"Captain," said Olvir, "he smells like a man long dead. I didn't notice at first, over the stench of the others, but he reeks like he's been a few long days in the grave."

Runolf walked over to the body. He looked pale and a little green, but he looked at the body without flinching. "He has no flies."

Olvir looked again at the body. It was true; there were no flies on the corpse of the skraeling. Insects crawled all over the other bodies in the village.

"Bersi," called Olvir, "are there flies on the head?"

Bersi the Fair reached under the bush and grasped the head by the long black hair, and pulled it out. He lifted it up to look at it, and the teeth snapped and the eyes stared at him. He dropped it and jumped back, crying out in surprise as the eyes followed him still.

"The head still lives!" he cried drawing his blade. His sword swept down, crushing the skull, and he beat it again and again until it was completely ruined. No flies landed on it when he stepped back.

Shaken and panting, Bersi walked to where Yrsa was being tended and reached for some long grass to wipe his sword with. Yrsa's wound was ugly where the skraeling's teeth had broken his flesh and torn out a small bite.

"The bleeding will not stop," Arinbjorn told Bersi, as he wiped the blood away again and again. It was not a bad wound, nor very deep, but the bleeding could weaken Yrsa, and he was even more foul tempered when tired.

Olvir came closer and looked at the wound. "Use fire," he pronounced. Arinbjorn looked at Yrsa, who nodded through his gritted teeth. Quickly a fire was built among the huts from coals found in the longhouse and Olvir took a burning stick as thick around as his thumb and finger together, then he pressed the flame to the wound. Yrsa grunted, but he had been more sorely injured than this before and so took it well. Arinbjorn took this as an opportunity to teach Runolf about using fire to treat wounds.

As the sun started to set, the men gathered well outside the village, upwind and near the water, and built a new fire and made their meal. The horses were tethered to stakes in the ground nearby. Bersi sat across the low flames from Olvir and watched the old man chew his food and think. The captain, too, was deep in thought, and the mood of all the men was dark as the night began to cool.

Yrsa caught a fever before the moon rose, and took to his bed, complaining of chills and aches in his shoulder. Olvir went to check on him later on, and found him tossing restlessly as he tried to sleep. Bersi lay upon the soft earth, closed his eyes, and listened to

Olvir muttering to himself before he fell asleep. He dreamed of screaming and dark men with gleaming eyes.

Valgard shook Bersi awake and he realized the screaming was real. He had been hearing it for some time, and it had joined his dream to make it a nightmare. It was Yrsa screaming, incoherent and writhing upon the ground while both Arinbjorn and Olvir struggled to hold him down.

"Bersi," called Olvir, "bring me my knife! And a torch to see by!"

Bersi rummaged through Olvir's bags while Runolf took a torch to them so that they could see. Bersi's hand found the knife and he pushed past Valgard to kneel by Yrsa's left side. The wound was even uglier now. The flesh around it was puffy and sore looking and black ooze ran from the edges of the bite. The wounded man's flesh was red and hot, and Bersi could feel the fever as Yrsa writhed. Yrsa screamed and fought and his agony made him blind. The captain and Olvir together managed to hold him down, but he still fought like a berserker.

"Cut the wound, Bersi," Olvir told him. "It is fouled, and we must drain the pus or he will likely die."

With Runolf holding the torch, Bersi did what he could, cutting the bad flesh away and washing out the dark pus with clean water. Yrsa stopped screaming partway through and his struggling quieted, for which all his companions were grateful. He stopped reacting to their ministrations even when a torch was reapplied to the wound. He lay quiet and his breathing was shallow. Olvir watched over him for a time and then told the others that Yrsa would most likely die that night.

"You are sure?" Arinbjorn asked. He looked at Yrsa and frowned, shaking his blonde head slightly.

"Yes. His fever still burns. I think he is too weak now to keep screaming."

Valgard cursed and stalked away into the darkness. He preferred to keep a distance from the dying and doubted that Yrsa would want to see his glowering face before he went to join the dead in Valholl.

Bersi shrugged. Such was the skein of a man's life laid out. If it was Yrsa's destiny to die here, then he would, and nothing his fellows did would stop it from happening. He lay back down near the fire and soon fell asleep again. And once again, Valgard shook him awake. It was near dawn and the sun was lighting clouds out over the sea to the east.

"He's dead." Valgard then stood and walked to where the other men had gathered over Yrsa's body. Bersi stretched and joined them.

Yrsa lay cold and still on the ground where he had slept. His eyes were open and he was not breathing.

He looks smaller, Bersi thought.

Arinbjorn knelt, closed Yrsa's eyes and turned to Runolf.

"Gather wood for his pyre," Arinbjorn told the boy and then looked to Valgard and said, "Fetch his weapons and his property." Bersi stood to go with Valgard and Olvir walked after Runolf to help with the wood gathering, leaving the captain with the body.

"When did he die?" Bersi asked his friend as they gathered the dead man's possessions.

"Just before I woke you."

Bersi lifted Yrsa's sword, still in its leather scabbard, and bent to pick up his small shield as he looked over at Arinbjorn. What he saw made his blood chill in his veins. Arinbjorn stood looking east towards the sunrise and behind him dead Yrsa was sitting up. Bersi's voice caught in his throat and only a strangled moan came out as he watched the body of Yrsa climb unsteadily to its feet.

As dead Yrsa looked around, his eyes fell on Arinbjorn, and he lurched toward the captain, arms outstretched and his mouth opening. Bersi finally found his voice, and yelled, "Behind you! Look out!"

Arinbjorn whirled and seized Yrsa's arms just as the dead man grasped at him, pushing the captain over backwards. The two figures fell together onto the ground as Bersi and Valgard ran towards them over the moss covered rocks of the shore. Bersi was still holding Yrsa's sword in his hand, forgotten, as he watched the dead man struggle with Arinbjorn. Yrsa was struggling to bite the captain and Arinbjorn struck him repeatedly in the face and neck with his fists. The dead man seemed not to notice, even when Valgard seized him and threw him off.

Yrsa fell into a pool of brackish water and began to get up again and Bersi helped the captain stand. The three men watched as Yrsa, grey and bloodless, eyes sunken and flesh cold, regained his feet and staggered towards them.

"Yrsa! What are you doing?" called Bersi, backing away with the others. His skin was crawling, and there was no sign of recognition in the dead man's eyes. Only the same expression as the skraeling in the village had worn. He remembered his sword finally and flung the sheath aside. Bersi stepped forward and thrust the tip of the blade into Yrsa's chest, the sword sliding between ribs to pierce the heart.

Yrsa ignored the blade, grasping at Bersi with his hands as he tried to pull him closer. Bersi noted that only a little dark and thick blood came from the wound, far too little for the severity of the injury.

Batting away Yrsa's clutching hands, he pushed the blade deeper and tipped the dead man over yet again. As he did so, Valgard appeared at his side holding a large rock, which he smashed into the side of Yrsa's head.

The dead man rocked at the impact to lay twitching on the ground, his arms and legs flailing until Valgard struck him three more times on the head with the rock, Yrsa's brains now scattered and bloody outside his skull.

What is going on? Bersi thought. Why did the sword not kill him? Then he remembered the head of the skraeling in the village and the seed of understanding took root in his mind.

He was deep in thought as Olvir and the boy returned.

\* \* \*

It was past noon and the pyre of Yrsa still smoldered. They had heaped the wood over him and lit the fire, leaving his sword still in his chest. No one had wanted to touch the body again and the prayers had been brief.

"I think we know why the skraelings have vanished," Olvir said to them all. He was standing near the water, tossing small rocks into the waves. He had been silent for some time, thinking.

Bersi looked up. He had been thinking also. He didn't like what his intuition was telling him, but he chose to hear what Olvir had to say before offering his thoughts.

"Tell us, old man," said the captain. Never a deep thinker, he respected Olvir for his reasoning and always took his counsel.

"This plague," Olvir began, "or curse, whatever it may be, has spread through the tribes. The curse makes the dead rise up again."

Runolf spoke up, his voice quiet. "To what end? Why would the gods do this?"

"Oh, I fear this has nothing to do with the gods, Runolf," said Olvir kindly. He liked the boy, as did all the men. Olvir spoke again.

"What did the skraeling do to Yrsa?" he asked.

"Bit him," Valgard replied, like it was the most obvious thing in the world.

"And Yrsa died from it," said Runolf.

"Yes," said Olvir, warming to the subject as he led the rest of them to his own conclusions. "And then he got up after he was dead and tried to bite the captain."

"Then you are saying if I would have died, I would have arisen after and tried to bite those near me?" Arinbjorn asked

Olvir smiled and it was a grim smile. "Such are my thoughts. This curse has spread among the skraelings this way, through the bites. Perhaps some have survived, but I think many are now dead and walking still. Many have been eaten."

"Of course. The bodies in the village." Valgard looked away, shaking his head. "They had all been torn apart and devoured."

The men looked at each other. Horror was dawning on their faces as they realized what this could mean for the colony.

"It is worse than you think," said Bersi, the first time he had spoken since the pyre was lit.

"What does that mean?" Valgard stared at the pyre, but his question was clearly heard.

"The dead men are impervious to our weapons. Yrsa's blows to the skraeling had no effect until he cut off its head. Even then, the head was still trying to bite me when I picked it up. And then with Yrsa I pierced his lungs and heart and he ignored the wounds until

Valgard smashed his brains. We cannot kill them except by taking the heads and bashing out the brains."

Olvir was nodding. He had come to the same conclusion.

"There is more," Bersi said, not wanting to think too hard about this part. "We must hunt them all down and destroy them. If there are any nearby, they must be all killed. Even if we ourselves all die in the attempt, it must still be done. Imagine what would happen if one of those dead men were to get onto a longship that somehow found its way back to Greenland or the mainland. What if it were someone only bitten amongst the crew? By the time they drifted back to home the entire crew would be dead and just waiting for someone new to bite."

"The curse would spread through the people of home as it has here and then onwards, until the entire world was nothing but walking dead men." Olvir shook his head and swore loudly. "Yes, we must destroy them all."

*  *  *

Bersi the Fair frowned as he looked out over the land. No birds sang this afternoon, and the forest was dark and home to horrors he did not want to imagine. The horses had been left behind, and the men were on foot. They followed the trail left by many feet, a trail spotted with blood and the dusty footprints of the walking dead. Olvir had looked at the trail in several places and said that the dead skraelings were following someone.

A single set of footprints, a woman by the look of them, turned occasionally to look back, something the dead ones never did. It was from the living woman that the blood trail came. She was wounded and tired and not far ahead of the dead ones, but the tracks were well over a day old.

All the men carried shield and sword now and wore helms and tough leathers. Olvir brought his long bow and some arrows. Valgard, following behind Bersi, scowled even deeper than usual as he listened to the silent forest, hoping for some sign that they were near their prey. Arinbjorn, leading the group, also wished silently for the success of their mission.

Runolf and Olvir brought up the rear, Olvir stopping to listen to the woods every so often, his old but sharp eyes catching every detail of the trees and land.

Finally, after three miles, Arinbjorn held up a clenched fist and sank to the ground quietly. The others stopped where they were and crouched as well. Bersi came up crouching beside the captain and squinted into the clearing ahead, where three dozen skraelings stood, or wandered about as if in a daze. In the middle of the clearing was a large boulder, and about it a great amount of blood lay scattered, broken bones lying here and there. Some of the dead men were still gnawing on bits of tissue on the bones, and all of them had fresh blood smeared across their faces from the feasting.

Bersi felt his stomach heave, but fought it back down. Truly the skraeling curse was evil beyond imagining. The woman trying to escape had been caught here by the skraeling dead, it seemed, and torn apart to feed their hunger.

Bersi felt himself grow enraged and slid his sword gently from his scabbard as he watched the abominations in the clearing. The others did the same and Arinbjorn pointed to the left, then at Olvir. He pointed right and then at Valgard.

Bersi, Runolf, and himself he gestured to attack from the center and they all stood to charge. Olvir drew an arrow to his cheek and loosed it, the shaft striking an unlucky skraeling in the right eye, passing through bone and brain to emerge out the back of the skull, the dead man flopping backwards to land on the earth.

Bersi ran forward with a cry on his lips and his arm already swinging. He cleaved the skull of the nearest dead man, knocking the creature to the ground. His next swing sliced the neck of the dead woman who had been standing beside the man but then arms were grabbing at his hands and sword. He stepped back and swung overhead, crushing the skull of another dead skraeling, pushing three back by running forward behind his shield.

Valgard slew the rightmost of the three dozen walking dead, then cut the legs out from below the next one with a backswing that ended by cutting into the hip of the third. Hands grasped at his arms and the soft moaning grew louder as the dead skraelings sensed more food. Valgard heard a cry from his left and saw

Arinbjorn fall backwards under a pile of skraelings, all grasping and trying to bite.

Bersi threw off one dead man and stabbed into another's neck with his sword point, then leapt frantically backwards as another three stepped forward to seize him.

He and Runolf came up back to back, fighting desperately to not be surrounded. The young man fought well, but the dead men were not normal foes. Blows that would kill a living man did nothing to the skraelings but slow them a little.

Olvir faired better. Having decided from the start that his own life meant nothing if the dead men spread their curse to the colony or the mainland, he loosed arrows with all the skill and wit he could summon. Shaft after shaft landed on the skraelings' dead skulls and many fell before him. His focus was shattered only when he heard Arinbjorn cry out in pain and turned to see the captain under a pile of attacking dead men. Worse still, one of them was worrying the captain's neck with its teeth. Blood flowed freely as Arinbjorn pushed the dead man away and twisted its neck with his hands. The spine snapped and the skraeling's body stopped moving, but others descended on Arinbjorn where he lay on his back and he screamed as they bit into his flesh.

Olvir dropped his bow and charged, swung his sword as fast as he could, and slew three of the foe, then grasped the captain's hand. Bersi and Runolf fought together, driving the horde of dead men and women away from the captain, but both were tiring.

Valgard had dropped his own sword, having wedged it into a skull. His heavy knife he used to slash at faces and eyes, hoping to blind the dead things. When Arinbjorn fell, Valgard was separated from him by a gang of the foe, and was nearly overwhelmed by rotten hands and biting teeth. One skraeling bit down on his shield arm, but the tough leather shirt resisted the teeth and Valgard punched the face away, pulping the nose and making the creature fall back. Another grasped his shoulder from behind and he felt the fingers clench as it tried to pull him over. He spun and smashed the arm with the edge of his shield, then drove the knife up under the thing's chin. He grinned as it fell away.

Bersi looked around and realized they would all die if they kept fighting. The captain was down and the curse was in him and

Runolf was tiring and making errors in his blows, striking more at limbs and chest rather than the skull. Olvir was helping Arinbjorn to his feet, but the dead men were moving closer to surround them. And Valgard, grinning with joy as he swung his knife, was tripped and fell to then vanish under half a dozen of the dead things. His shouts of rage lasted only moments as his throat was torn out by the skraelings' teeth. He coughed a great gout of blood, swung the knife into the eye of one last foe, and died on the sandy ground. Immediately the dead men began to feed.

"We must go!" called Bersi, and shoved his sword into the eye of a dead skraeling woman in front of him. "Quickly!"

Olvir agreed and started pulling the wounded Arinbjorn with him. The captain shoved him off, though, and grasped his sword again. "I am cursed now! You must find a way to stop them! Go now and I will hold them as long as I can!" And with that he turned back to the dead things as Bersi and Runolf ran past him. Together with Olvir, they leapt into the trees and turned to see the group of the dead converge on Arinbjorn. The captain was a good fighter, but bloodied now and weaker. He slew five more of the creatures before they dragged him down, but he did not scream or cry out. He called at the last, "Valholl! Father, I am coming!"

"Damn," swore Olvir, who picked his bow and a few arrows up off the ground and turned to run with Bersi and Runolf, who was limping and near exhausted. All three were splattered with the blackened blood of the foe and Olvir with the red blood of his dead captain.

They ran a mile and stopped for breath. After gasping and looking back along the trail, they held conference amidst the trees.

"We killed half, I think," said Olvir, panting, "if not more."

"Yes. Half at least. And we lost Valgard and Arinbjorn doing it." Bersi scowled and shook his head. He kicked a stone on the ground in frustration. At least Arinbjorn and Valgard would be welcomed in Valholl as heroes by the Valkyrie and the All Father.

The men caught their breath, cleaned themselves of the foul blood of the dead until Olvir held a hand up, silencing them all. The men listened and in the distance they heard a low moaning.

"They follow us," Olvir declared, "but I have a plan."

"What plan? That last plan of Arinbjorn's did us little good."

"We need to kill them all swiftly and I am nearly out of arrows," Olvir said, holding up only four shafts. "We must lure them into the skraeling longhouse at the village and then fire it."

Bersi considered it and liked the plan. There were only two entrances to the longhouse and they could be blocked once the dead men were inside with logs and branches, then the whole structure could be lit with a torch.

"Look!" cried Runolf, his voice free of fear. Bersi was proud of the boy for that as he looked where the youth pointed. Back down the trail, a dead skraeling had lurched into view and was walking stiffly towards them. More followed behind the first.

"See how slow they are? I saw that when we fought them in the clearing," Runolf said, and he was right. The dead men lurched and staggered, moving slowly. A dozen were visible now through the trees, all of them walking straight towards Bersi, Runolf and Olvir.

"They know we are here. They have our scent, perhaps," Bersi observed. He thought some more on the plan as the dead men slowly advanced, then turned to Olvir. "Take Runolf and run ahead. Make a fire and block the entrance of the longhouse, the one nearest the water. I will lead them to you and into the longhouse. Hide, and once they are inside with me fire it and block the other entrance."

Runolf frowned in a fair approximation of Valgard. "But you will be killed," he said.

"The dead men need bait inside if they are to follow into the trap. I have no fear of death, and I will be able to tell Valgard and the captain that we killed those who killed them!"

Olvir nodded, embraced Bersi followed by Runolf. Then the old man and the youth ran off without looking back and Bersi knew he would not see them again. He turned and patiently waited for the dead skraelings to get closer.

\*     \*     \*

Olvir and Runolf ran to the village two miles from where they had left Bersi the Fair. It was as dead and quiet as when they had left it and the whole way there Olvir was deep in thought.

Should he send Runolf back to the colony on his own to warn them? Should he try to think of a way to get Bersi out before they fired the longhouse? Would fire even kill the dead again? In the end, he elected to keep Runolf with him and keep to the plan as Bersi had instructed. And so, he sent Runolf to gather sticks and logs from the huts, then set about building a barricade at the entrance nearest the water. The opening in the longhouse wall was small, and Olvir and Runolf were able to use spears, logs, and even the woven nets the skraelings used to catch fish to block it off.

Once Olvir pronounced it solid, he sent Runolf to make a fire, prepare torches, and move with more logs and nets to the other entrance. His bow he placed on the ground nearby as he wove sticks and branches into the netting and tied one side off to the longhouse. The smell of fresh smoke over the stench of the dead told him that Runolf had built a fire.

Olvir looked at the sky, judged the time, and decided they had best hide soon. Enough time had passed that even the dead could walk two miles. He took up his bow and as he turned, he heard a cry. A dead man was grappling Runolf near the fire and the boy was outweighed by the skraeling corpse.

Olvir ran forward, cursing his inattention, and drove his shoulder into the naked dead man as Runolf struggled to push him away. All three fell down, and Olvir came up with his knife, plunging it into the face of the corpse, the blade bursting through the eye socket and into the brain beneath. Black blood oozed out onto his hands and he recoiled in disgust, leaving the knife where it was as the skraeling fell back and twitched in the dirt.

"Are you well, boy?" he asked, and Runolf shook his head, holding up a bloody scratch on his arm. The teeth of the dead man had only just broken the skin, but Runolf had the curse. Olvir was deeply saddened by this and Runolf himself was greatly distressed, but he worked hard to smother his fear.

"I am sorry, Runolf," he said. "Surely you will be welcomed in Valholl and great songs sung of your deeds here."

They stood and Runolf said, "I do not wish to die as the others, devoured by corpses or in a fever. Will you take my head, Olvir? When the time comes?"

"I will, lad," Olvir said kindly. "When the time comes. Until then you can still fight."

At that moment Bersi ran from the woods and straight into the longhouse, all the while shrieking loudly and calling upon the dead to follow him!

"In here! This way, damned things! Follow a Northman to your doom if you dare!" He stood in the archway and shouted at the woods and soon the dead followed him. Olvir and Runolf dropped to the ground and hid in the rocks, watching as the dead followed Bersi. He stood inside and slew as many as he could, using shield and sword to good effect as his war cries echoed amongst the huts.

Olvir counted nearly thirty dead things following Bersi, and once they were all inside, he got up and ran for the fire. Runolf ran to the barricade and shoved it over the entrance, risking a glance inside. Bersi stood within, covered in the blood of the dead, his shield on the ground. The dead skraelings were upon him and he called out no more, merely swung his blade in wide arcs, but still many of the dead still stood and encircled him.

Runolf shoved the barrier once more, driving it into place.

Olvir took up two burning branches and threw one to Runolf, who caught it, and they immediately fired the roof and walls of the longhouse, Bersi still fighting within. Smoke curled up with the flames, and soon the whole roof was ablaze, the two warriors standing back to watch. The roar of the flames drowned out any cries from within, and the roof collapsed shortly after, sending sparks and embers into the sky with the smoke.

A fitting pyre for Bersi, thought Olvir. The walls soon collapsed, and they threw more wood onto the fire from the huts. The fire burned for several hours, into the darkness that fell, and still they watched.

Near midnight, as the embers glowed and the smoke lessened, Runolf turned from where they stood watching and said to Olvir, "I have the fever." Olvir nodded and drew his heavy blade.

"This will be your pyre also then and I will sing your name to the All Father."

Runolf smiled, his eyes leaking tears, but only from the smoke. He turned back to look at the fire again, and said, "I..."

Olvir stuck swift and true, his blade slicing into Runolf's head below the ear and crushing jaw, brain and bones in one savage, merciful swing. Olvir shook the body off his blade and sighed in remorse. Picking up the corpse, he stepped toward to the fire while holding the boy in his arms.

"All Father! I give you Runolf this day! Brave and valiant, he is worthy to join your ranks in Valholl!"

He threw the body into the pyre and then the lad's weapons followed. He tore down two huts to throw more wood onto the flames, and then sat watching it all burn until dawn, not moving until only smoke remained.

When nothing stirred in the pyre, Olvir was satisfied that fire could indeed kill the living dead again.

*Have I killed them all?* he wondered. *Has the curse already spread to all the villages? Has it reached the colony?*

These thoughts troubled him as he gathered the horses, readying them for the long trip northwards to home. Once he was mounted, he rode forward, stopping beside the pyre, the reigns of the other horses tied in a string behind him.

"Bersi the Fair," he said to the pyre, "and Runolf, young lad. Tell the All Father I may be coming soon. Tell him!"

With that he turned north and rode away without looking back.

# DAYBREAK

### ALVA J ROBERTS

The gray light of security cameras fitfully illuminated the tiny office. The room was cold and empty, the only furnishings were a large office chair and six flat screen monitors.

Mike Stanton ran his hands through his thick brown hair. God, he was tired. He was not used to these overnight shifts. He sipped his coffee and ate the last of his bag lunch.

He started a few weeks ago, but as it turned out, no one wanted to rob Consumer Paper Incorporated. The pay was crap and the only challenge was staying awake until the morning shift arrived.

Mike glanced at his watch. Billy was late again. Like every other Saturday morning, he would stumble in reeking of beer and stale cigarettes from the night before.

It was a half-hour past shift change. Mike decided in another ten minutes he would call his supervisor and leave. CPI didn't have the resources to pay him overtime. Hell, they barely had the resources to continue making toilet paper.

"Screw it," Mike said, dropping his clipboard.

He would leave and if Billy showed up, he could take over. Mike was done. He had his MBA, and this job was crap anyway. If the damn economy hadn't tanked he would still have his office downtown.

Gathering his stuff, he headed for the door. The side door to the warehouse opened with a groan, the hinges protesting the movement as the harsh light of the morning sun pummeled Mike's face. He staggered a few steps, half-blinded as he adjusted to the light.

The door slammed closed behind him. He checked the handle to be sure it was locked. Billy had his own set of keys.

His car sat in the huge, empty parking lot. CPI was closed on Saturdays. Billy would be the only person in the warehouse, if he ever showed up.

At least Mike's commute was short. His apartment was only ten minutes from the CPI warehouse.

Maybe he would get some drive-thru on his way home. Mike knew he should eat something, but the change in his sleeping schedule had messed up his digestion and he now suffered horrible bouts of heartburn paired with a loss in appetite.

"Help! Help! God!" a woman's voice yelled.

Mike stopped walking and turned toward the sound. It was coming from around the corner of the building. The neighborhood was a checkerboard of empty lots and warehouses. Mike knew there were a lot of homeless people who lived in the area.

He crept toward the screaming, debating if he should help or call the police and leave. He had heard on the news that some muggers were baiting people by pretending to be hurt. After a couple of moments of hesitation, Mike's Midwestern upbringing won out and he rushed around the corner, sprinting to make up for the time he'd wasted deciding.

The woman's screaming faded into unintelligible shrieks of agony.

"I'm coming! Hold on!" Mike shouted as he rounded the corner of the warehouse.

Mike stopped, his mouth gaping.

The woman lay on the ground and men dressed in the worn dirty garb of the homeless hunched over her prone form. Blood dribbled down their chins and covered their clothing. The woman's intestines spilled out into the street and Mike could see gravel and dirt sticking to the organs. The homeless men dipped their hands into her body cavity, scooping out the soft flesh and bringing it to their mouths.

The woman made soft whimpering noises as her arms twitched fitfully.

Good God, she was still alive!

Not able to take the sickening scene, Mike leaned over and heaved up his bag lunch and coffee.

The homeless men raised their heads at the sound of Mike's vomiting and immediately looked in his direction. Slowly, they rose to their feet, skulking towards him on unsteady legs. One of them had a broken arm, the bone standing out jagged and white in the morning sun while another had a large gash in his throat.

"Shit!" Mike screamed, running for his car as spittle slid down his chin.

He hurled himself inside his silver Pontiac. There was a reassuring click of the doors locking. He slid his key into the ignition as he threw it in drive.

*What the hell was that?* he thought as he stared into his rearview mirror.

Mike sucked in a deep, unsteady breath in an attempt to calm his frayed nerves.

That's what he got for trying to help someone. It could get you killed. With one eye on the road ahead, he pulled out his Blackberry, dialing 911 as he fled the parking lot.

The cops could handle it. He just wanted to go home, get some sleep, and try to forget what he had just seen.

The phone whined a busy signal. He hung up and tried again but got the same busy signal.

*I can call back later*, Mike thought.

As he looked up from his Blackberry, he had to slam on his brakes as a teenager ran across the street. She was dressed in a cheerleader's uniform and couldn't be more than sixteen years old. Then she was gone, lost around a corner in the road.

*What was she doing running around this neighborhood?* he wondered.

Then, from behind her, a group of boys staggered into the street, wearing green and yellow letterman jackets stained red. Blood ran down their chins, dripping to the ground, their faces drawn and slack.

One of the boys turned toward Mike.

Mike gasped when he saw that the boy's left eye hung out of the socket, bouncing against his cheek as he moved. There was a gaping hole in his throat where his Adam's apple should have been.

Shaking his head in disbelief, Mike punched his foot down on the gas pedal. The Pontiac jumped forward, tires squealing.

Mike turned the corner, stopping next to the girl as she ran.

"Get in!" Mike yelled, reaching over and throwing open the door.

The girl hurled herself into the back seat as the tires on the car spun madly, throwing dirt and gravel into the air.

"What the hell's going on?" Mike shouted.

"I don't. I don't know. God!" There was a frantic, breathless tone to her voice. "We were coming home from the game last night. Someone ran in front of the bus, and the driver swerved. The bus tipped over. When I woke up the whole frickin' second string was trying to eat me."

"Calm down. What's your name?"

"Sara. I'm Sara."

"It'll be okay Sara. My name's Mike. We have to be calm. Just because everyone is turning into flesh-eating zombies, there's no need to panic."

"Zombies? That's crazy," she remarked but her eyes said differently.

"Oh, then how do you explain those people following you with their massive wounds and dead faces?"

"I...I can't," she said softly.

"Exactly. We're going to the police station," Mike said trying to sound confident. But he looked away from the road to talk to her and he didn't see the dead man standing in the middle of it.

Suddenly there was an explosion of glass and the sound of crunching metal as the man crashed down onto the hood of the car. Mike swerved all around the road, fighting the wheel as Sara cried out in terror.

No sooner did Mike regain control, then a bloody hand clawed its way up the cracked windshield, leaving a trail of crimson in its wake.

The hand pummeled the broken safety glass, blood spraying through the air as the small bones and flesh of the fingers shattered. Mike slammed on the brakes, the man flying off to roll across the road, only stopping when he hit the curb. But the zombie was soon up again and shuffling towards Mike, albeit now with a broken leg it dragged behind him.

Mike punched the gas pedal, ramming the front grille into the slowly rising figure with a crack of breaking bones.

Steam billowed out from under the hood as the Pontiac rolled to a stop, the engine making a grinding sound before dying completely. The stump of an arm raised itself over the hood, and blood smeared the car's finish beneath the man as he flopped his way onto the hood of the car like a fish.

"Run for it!" Mike shouted, fear churning inside his belly.

With car doors thrown open, Mike and Sara took off sprinting down the open road, Sara a few steps behind. The broken thing that was once a man lunged off the hood of the car, his mouth snapping at them as they passed by, but he was too slow.

The wind whistled by Mike's face as he ran, his leg muscles straining. As he ran, a sharp pain developed in his right side but he ignored it. After a few blocks he slowed his frantic speed, his breath coming in heaving gasps, sweat pouring down his face.

He stopped to lean against the facade of an empty store, trying to catch is breath as his heart pounded in his chest. He ripped open his blue, button up uniform shirt and tossed his tie to the side.

The street was empty, not a person in sight. Mike couldn't help but think of that as a blessing. They were out of the warehouse district now, and the streets were lined with dirty, vacant storefronts. Once this part of town had been a thriving community, but now it was just the empty place that corporations bought to build storage facilities.

"Why are we stopping?" Sara asked when she reached him. She didn't seem out of breath and looked like she could go for another two miles.

"Because I'm not a damn teenager anymore and I need to catch my breath," Mike answered angrily. He pulled his Blackberry out and dialed 911 again. It was still busy. "Damn, phone must be broken or something. Okay. Okay. We need a plan," he said.

"Yeah. Uhm. What do you think we should do?" she asked.

"My apartment isn't far from here. There's a Double Burger and a Super Cost Saver on the way there. Then we can get to a phone and get a hold of the police." He pushed off from the storefront, ready to head out. "Let's get going," he said while trying to sound confident.

It was as he took his first step to leave that the window next to Mike shattered, glass shards spraying out across the street. A groping, bloody hand reached out for him, chunks of glass embedded in the knuckles. When the hand grasped Mike, he fell away instinctively, and the hand tore a large piece of his uniform away.

Sara let out a terrified shriek and took off running, Mike close behind her, as more of the creeping figures appeared on the street.

Most were dressed in the tattered clothing of the homeless but all were covered in a thick layer of blood. Mike's heart thundered in his chest. He could see the Double Burger up ahead. Once there he could call for help and he'd be safe.

A white two-door car pulled up to the open drive-thru window. The driver, a fat man wearing a cowboy hat, hammered the horn of his car.

Mike sprinted forward, thank God that not everyone was dead. For a little while there it sure felt that way.

A figure wearing the red and gold of a Double Burger employee dove through the open window, attacking the customer in a ravenous frenzy. The fast food worker's legs thrashed and kicked, still half inside the building.

"Zombie drive-thru. All you can eat." Sara whispered as she watched the carnage.

"What the hell is going on around here?" Mike shouted. He felt like he was going to cry, but then he glanced back at Sara's slight form and tried to stay calm, not wanting to look the wimp in front of her. It was a male thing, pure and simple.

*Keep it under control, Stanton. You got to keep it under control*, he thought.

"Come on, we can take a left down 52nd street. Then we can cut through a couple of empty lots and be at the Super Cost Saver."

"Why the hell do you think the Super Crap Saver is going to be any different? Everyone's going crazy! There are goddamned zombies everywhere!" she yelled, on the edge of hysterics.

"I don't know if it's going to be any different. But we can either wait for the Double Burger staff to come out and rip us apart or we can keep moving."

Sara reluctantly nodded her agreement.

"How are we going to tell the difference between the killer zombies and the Crap Saver employees?" Sara quipped.

"One thing at a time," Mike told her.

They hurried down the empty street, there eyes searching every corner and alleyway. The air began to grow hazy as a great billowing dark cloud rose up across the city.

The refuse of civilization lay scattered about the empty lots. Stained mattresses and rusting refrigerators stood next to piles of old newspapers and beer cans.

Mike stopped as he entered the lot, bending over to pick up a rusty, three-foot length of lead pipe. He swung it experimentally. It felt cool and reassuring in his white-knuckled grip.

The pile of trash next to him rustled. Mike let out a yell, swinging his newfound weapon at the pile of newspapers again and again until a large rat scurried out from under the pile.

Sara stared at him, her mouth hanging open, her hands shaking and pointing.

"Just a rat," Mike said with a sheepish shrug of his shoulders.

"Behind you!" Sara yelled.

Mike spun around, gripping the pipe like a baseball bat, ready to swing for the fences.

A blood-soaked figure staggered towards him. The man was about twenty years old with spiky blonde hair. The left side of his face was a raw, shredded mess. A large gaping hole showed his jawbone and back teeth. Strands of black, dirty flesh hung flapping as he came towards them.

His hands reached out, a low moan escaping his pursed lips. Stark white bone showed at the tips of his fingers. A torn blood-stained t-shirt proclaimed in thick block letters: **Shit Stains Happen**.

Mike screamed in fear and anger as he charged toward the man. The pipe connected with the zombie's skull with a resounding *crack* and the man dropped instantly. Mike kept swinging, bashing the corpse's head. Thick, black, half-congealed blood splattered outward, covering Mike's arms, chest and face.

"I think I killed him," Mike said while stumbling toward Sara.

"There's more of them coming," Sara said, pointing down the street.

Three more of the slow-moving zombies ambled toward them from half a block away. Mike and Sara turned, rushing through the empty lots. There were three lots all side by side. Trash littered their path, but they didn't see anymore of the creatures in the open space.

"Is that a park?" Sara asked.

"Sort of. The Super Cost Saver bought the land around it and planted a bunch of trees and bushes to hide the warehouses from their customers. If we make it through there, we'll be in the parking lot."

The shaded ground beneath the trees looked as if it was a popular hang out. There was an old, faded plaid couch that had been set on fire at some point. Used dirty condoms, cigarette butts, and beer cans littered the ground. Odd colored patches on the edge of the clearing testified to incidents of vomiting and diarrhea.

"Unnnghhh."

Mike heard the tell tale moan of the undead as ten, rough looking bikers rose from the nearby bushes. They wore grungy leather clothing, tattoos covering most of their visible skin.

The one nearest Mike had the handle of a knife sticking out from his chest. Next to him, a skinny, worn-out looking woman in bright red bra and leather pants gnawed on a dismembered hand.

"Run for it, Sara!" Mike yelled, raising his pipe.

"I can't! They're all around us!"

Mike glanced over his shoulder to see more of the leather-clad zombies were coming up from behind them. Sara's shoulder blades met Mike's back.

He panted heavily, positive he was going to die.

As the bikers moved closer and Mike gripped his pipe tighter, the sound of gunfire tore through the clearing. The biker chick's head disappeared in a cloud of blood and brain matter as one after another, the zombies' heads exploded as bullets tore through them. The ground underneath the group behind them was quickly covered in pieces of the bikers.

Mike stared around in wonder. They were all dead. Blood and brain tissue dripped from the trees overhead like gruesome rain.

"Looks like you guys could use some help," a man in army fatigues and combat boots said as he walked through the nearby bushes. "Lieutenant David Johnson, Special forces, retired."

The man was a walking armory. He carried the biggest gun Mike had ever seen. Two handguns rested in hip holsters, a shotgun and a rifle hung from his shoulders, and grenades were strapped across his chest. He had what looked like the handle of a sword sticking up over his left shoulder and a duffle bag was on his hip.

"I was on my way to the Super Cost Saver to gather some supplies," the soldier said. "Thought I'd try out one of my pipe bombs on that last group. Don't have enough grenades to last forever." The man lit a cigarette, taking a long drag. "Looks like we might have to find someplace to hole up for a while. Could use a few more eyes to watch my back. You stick with me and everything will be oka..."

The man's voice trailed of in a choked gurgle as the torso of a zombie dropped from the tree above, sinking its teeth into his throat. The zombie's intestines hung down the front of the soldier's neatly pressed uniform like garland.

Mike ran over, smashing the pipe into the skull of the ghoul. There was a loud crack, shards of bone flying into the air. Mike hit it a couple of more times just to be sure it was dead for good, then he gave the soldier a couple of good whacks to the head as well. Better safe than sorry.

"Help me grab his weapons," Mike told Sara.

They left behind the pipe bombs, the sword, the grenades and the massive gun. Mike wasn't going to haul around the heavy gun, and figured he would just blow his hand off with the explosives. The sword was worse than useless. He packed the length of pipe in the duffle bag, just in case.

"The parking lot should be just through these bushes," Mike said as he headed out.

Mike leveled the assault rifle in front of him, hoping it was loaded and there wasn't a safety or anything.

Sara nodded. She looked strange in her yellow and green cheerleader uniform while holding a shotgun. She now had a handgun strapped to her hip, but it was kind of nice, like an avenging football angel. Mike liked football.

They broke through the bushes and stopped dead in their tracks at the sight of more bedlam. The parking lot was a chaotic, bloody Hell. People ran screaming in every direction. Cars sped through the parking lot, slamming into the running people and each other in their frenzied attempts to escape. Hundreds of zombies shuffled their way through the parking lot, shoveling raw, bloody flesh into their mouths like it was an all you could eat buffet.

Blood filled the rain gutters, flowing into the storm drains. Chunks of flesh bobbed and floated along. Mike saw a foot with a pink flip-flop still on it jerking along next to the other refuse.

"Damn it. You said it would be safe here. I want to go home," Sara railed.

"The employee lot looks fairly empty. Let's take a car and get the hell out of the city."

"Yeah, okay," Sara agreed. "My parents have a cabin up in the mountains. We could go there."

"That would be perfect!" Mike exclaimed.

Mike ran down the small incline into the employee parking lot. A zombie shuffled toward them and Mike pulled the trigger of the assault rifle, bullets spraying through the air, peppering the zombie. Finally, one of the rounds hit its head and the ghoul dropped.

"God, what'd that take you, like forty bullets to kill one of 'em?" Sara gasped.

"You think you can do better? The closet I ever came to shooting a gun was in an arcade!" Mike shouted, running for the cars.

More of the tottering figures came into view. Blood smeared their bodies and covered their faces, broken limbs hanging at odd angles. They were of every size, height, and color. Some were dressed in worn, faded rags while others wore expensive business suits. Zombies didn't discriminate. You were either one of them or food.

Mike screamed, holding the trigger down. The rifle fire reverberated through the parking lot. Sara held the shotgun to her shoulder, blasting zombie after zombie. Flecks of sticky, cold blood sprayed through the air, covering them in a fine mist.

The assault rifle clicked. Empty. Mike pulled out the handgun.

It looked just like the ones the cops used on TV and he thought it might be a Glock. He fired a couple more shots straight into the heads of the oncoming figures and found he was a much better shot with the Glock.

The zombies lay in a pile of shivering flesh. Not all of them were dead, but the ones that weren't head shot were practically cut in half.

# DEAD WORLDS

"Come on!" Mike shouted.

Mike slammed his lead pipe through the back window of a boxy, early eighties model, Ford LTD, only to realize the car was unlocked. He opened the driver's side door, his face turning red. Sara hopped into the passenger seat.

"Why'd you pick a car that was made before I was born? This piece of crap isn't going to make it ten miles."

"Do you know how to hot wire a car? I sure the hell don't. I saw this in a movie once."

Mike slammed the pipe into the ignition. Nothing happened. Mike tried again. Nothing. Damn.

Sara reached over and flipped down the visor and keys fell into Mike's lap.

"Never take up a career as a car thief," Sara said. "Let's get the hell out of here."

"Buckle up," Mike told her, feeling like some action hero from a bad movie.

The big V8 engine rumbled to life with a belch of smoke. Mike threw the massive car into gear, his foot slamming down on the gas pedal. Clouds of smoke rose from the rear wheel wells as the car hurtled forward, picking up speed.

A disheveled figure bounced off the front bumper, spraying the windshield with blood. Mike hoped it was a zombie, but couldn't be sure. He turned on the windshield wipers.

More men and women lurched toward them. Mike punched the gas, crashing into the crowd with a spray of blood and crunch of broken bones.

Sara screamed when a small woman jumped on the hood of the car, her lower jaw dangling by scraps of flesh. She pounded and clawed at the windshield, her finger nails tearing off as she tried to scratch her way through the glass. Mike cranked the wheel. The woman tumbled off the car, falling hard on the asphalt.

The tires screeched as Mike made the turn onto the highway. Cars were scattered across the road and Mike had to swerve around the smoking, wrecked heaps.

"Which way?" he asked.

"Just keep going until you hit the Exeter Expressway. That'll take you out of the city. Then we'll have to take a right onto a rural highway. Just turn at the sign for Crystal Lake," Sara said, breathing deep. She leaned over and pushed the eight track into the player and loud seventies rock blared through blown speakers. She laid her head back and closed her eyes.

Mike kept driving, trying to ignore the carnage he saw. Thousands of people, no hundreds of thousands of people, were dying around him. Wrecked and stalled cars littered the highway. They were better to look at than the ruined bodies that hadn't yet risen or the lurching staggering undead.

A few hours later, the cabin came into view. Mike hadn't seen any of the walking dead since leaving the city. When Sara fell asleep, he tried the AM radio, but couldn't find a station. His Blackberry lay on the seat beside him, a spider web of cracks crisscrossing the screen.

"This is where we spent most of our summers. There're vacation cabins and summer camps all around the lake. About ten miles down the road there's a little town. Hey, that's my parents' car!" Sara's voice vibrated with excitement.

He parked the car outside the cabin. It was a large building, with a stone facade and a huge wrap around deck. There were granite counters by the massive propane grill. Steam rose from a Jacuzzi on the side.

Mike and Sara hurried through the unlocked front door.

"Mom! Dad!" Sara shouted, running through the huge living room.

A sectional sofa and two armchairs faced a fifty-two inch plasma TV. Mike walked over to the fully stocked bar and poured himself a shot of whiskey.

"Sara? Is that you? Oh thank God." A voice called from the next room.

Sara's father ran into the room, scooping Sara up in hug.

"Dad, this is Mike. He saved my life. Where's Mom?"

"All the excitement gave her one of her migraines. She's lying down."

"I'm going to go check on her," Sara said, tears of joy glistening in her eyes.

Sara's father turned his attention to Mike. "How can we ever repay you?" he asked.

"It's okay," Mike said, feeling slightly uncomfortable.

"You're welcome to stay here. We have plenty of food and water and we're miles from anyone."

Sara's scream shattered the uncomfortable feeling in the air and Mike heard her Glock fire three times in rapid succession. Mike ran to the bedroom, pulling out his own gun while Sara's father followed close behind.

"What's wrong?" Mike shouted, surveying the room.

"A mouse! A fucking mouse!" Sara yelled.

"You watch your mouth, Sara Jane Mitchell," said an older woman on the bed, her hands clutched to her ears.

Mike started to laugh, holstering his gun. Everything was going to be okay.

No sooner did Mike holster his gun then the window behind him exploded, glass showering the room. Rough hands grasped his shoulders, pulling him out of the house.

He managed to let one scream of panic escape his lips before sharp teeth dug into the tender flesh of his neck.

# BRIDESHEAD BEACH

## TOM HAMILTION

### 1

"Look," Kathryn said, "this one has the keys in it."

"It's probably out of gas," Maureen acknowledged, "most of the ones with the keys left in them are out of gas."

"Well," Kathryn stripped off her business suit jacket and searched the mercifully empty streets, "we're gonna have to give it a try." She climbed behind the wheel and unlocked the passenger door so that Maureen could climb in the other side.

"I never thought that I'd be caught dead in a Hyundai," Maureen said as she shut herself in.

"Yeah," Kathryn commented, "but I'd rather be caught dead in a Hyundai then caught by the *living* dead." She tried to turn the ignition over but the car coughed like a sick old woman.

"See," Maureen said, looking around cautiously, "the piece of shit's dead. Now let's get the hell out of here; we're makin' way too much noise."

Instead of answering, Kathryn tried to turn it over again, and this time the car sputtered to life.

"Hot damn!" Maureen said and squeezed Kathryn's arm. "Let's cruise."

Maureen was a huge woman; bordering on morbidly obese. Her thin, patchy, gossamer strands of blonde hair framed her red face and the blotches of psoriasis which traveled up and down her exposed arms were shaped like small countries on an oceanographic map.

Kathryn was glad that they had found a car, not for her sake, but for Maureen's. She wasn't sure that the heavily breathing fat woman could escape quickly enough in the dreaded event they should become cornered.

But now that Kathryn had the compact car started, she was faced with a new problem. This model was equipped with a stick shift; a four on the floor.

"You know how to drive one of these?" she asked Maureen.

Maureen looked at her, confused. "Put it in drive," she said.

"Well, hell, I've never driv..." Halfway through Kathryn's sentence the passenger side window shattered and a white arm roughly grabbed Maureen by the hair. The big woman screamed, scratched and pushed at the chest of an attacker who's face couldn't yet be seen.

"Go! Go! Go! Go!" Maureen shouted.

Kathryn threw her arms up in vexation and scanned the car's controls. But she may as well have been staring at the console of an airplane, and her panic was giving her even less chance of figuring it out.

"Go, Kathy, go!" Maureen continued to buck and kick at the body which was trying to enter the cab.

"I'm trying! I'm..." As she pawed the gear shift, the clutch inexplicably popped and the little car scooted a few feet, momentarily shedding the assaulter whose gruesome white face then came into view as it stumbled along with the vehicle.

One eye was gone from a rifle shot which must have missed the brain, yellow pus dripping from the socket. But the car soon stalled and the abomination was on them again. Maureen scooted across the seat in an effort to avoid the cold, white hands of the zombie, but this move only squashed Kathryn up against the driver's door; making it impossible for her to try the ignition again.

For several seconds all she could do was try and catch her breath as her friend fought for her life against one of the living dead. She couldn't even reach the door handle. But then, just as she was contemplating what it would be like to roam the city as a shuffling corpse, the sound of a gunshot reverberated off of the high buildings. And she heard Maureen's voice go from high-pitched wails of terror to sobs of relief. A second later she felt the considerable bulk of her robust friend ease up and off of her. Maureen was shivering as if she were wearing soaking wet clothes in sub zero temperatures.

"Oh, Jesus, Oh, Jesus, Oh, Jesus," Maureen kept repeating.

When Kathryn could turn around again, she saw that the back window of the Hyundai was smeared with bright red flecks of rose-colored blood. As Maureen recovered enough to climb out of the car, Kathryn leaned over across the upholstery and inspected the slumped over body of the *dead*, dead man. His second eye was now shot out also. She tried to start the Hyundai again, but it was as dead as the felled ghoul; out of gas after all. Kathryn got out of the driver's side and looked back over the roof of the car towards the source of the sniper.

"Just in the nick of time," an approaching voice said and Kathryn locked eyes with a man in a plain green soldier's uniform with a matching helmet. A long rifle hung from a strap around his neck. This was obviously the marksman who had re-executed their deathly pale stalker. The man's round and puffy face seemed much too swollen for his trained and trim body.

"Oh, thank you, thank you, sir!" Maureen gushed as she took two uneven steps over trash and rubble towards her savior. Kathryn suspiciously brushed her long brown hair off her alabaster cheek.

"How will we ever be able to make it up to you?" Maureen continued.

"Well," said the man, "I'm not sure that you can." And Kathryn was wary of his weird grin and the facetiousness which she sensed in his tone. She walked around the deceased car and stood at her friend's side; her taut yet curvy body evident even under the business skirt and long sleeve white blouse.

"But I might be able to think of something your friend here can do," the man quipped, his eyes looking Kathryn up and down.

Kathryn understood what he was getting at perfectly, but Maureen didn't seem to get the gist of it. She took another step towards the man and was now standing no more than four feet from him.

"Well," she smiled, "if there's anything that we can do, I'm sure... I mean, you saved us. We really don't know how to thank you," Maureen said.

"Hey," the man held his palms out innocently and continued through an earnest smile, "don't mention it." He then quickly raised the rifle and shot Maureen in the throat. She didn't fall at once, but could only stand back and cover the wound in shock. Then she took her hands away from it for some desperate reason and a straight line of blood shot ten feet across the asphalt every time her heart beat. Kathryn rushed to her friend's side and dropped to her knees, almost catching her as she collapsed onto the cluttered street.

Oblivious to the gunman, Kathryn tore off a strip of her blouse and pressed it against the wound, but Maureen only gaped for air, her mouth opening and closing like a manatee out of water. Kathryn heard a second loud boom, as if she were an inch from two cars colliding, and now there was a hole in Maureen's forehead to match the one in her throat. The big woman's eyes grayed over and stared into the distance of the next world.

Kathryn scooted away from the body and stared up at the murderer from the seat of her skirt. He was chuckling, yet his weapon was pointed at the ground.

"You're not going to kill me?" she asked.

"Why would I shoot a smokin' hot fox like you?" the man answered.

"But um... but I... you shot... killed her. Why did you kill her?" Kathryn stuttered through the shock.

"I was doin' her a favor."

Kathryn mulled this over for a few seconds. "And you won't do me the same favor?"

"No," the man answered, "I'm not going to shoot you." A gleam twinkled in his eye that must have been similar to the one Adam and Eve saw as they bit into the apple. "But don't worry," he finished, "there'll certainly be favors involved. Now march!" He raised the gun again.

"No!" Kathryn resisted defiantly, "kill me here but I'm not going with you." She meant it. She didn't want to see what this violent cretin had in store for her.

"Look, bitch," he began, "there are worse things than gettin' shot, now get up and make that nice ass as yours march before I show you what those things are." Kathryn didn't move.

"March, goddammit!" This mean bellow frightened her enough to where she got up and began marching in the general direction of where he had his gun sight pointed. They walked for perhaps ten blocks without speaking, around stalled cars, crude makeshift sandbag forts and fire blackened barricades.

Finally they rounded a corner and Kathryn found herself staring at a huge edifice of crushed cars. They stretched in between two buildings to create an impressive blockade. There was a doorway sized opening which had probably been left there intentionally by the crane operator. A second soldier stood in this entrance, listlessly smoking a cigarette. The men nodded at each other as they passed. On the other side of the junker wall there was a long segmented vehicle painted camouflage and covered with nets of black mesh. It reminded Kathryn of a mechanical caterpillar. Reacting to a shuffling sound off to her left, Kathryn caught sight of a walking dead man in a suit and tie as he stumbled out of an office building. He didn't have to push the exit lever since all the glass doors had been busted or shot out.

Before Kathryn could cry out, yet another boom raped the silence and the zombie jumped as a head shot met with its scalp. A JFK sized flap jutted out from the side of its exposed skull right before it fell. There was a sniper atop the caterpillar which Kathryn had failed to notice, and he'd skillfully lopped the dead man's brain off.

There was a wrought iron door in the center of the long bus which opened down like a draw bridge. The soldier softly tapped Kathryn in the small of the back with the tip of the powerful gun. Feeling that she had little choice, she climbed inside. There were several other women within the capsule/cell. They laid haphazard under freckled spots of sunlight which circled in through small, perfectly round holes in the wall, as if coin blanks had been knocked out of them. None of the women spoke to Kathryn or offered up any theories in the way of explanation of why they were there. Some of them wore clothes which were dirty and disheveled, others still looked halfway presentable. The soldiers were obviously on patrol to collect prisoners and this made Kathryn wonder why Maureen hadn't been spared as well? The draw bridge like door clanged closed behind her.

Then, as she looked around the cell, the similarities began to hit her. Even with their tatted hair and torn clothes; even with their grimy skin and smudged mascara; even with their stinking underarms and chipped nails, all of the women confined within the cell were at least fairly attractive.

2

"Well it has to be better than wandering around out there," a pale girl with tired, purple chevrons underneath her pretty hazel eyes was saying. "I mean, at least we're away from those dead things."

Some of the women nodded their heads yes, but most were too exhausted to answer. Kathryn and the others had been led into a brightly lit room where they were made to sit down at small exam desks like school children. There was a blackboard on the wall but there wasn't anything written on it and no chalk could be found on its built in shelf. There was no apple nor was there a teacher's desk to place one on. The room had no windows but there were two doors; one which they had been led through after exiting the caterpillar and a second door which was in the complete opposite corner. On each desk a glass of ice water had been placed and most of the women drank greedily.

After about fifteen minutes, the door they had been led through opened and a man sauntered in. He wore a similar uniform to the one sported by the man who had captured Kathryn, only this man had a baseball cap on rather than a helmet, and there were two silver bars on the shoulder of his long sleeve shirt. His polished boots were free of dust and grit and tufts of thick black hair sprouted out from underneath the hat at wild intervals. He looked the ladies over with maddening turquoise eyes, and even though his movements were controlled and strict, Kathryn sensed he was deranged inside his mind.

"Hello, ladies," he began, "my name is Captain Enervy." The women straightened up and cocked their heads to listen even though he was speaking at a drill sergeant's pitch. "I have some very good news for all of you. We are now inside a guarded and heavily armed compound. You are completely safe from the walking dead which have, unfortunately, taken over a large part of our city. This is a situation that our forces are working hard to rectify. In the meantime, you will be given food, lodging, and you will be able to wash whenever you wish. You will also sleep in a warm bed." He paused here and some of the women began to rejoice; clutching each other's hands, cheering and even crying. But Kathryn, who had watched her friend executed, didn't join in the celebration. "All that we ask in compensation is that you women comply with our orders, which includes supplying companionship to and satisfying the needs of our troops." The joyful chatter ebbed quickly and the happiness decelerated down into a bleak silence. Captain Enervy proudly surveyed the scene, ready to gauge the women's reactions and field objections. After a few confusing seconds, one woman stood up.

She wore nothing but a grungy tank top and a pair of tattered Levi's. Her hair was cropped into an extremely short crew cut. But even in this unflattering apparel she was a breathtaking beauty; large brown eyes atop chiseled cheekbones.

"You mean," she said, "that you want us to have sex with them." Captain Enervy looked the woman right in the face and Kathryn saw a flash of the temper which he was making an effort to conceal.

"Yes," he answered simply, "we want you to have sex with them."

"Jesus," the standing woman said, "you guys are unbelievable. Instead of using your weapons to help people, you want to turn the world into one big brothel." Kathryn felt like telling the dissident to pipe down; she was sure that the girl didn't realize how hot the fire she was playing with could scorch. Perhaps her introduction to this army had been kinder than Kathryn's violent, murder splattered initiation.

Oblivious to these grave dangers however, the girl continued. "Well I won't do it. I refuse! I will not! I will not! I'd rather take my chances with the walking dead than have some sweaty grunt rape me every night. At least the dead are honest and up front about their intentions."

Captain Enervy slowly strolled around the room, addressing everyone except the short haired woman. "I strongly suggest to all of you that you stay here with us in comfort and safety. I'm sure that, at some point, some of you may have to perform acts which you might find distasteful or immoral, but I assure you! There will be no rough stuff and you will be treated with respect as brides of the regiment. And I implore you..." Here he paused for effect, "I implore you to consider the heinous alternative." The room fell silent as the women's troubled, overloaded minds contemplated this difficult choice. The defiant woman continued to stand but she didn't shatter the silence. Finally, after about half a minute, Captain Enervy seemed to be speaking for her.

"Of course, if anyone feels that they have a better chance out there, with those shuffling ghouls, then they're free to go. Private Gliet!" He called out to a man at the back of the room. Kathryn hadn't noticed the man before and she wondered how long he'd been standing there. She supposed it was possible he'd been there for the duration of Enervy's announcement, but she didn't think so. He was a tall soldier, perhaps six foot two or three, in marvelous physical condition. Though his features seemed tainted by a trace of mental retardation; almost as if he were a mongoloid.

"Show this nice young lady the way out." Captain Enervy said as Kathryn shivered and trepidation traveled up her delicate spine. Private Gliet nodded and gestured towards the standing woman like a waiter ready to show someone to their table. He held his arm out towards the second door; the one located on the opposite side of the room from which they'd entered. The woman took a few timid steps, perhaps starting to sense what Kathryn already knew; that this seemingly carefree release from the regiment was too good to be true. And so it was.

As the woman approached the threshold, Private Gliet simultaneously accosted her while swinging open the door. The sunshine which flooded in was even brighter than the room's white lights. There was no floor or stairway beyond the frame, just the thin air hanging over a twenty five foot drop. Before the short haired woman even had a chance to scream, Private Gliet hurled her out head first. When she did scream, it sounded as if her voice was floating up and out from an elevator shaft. At the bottom of her drop were the dead; hundreds of them crawling and falling over each other like salamanders in the mud. They didn't have the sense to catch her or break her fall. So when her vivacious frame met with the hard, packed down sand, something could be heard snapping, perhaps an arm or a leg. They converged upon her quickly however, pulling her apart like lions raking at a bison carcass. Mercifully the screams didn't last long as they soon pulled out her voice box. Her clothes quickly disappeared along with her skin. The carnage ended as a ghoul who had once been a person ate her beautiful face.

In the confines of the room, panic ensued. Private Gliet, his mission accomplished, stood at attention with his back to the wall. The women roared and screamed and cried as several of them stood up on their chairs. They stomped their feet on the seats like cartoon wives in white aprons afraid of a kitchen mouse; as if they were trying to put as much distance between themselves and the dead pit as possible. Kathryn didn't get up, but she buried her face in her hands and tears sizzled out from in between her fingers. Captain Enervy stood upright with his hands still clasped behind his back. The mad violence which always seemed to be spinning in his eyes momentarily quelled.

"Now!" He shouted spiritedly, "if there are no more conscientious objectors, I suggest that you all get some sleep." He paused here to salute the moaning women. "Report for makeovers at 0900."

3

The salty smell of the nearby sea tickled their nostrils and billowy strips of evaporating clouds dissolved in front of the unbridled sun. The group rode on the back of a flatbed wagon; much like a hayride only devoid of any leisure or fun. They were being pulled along by a tractor which was driven by a heavy set, thick legged matron who was also wearing the now familiar uniform of the regiment. Only this version came with a skirt instead of pants. She had no holster for a gun, but a long truncheon hung from a loop on her accessory belt. The words: *PENIS ENVY* had been carved neatly down its shaft.

All of the women had gotten a chance to shower and were furnished with toothbrushes, deodorants and other sundries. Not having a fresh change of duds however, they'd had to put their soiled clothes back on. They didn't see any soldiers along this path save for the matron and talk among the passengers soon turned to crude escape plots.

"I wouldn't," said Kathryn. Then she pointed to a distant tree line. Barely visible in the rising haze was a tall chain link fence with looping scribbles of razor wire and spikes at its highest point. As they got a little closer to that spot and rounded a bend, the dead could be seen clinging to its tiny octagons in between crawls of climbing vines; like grotesque butterflies on a screen door.

"We're still inside the compound," she whispered. "They must have gunners perched atop the perimeter. Not so much to keep us in as to keep the dead out, but I'm sure they'd shoot anything that moved." As if on cue, a distant spit of machine gun fire crackled in the morning air and the peering dead peeled off the fence. It was 8:45 AM.

Finally, the tractor ground to a halt in front of what had been a department store. Mannequins stood naked in front of the shattered out display windows and fallen clothes littered the aisles. Some of the panels were missing from the ceiling and sunlight made its way through the voids, taking over the job of the snuffed electricity. Otherwise, it looked basically all right. The heavy set matron hopped down from the tractor seat.

"My name is Sergeant Marge," she shouted. "What I need for you ladies to do is go inside there and pick yourself out some clothes. If I were you, I'd select something short, bright and sexy. You'll also find a large assortment of cosmetics inside. I suggest that you paint those pretty faces up bright and rosy; the more the soldiers like you the faster they'll be finished with you and you can go on back to your barracks. Don't use hairspray as the men don't like the way it feels and *do not* select any outfits with pants. *Dresses* only! Don't worry about the living dead as this sector has long been cleared and you're behind friendly lines."

One of the women, a thirty something brunette with thick, preened eyebrows, scoffed and whispered to her friend: "Yeah, real friendly."

This prompted Sergeant Marge to stop her instructional speech and walk through the crowd where she met the brunette. She put her chin one centimeter from the woman's cheek and spat at the side of her face, "*Do not* interrupt me!" The woman froze and stood at attention. The big woman turned as if to walk away, before quickly spinning around, drawing her club, and bringing it around in a three quarter circle onto the back of the woman's leg. The brunette hit the street and cried out in agony as she tried to massage life back into her throbbing calf. Satisfied, the sergeant continued.

"So," she picked up her lost thought. "You'll be safe at all times. You're all welcome to try and escape, although I can assure you that it's impossible and even if you did manage to breech our security you'd still be without food, water or shelter. Not to mention that you would be at the mercy of the living dead, who, as we all know, aren't capable of mercy." She paused here, and looked around, waiting for her words to sink in. "While, on the other hand, if you're smart and go along with our curriculum, you'll be well fed, comfortable and in no danger. Hell," before finishing this sentence, she even had to scoff at herself, "you might even find that, after a while, you begin to enjoy it."

The women said nothing, although the way most of them shuffled in place clearly indicated they had their doubts.

"All right! I need you little whores to make yourselves beautiful. I'll expect to see you back here and lookin' like super models at 1100 hours."

4

When the sun was at its pinnacle, Sergeant Marge led Kathryn and the others down towards the beach on foot. It was a little treacherous walking on the sands since some girls had selected high heels or pumps. As they approached a sentry post which led onto the dunes, two guards looked Kathryn and the others over lustfully. A wolf whistle was heard as one of the men feigned masturbation and leered like a chimp. Some of the girls had a little trouble climbing a high sand cliff in their prissy shoes. But the ground leveled off at the top and they all looked out over the omniscient ocean. A chubby cloud suddenly blocked off the sun's rays and the waves whipped a dark blue like an endless dream of troubling shadows.

The soft and salty squalls teased the hair of the conscripted prostitutes as they were led towards several tents. The structures were small and circular, lavishly draped in velvet like a knight's quarters. Triangular flags tugged straight out by the ample winds, flapped atop each bungalow. As they approached the initial doorway, the first woman was ordered inside. She put up no opposition and disappeared behind the curtain. It didn't take much imagination on the part of the group to know what was going to happen to her next, and even if it would have, they would soon be experiencing similar treatment themselves and would have no need to vex their imaginations. After three more stops it was soon Kathryn's turn and she was ushered into one of the tents.

A black man sat on the edge of a wide cot, wearing only an army green t-shirt, dog tags and loose fitting boxing shorts. He was slowly breathing through a cigarette and made no more movement than a waiting spider. There was no floor save for the sand of the beach as Kathryn demurely stepped inside. There was a bottle of Crown Royal sitting on a nearby backpack and two collapsible director's chairs across from and facing the cot.

At last he moved a little. "Sit down," he said. "You want a drink?"

Kathryn thought about this for a beat, decided she'd never wanted anything more, and nodded her head yes. Although the man had yet to look at her, he somehow caught her nod and poured her a sip in a plain plastic glass. She sat down across from him in one of the chairs.

"Stuff'll be gone pretty soon," he said, "be a real shame to never drink Crown Royal again. Who knows what kinda shit we be resortin' to drinkin' after that. Motherfuckers be goin' blind and shit."

Kathryn didn't answer or react in any way. After a few seconds, she took a sip of the hard brown liquid. When she commenced coughing, the man spoke again. "Yeah, I know you're scared, but you got to ask yourself, who worse? Me or them hordes out there? Any sane person know the answer. If there're any sane people left that is. Hell, I ain't that scary."

In the pause, the man poured himself another. "What's your name?" he asked.

"Kathryn," she replied blandly.

"Hmmm, how you feelin', Kathryn?"

It was an odd question, and after mulling it over for a couple of seconds, Kathryn just felt compelled to answer honestly. "I feel a little under it," she whispered.

"Yeah," he half laughed, "no wonder, me too."

He got up and walked over to a basin of water; bending over to splash some onto his tough, leathery features.

As he toweled off he said, "Well, we best be gettin' on with it. Climb up on that cot over there."

Without much vigor, yet resolved to her fate, Kathryn walked over and lay down on her back. She barely had a chance to settle in before the man was on her; his service revolver pressed up against her temple and his breath on her cheek.

She gasped in shock.

"What you think, huh?" he raved, "you think I'm like these animals roun' here, huh! You think I force myself on some poor girl ain't willin', huh!"

Kathryn's only defense from this offbeat attack was to close her eyes tight, forcing a hot tear to leak out and streak across her cheek.

"What I want with you white bread? Me I gots... I mean I had... a wife and baby a my own. I know they out there somewhere," He waved his arm in a gesture which represented everywhere. "I know they..." He stopped talking and jumped up suddenly.

Kathryn rose up to a sitting position as he knelt down in the corner of the hut and began to weep roughly. When he'd quieted some, she got up from the cot and walked over to where he was doubled over. Putting her petite hand in between his muscular shoulder blades, she softly spoke.

"It's okay," she said, "We've all lost someone that we loved."

After a couple more minutes of sobbing, he slowly picked himself up and walked back over to sit on the cot. Kathryn stayed where she was, her knees in the sand. He swallowed the final gulp of whisky and began speaking on a new subject.

"Enervy is a monster," he said, "not just a close minded grunt, but a dangerous killer. When he picks you, and sooner or later he will 'cause he always picks the pretty ones, you as good as dead."

Kathryn could only stare at him.

"He like to make porno and snuff films; force chicks to fuck the dead, evil shit like that. I only wish there was somethin' that I could do for ya."

Kathryn shrugged and smiled faintly.

"Wait a minute," he said suddenly as if a thought just occurred to him. "Wait a minute." He leaned over and reached into his backpack; retrieving a handsome military issue buck knife complete inside a camouflage sheath. He got up quickly and offered it to Kathryn. "Hide this, don't show it to that dyke Marge, don't show it to any of the bitches in your barracks, don't show it to no one. When Enervy picks you, wait until you get him by himself. When he turn around, you bury this spike in his black heart, ya hear me? It's your only chance."

Kathryn stared at the knife. It was long and intimidating, but she supposed it could be hidden inside her underwear bottoms. She smiled gratefully and took the bracketed blade.

"Thank you," she said.

"Yeah, all right," He sauntered back over and reclined on the cot. His relaxed posture was a sharp contrast to the madness he'd demonstrated throughout their rendezvous. "By the way, Kathryn, my name's Granderson. Pleased to meet ya."

"Pleased to meet you," she said.

"When that dyke Marge comes back you tell her everything was cool; you had a good time."

She nodded.

## 5

Several days passed inside the stainless steel barracks which may have been more accurately described as a prison. Kathryn didn't do much of anything during this interlude; aside from lying forlornly in her bunk and praying she wouldn't be selected for a second and surely more intimate date. Now and then the dull mirrored door would roll open and Sergeant Marge would call out the name of the next unfortunate escort.

Kathryn didn't make many friends throughout this period, nor did she want to. Sporadic spurts of conversation floated past her ears intermittently, but the topics were limited to such small talk as the good condition of the food, the affable temperature of the cell, and the crisp and clean sheets. No one seemed eager to touch upon the subject of their forced sexual encounters or the horrific encounters they'd had with the dead which had led to their imprisonment. Kathryn didn't want to talk either, even though she'd been fortunate enough to avoid being blackmailed into intercourse; at least so far.

She hid the buck knife underneath her mattress since that was the only place to hide anything. At times when she felt the most dread, she would finger the blade which Granderson had given her, praying she would have the courage to use it when the crucial moment came. Then she closed her eyes and drifted into a restless daydream.

In the dream, she was trapped inside a burning mobile home which was surrounded by the dead. She could see the tops of their squash-colored heads moving past the small, weak, roll out windows. She fled into the hallway bathroom and closed herself off inside a cramped closet. But the moaning marauders were relentless. They shredded their hands and forearms, even bashing their soft heads against the aluminum siding until she could sense that the panels were starting to give. Then they were walking inside the blaze; becoming the fire, awash in flames, willing to endure any hellish barrage to get at her.

Until at last they wrapped their cold burning arms around her and the last sound she would ever hear were chained up dogs howling in the distance. She awoke to Sergeant Marge calling out her name in the same gruff pitch as the pit bulls from her nightmare.

She rolled over on her side before rising and slid the knife down inside her pink underwear.

Once outside, she discovered it wasn't night after all as the hot sun blushed in an endlessly clear sky. There was no clock or fixed schedule inside the barracks, making it impossible to tell the time of day. They didn't return to the tents, but rather walked for a short stretch along the shore until they came to a lavish beach house. Its picturesque balustrade afforded any onlooker a scenic view of the tumultuous pacific.

As Kathryn climbed the wooden stairs which led up from the beach, she recognized Captain Enervy sitting leisurely on a deck chair. His tan and muscular body was covered only by a pair of oak green army issue swimming trunks.

"Hello," he said with surprising friendliness, and then as he glanced past Kathryn, "That will be all, Marge."

The Sergeant saluted and said, "I'll be at the bottom of the stairs if you need me, Captain." With that she turned and exited.

Enervy studied Kathryn for several seconds before sipping an icy drink in a tall glass. His gaze didn't seem as disquieting in this relaxing setting although he didn't ask her to sit down or offer her a beverage.

Finally he said, "Do you know why you've been brought here?"

Kathryn's mouth turned up at the corners. "For sex," she said bluntly.

Enervy chuckled petulantly. "Because there are some things going on here at the base that I think you should know about."

"Why tell me about them?"

Enervy got up and began to pace. This reminded Kathryn of the military manner which he'd displayed in the classroom and of his potential for being gravely dangerous.

"Because I like you. I've liked you from the first time I saw you."

"That's nice," Kathryn said sarcastically. He seemed to get a little peeved at this.

"You don't understand, there are dangers everywhere. My offer to you could save your life."

"Offer?"

"You could become an exclusive. An officer's mate if you will. A position which would give you a chance to get out of the barracks. You could live in an officer's quarters with only one man. In a monogamous relationship. Yet before I can offer up these luxuries, I need to have a sense of your attitude towards this promotion. Not everyone gets a chance to avoid the camp's pitfalls."

"You mean like the pit that women fell into when you ordered her murdered."

Enervy grimaced again; he seemed to be getting annoyed at the way she kept shooting him down.

"That was very unfortunate," he said. "But she was trying to instigate a riot. We can't have anybody stirring up controversy or inciting rebellion. *Discipline!*" He shouted with such force Kathryn was taken aback as he began raving, "We must have order here or else every woman in that room, including you, would have had to die! Every woman in that room would have to be sacrificed to preserve order and...wouldn't that be a shame to waste all that beauty?" Here he smiled slyly and with a wave of his hand finished. "One bad apple, you see." He sat back down and took a sip of his drink, his anger having passed as quickly as it came about. This gave Kathryn the courage to say, "So you're a good guy, is that it?"

He hatched a peevish grin, "There are no good guys or bad guys, only survivors." He got up from the chair and stepped towards her. "It's a difficult call, I understand. But I'm afraid that it's one you'll have to make rather quickly." He was standing right in front of her now and she tried not to step back from him or seem intimidated. "I'm afraid that humanity no longer has any time for courting. And I personally have many responsibilities here at the base, so I won't be able to wine and dine you." He took her firmly by the shoulders and kissed her softly on the mouth. Her heart began to beat as if she were searching for a bomb in a maze of industrial pipes. She could feel the knife pressing against her abdomen as his hands traced down the small of her back and squeezed her buttocks. She knew the time for action was now; it would only be a few seconds before he pressed against her and discovered the knife. But she was frozen by fear and stress. She leaned back, almost fainted, and then was righted by his strong arm. When she went limp however, her muscles contracted and the knife slipped and dislodged from her underwear. It hit the wooden deck with an audible thud. It then bounced under the railing and onto the sands below.

"What was that?" he shouted, "You bitch you... who sent you here to kill me?"

Kathryn couldn't answer, the scene was too much for her nerves and she was going in and out of consciousness. He let her go and she collapsed onto the deck. Enervy abandoned her felled frame and walked over to the railing.

"Sergeant!" he shouted. Marge walked out from under the deck into view and looked up at him.

"Yes, Captain."

"Fetch me that weapon."

She looked to where he was pointing and walked towards the knife. Enervy stormed back over and lifted Kathryn's dizzy head off the wood planks.

"Now bitch," he began, "you're going to tell me what you're doing here or I'm going to cut your fucking eyes out!"

Marge stomped up the stairs then. "Hold her down, Captain," she said. "I'm going to teach this little hussy a lesson."

He did so. "Don't kill her, Sergeant," he said. "I need to find out some information from her."

"Oh, don't worry, Captain, don't worry about anything."

What happened next flabbergasted Kathryn to the point where she didn't know if it was real or imagined. Sergeant Marge stepped around Captain Enervy and, in one swift motion, plunged the buck knife into his unprotected eye. He wavered and a stream of yellow liquid shot out from his retina. Sergeant Marge quickly reached over and extracted the knife before plunging it back in again as if she were hacking through a watermelon.

This time the Captain fell; the blade still protruding from his eye; its handle covered by a wash of blood and other internal fluids which dripped down onto the deck and Kathryn's forehead.

She could feel his heavy body pinning her down, and before her mind revolved into blackness, she heard Sergeant Marge say, "Get up murderer, you're going to have to answer for killing the captain."

6

After Kathryn awoke, she was marched down the beach. Sergeant Marge had her arm twisted behind her back; tangled in with the club like a splint.

"March, whore! March, whore!" She kept shouting and finally Kathryn's feet began to walk for themselves, even though she had lost her shoes at some point and the grains of sand felt like miniscule shards of glass.

They soon abandoned the beach however and the soles of Kathryn's feet burned on the hot asphalt. Before long they came to a block building with the anagram Y CA hanging from the second story bricks. The second letter in the abbreviation was obviously missing with two bare, rusted prongs sticking out between the Y and the C. As Kathryn was marched through a locker room, she began to hear the moans. To her it sounded like the cries from the prisoner's in Dante's Inferno. She tried to run then but Marge tightened the splint. "Don't even think about it, bitch."

They came to the room which was the source of the ungodly noises. There had once been an Olympic swimming pool at its center but the water had long been drained. Now the dead were crawling around on the pool floor, trying to climb out only to slide back down the walls and falling over each other; writhing like fat snakes.

Marge marched Kathryn right to the edge of the pool. The dead made no reaction aside from continuing to try to escape. Kathryn braced herself for the cruelest of deaths but before she could be thrown in, she heard the sound of applause or rather, one man clapping.

Sergeant Marge whirled around as Granderson walked out of the shadows, laughing heartily.

"Captain Granderson," she said, "this woman murdered Captain Enervy and then tried to attack me. I was taking her to the pool."

Kathryn stared at Granderson, desperation in her eyes. He shot her a reaffirming look that gave her hope.

"How was he killed?" he asked Marge.

"With this, sir, she must have stolen it from one of the officers."

Granderson nodded and retrieved the gore splattered knife from the sergeant. "Yes, that must be it," he said.

"Captain Granderson, this may be an inopportune time to bring this up. But you'll be needing a replacement for Captain Enervy. I'd like to respectfully submit my name for serious consideration."

"Don't worry, Sergeant Marge," he answered. "You'll get what's coming to you."

"I'm glad to hear that, sir. I've done my best for the regiment."

"Mmm hmm, mmm hmm," Granderson was staring at the knife and seemed to be thinking about something else.

"What about this wretched underhanded bitch, sir? Do you want me to toss her into the pit?"

Kathryn stiffened in terror.

"Well," he said while hatching a smile. "Why don't you let me worry about her?"

Marge looked around slightly confused and then, perhaps not wanting to defy the captain, she released Kathryn from the wrestle hold.

"Will there be anything else, Captain?"

"I don't think so," he said before quickly pulling out his service revolver, "at ease, Sergeant." He pointed the gun and shot the thick bodied soldier right between the eyes. The back of her head exploded before she blinked once in shock and fell onto the tiles like a folded up lawn chair. Kathryn stepped back agape. This was the third time in less than a week she'd watched someone executed at point blank range before her very eyes, and the impact which the shock had upon her didn't lesson with repetition. Granderson casually strolled up to them and nudged her body over the edge of the pool with his boot. She hit the pond of roiling dead and bounced around like a dingy in a hurricane, before her body went under their solid surface and disappeared in a violent whirlpool of gore.

He then looked at Kathryn and smiled widely.

"Ah, thank you, thank you so very much, Kathryn, for doing what I couldn't. I've wanted Enervy out of the way for some time now. But the sycophants within his faction never would've stood for it. I would've been tried for it and well... the trials around here usually end the same." He gestured towards the pool. "But this...this senseless self defense at the hands of a whore. Why, it's practically perfect and I even get rid of that dyke Marge to boot. Too ambitious that one. Now I'll follow you through those doors," he said before sticking the revolver in between her shoulder blades.

As she'd done so many times in the last few days, Kathryn began to march.

"And with Enervy out of the picture my faction will take over the entire compound with me as commander in chief," he said. "I'll be tantamount to a king nowadays."

Kathryn noticed for the first time that the colloquial street lingo he'd been using back in the tent was gone and he was now talking with the brio of a college professor. They crossed through a tiled opening which had no door and into a shower room.

"As a reward for so bravely assassinating my biggest political rival I'm prepared to make you a star," he said.

Kathryn rounded another corner, and standing in front of a row of shower stalls, she saw a video camcorder perched atop a tripod.

"A porn star maybe, but a star none the less," he grinned.

Kathryn could hear an awful gurgling sound coming from one of the stalls which was obscured by a curtain. It reminded her of the sound a dog would make had it been run over by a milk truck, to be left whimpering and wounded on the road. She slowed down as she approached the source but Granderson urged her on with the gun.

"I'd like to introduce you to someone," he quipped. Grabbing her mane tightly so she couldn't run, Granderson pulled back the shower curtain to reveal a monstrous spectacle.

There was a purple-faced dead man standing in the shower stall. He was held in place by an intricate web of barbed wires which made deep lacerations in his beige skin. There was no blood flowing from these fresh cuts however and his upper lip had been either lopped off or had disintegrated from decay. There were no teeth in his mouth and both of his arms had been surgically amputated at the forearm.

He looked up at them with a savage longing in his bright teal eyes.

"This is Corporal Johnson," Granderson said, "he may be dead, but he does have one attribute that not every zombie has." Here, Granderson paused and pulled a toga off of the hideous creature's midsection. "You see, old Johnson here still has the fire down below."

Kathryn tried to bolt, but this only tightened the grip Granderson had on her long hair.

He continued as if she hadn't tried to escape: "That's right: Johnson here, long lost buddy of ours, will respond to sexual stimulation."

Kathryn struggled and cried, but the captain was much too strong for her.

"So what I want from my actress is very simple, Kathryn." He reached up over his head and switched on a boom box which was sitting atop the block divider wall. The familiar riffs of the *Rolling Stones: Start Me Up* strummed out. "You just listen to old Mick Jagger here, where ever he may be. Because he's got some good advice for you and we're gonna find out if you're hot enough." He switched on the camcorder. "We're gonna see if you can make a dead man cum."

## 7

Private First Class John Wilkes Scooter Benson was glad he'd joined the army a year ago. God knows where the hell he would have ended up if he'd went to college with his pencil-necked high school buddies who were even now probably roaming the streets like some possessed puppet, looking for some poor bastard's entrails to munch on.

Whew, he shivered. As it were he was situated inside a safe compound. He slept in a firm but comfortable bed inside a five star barracks, chowed down on a hot breakfast before reporting to his cushy duty, and while there was still poor bastards out there somewhere, scavenging for their very lives, he pulled on clean, laundered and starched socks every morning.

Hell, next week it was going to be his company's turn with the women.

His thoughts were interrupted by a flash of motion on the far right of his peripheral and a quarter of a second later he emptied a clip into a walking corpse which had once been a very attractive woman in a yellow sun dress. Not long after the big slender bullets ripped her apart, his two-way crackled out a garbled spiel.

"What's goin' on over there, tower sixteen? Over."

Scooter picked up the two-way. "What the hell do you thinks goin' on? I got a walker two blocks northwest and I just took her head off. Over."

There was a brief pause and the radio barked again, "10-4. Over."

Scooter had seen the women riding by on the back of the flat wagon. Jesus, they had looked good; some of those dresses didn't cover much more than a napkin would have. They must have sent a rescue squad over to the Playboy Mansion to come up with those bitches. One more work week and he would get to sample the goods; if you could even call this work that is. Sitting in an armored tower shooting at these slow, stupid, mothers like they were clay ducks. He'd played video games which were ten times harder. Hell, some of the guys were even bringing twelve packs up into the towers with them. May as well drink as many cold ones as possible before the supply was gone forever. Sniper command knew about it but they didn't give a shit. Hell, some of the guys aim were even a little sharper with a couple beers in 'em; took the edge off.

His thoughts were boggled again by a stir of dust a great distance away, out past the old fish hatchery, which was barely visible on the farthest rim of the firmament.

It looked like a dust storm was kicking up or fog maybe.

"What the hell?" Scooter muttered and picked up his binoculars. But he wasn't really prepared for the sight he beheld once he lifted the field glasses to his eyes. The living dead!

Hundreds of them, thousands of them, millions of them, all marching across the exposed prairies down past the old dilapidated foundries towards the outskirts of the town. Like maggots on the carcass of a deceased world, shaking and squirming and deathly white; ready to attach themselves to any living or dying population.

Scooter lowered the field glasses.

"Holy fucking shit!" he said.

8

In her bare feet, Kathryn scrambled across a high asphalt parking ramp. She couldn't see the beach, but she could hear the roar of the ocean splashing against the concrete barriers and continuing on up underneath the beams which held the structure she was standing on in place. The drum-like pop of automatic gunfire came from every direction, challenged in pitch only by the locust-like drone of the moaning dead.

Back inside the Y CA from where she'd just fled, Kathryn had stood up straight in front of Captain Granderson and told him to shoot her in the chest rather than force her to copulate with the grotesquely disfigured and demonized Corporal Johnson.

The captain had looked out from behind the camcorder and grinned like a hyena, but just as he was preparing a fresh wisecrack, an invisible force slammed into his shoulder. He screamed in agony as a small geyser of blood leaped from the new wound in a vivid splash. Before he could collect himself, a second projectile struck him in the opposite shoulder, causing him to fold down onto his knees. Kathryn took a step towards the front of the stall as the shooter came into view. With his one eye twisted into a cruel, taffy-like laceration, which resembled a mass of egg yokes mixed with ketchup and tarter sauce, Captain Enervy approached them. Thick spiraled designs of dried blood coated his bare chest. His good eye was shining as blue as a whirlpool whipped by a cyclone, relishing the prospect of retribution and vengeance.

"Hello, Granderson," he said, "didn't think you were going to get rid of a soldier of my caliber that easily did you?"

Granderson didn't answer but only writhed in agony on the hard shower floor, a huge circumference of gore widening around him.

"You think I don't know the people who want me out of the way around here? Your coup is through, asshole, and another bullet's too good for you. Now get up and march to the pit."

Kathryn would have backed into the stall and hid, but with Corporal Johnson in the booth she had little choice but to stand her ground. Finally, Enervy noticed her and turned to face her.

"Ahh, the little bitch," he said. "Still think you're an assassin? I ought to throw you in the pit, too."

Kathryn said nothing, but could only stand dumbfounded by the awful sight of the maimed soldier.

"Nah," he said after a few seconds. "I think I'll just blow your fucking head off." But even as he pointed the gun at her to carry out his threat, Granderson sprang up from the floor. The two men locked onto each other as the gun went off again. The bullet ricocheted throughout the block partitions before hitting Corporal Johnson in the head. His brain exploded like a stink bomb full of thick black ink and his body collapsed only to be held up by the web of wires. This sight drove Kathryn into a near frenzy of fear and she dashed around the two struggling men to escape down the hallway. She heard several more gunshots as she exited the building but would never know who shot whom.

Now she was crossing over from the asphalt and back onto the beach, grains of sand digging into the balls of her red feet like metal shavings. Wasps sang around her and she slapped at her head dizzily. It was then she realized with a rising sense of terror it was gunfire in the air which was making the buzzing noise; gunfire which was narrowly missing her head.

She dropped onto her stomach to avoid the bullets, but a lump in the sand brushed up against her. It was a severed head with a hole the size of a grapefruit underneath its blood soaked hair line. She screamed and rose again, running down the beach in an aimless panic.

She ran for a great while without reason or direction, zigzagging through a field of the living dead. But they were slow and cadaverous and she managed to avoid them easily. Periodically, some of them exploded and were hurled fifteen feet into the air, their frail bodies cracking apart like wooden figures on a firing range. Although Kathryn, in her distress, had no idea she was running through a mind field.

Ultimately, she came along to a line of soldiers who were slowly retreating as a massive front of the dead converged on them. They fired their impressive weapons continuously, the large pellets seeming to evaporate in the cold flesh of the zombies like snow melting onto a hillside; only the occasional shot finding its target and obliterating a fetid brain.

They also coated the zombies with the incinerating spittle from a squadron of flame throwers. But, just as in the dream which Kathryn was now recalling in a deja vu, the wall of flames had a minor effect in slowing them down.

After Kathryn ran around the edge of the battle, the soldiers began to be overrun. The sheer numbers of their maggot-ridden opponents defeated their ample firepower. As the dead swarmed over the soldiers like the tide washing out the sands, their screams pierced the air like sharp teeth pinching through flesh.

Kathryn continued on at a full sprint; darting in a line concurrent with the fence. The dead clung to the links like fancy colorful insects pinned to a cloth, an endless mass of their decaying brethren swelling against the ramparts behind them. Hundreds of thousands of white ghouls as far as the eye could see. Kathryn fell for the second time, spraying her eyes with the coarse sand. For a few seconds she could only crawl slowly before she sensed a great violence around her and rose to run down the beach blindly. She bounced off mysterious forms now and then but had no way of knowing whether or not it was one of the soldiers or one of the walking dead. After a few frightful seconds of this she could feel the warm ankle deep waters of the Pacific sloshing through her toes. She dropped to her knees and frantically washed the sand out of her eyes. When she could open them again, she saw the flags of the tents, the knight's quarters where she had first encountered Granderson and the girls in her group had first encountered the lust of the regiment. The fabric was being ripped apart by the dead, who were perhaps hoping to find even more quarry inside the makeshift huts.

Instinctively, she began slowly backing into the waves until the warm waters were at her waist. Thankfully, the flesh eaters didn't seem to be following her into the water.

Most of the soldiers gamely fought on against long odds rather than flee into the ocean. Perhaps the instincts instilled in them during their training spurred them on to make a stand or maybe they just didn't want to get their precious guns wet. Now the water was at Kathryn's neck as she watched the fence collapse in many sections under the great push of the lifeless yet living throng. The zombies crawled across the hot sands as if blind and hungry, like a million infant crabs searching for a slimy meal in the wet sand.

The death shouts of the regiment were somehow louder and more painful than the steady moan of the undead crowd, as if the souls of the soldiers were suffering more misery than even the tortured, souls who confronted them.

But even if they could defeat the living dead in terms of agony, they couldn't defeat them in battle. In no time the last pocket of the regiment was cornered and torn apart like strips of red rags.

Kathryn sighed, nearly cried, and then turned from the horrid scene and began to swim.

# CRUISE OF THE LIVING DEAD

SCOTT BAKER

The briny smell of salt water drifted in through the porthole. Carissa Banning stood by the opening, inhaling deeply. Several decks below, she could hear the ocean slapping against the side of the cruise ship.

A feeling of utter contentment washed over her. She loved the ocean, which was not surprising since she had grown up in the coastal city of Rockport, Massachusetts. It was one of the reasons she had gone to medical school, to help her fellow man while making enough money so she could eventually retire to the New England coast. Then, during her last year of residency, she got an epiphany. Why spend twenty or thirty years in some clinic treating colds and mending broken bones, hoping someday to live by the sea, when she could fulfill both desires as a cruise line doctor? Finding an available position was difficult, but between her grades and some glowing recommendations from the hospital where she interned, six months ago she finagled a position aboard the S.S. *Sea Princess*.

Now, every day she stood by the porthole to take in the sights and sounds of the ocean, marveling at her good fortune. Carissa was exactly where she wanted to be.

The door to sick bay abruptly opened, snapping Carissa out of her reverie.

"Hey, Doc. I got a couple of patients for you." The voice belonged to Bobby, one of the ship's stewards. He frequently dropped in to say hello and bring her coffee. Carissa knew that Bobby liked her, but was too shy to ask her out, probably because she was ten years his senior. Today he had an unusual urgency in his voice.

"Coming." Carissa moved away from the porthole and stepped into the examination room.

Bobby helped a middle-aged man up onto the exam table. A large wound on the man's shoulder and a smaller one on his right forearm oozed blood, the former staining his Hawaiian shirt. A woman with shoulder-length blonde hair stood nearby, cradling her left arm, which also dripped blood from a nasty looking wound near her wrist. A boy about eight years old and his older sister stood off to the side, the girl nervously twirling her auburn pony-tail.

Carissa stepped over to the exam table, pulled a pair of white rubber gloves from a cardboard storage box, and slid them on. "Who do we have here?"

Bobby stepped aside so Carissa could examine the man. "This is Mr. Lansdowne and his family. He and Mrs. Lansdowne were bit by some nut while ashore."

"Everything'll be all right, so just relax." Carissa adopted her most soothing bedside manner. She gently slid off Mr. Lansdowne's shirt, pausing only when he winced from the pain. "Tell me what happened."

As Carissa examined the wounds, Mr. Lansdowne related how he and his family had gone ashore that morning to visit the Bermudan countryside. While touring an old sugar plantation, the family had come across a man dazed and bloodied. When they tried to see if he needed help, the man attacked them, biting the father in the shoulder and trying to tear out a chunk of flesh. Mr. Lansdowne held the attacker's head in place with his left hand while punching him with the right, which was when the attacker bit his arm. Mrs. Lansdowne received her bite when she tried to pull the attacker off her husband. Mr. Lansdowne eventually crippled the man with a kick to the knee, rushed his family back to the car, and returned to the ship.

The wounds were deep and would definitely leave scars, but thankfully none of the injuries appeared to be life threatening. Carissa irrigated the bites with a diluted water povidine-iodine solution, stitched the wounds closed, and gave father and mother a heavy dose of penicillin to fight off infection.

"Any idea why he attacked you?" asked Carissa as she stuck a syringe into Mrs. Lansdowne's arm and pressed the plunger.

"None." Mr. Lansdowne sat in a chair, cradling his right arm and massaging the area around the dressing. "Other than that he was a friggin' nut."

"He didn't say anything?"

"Just moaned a lot, like he was in pain. He had several bite marks on him and was covered in blood. And he looked sick."

"How so?" Carissa removed the syringe from Mrs. Lansdowne's arm, placed the cover over the needle, and tossed it into the bio-hazard bin.

"His skin was blotchy and discolored." Mr. Lansdowne closed his eyes and twisted his neck.

"Are you okay?"

"Just a little stiff and light-headed. Probably stress catching up with me."

"Maybe," said Carissa. She stepped over to Mr. Lansdowne and placed her palm against his forehead. "You're running a fever."

"Is that bad?"

"With your other symptoms, I can't rule out the possibility the man who attacked you may have given you rabies."

Mrs. Lansdowne gasped. "Isn't that fatal?"

"It's not as bad as it sounds." Carissa smiled in reassurance. "You and your husband only just got bit, so there's little chance the infection has become acute, assuming you even have rabies. I'll take some saliva, blood, and skin samples from both of you for testing. In the meantime, let me start you on a regimen of vaccines and rabies anti-bodies."

Carissa went about taking the samples and administering the shots as casually as possible, assuring the family that in a few days they would be lounging around the pool with this unfortunate event behind them.

* * *

Two days passed before Carissa thought of the Lansdownes again. The *Sea Princess* left Bermuda the same night she treated the father and mother. Over the next two days, Carissa spent her time treating a drunken idiot who gave himself alcohol poisoning during a drinking binge on shore, a retiree who developed a severe food allergy, and a college student who required stitches after cracking her head on the diving board. It was not until their second day out of port that Carissa realized the Lansdownes hadn't come by for their follow-up visit. After lunch, she prepared a set of syringes with the second round of vaccines and rabies anti-bodies, packed them into a portable medical bag, and went to pay a cabin call.

As Carissa entered the main deck, she ran into Bobby, who greeted her with a smile. He gestured toward the medical bag. "Who's sick?"

"I'm checking on the Lansdownes."

"Lansdownes?" Bobby mentally sorted through the passenger list until the name finally registered. "That's the family that was attacked back in Bermuda."

"The same." Carissa lifted the bag. "It's time for their next round of shots."

"Come to think of it, no one's heard from them since we left port. Mind if I tag along to check on things?"

"No problem."

As they approached the Lansdownes' cabin, Carissa noticed a maid service cart sitting out front. As the more petite of the two maids arranged cleaning supplies, her raven-haired companion knocked on the door. When the maid received no response, she unlocked the door, pushed it halfway open, and leaned into the room.

"Room service. Can we come in and cl..."

The maid's question devolved into a scream. Mr. Lansdowne shoved the door open and stumbled out of the room, snarling at the four people gathered in the corridor. Everyone paused, taken aback by his appearance. A bluish-black discoloration covered his exposed skin. At first Carissa thought the rabies had progressed more rapidly than normal, until she caught a whiff of the odor. It had been a while since she'd last smelt it, dating back to her internship in the Pittsburgh Hospital Emergency Room, but she could never completely force from her memory the sickeningly sweet smell of rotting flesh.

Before anyone could react, Mr. Lansdowne shoved the raven-haired maid against the wall and plunged his teeth into her face. He flicked his head to the side, ripping off the maid's nose and upper lip. The maid screamed even louder, an anguished howl of terror and pain. Blood spurt from the wound, splattering across the walls as the maid thrashed around, trying to break free. The violence of the assault shocked Carissa into inactivity, but that numbness lasted only a few seconds. She dropped to her knees and vomited when Mr. Lansdowne swallowed the maid's flesh.

The petite maid reacted first. Stepping behind Mr. Lansdowne, she wrapped her left arm around his neck, careful to keep away from his mouth, and tried to pull him off of her coworker. Mrs. Lansdowne emerged from out of the room, grabbed the petite maid by the shoulders, and chomped into the back of the neck, yanking off a chunk of flesh and chewing it. Releasing her grip from Mr. Lansdowne, the petite maid used her hands to batter at the wife's face, trying to break the death grip. Mr. Lansdowne turned around and shoved the petite maid, who banged into the cleaning cart and toppled over backwards. The two Lansdownes fell upon her, fingers and teeth tearing into the anguished woman's stomach.

The raven-haired maid slid down the wall and sat in a growing pool of her blood, slipping into shock.

Carissa snapped herself back to reality and moved to help the maids, but Bobby grabbed her by the arm.

Carissa jerked free. "What are you doing?"

"I'll handle this. You get the other passengers off this deck, then go warn the captain."

"What about the kids?"

A set of high-pitched moans came from the cabin. Carissa and Bobby watched as the Lansdowne children, or what remained of them, stepped into the corridor. The girl's right arm hung limp by her side, most of the skin and muscle having been chewed off below the elbow, leaving only strips of flesh and tissue dangling from where it was attached to the bone. Her brother stood to her rear, swaying unsteadily, several feet of intestine dangling out of a hole gnawed into his abdomen. The siblings stared at Carissa and Bobby through lifeless grey eyes. Before either could attack, the raven-haired maid leaning against the wall groaned, attracting their attention. The siblings set upon the maid, each feeding off of her face wound.

"Warn the others!" ordered Bobby.

Carissa barely heard him. She mentally tried to force the grotesque image from her mind, but it burned itself into her psyche, closing down her mental processes and paralyzing her with fear.

Bobby spun her around to face him, and slapped her hard across the face. The stinging brought Carissa back to her senses.

"You need to get everyone off this deck! Now!"

Carissa nodded weakly and backed down the corridor toward the elevator. She watched as Bobby raced into the carnage. He grabbed the little girl by the ponytail and half-eaten arm and pulled her off of the raven-haired maid. Raw flesh and muscle separated from the woman, the chunks still clenched between the girl's teeth. The maid showed no reaction. Bobby flung the girl back into the cabin and then turned to grab her brother.

Carissa moved down the corridor, pounding on each door she passed. Thankfully, most passengers were topside enjoying the cruise. Those who emerged from their cabins only needed to glance down the corridor and were more than convinced to leave. Carissa got as far as the fifth cabin when yelling distracted her.

"Stay back!" Bobby was yelling to a burly man in sweat pants and a Patriots t-shirt who ran down the corridor from the opposite direction to help. The Lansdowne parents stood and lumbered toward him. Each one grabbed hold of the burly man and dragged him to the floor, tearing into him with teeth and fingers. As Carissa watched, Bobby pushed past the cleaning cart to help, but never made it. The raven-haired maid darted out a hand and clasped Bobby by the ankle, holding him in place with a lifeless hand. Reaching up with her other hand, the maid grabbed Bobby by the pant leg and pulled herself up, hand over hand, clawing her way up his belt and shirt until she stood erect. Bobby tried to shove her off, but couldn't get enough leverage. With an animalistic snarl, the maid sank her teeth into Bobby's throat. He cried out, his howl drowned out by a gurgling as blood filled his throat.

"Bobby!" Carissa started back down the corridor to assist her friend, stopping short when the Lansdowne children stepped out of the cabin and fixed their gaze on her. Their mouths chewed in anticipation, spilling blood and gore across decaying lips. Carissa gasped when the children plodded toward her. She moved down the corridor, keeping her back against the wall, never taking her eyes off of the children.

Something metal slammed into Carissa's back. Looking over her shoulder, she saw a wall-mounted fire extinguisher pressing against her. Grabbing it, Carissa aimed the nozzle at the girl's snarling visage and squeezed the trigger. A blast of $CO_2$ hit the girl square in the face, momentarily blinding her. She veered to the right and smacked face first into the wall, grunting in frustration. Carissa shot another blast of $CO_2$ into the girl's face and took a few steps toward the approaching brother, then blasted him twice. As the children tried to regain their orientation, Carissa moved back down the corridor, knocking on doors to alert passengers to the danger.

Seven cabins and two more evacuated families later, Carissa arrived at the last door and knocked frantically.

A voice from deep inside the cabin yelled, "Piss off, asshole."

"Open up!" Carissa banged on the door even harder. "This is an emergency!" Three more pounds. "You have to evacuate this deck now!"

The cabin door swung open violently. A man, naked accept for a towel wrapped around his waist, stood in the doorway. "Are you deaf, bitch? I told you to..."

A collective set of moans cut off his tirade. Carissa and the naked man both glanced down the corridor to see a hoard of living dead swarming towards them. The Lansdowne family and the two maids spread across the corridor, with the burly would-be rescuer limping along behind on a badly-chewed leg, struggling to keep up.

The naked man's jaw dropped open. "What the...?"

"We have to make a run for it."

"Let me get my wife." The naked man ducked back into the cabin, yelling for his wife to hurry up.

Carissa raised the nozzle of the fire extinguisher and stepped forward to confront the living dead. She gave each of the Lansdownes and the maids a three-second burst to the face, slowing their advance. At best, she bought herself a few seconds. Looking over her shoulder, the naked man and his wife still hadn't left their cabin.

"Hurry up!" Carissa yelled as she aimed the nozzle at Mr. Lansdowne and blasted him in the face a second time.

The raven-haired maid let out an angry growl and lunged at Carissa. Carissa raised the nozzle and pressed the trigger, but nothing came out. A quick glance at the pressure indicator confirmed her fears. The extinguisher was empty. Raising the cylinder, she slammed the base of it into the maid's jaw, shattering several teeth and fracturing the exposed skull; yet the injuries barely slowed her down. Carissa backed up toward the cabin.

"We're out of time!" she yelled when alongside the open door.

The man emerged from his cabin, this time wearing trousers, pulling along an attractive brunette who was yanking her jeans up over her thighs. When the brunette saw the living dead only a few yards away, she screamed and ran back into the cabin. The Lansdowne children and the petite maid pushed their way inside the cabin after her. Crying out for his wife, the man tried to pull the three living dead back into the corridor, only to be set upon from behind by the rest of the Lansdowne family and the raven-haired maid. They dragged him to the floor and clawed open his chest. The terrified screams of the wife and the howls of pain from her husband drowned out all other sounds.

Carissa turned and ran down the corridor until she reached the forward bank of elevators. She frantically jabbed at the call button until she heard the car begin its descent to her deck.

A groan caused her to spin around. The burly man with the half-eaten leg made his way by the feeding frenzy and staggered toward her, seeking fresh meat. He was only three yards away. Carissa glanced up at the indicator. Three decks to go. The elevator would never get here in time.

Carissa raised the fire extinguisher and drove the base into the burly man's face. It barely fazed him. Carissa smashed him in the face again, only this time harder. The burly man swayed momentarily, and then lunged. In desperation, Carissa swung the extinguisher like a bat, connecting with the side of his head. This time the blow knocked him against the wall where he dropped onto his good knee. Carissa swung the extinguisher again. A loud *crack* echoed down the corridor as the burly man's skull shattered, driving fragments of bone into his brain. He convulsed several times before falling to the ground, motionless.

A metallic ping announced the arrival of the elevator. As the doors slid open, Carissa ran inside, pressed the button for the main deck, and then flung herself against the rear wall.

Only when the doors closed and the elevator began its ascent did Carissa drop to her knees and sob uncontrollably.

* * *

By the time Carissa entered the bridge, news of the carnage on the main deck had already arrived. Uneasiness gripped the crew, charging the air like static electricity. The tension was palpable, with the crew self-consciously going about their business, looking to each other for reassurance rather than performing with their usual confidence.

Carissa had seen them like this once before when the ship got caught in an unexpectedly violent storm that almost floundered the vessel. It did nothing to calm her anxiety.

The only person who didn't appear to be in a state of near panic was Captain Jurgensen, a veteran of twenty-six years with the cruise line. He stood by the command chair, the ship's intercom phone wedged between his shoulder and ear. After several minutes, the captain replaced the receiver and turned to the bridge crew.

"Okay, ladies and gentlemen. We have a situation developing down on the main deck that includes casualties and possible fatalities. A disturbance has broken out and passengers are attacking each other."

"They're eating each other," announced Carissa. The crew looked at Carissa as if she had lost her mind. The captain folded his arms across his chest and glared at her through squinted eyes, barely concealing his anger at having to deal with such nonsense.

"Explain."

"I was down on the main deck when this started. I went to check on the Lansdownes, who came to the infirmary two days ago after having been bitten by some nut back in Bermuda. When the maids opened the door to their cabin, the family attacked and began eating the maids and several passengers."

"Eating?" Jurgensen's tone warned Carissa that she ran the risk of being thrown off the bridge.

"Captain, I know it sounds crazy. But I saw the whole thing. The Lansdownes attacked and ate Bobby, two maids, and several passengers. Several minutes after being killed, the maids and passengers came back to life and attacked other passengers. Just like in one of those zombie movies."

A chorus of snickers floated through the bridge. For a moment, Carissa thought she'd overplayed her hand and expected to be escorted back to her cabin. Instead, Jurgensen unfolded his arms and looked out over the ocean. The snickering at her expense suddenly stopped.

After nearly a minute of silence, the first mate, Commander Travis, stepped over to Jurgensen. Though he spoke in a soft voice, his words carried through the deafening silence on the bridge. "Is everything all right, Captain?"

"Far from it." Jurgensen turned and crossed the bridge to Carissa. "You said the Lansdownes were infected prior to their attacking the others. With what?"

"At first I thought it was rabies. But the infection spread too quickly," she said. "Besides, rabies can drive its victims insane and make them vicious, but I've never heard of a case where it caused its victims to eat each other."

"Then what's your assessment?"

Carissa inhaled briskly, not quite certain how to answer. "I have no idea what type of infection we're dealing with. But from what I've seen, it's highly virulent. Even a single bite causes death in as little as a few minutes, depending on the severity of the wound."

"What are the chances of stopping the infection?"

"Maybe it shouldn't be stopped." The statement came from Reverend Stiles, the ship's chaplain and a devote Baptist. Stiles stood by the entrance to the bridge.

"What's that supposed to mean?" Jurgensen demanded.

"Maybe this isn't an infectious outbreak after all." Reverend Stiles advanced toward the captain, summoning his courage. "Perhaps we're witnessing some sort of miracle, a divine retribution to punish us for our sins."

"You can't be serious?"

"Doubt if you want," Reverend Stiles responded accusatorily. "But if you've read the Bible, you'd realize resurrection is a common theme. Lazarus was brought back to life. And Jesus himself rose from the dead on the third day."

"I do read the Bible. I just don't recall Jesus rising from the dead and then eating his disciples." Jurgensen focused his attention back to Carissa. "Miss Banning, I'll ask again. What are the chances of bringing this outbreak under control?"

Carissa sighed and shook her head. "I don't have the expertise to handle something like this, so our chances of stopping it are next to impossible. Best we can do is to contain its spread and get the uninfected off the ship as soon as possible."

Jurgensen stared at Carissa. She couldn't tell if his cold, hard eyes reflected his disappointment with her lack of capabilities or his acceptance of the harsh reality. In either case, Carissa felt humiliated; a useless fraud completely out of her element. None of which was assuaged by Jurgensen's response.

"Head below and try to get as many passengers topside as possible. God help you if you're wrong, Miss Banning."

The captain walked past Carissa, pausing just long enough to place a reassuring hand on her shoulder. "And God help us all if you're right."

*   *   *

It took less than an hour for Carissa to clear all the passengers off of the guest decks, or more precisely, those passengers who had survived the outbreak. Most of the passengers on the upper decks were already alerted to the carnage taking place below them, and as such were easily removed to the boat deck, one level above the main deck.

Checking on the lower decks was more problematic. Every major stairwell was filled with the living dead from main deck on down. Carissa reasoned that because of their limited mobility, it was easier for the living dead to descend rather than climb them. She scanned the lobby deck looking for a safe way down, eventually finding a service stairwell not infested with zombies, and descended to the lower decks. Carissa walked into a charnel house.

The main deck and the one beneath were completely overrun by the living dead. At each level, Carissa carefully opened the service door and peered into the corridor. On each level, she found scores of zombies roaming the corridors and feeding off of the passengers unfortunate enough not to have escaped.

Muffled screaming and cries for help warned her that some passengers remained trapped in their cabins. However, with each deck swarming with zombies, and with the only weapon at her disposal being the semiautomatic pistol issued to her from the ship's arms locker, any attempt to save them would have been suicide. On the last deck she checked, Carissa quietly closed and locked the service door, rationalizing her decision by telling herself the surviving passengers would be safer in their cabins until a full-scale rescue could be mounted.

After disconnecting the power to all the elevators between the passenger decks so no zombie could inadvertently make its way topside, Carissa returned to the bridge. She found the situation there bordering on breakdown. Jurgensen stood by the main console, yelling into the ship's intercom phone every few seconds, demanding that someone answer. His usual confidence had given way to a fear and frustration that infected the rest of the bridge crew. They nervously glanced back and forth to each other, trying to find strength amongst themselves, but only found mutual uncertainty and despair. Even Commander Travis seemed at a loss for action, hovering a few feet from the captain but too nervous to approach.

Carissa slid up beside the first officer. "What's going on?"

Travis shrugged. "The captain got a call from shore about five minutes ago that upset him. He's been trying to call the engine room ever since, but with no luck."

"Any idea what the call was about?" she asked.

"None. But the capt..."

Jurgensen slammed the receiver back into its cradle, cursed under his breath, and then stared out over the ocean.

Travis cautiously stepped forward. "Is everything all right, Captain?"

"No," Jurgensen sighed. He faced the bridge crew. "I just got off the phone with Norfolk. I've been advised that the Navy is sending the *Mitscher* out to meet us, and that we should hold our position until they arrive."

"That's good news, right?" Travis looked to the crew, hoping to bolster their morale.

Jurgensen looked at Travis the way a strict schoolmaster would a student who had blurted out a wrong answer in class. "The *Mitscher* is a destroyer. The Navy's not coming here to rescue us. They're coming to sink us."

"Why would they do that?" asked Travis.

"To keep the infection from spreading to the mainland," answered Carissa. She felt a cold shiver race down her spine as the full impact of the words set in.

"What the hell do you know?" snapped Brian, the navigator.

"Miss Banning's right," Jurgensen said with a quiet resignation to his voice. "If this outbreak ever reached a populated area like Norfolk, it could spread across the United States in a few months. Washington can't take that risk. And I don't blame them."

"So what do we do now?" Travis asked. "Try to outrun them?"

Jurgensen shook his head. "If we run, the Navy'll hunt us down and sink us without a second thought. Our only chance is to come to a full stop, put the uninfected in lifeboats, and set them adrift. Once the Navy has sunk the *Sea Princess*, maybe we can convince them to bring the survivors aboard one at a time, check them for wounds, and rescue those who aren't infected."

"Makes sense," Travis agreed.

"Except I can't reach the engine room." Jurgensen rested his hands on the edge of the control console and bowed his head while he contemplated his next move. It only took him a few seconds to formulate a plan of action. When he next lifted his head, the usual confidence had returned to his eyes, only now bolstered by a determination not to give up without a fight.

"Mister Travis, head down to the engine room. Find out what's going on and stop this ship. I don't care how you do it. Every minute we're moving decreases our chances of getting out of this alive. Take Miss Banning and Mister Kennedy with you. I'll have the crew prepare the passengers to abandon ship. Once you've stopped the ship, we'll get the uninfected to safety. Any questions?"

Travis stood at attention. "None, sir."

"Good. Move out."

With Travis leading the way, the engine room team headed out. As they were about to exit the bridge, Jurgensen called out to his first officer.

"Mister Travis, be careful. God knows what you'll find down there."

\* \* \*

The team made their way from the bridge toward the stern. As they exited the ship's interior onto the promenade deck, a terrible din greeted them from below. Carissa moved to the outer edge of the deck and peered over the railing. Two stories below, on the boat deck, over fifteen hundred passengers filled the ship's length, crowding into every available space. Even from up here, Carissa could sense the fear and uncertainty smoldering among the frightened passengers, threatening to ignite into full panic. Scattered throughout the throng, crew members tried to calm the passengers, promising they would soon be boarding the lifeboats and moving away from the liner to safely wait for rescue. The crew succeeded in talking down the passengers for now, but the terror still simmered beneath the surface, ready to be set off by the slightest provocation. Carissa and the others had to stop the ship soon. Just forward of mid-ship, Travis led the team back inside and guided them to a service elevator. Removing a key from his pocket, he inserted it into the control panel and turned it to the right. The doors slid open. Travis entered first, followed by Carissa and Kennedy. The first officer inserted the key into the inner control panel, turned it to the right, and pressed the button for the lowest deck.

As the elevator began its jerky descent, Travis removed his semiautomatic from its holster, flipped off the safety, and clasped the weapon in both hands, ready to quickly aim.

"Is that necessary?" asked Carissa.

"Something cut off communications with the engine room," Travis answered sternly. "How confident are you it was just mechanical failure?"

Carissa withdrew her own side arm and checked the safety.

The elevator came to a halt on the lowest deck of the ship and the doors slid open. Carissa half expected a hoard of zombies to swarm in on them. Instead, the team was greeted with an eerie stillness that sharply contrasted with the frenetic energy topside. They stepped out into the passageway, side arms at the ready. Carissa peered down the passageway in both directions, surprised to find no signs of life. Usually the engine room was one of the busiest areas of the ship, but now there were no indications that anyone was ever down here. No movement. No noise. The only sound came from the steady background hum generated by the engines, which reverberated through the hull.

Travis used the key to lock the elevator into place and then slid it into his jacket pocket. He pointed to the stern and set off for the engine room.

The passageway stretched for nearly one hundred feet before ending against a bulkhead. The three crewmen slowly moved forward, pausing at each hatch to make certain it was secure. Every few seconds, Carissa glanced over her shoulder to see if anything was following them, relieved to see nothing there.

At the end of the passageway, a small flight of iron steps led up to the hatch in the engine room bulkhead. Travis grabbed the wheel lock and pulled. The heavy metal hatch swung open.

Kennedy stepped up beside Travis and whispered, "I thought the engine room was battened down?"

"It's supposed to be." Travis pulled the hatch all the way open and stepped through, followed by Kennedy.

Carissa took the side arm in her left hand, rubbed her right palm against her skirt, then switched it back. With a deep sigh to steady her nerves, she stepped through the hatch.

They stood on a grated metal landing just inside the hatch. The engine room was cavernous compared to the rest of the ship. The room was thirty feet high and extending back a hundred feet, dominated by two enormous diesel engines. Pipes, air ducts, and steel supports for the catwalks crisscrossed the area, blocking their full vision. The roar of the engines drowned out all other noises. Carissa had been down here three months previous to tend to an engineer who had gotten an arm caught in some machinery. Everything was as she remembered it except for one factor. This time, mixed in with the smells of oil, diesel fuel, and sweat was a coppery odor she knew all too well...blood.

Travis led the way along the catwalk deeper into the engine room, then suddenly stopped and held up his left hand for the others to do likewise. He pointed toward the base of the metal stairs in front of them. Carissa followed his line of sight. In front of the engine's command console, five of the engineering crew lay scattered across the floor, their torsos torn open and their intestines yanked out. Organs and severed limbs were strewn around, the entire carnage coated in blood that dripped from the metal gratings.

There were three zombies still amongst the bodies, feeding off of the dead.

Travis glanced at Kennedy and Carissa. He lifted his forefinger and pointed to each of the zombies as he mouthed the words, "One shot each to the head."

Carissa shook her head repeatedly. "I'm not a good shot," she whispered. "I can't do it."

The look of disgust Travis flashed her hurt more than her own sense of uselessness. Travis focused his attention on Kennedy and spoke in a hush. "You take the middle one. I'll get the two on each end."

Kennedy nodded and raised his side arm, aiming at the center zombie's head.

Carissa winced as the gunshots rang out, the sound amplified many times in the confined space. The heads of the two closest zombies exploded, their bodies spasming for a second before slumping down over the fallen crewmen. Looking up from its meal, the third zombie snarled at them. Travis fired a single round into its face, blowing the back of its skull and brains across the engine room. With Travis in the lead, they ran down the stairs toward the console. Carissa felt her shoes squishing on the gore as she crossed the landing.

Kennedy looked down at one of the zombies. "How the hell did these *people* get in here?"

"It doesn't matter now," Travis said. He slid his side arm between the waistband of his trousers and the small of his back. "Help me shut down the engines. Carissa, keep your eyes open for any more of those *things*."

As the two men went about their business of shutting down the engines, Carissa scanned the compartment. She thought she heard a faint moaning, but couldn't be sure where it came from. She stepped to the opposite end of the landing, thinking maybe a wounded crew member had crawled away to safety, but saw nothing. The moaning sounded again, this time louder. Then a second and third set of moans joined in the ghastly chorus. A metallic clank from overhead caught her attention. Carissa looked up to see three zombies dressed in engineer jumpsuits moving along the catwalk above her, their lifeless eyes fixed on the three humans below.

"We've got company!" she yelled.

"Stop them!" Travis cried, working frantically. "We need a few more minutes."

Carissa saw that the catwalk led to the landing by the main hatch. She raced to head off the dead engineers. By now the first of the zombies had reached the stairs, swaying from side to side as it descended. Carissa raised her firearm and pulled the trigger. The round hit the zombie in the right shoulder, punching a chunk of rotten flesh out of its back and knocking it off balance, but doing nothing to stop its advance. She raised the muzzle a little higher and fired again. The round whizzed by the zombie's head. By now it was only a few feet away. Carissa stepped forward and shoved the barrel into the zombie's face. It snarled and lunged just as she pulled the trigger. The round tore into the engineer's brow between the eyes, disintegrating the head. The body dropped to the landing with a sickening thud.

Swallowing the bile rising in her throat, she aimed the firearm at the second zombie and waited until it was five feet away. The round tore off the zombie's jaw and blew off the back of its head, knocking it backwards onto the stairs. The third zombie lunged at Carissa, tripping over the bodies in front of it. Carissa jumped back as the third one nearly fell on top of her. Before it could get up, she placed the barrel against the back of its head and squeezed the trigger. The skull exploded like a ripe melon, showering her in gore.

A new set of moans caught Carissa's attention. She looked up to the catwalk in time to see four more zombies lumbering in her direction.

"I can't hold them off much longer!"

"Got it." Travis' voice echoed through the compartment as the first engine went silent. "Let's haul ass. Hopefully one's enough."

Travis and Kennedy raced for the main hatch, taking the stairs two at a time. Carissa fired at the lead zombie as it started down the stairs, but her aim was low. The round shattered its knee cap, causing it to tumble forward and crash to the landing in front of her. Before she could fire again, Travis pushed her toward the hatch.

"Go. I got this."

She climbed through the hatch into the passageway, with Kennedy close behind. Travis took down the second and third zombie with head shots, then turned to join the others. As he bent to exit through the hatch, the zombie Carissa had only wounded in the knee cap grabbed Travis by the ankle and pulled itself up his leg. Travis spun the firearm to shoot it just as the fourth zombie lumbered off of the stairs, landing on top of him. Travis fell back against the hatch, slamming it shut. Two sets of teeth bit into Travis' flesh. Carissa headed back for the hatch, but before she could open it, Travis spun the wheel from inside the engine room, locking the bolts in place.

"Travis!" Carissa pounded on the steel hatch.

Kennedy placed his hands on her shoulders and pulled her away, gently backing her down the stairs. "It's no use. You can't help him now."

More moaning caught Carissa's attention. She glanced down the passageway to see a dozen zombies heading in their direction. They were already less than fifty feet away, halfway between them and the elevator. All wore the garb of the ship's passengers. Bright colored shirts, bathing suits, and a few wore bathrobes.

Carissa slumped to the deck. "We're trapped."

"No, we're not," Kennedy said and grabbed Carissa by the arm and forced her to her feet. He led her down the passageway toward the zombies, stopping at the first hatch on the right. "We still have the emergency ladder."

The two made it to the hatch to the emergency ladder seconds before the zombies. Kennedy spun the wheel, undogged the bolts, and pulled open the hatch. Using the hatch for cover, he aimed the side arm down the passageway and fired off a rapid volley at the approaching hoard. Several of the living dead sustained head shots and dropped to the deck.

"Hurry!" Kennedy yelled.

Carissa climbed through the opening. The space was only three feet square and lit by a single emergency bulb encased in a dirty plastic cover. A metal ladder on the opposite wall ascended up through the decks. She started climbing, pausing after a few feet to yell out, "Come on!"

Jumping into the confined space, Kennedy tried to close the hatch behind him. Three sets of dead hands grabbed the hatch rim and yanked it open, knocking him off balance. Before he could regain his footing, one of the zombies reached in and clasped him by the arm with both hands. Kennedy placed the barrel of his side arm against one of the zombie's wrists and pulled the trigger, severing the dead hand. When he placed the firearm against the other wrist, he saw that the bolt was locked back in its open position, signifying he'd expended his ammunition.

Carissa heard Kennedy curse. She looked down just as a second zombie leaned through the hatch and grabbed Kennedy's other arm. Together, the two zombies pulled Kennedy through the hatch into the passageway where the living dead began to feed off of him. Carissa started down the ladder to see if she could help. Just then, a third zombie fell through the open hatch onto the floor of the enclosed compartment. When it caught sight of Carissa, its mouth opened, the gnawed-away lips giving a clear view of gums and gore-covered teeth as it chewed the air. She withdrew her side arm and fired the remainder of the magazine into its face, pulverizing the head into red pulp. Dropping the side arm onto the lifeless body, she continued her climb to safety.

Halfway up the ladder, far enough away so she could no longer hear the carnage taking place below, tears suddenly filled Carissa's eyes. She paused, wrapped her arms around one of the rungs and sobbed. She had failed. The team had shut down only one of the engines, and lost two good men in the process. Kennedy probably would be alive right now if he hadn't been looking after her, and if he had lived he might have been able to shut down the other engine. Because of her, everyone was now stuck aboard ship. A part of her wanted to just drop back down to the lower deck and let the zombies put her out of her misery. Yet she couldn't let go because deep down she knew that would be just another wasted life. So far she hadn't accomplished much, but at least topside she might be able to give solace to those waiting to die.

Wiping her eyes on the sleeve of her blouse, Carissa resumed climbing. The ladder ended in another narrow compartment overlooking the promenade deck. After closing the hatch to block access to the ladder, Carissa exited the compartment. After being stuck for so long in the claustrophobic confines of the engine room and escape ladder, she yearned for the sound and smell of the ocean.

Instead, she was greeted by terrified screams and inhuman moans. The stench of decay and shit assaulted her senses. Summoning every ounce of will, Carissa forced herself to move to the edge of the promenade deck and peer over the railing to the boat deck below.

Scores of zombies from the lower decks had made their way onto the boat deck fore and aft. They fed on the hundreds of passengers jammed along the deck from gunwale to bulkhead. Those passengers who tried to defend themselves were quickly overrun by the living dead, dragged to the deck, and slaughtered. Others dropped to their knees and awaited the end, some praying for salvation; some crying or screaming, too terrified to move. Some merely stared blankly into space, having lost their sanity.

The rest ran around in a frenzy, trying to escape, knocking over those around them to be crushed by the panicked throngs or pushed down and trampled. As the zombies made their way along the deck, they left dozens of ravaged bodies behind them. A few were so savagely devoured that nothing remained to turn into the living dead. Most of the others quickly reanimated, stumbled to their feet, and set off to feed on their fellow passengers.

Despite the ship still sailing ahead at close to full speed, several crew members had loaded one of the lifeboats with women and children and were carefully lowering it to the ocean's surface. As the lifeboat disappeared below Carissa's line of sight, half a dozen zombies swarmed over the crew members. Four other zombies lumbered over to the edge of the deck and toppled off the side into the lifeboat.

Farther forward, a dozen passengers commandeered a lifeboat and were trying to lower themselves to safety. They might have made it if anyone aboard had experience working with the pulley system. After only a few feet, a young woman on the aft end of the lifeboat loosened the lines too much. The rear of the boat dropped, spilling everyone into the ocean. Carissa watched the passengers float alongside the length of the ship, for a moment thinking they might make it. As they passed by the stern, each passenger got caught in the ship's undertow and was sucked into the propellers. The ship's wake turned crimson.

Carissa became aware of moans much louder than the others. Facing forward, she saw four zombies approaching her, fifty feet away and closing fast. Rather than try and escape, she stood still. Where would she run to? With the ship overrun by the living dead, running would only delay the inevitable.

An explosion rocked the ship. A fireball formed on the boat deck just aft of mid-ship, instantly incinerating dozens of passengers and zombies. The concussion hurled Carissa backwards against the outer bulkhead, knocking the wind out of her. She rolled onto her hands and knees, too dazed to stand. A loud ringing in her ears blocked out all other sounds. When she opened her eyes, the wooden deck seemed to spin beneath her. Carissa squinted and crawled toward the railing. She was vaguely aware of other explosions rocking the ship, feeling the reverberations through the hull.

Reaching the railing, Carissa pulled herself to her feet and steadied herself against the metal rung. Slowly, her senses returned. Looking up and down the length of the boat deck, Carissa saw the cruise ship in flames. Pillars of black smoke billowed from four gaping holes along the starboard hull below the waterline. The nearest explosion had collapsed a twenty-foot section of the promenade deck, including the portion with the zombies coming after her. Bodies and debris littered the water to starboard. Dozens of zombies grasped for something floating around them, either survivor or debris, but failed miserably to sink beneath the surface, their arms flailing away uselessly. Not that this gave the survivors in the water a reprieve. They tried swimming away, only to get caught up in the water rushing into the breaches in the hull, sucked back into the sinking ship.

Scanning the horizon, Carissa saw the source of the explosions. A warship flying the U.S. flag sailed about a mile off the cruise ship's starboard beam. The warship came out of a sharp turn to port that reversed its direction so it could make another pass.

The cruise ship already had developed a five-degree list. Metallic creaks and groans echoed from the interior loud enough to rival the mayhem topside. At this rate, the ship would sink in minutes. Carissa noticed the ship was slowing down. A glance aft confirmed it, for she no longer saw a wake. The explosions must have knocked the remaining engine off line, which was lucky for her. She now had a fighting chance.

Racing along the deck, Carissa made her way toward the stern. Thankfully the farther aft she went, the fewer zombies she encountered, most of the living dead congregating mid-ships where the surviving passengers were. She reached the stairs leading down to the boat deck, rushed down them, ran over to the guardrail overlooking the stern and climbed over. It was a fifty-foot drop to the ocean, but if she jumped correctly, she should be able to make the dive without hurting herself. At least she no longer had to be concerned about being chewed up by the propellers.

Carissa heard the zombie a moment before it grabbed her by the shoulders. Clutching the guardrail with her right hand, Carissa jerked her body to the left to break its grip. The maneuver worked, but only for a second. Driven into a frenzy by its insatiable hunger for flesh, the zombie continued to grasp at her. Alerted by the noise, five more zombies moved in her direction. She might be able to hold off one of the living dead, but not half a dozen.

Two more explosions rocked the cruise ship. Carissa felt the stern rise out of the water and crash back down. The jolt knocked her right hand from the guardrail and she plummeted backwards. Unable to execute a dive, Carissa struggled to keep her feet pointing down. She hit the water harder than anticipated and felt a sharp pain shoot through her side. The entire world closed in around her as she sank beneath the surface.

For a moment, Carissa became dangerously disoriented, unable to determine the way to the surface. She frantically looked around to get her bearings, finally spotting the sun's reflection above her. She swam toward the light, but slowly, finding it difficult to move her right arm. Each stroke sent a wave of pain across her chest, driving air from her lungs at an alarming rate. Her lungs strained to inhale. Unable to hold her breath any longer, Carissa sucked in a mouthful of air just as she broke the surface.

The cruise ship pulled away from her, now much slower, being propelled only by its momentum. Its list had increased by more than twenty degrees. Passengers clung on to fixtures and guard-rails as zombies toppled over the side, occasionally clutching onto one of the living and pulling them to a watery grave.

The ship drifted along for another quarter of a mile. Suddenly, the moaning of strained and twisted metal emanated from deep inside the hull and the ship's list increased sharply. Carissa watched as the cruise ship rolled onto its side, spilling everyone still on deck into the ocean. Terrified screams and cries for help mixed with the ship's death throe. The bow slid beneath the surface, followed a moment later by the stern lifting out of the ocean at a forty-five degree angle, its propellers pointing skyward. The cruise ship slid beneath the surface, the undertow pulling both the living and the living dead into the murky deep.

Seconds later, an unnatural silence descended across the ocean.

A half-flooded lifeboat that had broken loose from its moorings floated a few hundred yards away from her. With the last of her strength, Carissa swam to it, crawled inside, and collapsed in the water-filled bottom, exhausted and panting from the pain in her side. Despite the throbbing, she felt a sense of relieve.

She made it. She was alive.

But her spirits sank when she glanced up to see the U.S. war-ship gliding to a stop alongside her. Half a dozen sailors lined the starboard beam, each training an assault rifle on her. A young ensign stood amongst them, a bullhorn clutched in his right hand. He raised it to his mouth. Carissa winced, expecting to be cut down. Instead, the ensign yelled down to her.

"Are you infected or wounded in any way?"

Carissa shook her head vigorously so as to be seen from the deck.

"Okay, ma'am. Listen carefully. We're going to lower a ladder to you and bring you on board. Do exactly as you're told and make no sudden movements, otherwise we'll be forced to shoot you. Do you understand?"

Carissa nodded vigorously.

The ensign lowered the bullhorn and issued orders to the men on deck. Three of them raced off to get the ladder while the others kept their assault rifles trained on her. At this moment, she was in too much pain to care. All that mattered was that she had survived both the outbreak and the sinking of her cruise ship, the only one of almost three thousand people to do so.

Most importantly, the zombies had been sent to the ocean bottom and would never be able to infect the land.

\* \* \*

Ten days later.

Virginia Beach. The sun had set hours earlier, driving the late summer vacationers off of the beach and into the restaurants and clubs along Atlantic Avenue. No one was around to notice the lone figure that emerged from the ocean and stumbled its way onto the sand. It wore the remnants of a cruise ship captain's uniform. After more than a week walking along the ocean floor, much of its skin that wasn't already eaten by sea life now sloughed off it from being waterlogged. Pausing on the sand, the zombie adjusted to this new environment.

A moment later, a second zombie emerged from the ocean, this one a woman in the tattered remnants of a sun dress, its gut torn open and its abdomen empty of all internal organs. It dragged itself across the sand and joined the first zombie.

Up and down the length of the beach, more and more of the living dead trudged out of the watery depths. After a few minutes, more than fifty zombies stretched out along the beach for a quarter of a mile. They all stood tottering on the sand, looking around and getting their bearings. Almost as one, their collective attention was drawn toward Atlantic Avenue.

The zombie in the cruise ship captain's uniform gurgled a moan, as if it was issuing a command. One by one, the zombies set off up the beach, stumbling for the lights and sounds along the boulevard that signified where they could find food.

# ABOUT THE WRITERS

**Scott Baker** was born and raised in Everett, Massachusetts. He now lives in northern Virginia with his wife and six house rabbits. His previous writing credits include *Rednecks Shouldn't Play With Dead Things*, which was published in the autumn 2008 edition of *Necrotic Tissue magazine*. He is currently working on a trilogy of novels about a small band of humans hunting vampires in Washington D.C.

Please contact him at http://www.horror-mall.com/haunt/zombiebunnies.

**Eric S. Brown** is the author of numerous zombie books including *Season of Rot* (Permuted Press), *World War of the Dead* (Coscom Entertainment), *War of the Worlds Plus Blood Guts and Zombies, Unabridged Unabashed, and Undead*, and *Barren Earth* to name only a few. His short fiction has been published hundreds of times in magazines and anthologies like *The Undead, Dead Science, Zombology, Dark Wisdom, The Blackest Death*, and *Post Mortem* magazine. He was also featured as an expert in the zombie genre in the book Zombie CSU. He is 34 years old and lives in NC with his wife and son.

**Francesco Collia** is a writer and librarian born and raised in Staten Island, NY, but now living in Tampa, FL. There's more but you get the idea.

**Anthony Giangregorio** is the author and editor of more than 25 novels, almost all of them about zombies. His work has appeared in *Dead Science* by Coscomentertainment, *Dead Worlds: Undead Stories Volumes* 1, 2 , 3, and 4, *Book of the Dead* and an upcoming anthology (Zombology) by Library of the Living Dead Press and their werewolf anthology titled *War Wolves*. He also has stories in *End of Days: An Apocalyptic* Anthology Volumes 1 &2

Check out his website at www.undeadpress.com

**Tom Hamilton** is an Irish Traveler. His work has appeared in over one hundred publications around the world. Including the *Rockford Review, Red Wheelbarrow Literary Journal* and *Sinister City* among many others. He has two poetry chapbooks published. *'The Rain Draw Bridge'* from 'Alpha Beat Press' and *'The Last Days of My Teeth'* from 'Budget Press' His short story *'The Spider'* is available as an E-book from 'Curious Volumes Publishing'. He also has stories in *Dead Worlds 1 and 2* and *Book of the Dead* by Living Dead Press.

Along with his wife Mary Theresa and their three small daughters, Tiffany, Hope and Catalina, he lives in Loves Park IL. USA.

**Kelly M. Hudson** grew up in the wilds of Kentucky and currently resides in California. He has a deep and abiding love for all things horror and rock n' roll, and if you wish to contact Kelly or find links to other stories he's had published, please visit www.kellymhudson.com for further details. He thanks you for reading his dumb old story and wishes you and yours a very happy day!

**Mark M. Johnson's** writing credits include: *The Black Empty's Letters From the Dead*, read by Doctor Pus on the Library of the Living Dead podcast. Short stories in, *Bits of the Dead* from Coscom Entertainment, *Zombology* from Library of the Living Dead Press, and *Dead Worlds Volume 2* from Living Dead Press.

**Keith Adam Luethke** attends the University of Tennessee and is pursing an M.A in writing. Previous works include: *The Dweller, Wait until Dark, Dead Roads*, and *The Tormented*, all of which sell on Amazon. He is currently working on a four book series entitled *Shelter from the Undead*. He loves new fans and can be reached at kluethke@utk.edu.

**Catherine MacLeod** lives and writes in Nova Scotia. Her publications include short fiction in "On Spec," "TaleBones," and several anthologies, most recently "Tesseracts Thirteen." She shares a birthday with Bram Stoker, a fact which delights her no end.

**Rick Moore,** originally from Leicestershire, England, moved to the US ten years ago and now lives in Phoenix, AZ. Rick's fiction has appeared in numerous zines and anthologies, including *Dead Worlds Volume 2 & Book of the Dead* by Living Dead Press, *The Undead: Flesh Feast, History Is Dead, The Beast Within, Cthulhu Unbound, Harvest Hill, Dark Animus*, the 2009 Stoker nominated *Horror Library 3* and *Bound For Evil* (his inclusion in which still regularly sends Moore into a geekified frenzy of frothing at the mouth fanboy excitement as the collection also contains fiction by two of his childhood heroes, H.P. Lovecraft and Ramsey Campbell). To earn his daily crust, Rick works for the Arizona State Hospital as a Mental Health Specialist. Visit him online at http://www.myspace.com/zombieinfection

**Michael Presutti** has been writing since the age of 19. He lives in Worcester county Massachusetts. His book *Last Words* that was released in November 2008 has been receiving excellent reviews. The sequel *Shadows and Ashes* will soon be finished. He is also working on a book of short stories. His stories are also featured in anthologies. The latest 2 are *End of Days: An Apocalyptic Anthology* and *The Book of the Dead* by Living Dead Press.

**Alva J. Roberts** lives in a small town in Western Nebraska with his wife and two dogs. When he is not writing, he works as a librarian at the public library. Daybreak is his first published story.

**Jessy Marie Roberts** lives in Western Nebraska with her husband and two dogs, Tucker and Snags. When she isn't writing, Jessy enjoys cooking, gardening, and reality TV.

**Rob X Román** (a.k.a. Doc Monster) has written for *Lady Vampré* and *Hari Kari* (Blackout Comics). He's proud to be the "script doctor" for Carl Anders *Aabø's Jon Pay: Private Investigator* (BDP Comics) and editor for Robert Freese's *Shivers* (eTreasures Publishing). As a cartoonist, he's worked for musical artists like Mike Dalton Band, Steps, Li'l Mama and Bowling for Soup. His pin-ups have been printed in Billy Joe Van Helsing - *Redneck Vampire Hunter* (Alpha Productions), *Ripperman* (Chanting Monks Press), *Shadowflame: 10th Anniversary Edition* (Bloodstained Productions) and *Electric Frankenstein* (Dark Horse Books).
You can read his *House of Scares* and *Jonny Horrors* comics in Scary Monsters Magazine (issues 40 – 45 and the 2001 yearbook) and *Shadowflame: The Spud Adventures*, currently on www.arcana.com.
Check out his animation at www.docmonster.com.

**Michael Simon** lives and works in eastern Canada with his wife and three children. Published works have appeared in *Apex: Science Fiction and Horror, Andromeda Spaceways Inflight Magazine, The Sword Review, Ragged Edge, Drabble, Mindflights and Art and Prose.* He has been short-listed for the AEON Award and Writers of the Future and has contributed to several anthologies including *Travel a Time Historic, Tall Tales and Short Stories, The Unknown, Dead Worlds: Undead Stories (Volume 1 and 2)* and *Book of the Dead*. Nonfiction articles have appeared in Stitches Magazine, *The Physician's Chronicle, Physician`s Review, Caregiver Magazine, The Medical Post* and *Hockey Net.*
To find out more visit his website at michaelsimonweb.com.

**Gareth Wood** is a Canadian writer of horror and science fiction who lives in Calgary, Alberta. *The Unlucky* is his first published work.

# REVOLUTION OF THE DEAD
by Anthony Giangregorio
## THE DEAD SHALL RISE AGAIN!

Five years ago, a deadly plague wiped out 97% of the world's population, America suffering tragically. Bodies were everywhere, far too many to bury or burn. But then, through a miracle of medical science, a way is found to reanimate the dead.

With the manpower of the United States depleted, and the remaining survivors not wanting to give up their internet and fast food restaurants, the undead are conscripted as slave labor.

Now they cut the grass, pick up the trash, and walk the dogs of the surviving humans.

But whether alive or dead, no race wants to be controlled, and sooner or later the dead will fight back, wanting the freedom they enjoyed in life.

The revolution has begun!

And when it's over, the dead will rule the land, and the remaining humans will become the slaves...or worse.

# DEAD RECKONING: DAWNING OF THE DEAD
by Anthony Giangregorio
## THE DEAD HAVE RISEN!

In the dead city of Pittsburgh, two small enclaves struggle to survive, eking out an existence of hand to mouth.

But instead of working together, both groups battle for the last remaining fuel and supplies of a city filled with the living dead.

Six months after the initial outbreak, a lone helicopter arrives bearing two more survivors and a newborn baby. One enclave welcomes them, while the other schemes to steal their helicopter and escape the decaying city.

With no police, fire, or social services existing, the two will battle for dominance in the steel city of the walking dead. But when the dust settles, the question is: will the remaining humans be the winners, or the losers?

When the dead walk, the line between Heaven and Hell is so twisted and bent there is no line at all.

# RISE OF THE DEAD
by Anthony Giangregorio
## DEATH IS ONLY THE BEGINNING!

In less than forty-eight hours, more than half the globe was infected.

In another forty-eight, the rest would be enveloped.

The reason?

A science experiment gone horribly wrong which enabled the dead to walk, their flesh rotting on their bones even as they seek human prey.

Jeremy was an ordinary nineteen year old slacker. He partied too much and had done poorly in high school. After a night of drinking and drugs, he awoke to find the world a very different place from the one he'd left the night before.

The dead were walking and feeding on the living, and as Jeremy stepped out into a world gone mad, the dead spotting him alone and unarmed in the middle of the street, he had to wonder if he would live long enough to see his twentieth birthday.

# DEADFREEZE
by Anthony Giangregorio

**THIS IS WHAT HELL WOULD BE LIKE IF IT FROZE OVER!**
When an experimental serum for hypothermia goes horribly wrong, a small research station in the middle of Antarctica becomes overrun with an army of the frozen dead.

Now a small group of survivors must battle the arctic weather and a horde of frozen zombies as they make their way across the frozen plains of Antarctica to a neighboring research station.

What they don't realize is that they are being hunted by an entity whose sole reason for existing is vengeance; and it will find them wherever they run.

# DEAD WORLDS: Undead Stories
## A Zombie Anthology Volume 1
### Edited by Anthony Giangregorio
Welcome to the world of the dead, where the laws of nature have been twisted, reality changed.

The Dead Walk!

Filled with established and promising new authors for the next generation of corpses, this anthology will leave you gasping for air as you go from one terror-filled story to another.

Like the decomposing meat of a freshly rotting carcass, this book will leave you breathless.

Don't say we didn't warn you.

# VISIONS OF THE DEAD
## A ZOMBIE STORY
by Anthony & Joseph Giangregorio

Jake Roberts felt like he was the luckiest man alive.

He had a great family, a beautiful girlfriend, who was soon to be his wife, and a job, that might not have been the best, but it paid the bills.

At least until the dead began to walk.

Now Jake is fighting to survive in a dead world while searching for his lost love, Melissa, knowing she's out there somewhere.

But the past isn't dead, and as he struggles for an uncertain future, the past threatens to consume him.

With the present a constant battle between the living and the dead, Jake finds himself slipping in and out of the past, the visions of how it all happened haunting him.

But Jake knows Melissa is out there somewhere and he'll find her or die trying. In a world of the living dead, you can never escape your past.

**THE NEXT EXCITING CHAPTER IN THE DEADWATER SERIES!**
# DEAD VALLEY   BOOK 7
### by Anthony Giangregorio

After nearly drowning in the icy waters of the Colorado River, the six weary companions come upon a beautiful valley nestled in the mountains of Colorado, where the undead plague appears to have never happened.

With the mountains protecting the valley, the deadly rain never fell, and the valley is as untouched as the day it was created.

But the group is soon captured by a secret, military research base now run by a few remaining scientists and soldiers.

On this base, unholy experiments are being carried out, and the group soon finds themselves caught in the middle of it.

Mary, Sue, Raven and Cindy are taken away to be used as breeders, the scientists wanting to create a new utopia, which the living dead can't reach, but the side effect of this is the women will lose their lives.

Henry and Jimmy, now separated and captured themselves, must find a way to save them before it's too late; the scientists unleashing every conceivable mutation at their disposal to stop them.

In the world of the living dead, the past is gone and the future is non-existent.

## ROAD KILL: A ZOMBIE TALE
### by Anthony Giangregorio
**ORDER UP!**

In the summer of 2008, a rogue comet entered earth's orbit for 72 hours. During this time, a strange amber glow suffused the sky.

But something else happened; something in the comet's tail had an adverse affect on dead tissue and the result was the reanimation of every dead animal carcass on the planet.

A handful of survivors hole up in a diner in the backwoods of New Hampshire while the undead creatures of the night hunt for human prey.

There's a new blue plate special at DJ's Diner and Truck Stop, and it's you!

## DEAD WORLDS: Undead Stories
## A Zombie Anthology Volume 2
### Edited by Anthony Giangregorio

Welcome to a world where the dead walk and want nothing more than to feast on the living.

The stories contained in this, the second volume of the Dead Worlds series, are filled with action, gore, and buckets and buckets of blood; plus a heaping side of entrails for those with a little extra hunger.

The stories contained within this volume are scribed by both the desiccated cadavers of seasoned veterans to the genre as well as fresh-faced corpses, each printed here for the first time; and all of them ready to dig in and please the most discerning reader.

So slap on a bib and prepare to get bloody, because you're about to read the best zombie stories this side of Hell!

# THE DARK
## by Anthony Giangregorio
### DARKNESS FALLS

The darkness came without warning.

First New York, then the rest of United States, and then the world became enveloped in a perpetual night without end.

With no sunlight, eventually the planet will wither and die, bringing on a new Ice Age. But that isn't problem for the human race, for humanity will be dead long before that happens.

There is something in the dark, creatures only seen in nightmares, and they are on the prowl. Evolution has changed and man is no longer the dominant species. When we are children, we're told not to fear the dark, that what we believe to exist in the shadows is false.

Unfortunately, that is no longer true.

# SOULEATER
## by Anthony Giangregorio

Twenty years ago, Jason Lawson witnessed the brutal death of his father by something only seen in nightmares, something so horrible he'd blocked it from his mind.

Now twenty years later the creature is back, this time for his son.

Jason won't let that happen.

He'll travel to the demon's world, struggling every second to rescue his son from its clutches.

But what he doesn't know is that the portal will only be open for a finite time and if he doesn't return with his son before it closes, then he'll be trapped in the demon's dimension forever.

SEE HOW IT ALL BEGAN IN THE NEW DOUBLE-SIZED EDITION!
# DEADWATER: EXPANDED EDITION
## by Anthony Giangregorio

Through a series of tragic mishaps, a small town's water supply is contaminated with a deadly bacterium that transforms the town's population into flesh eating ghouls.

Without warning, Henry Watson finds himself thrown into a living hell where the living dead walk and want nothing more than to feed on the living.

Now Henry's trying to escape the undead town before he becomes the next victim.

With the military on one side, shooting civilians on sight, and a horde of bloodthirsty zombies on the other, Henry must try to battle his way to freedom.

With a small group of survivors, including a beautiful secretary and a wise-cracking janitor to aid him, the ragtag group will do their best to stay alive and escape the city codenamed: **Deadwater.**

# DEAD END: A ZOMBIE NOVEL
### by Anthony Giangregorio
## THE DEAD WALK!

Newspapers everywhere proclaim the dead have returned to feast on the living!

A small group of survivors hole up in a cellar, afraid to brave the masses of animated corpses, but when food runs out, they have no choice but to venture out into a world gone mad.

What they will discover, however, is that the fall of civilization has brought out the worst in their fellow man.

Cannibals, psychotic preachers and rapists are just some of the atrocities they must face.

In a world turned upside down, it is life that has hit a Dead End.

# DEAD RAGE
### by Anthony Giangregorio

An unknown virus spreads across the globe, turning ordinary people into bloodthirsty, ravenous killers.

Only a small percentage of the population is immune and soon become prey to the infected.

Amongst the infected comes a man, stricken by the virus, yet still retaining his grasp on reality. His need to destroy the *normals* becomes an obsession and he raises an army of killers to seek out and kill all who aren't *changed* like himself.

A few survivors gather together on the outskirts of Chicago and find themselves running for their lives as the specter of death looms over all.

The Dead Rage virus will find you, no matter where you hide.

# FAMILY OF THE DEAD
## A Zombie Anthology
### by Anthony, Joseph and Domenic Giangregorio

Clawing their way out of the wet, dark earth, these tales of terror will fill you with the deep seated fear we all have of death and what comes next.

But if that wasn't bad enough to chill your soul, these undead tales are penned by an entire family of corpses. The zombie master himself, Anthony Giangregorio, leads his two young ghouls, his sons Domenic and Joseph Giangregorio, on a journey of terror inducing stories that will keep you up long into the night.

As you read these works of the undead, don't be alarmed by that bump outside the window.

After all, it's probably just a stray tree branch...or is it?

# The Lazarus Culture
## by Pasquale J. Morrone

Secret Service Agent Christopher Kearns had no idea what he was up against. Assigned on a temporary basis to the Center for Disease Control, he only knew that somehow it was connected to the lives of those the agency protected...namely, the President of the United States. If there were possible terrorist activities in the making, he could only guess it was at a red alert basis.

When Kearns meets and befriends Doctor Marlene Peterson of the Breezy Point Medical Center in Maryland, he soon finds that science fiction can indeed become a reality. In a solitary room walked a man with no vital signs: dead. The explanation he received came from Doctor Lee Fret, a man assigned to the case from the CDC. Something was attached to the brain stem. Something alive that was quickly spreading rapidly through Maryland and other states.

Kearns and his ragtag army of agents and medical personnel soon find themselves in a world of meaningless slaughter and mayhem. The armies of the walking dead were far more than mere zombies. Some began to change into whatever it was they ate. The government had found a way to reanimate the dead by implanting a parasite found on the tongue of the Red Snapper to the human brain.

It looked good on paper, but it was a project straight from Hell.

The dead now walked, but it wasn't a mystery.

It was The Lazarus Culture.

# END OF DAYS: AN APOCALYPTIC ANTHOLOGY
## Edited by Eric S. Brown
### With a story by Anthony Giangregorio

Our world is a fragile place.

Meteors, famine, floods, nuclear war, solar flares, and hundreds of other calamities can plunge our small blue planet into turmoil in an instant.

What would you do if tomorrow the sun went super nova or the world was swallowed by water, submerging the world into the cold darkness of the ocean?

This anthology explores some of those scenarios and plunges you into total annihilation.

But remember, it's only a book, and tomorrow will come as it always does.

Or will it?

# DEADFALL
## by Anthony Giangregorio

It's Halloween in the small suburban town of Wakefield, Mass.

While parents take their children trick or treating and others throw costume parties, a swarm of meteorites enter the earth's atmosphere and crash to earth.

Inside are small parasitic worms, no larger than maggots.

The worms quickly infect the corpses at a local cemetery and so begins the rise of the undead.

The walking dead soon get the upper hand, with no one believing the truth.

That the dead now walk.

Will a small group of survivors live through the zombie apocalypse?

Or will they, too, succumb to the Deadfall.

# DARK PLACES
By Anthony Giangregorio

A cave-in inside the Boston subway unleashes something that should have stayed buried forever.

Three boys sneak out to a haunted junkyard after dark and find more than they gambled on.

In a world where everyone over twelve has died from a mysterious illness, one young boy tries to carry on.

A mysterious man in black tries his hand at a game of chance at a local carnival, to interesting results.

God, Allah, and Buddha play a friendly game of poker with the fate of the Earth resting in the balance.

Ever have one of those days where everything that can go wrong, does? Well, so did Byron, and no one should have a day like this!

Thad had an imaginary friend named Charlie when he was a child. Charlie would make him do bad things. Now Thad is all grown up and guess who's coming for a visit?

These and other short stories, all filled with frozen moments of dread and wonder, will keep you captivated long into the night.

Just be sure to watch out when you turn off the light!

# THE MONSTER UNDER THE BED
By Anthony Giangregorio

Rupert was just one of many monsters that inhabit the human world, scaring children before bed. Only Rupert wanted to play with the children he was forced to scare.

When Rupert meets Timmy, an instant friendship is born. Running away from his abusive step-father, Timmy leaves home, embarking on a journey that leads him to New York City.

On his way, Timmy will realize that the true monsters are other adults who are just waiting to take advantage of a small boy, all alone in the big city.

Can Rupert save him?

Or will Timmy just become another statistic.

# DEAD TALES: SHORT STORIES TO DIE FOR
By Anthony Giangregorio

In a world much like our own, terrorists unleash a deadly dis-ease that turns people into flesh-eating ghouls.

A camping trip goes horribly wrong when forces of evil seek to dominate mankind.

After losing his life, a man returns reincarnated again and again; his soul inhabiting the bodies of animals.

In the Colorado Mountains, a woman runs for her life, stalked by a sadistic killer.

In a world where the Patriot Act has come to fruition, a man struggles to survive, despite eroding liberties.

Not able to accept his wife's death, a widower will cross into the dream realm to find her again, despite the dark forces that hold her in thrall.

These and other short stories will captivate and thrill you.

These are short stories to die for.

**THE PLACE TO GO FOR ZOMBIE AND APOCALYPTIC FICTION**

  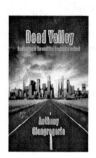

  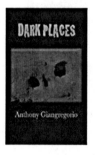

# LIVING DEAD PRESS

## WHERE THE DEAD WALK
### www.livingdeadpress.com

CPSIA information can be obtained at www.ICGtesting.com
Printed in the USA
BVOW01s0245130315

391574BV00010B/88/P

9 781935 458265